An
Untamed
Heart

Books by Lauraine Snelling

An Untamed Heart

RED RIVER OF THE NORTH
An Untamed Land • *A New Day Rising*
A Land to Call Home • *The Reapers' Song*
Tender Mercies • *Blessing in Disguise*

RETURN TO RED RIVER
A Dream to Follow • *Believing the Dream*
More Than a Dream

DAUGHTERS OF BLESSING
A Promise for Ellie • *Sophie's Dilemma*
A Touch of Grace • *Rebecca's Reward*

HOME TO BLESSING
A Measure of Mercy • *No Distance Too Far*
A Heart for Home

WILD WEST WIND
Valley of Dreams • *Whispers in the Wind*
A Place to Belong

DAKOTAH TREASURES
Ruby • *Pearl*
Opal • *Amethyst*

SECRET REFUGE
Daughter of Twin Oaks • *Sisters of the Confederacy*
The Long Way Home • *A Secret Refuge 3-in-1*

*Golden Filly Collection One**
*Golden Filly Collection Two**
*High Hurdles Collection One**
*High Hurdles Collection Two**

*5 books in each volume

With joy and delight I dedicate *An Untamed Heart* to my aunty Inga and to my mother, Thelma, who are my heroes and who became Ingeborg. What a wealth of love and encouragement they have always been for me.

An Untamed Heart is also dedicated to my Norwegian friend Gunlaug Noklund, who not only helped me with the accuracy of this book but allowed me to use her name as Ingeborg's cousin and dearest friend.

An
Untamed
Heart

LAURAINE
SNELLING

BETHANYHOUSE
a division of Baker Publishing Group
Minneapolis, Minnesota

© 2013 by Lauraine Snelling

Published by Bethany House Publishers
11400 Hampshire Avenue South
Bloomington, Minnesota 55438
www.bethanyhouse.com

Bethany House Publishers is a division of
Baker Publishing Group, Grand Rapids, Michigan

Printed in the United States of America

Library of Congress Cataloging-in-Publication Data
Snelling, Lauraine.
    An untamed heart / Lauraine Snelling.
        pages cm
    Summary: "After the loss of her first love, is Ingeborg Strand willing to
marry a sranger—however kind—for the promise of a new life in America?
The prequel to the RED RIVER OF THE NORTH series"— Provided by
publisher.
    ISBN 978-0-7642-1151-5 (cloth : alk. paper)
    ISBN 978-0-7642-0203-2 (pbk.)
    1. Single women—Fiction. 2. First loves—Fiction. 3. Widowers—Fiction.
4. Families—Fiction. 5. Farm life—Fiction. 6. Norway—Fiction. 7. Domestic
fiction. I. Title.
PS3569.N39U56 2013
813'.54—dc23   2013023297

Scripture quotations are from the King James Version of the Bible.

Cover design by Jennifer Parker
Cover photography by Mike Habermann Photography, LLC.

13   14   15   16   17   18   19   7   6   5   4   3   2   1

1

"Oh, Gunlaug, you are so funny." Ingeborg Strand grinned at her cousin, who was not only her best friend but her only real confidante. The two had been born within days of each other and had always shared a crib or blanket on the floor when their mothers were together. They had grown up with a bond closer than sisters.

"But, Ingeborg, you can't marry someone just because your mor thinks he is perfect!" Sitting on the still slightly damp earth, Gunlaug locked her hands around her knees and rocked back, at the same time raising her face to the sun.

"And I will not. Perfect is in the eyes of the beholder—my eyes, not hers. I think Per Tollefson is worse than scraping the bottom of the apple barrel."

"Well, you have to admit, he's not rotten." Gunlaug snorted behind her hand.

The two giggled again. "No, not rotten. He is almost a man of honor, but he can't string two words together without stuttering, stumbling, and blushing. Why, a conversation comes to a halt when he tries to talk."

"'Almost a man' is surely right. And you love words, so you would go so crazy you'd run screaming out the door on a long winter's night."

"Or curl up and die of boredom." Ingeborg shook her head. "Surely there is a man somewhere who is no longer a stumbling boy and can make decisions and carry on a decent conversation."

"Tall and good looking would help." Gunlaug closed her eyes and smiled with the dreamy, dopey gaze that told Ingeborg she was thinking of Ivar, her current man—er—boy of the moment. He was not nearly as ideal as Gunlaug thought, but Ingeborg had not the heart to smash her cousin's latest dream.

"Come along. Mor is going to be wondering where we are." Ingeborg stared east across the valley to the mountain peaks still wearing their winter finery, glistening white in the brilliant spring sun. Here it was her twentieth birthday with no marriageable man in sight. Her mother was growing frantic. She often accused her daughter of deliberately offending all the young men the entire community paraded before her. It seemed every mor in a five-mile radius knew of someone who would be ideal for Ingeborg.

The call came across the crystal air. "Ingeborg, Gunlaug, where are you gone to?" It was her mor. Hilde's voice carried the oft-disgusted sound she used with her oldest daughter.

"Picking dandelion leaves," Ingeborg called back, pointing to the patch of dandelion leaves out beyond the barn that she and Gunlaug were supposedly harvesting. The two covered their snickers with hands not full of green leaves, nor were their baskets. This first gift of the growing season was prized both as a tonic and a vegetable and, when dried, a medicinal tea that carried healing properties to a people starved for something green. Serve something fresh, and everyone sighed in bliss.

"I can't wait for the dance." Gunlaug clipped leaves as she dreamed. "I can see Ivar again."

Ingeborg rolled her eyes and tossed some leaves into the bent-willow basket. With the back of her hand she pushed the strands of wheaten hair off her now perspiring forehead. How wonderful the sun felt on her back. If a storm didn't come roaring in and surprise them all, they'd all be able to strip off their woolen undergarments and bask in the freedom of lighter clothing.

"I think I won't go."

"You're crazy. Your mor will never forgive you." The shock on Gunlaug's face made Ingeborg laugh again. "Besides, you know how you love the music and dancing."

"I know." Whirling around a dance floor did indeed make her feel light as a butterfly. At five feet seven, Ingeborg was plenty tall and not willowy like one of their other cousins. *Sturdy* and *wholesome* were two words she frequently heard. But she never lacked for dance partners, since dancing with her made her partners look good too.

She sat back on her heels and studied their baskets. Did they have enough? "Did your mor want some of these?"

"No, she sent Hamme out to our patch. She thought I was going to help, but I told her Tante Hilde had asked for me."

"Well, she did, sort of. She said, 'You two girls,' and she was looking at us."

"Right." The two exchanged a look that would do a conspirator proud.

When Hilde called again, Ingeborg reluctantly rose to her feet, glancing around at the green carpet with bright yellow suns sprinkled throughout. "We pretty well cleaned this patch out, so let's take our bounty up to the house."

Swinging their baskets, the two strolled across the rapidly greening pasture. Several lambs were nursing, while others gamboled beside the ewes or chased each other. The ewes kept grazing, pretty much ignoring their offspring until one got too near the fence. Then the mother sent out a warning bleat. The lamb scampered back, making the girls look at each other and laugh. Spring lambs could always make them laugh; their antics were such a delight.

Ingeborg clasped her basket handle with both hands and swung it in a circle. "I love spring."

"Me too. Spring, the time of love."

"You're in love with *being* in love."

Gunlaug stopped, her face suddenly turning serious. "You really think so?" She shook her head. "I know you don't like Ivar much, but—"

"Do not fret, my dear cousin. I just don't think he's good enough for you. Surely there is someone more grown up. Ivar is such a mama's boy."

Hjelmer, her brother, came running across the pasture. "Ingeborg, Mor said to come quick. The Gaard baby is on the way, and she is afraid there will be trouble."

Ingeborg and Gunlaug broke into a run. "Has Mor left yet?"

"She is waiting for you. Give me your baskets." They handed them off and ran on.

Ingeborg knew that unmarried young women usually weren't allowed at a birthing, so if Mor told her to hurry, there would surely be trouble. Hilde Strand had a special sense for that, which was one of the reasons she was in such demand as a midwife. The girls were both out of breath by the time they reached the house, where Hilde met them at the door.

"Gunlaug, you go home and ask your mor to pray for this baby. She can pass on the word." As she spoke, she was shaking her head.

"Ja, Tante." Gunlaug set off for home, heading north while Ingeborg and her mother turned south at the road.

"Why did we not take the buggy?" Ingeborg asked, as they walked so fast they were nearly trotting.

"Because we can cut across the south field and get there more quickly. We might have to turn this baby, and that will take both of us. Her mister is worthless in the birthing room, as are most men."

Ingeborg nodded. She had already learned that. The busier the husband kept, outside preferably, the better for all concerned. "What about the children?" The Gaards already had three youngsters, with the eldest a girl of six. Her mother had delivered all of them, because their mother was slim hipped with a definite lack of elasticity. "Has she already been in labor for a while?"

"Ja. She should have sent for me before, but Greta ran over, calling my name, and when I answered her, she turned back to help with the younger ones. She acts so much older than six, but that is often the case when the mother does poorly. It takes Trude a long time to come back to health after the baby is finally born." Hilde shook her head. "I warned them both that having babies so often like this, one of these times she might not make it."

Oh, please Lord, don't let this be the time. Ingeborg had already watched one mother slip into a comatose state and then death, and there didn't seem to be anything any of them could do. Mor had been morose for days afterward.

"How will I help you?"

"Remember how you turned that lamb inside the ewe? If it's the same problem, we will try the same thing. Your fingers are longer and your hands more slender than mine. And you are strong."

Ingeborg remembered the lambing like it had happened yesterday. The crying ewe, her far and brother holding the ewe still while her fingers searched for the lamb's nose amongst what seemed like all legs. How she did it one handed, she would never know. When the ewe gave another heave, the pressure on her arm was excruciating, but she held on somehow and the two front feet and the nose presented. Mother and baby did well. Her arm had bruises for a week, but she would never forget the immense welling up of joy she had felt when the lamb began to breathe and shook its head. Her far had been compressing the rib cage and muttering, "Breathe, little one, breathe."

Ever since, when there was any trouble in the lambing pen, Far called on his oldest daughter. When he said she would make as good a midwife as her mor, Ingeborg had been floating above the ground. Compliments from him were rare and to be treasured deep in one's heart. Why, once she had splinted a lamb's broken leg and fashioned a bandage that went over the shoulders and kept the splint and wrap in place. Now the lamb walked with nary a limp.

"Come quick. Please hurry." The older boy met them at the road. He was five and also grown up.

In spite of their puffing, Ingeborg and Hilde broke into a jog again, Mor carrying the basket with the necessary birthing accoutrements and some medicinal herbs for a tisane, a drink to help the mother regain her strength faster.

Ingeborg hung back so Mor could go into the house first, as was proper. After all, Mor was the midwife, not the lowly assistant. Hilde turned to her daughter before they entered the bedroom. "You keep praying until I call for you. We need our God to see us through this."

"Ja, I will."

Hilde closed the door behind her, then opened it again almost immediately and beckoned Ingeborg to join her. The room felt overwarm as Ingeborg entered. An older woman was sitting off to one side keening, with an apron over her head. The pregnant woman lay on the bed, clutching a rolled towel and clamping her teeth down on it when a contraction made her groan and weep. Hilde went to the head of the bed and spoke sternly.

"Now, I know you are miserable, but listen to me. I am here to bring you through this, but you must do as I say. Just like you have all the other times. We are a good team, you and I. Right?"

The woman on the bed nodded and fought against another contraction that rolled over her. "Ja, I know," she ground out. "But this one . . ." She clamped her teeth on the rag, and panted. "Something . . . is . . . wrong."

"I will see where you are." Hilde checked for the dilation, keeping her hand on the woman's huge belly. "You must get up and walk. You are not dilated far enough yet."

"You cannot be that cruel." The mother-in-law dropped her apron. "See how in agony she is."

Hilde turned to the woman. "Could you please go heat us some water? And bring me a bowl or jug of boiling water for the tisane. It needs to steep."

The woman muttered her way out the door, leaving her obvious feelings of dislike in the room behind her.

Hilde nodded to Ingeborg. "Come. We will walk her."

Ingeborg jumped to the other side of the bed, and together they lifted Mrs. Gaard to her feet.

The woman swayed between them, so Ingeborg wrapped an arm around her back to hold her up. They walked the length of the room and back, back and forth. Ingeborg glanced at her mother, who she could see was praying with each step. She knew her mother had learned to do that, but so far she was not able. Her mother said to ask God for help and to thank Him that He is God and able to do far beyond what they asked or believed. How could she pray that when she wasn't really sure God was listening? Sometimes she felt He did, but other times she was not so sure. Like right now. Could not He see the agony this woman suffered and come to their assistance without continuous prayer?

"No more. I cannot go on."

"Yes you can. You must, if you want to deliver this child."

Ingeborg tightened her grip on the woman's waist as another wave rolled over her. How long could this continue? She looked over at her mother, whose serene face belied everything that was going on.

Mrs. Gaard stumbled and became a dead weight between them.

"Trude, come, you will lie down now so I can see if the walking is helping you."

The mother-in-law brought in a jug of steaming water and set it on the table, her tongue clicking against the roof of her mouth, her frown enough to scare children.

"Takk." Hilde helped their patient back to the bed and

lowered her to sitting, then swung her feet up. She rolled onto her side, moaning, tears streaming down her face.

When the contraction had passed, Hilde rolled the woman onto her back and checked for the dilation. "The baby should be presenting by now, but even with all our walking, there is not sufficient change." With gentle fingers she pressed all around the mounded belly, searching for any information she could gain.

"Does the baby need to be turned?" Ingeborg whispered.

Her mother nodded but kept moving her hands. The woman groaned, so faint as to rather be a moan.

"We will have to turn her over." Hilde looked to her daughter.

Ingeborg nodded and sucked in a deep breath. "Ja."

Hilde leaned close to Trude's ear. "You must get up on your hands and knees."

Trude rolled her head from side to side. "No. No, I cannot."

"You must. We will help you." Hilde nodded to Ingeborg. "We will roll her your way."

Ingeborg nodded, her stomach clenching along with her teeth. Together she and her mother rolled Trude over.

"Stiffen your arms, Trude. And your knees. We will help you."

Ingeborg strained, assisting to lift the woman who was so weak she could barely move her arms. Once they had her upright, Hilde braced. "See if you can turn the baby like you did the lamb."

Ingeborg closed her eyes. *Please, Lord. Please, Lord. Jesus, help me.*

"Trude, you must breathe and do what we say."

"Ja." Her head hung. The sound of her panting filled the room.

15

Ingeborg felt with her fingers. A leg. An arm. A shoulder. She concentrated and imagined that she was working on the ewe. Slowly, gently. A contraction squeezed her hand. The head, she felt the head, like the baby was swimming. And turning. And . . .

"The head, the baby is turned."

"Thank you, Lord God. Thank you." Hilde sang her litany over and over. Trude fell on her side and rolled onto her back. An anguished cry ripped from her throat. Her body convulsed and the baby boy flowed into Hilde's hands.

"Usually we lay the baby on the mother, but . . ." Hilde handed the baby to Ingeborg. "Hold him while I cut the cord."

With the cord tied off and severed, she returned to her patient to stem the blood flow. "Help him."

Ingeborg shook the baby gently. "Breathe, baby, breathe. God, make him breathe." She tipped the baby up and down, then blew in his face. She remembered her father squeezing the lamb's ribs. She pushed on the baby's chest and released. Again. She covered his nose and mouth and blew. The tiny chest heaved, and the baby stiffened in her hands. Then relaxed. And cried, a mewling that sounded more like a kitten than a baby. He flailed his hands and cried again.

Ingeborg grabbed the flannel cloths Trude had laid out and wrapped one around the tiny body. Holding him close, she watched as her mother worked to stop the bleeding.

Mor kept up an even pace, speaking in a singsong to encourage the woman in the bed.

Ingeborg held the tiny body close to her and grabbed a small blanket to wrap around him. Would the bleeding never cease? How could her mor remain so calm? Her own heart seemed ready to leap out of her chest.

After what seemed forever and the pile of bloodied cloths growing by the bed, the flow slowly eased, and Hilde nodded.

"Thank you, Lord God, thank you." She packed clean cloths against the woman's body and heaved a sigh. "How is he?"

"Alive."

"Lay him on his belly on his mother's chest."

Ingeborg did as told. "I have not cleaned him yet."

"Call the older woman to bring us hot water and a tub, so we can get these sheets soaking."

Ingeborg crossed the room and found the older woman sitting just outside the door. "Can you bring in a tub and plenty of warm water? We need to clean her and the baby."

"Alive? The baby is alive?"

"Ja. They both are."

"Praise God."

"Ja, praise God." Ingeborg waited until she returned, then took the hoop handle to carry hot water in to pour into a dishpan. She added some cold until it was just warm.

"You may wash him," Hilde said.

Very aware of the honor, Ingeborg took the baby in both her hands and lowered him into the water. So perfect. Tiny fingers and toes, a button nose and pink lips. He no longer looked blue. Perfect. This baby. She had helped this baby so he was able to be born, when he could so easily have died. She couldn't stop the tears that dripped off her chin. He waved a perfect little hand, swishing it in the water. With a cloth she washed his face and over the top of his bald little head. Was there anything else in this world that could be even close to feeling like this?

She glanced up to see her mother watching her. The two

smiled and together dried the little baby and wrapped him again, to lay him at his mother's side. Her faint smile as she held him close brought more tears.

"Tusen takk." The words came faintly from the mother.

"Thank our God. I will tell your husband he can come in now." Hilde glanced around the now straightened room. All the bloody sheets and cloths were soaking in the tub. Ingeborg had been cleaning while Mor settled the baby with his mor.

Later, mother and daughter walked toward the east and home. Behind them the stars still hung in the cerulean sky, but to the east, a band of faint yellow heralded the new day. A breeze picked up and lifted the strands of hair that had pulled free from their braids.

"I want to learn it all."

"Ja, I am not surprised. You too have been gifted with the desire for healing."

"There can be nothing like this . . . this . . ." Ingeborg's heart felt like it was bursting.

"New life."

"Ja. New life. Death was so near, hovering around our shoulders." She shuddered in the predawn chill.

"But God answered our prayers."

"This time. But what about the times He does not answer with life?" Ingeborg waited, expecting the usual curt reply. Why her mother seemed always angry at her she could never understand. But now they were actually talking.

"He always answers. But sometimes we do not like the answer."

"Today we helped that baby live. I have to know more." Ingeborg turned it into a promise to herself. She would learn

all there was to learn. Was this what God wanted for her?
"Will you teach me?"

"Ja, but it is not easy."

"I understand. Takk."

Besides, she didn't need a husband to become a midwife.

2

"So how did it go for Mrs. Gaard?" Gunlaug asked later that day when she brought over a basket of små brød, each little cake glowing golden. "Oh, and tell your mor this is a new recipe, and Mor wants to know her opinion."

Ingeborg stared at her cousin. Still groggy from lack of sleep, she caught a yawn and shook her head. "Which do you want first?"

Gunlaug gave her a look of confusion. "Mrs. Gaard, of course."

"We saved the baby, and Mor kept the missus from bleeding to death after the baby finally came."

"I was afraid to ask in case one or both of them had died."

Ingeborg closed her eyes, feeling herself back in that room where death had hovered in the corners. "So close." Did she dare share with her innocent cousin what had gone on? "You cannot tell anyone if I tell you something."

Gunlaug's eyes widened. "Who would I tell?"

Ingeborg shrugged. That was true. The only ones they told were each other. "I . . . I turned the baby inside Mrs. Gaard like I did the lamb. I felt the baby turn, and there was his head. He was born just a few minutes later, and his mother nearly bled to death. Oh, Gunlaug, he is so perfect. And then he wouldn't breathe and I finally breathed for him and he went stiff and then started to breathe and he sounded like an angry kitten. Mor let me wash him, and oh, Gunlaug, helping a baby come into this world has to be the most wonderful thing I can do."

"You can do? Tante Hilde is the midwife."

"I know, but she said she would teach me all she knows if I really want to learn, and I do so want to learn all that I can."

"I think your mor wants you to get married more than she wants you to take over her job as midwife."

"But I could do this and not have to even think about finding a suitable man and getting married."

"Tante Hilde is married. I think you have to be married to be a midwife."

Ingeborg felt like stamping her foot. Why was Gunlaug being so stubborn?

"Besides, that means you'd have to spend all your time with your mor, and you and she don't always get along."

Now, that was an understatement. Ingeborg stared at her cousin. Sometimes she made really wise comments, and this was obviously one of those times. Mor found more fault with her than all the others put together. She'd often wondered why and finally figured it was because she had more flaws than anyone else. She was headstrong, stubborn, and argumentative at times, and had a curiosity bump that couldn't be stifled.

It was a shame her mor couldn't be more like her far. He let her try things that most fathers wouldn't, like helping birth the lambs and calves and learning how to notice and treat many of the animal ailments. While other fathers would not permit their daughters to study and learn all they could, instead consigning them to help their mors, her father encouraged her to think and question.

Through the years she and her oldest brother, Gilbert, had engaged in many discussions that sometimes grew rather heated. Gilbert, who was not only Ingeborg's older brother but was also the oldest of all the cousins, was a firm believer in doing things the same way they had always been done, and Ingeborg wanted them to try new practices she'd read of.

"Ingeborg. Ingeborg, come back from wherever you went." Gunlaug waved a hand in front of Ingeborg's face.

"Oh, sorry."

"I'm glad you were able to help Mrs. Gaard."

"Mor will go check on her in a bit. I'm hoping I can go along."

"If you do, I'd suggest you keep your torrent of questions to a minimum."

Ingeborg nodded. "You're right." She wrinkled her nose and made a face. "But how am I to learn it all if I cannot ask all the questions?"

"That's your problem." Gunlaug got that goofy look on her face again. "Just think, three more days until the dance. What are you going to wear?"

"Clothes."

"I will have my new blue skirt finished by then, and I am going to add some lace to that waist that is looking shabby."

Ingeborg grabbed her friend's hand. "Come with me. I need to check on the cow that is due to calve. She's out in the west pasture."

All the way out through the three gates and skirting around an area that had gone boggy with the spring melt, Gunlaug talked about Ivar. Ingeborg tuned out her cousin's voice and let herself ponder what had gone on during the night. What might they have done differently? First, how could they have made the woman more comfortable? Second, was there a way to prevent a baby from going breech and thereby sliding into the birth canal like God ordained for it to do? When did the baby turn wrong? Was it something the mother did? Her mor had said it was an act of God, but why would God step in and make a baby do something wrong? If it was the mother's fault, what had she done and when? In between her thoughts, she nodded and smiled at Gunlaug as if she cared to hear about Ivar, her latest beau.

They finally located the cow off in one corner behind a stand of willow brush, already nudging her calf toward the teats dripping milk. She lowed and tossed her head, warning Ingeborg to stay away.

"Easy girl, you did a fine job. How about we go on up to the barn, where you two will be safer?" The smell of blood could bring in all sorts of predators, many of whom would be very pleased to carry off the newborn calf. Ignoring the threatening motions from the cow, Ingeborg broke off a willow branch and walked around on the other side of the disgruntled mama.

"Aren't you going to let the calf get stronger first?" Gunlaug followed Ingeborg's lead and broke off a switch.

"I suppose I should, but we lost a lamb out here earlier. The scavengers pick up on a scent quickly."

Gunlaug looked over her shoulder, as if expecting a wolf to leap out from behind the brush at the end of the field.

Ingeborg rolled her eyes, something she did often when her cousin's many fears got in their way.

Ingeborg spotted another mat of dandelions. "We can fill our aprons with those while we wait."

"Who do you want to dance with?" Gunlaug adopted the dopey look again.

"The king of Sweden and Norway."

"Ivar is such a good dancer. What if I could dance every dance with him?"

"You think it will snow today?" Ingeborg tucked her chuckle back under her chin and added more handfuls of green leaves to the apron she'd removed and laid flat for carrying the greenery.

Gunlaug glanced toward her. "I'd let you dance with him, you know."

"Right. You know his mother would be sending darts at you if he didn't dance with others too."

"I don't think she likes me very much."

"She doesn't like anyone who catches her sweet baby's eye. You know that no one, even the queen mother herself, would be good enough for her precious son."

"True. But I love him, and he needs to be loved. Maybe then he will be happier."

Ingeborg glanced up to see the calf nursing, his tail doing the metronome swish. *Enjoy your first meal of colostrum, little fellow. It is your last. From now on, we'll be milking your mor and giving you what's left.* She felt almost guilty about it, but it had to be.

She sat back on her heels. In the blue arch of the heavens, she heard the scree of an eagle. The mountain peaks gleamed white, and the greening of the pastures not only charmed her eyes but tickled her nose. The smell of spring was one of her favorite scents. The pungent odor of the dandelion leaves only added another overlay of joy.

She mused, "Soon we'll be able to journey up to the seter. Freedom again. I can't wait."

Gunlaug wailed, "But then I won't see Ivar for weeks at a time, or even all summer."

Ingeborg ignored her and searched for the eagle. Wouldn't it be an amazing thing to find the eagle's nest in the crags of the cliffs? Her brother Gilbert had found one once and saw three hatchlings in the nest of sticks. He also found out that a furious mother eagle could inflict serious damage on a climber. He still bore the talon scars on one shoulder.

She picked up the corners of her apron and tied them together into a bundle. "Let's move her down now."

Together they drove the cow and calf down to the small fenced pasture behind the barn. The cow ambled over to drink at the water tank and didn't even notice that Ingeborg was shunting her calf off into the calf pen. Ingeborg made sure the gates were securely closed and took her bundle of greens up to the house.

"Mor said to tell you that you could have gone with her, but she couldn't find you." Mari, the baby of the family at ten, turned from checking the roast baking in the Dutch oven hanging over the coals of the fireplace. "She said that when you finally showed up, you should start the corn bread for supper." She wiped her hands on her apron. "You brought more dandelion leaves. Good."

As if Mor had looked for her. She'd said she was going to check on the cow. Had Mor waited until she left to go back to the Gaards'? No matter how many questions Ingeborg had, she'd not been able to ask them. The thought of Mor's frown warned her away.

"Bess had her calf way out to the end of the pasture. He'd just been born, so the walk down took awhile." She dipped water out of the wooden bucket into a basin and started washing the quickly wilting leaves. That was one thing about spring greens. It took a lot of them to feed the family even one meal.

⁓

Saturday blossomed under the spring rain that had been falling off and on for two days. The earth smelled fresh and new as Ingeborg carried the milk buckets up from the barn. She poured the milk through the strainer and into the pans to let the cream rise. She had enough cream already to make butter, and that was the next thing on her list to do for the day. Her mother had been called out again during the night but did not invite her to go along. Resentment nibbled at the edge of her thoughts like a mouse on cheese. How was she to learn if she was always left at home?

Berta and Mari were putting breakfast on the table by the time she walked into the house.

"Did you bring up the cream pitcher?" Berta asked over her shoulder from where she was lifting bacon from the pan to a platter.

"No. No one asked me to."

"We ran out." Mari headed for the door.

"Can you go call the men instead?" Berta swiped the back of her hand over her forehead. She sounded so much like Mor that Ingeborg did a double take. The same sound of dissatisfaction, as if Ingeborg should have known enough to bring up the cream pitcher without being told.

"I will, and I will get the cream pitcher." She knew she sounded aggrieved, but hearing it from Mor was bad enough. "You don't have to get all cross."

Ingeborg shook her head as she headed out the door. She retrieved the cream pitcher from the springhouse, called to the men working on a wagon by the barn, and returned to the house, reminding herself to just ignore tones and pay attention to words. The weeks to moving up to the seter were stretching longer and longer. Ah, the seter. That was the one place she was in charge, and no one whined at her or ordered her around. As Gunlaug had reminded her, at the seter they were free.

She resolved not to mention that she was disappointed not to be asked to go with Mor when she returned. She had plenty to do before they all had to get ready for the dance.

The dance. Such mixed emotions surrounded the dance. Many of the Christian families refused to attend dances. But it was a place for young people to meet and talk, so the Strands were among those who went. Quite possibly it was at Ingeborg's mor's instigation, for weddings were forged there. Gunlaug could not wait. Ingeborg could. She could read the looks her mor gave her well, and the most looks always came at dances. *Go find a husband. Be charming. Keep your questions to yourself.* Amazing how many different things could be read into one glance. Perhaps because she had heard them all so many times before.

Gilbert had not married yet. Why was he not getting the looks? Sometimes, really often, she wished she had taken Bjorn, the second son, eighteen months older than she, up on his offer to take her to Amerika with him, but then they'd never heard from him again. Mor and Far were sure he had died, since he'd not ever written. According to records, the ship had made it to Amerika, but perhaps he died on the voyage, or he had landed and something happened to him. They'd all heard the horror stories of people disappearing in spite of the advertisements by Amerikan railroads promising a land of streets paved with gold. But free land— that was what emigrants could work for. And what made the long journey and the dark, unknown dangers possibly worth it.

⅌

Ingeborg sighed, for at last the evening of the dance had arrived. Her sisters were all getting dressed, and she was sure Gunlaug was also ready long in advance. If there were any way out, Ingeborg would take it.

"Are you not ready?" Mor asked one more time.

"Nearly." Ingeborg wrapped her golden braid around her head and pinned it into place. Gilbert gave her a brief nod with an almost smile that showed her he approved. Gilbert and Ingeborg each picked up a basket of the food they'd prepared, as did their parents as they went out the door to walk the mile to the Geltlunds' place. The dance would be held in the barn loft tonight, for not only was it in town, it was nearly empty of fodder. Far had said they'd leave the horses to rest tonight.

The Strands met Gunlaug's family as they walked the road past their farm, and her cousin immediately fell into step beside Ingeborg.

"What if Ivar's mother gives me one of her looks for dancing too often with her son?"

"Ignore her."

"You might be able to do that, but she makes me quake in my shoes."

Ingeborg shook her head. *Silly goose, you better listen to what you are saying if you want to marry that mama's boy. His mother will run your life, or ruin it.* But she kept her thoughts to herself. Perhaps up at the seter, Gunlaug would get over this infatuation for Ivar.

They heard the music while they were still up the road a bit. Katrina, Ingeborg's next in line sister, hung back, and Oscar Boll, her intended, fell in step with her as they passed his farm. He was a bit slow but not a bad catch. Right now, he and his far were building a house for the new bride and groom, so they might not have to live with his parents. Since he was the eldest son, he would inherit the farm.

Couples were swirling around the well-swept area to the beat of a tune played by an accordion, a fiddle, and a guitar, which its owner insisted was imported from Germany. Someone thumped on a homemade drum. Ingeborg's feet seemed to have a life of their own. She never could keep still when the music played.

They set their baskets on the tables, and Gilbert grabbed her hand. "Come on, before you get told what to do."

Gratitude for her older brother swept her along with him as they picked up the pattern and let the music take them away. Both of them were content to enjoy dancing and not talk.

Ingeborg glanced off to the side. She had attracted the attention of Asti, a sort of friend, since they both knew everyone in the small community of Valdres. Asti wanted to be dancing with Gilbert, Ingeborg knew, and she tucked a smile away. Surely Gilbert might like to know this, if he didn't already.

Asti would be a good wife to her big brother. How could she work this out?

She stopped herself. Why would she work this out? She hated being pushed, hated being the subject of matchmaking. Surely Gilbert would like it no better. She missed a beat and shrugged up at him. When the music ended, she guided him over to where Asti and another friend were chatting. When Gilbert slowed down, she took his arm and kept him going. "Asti, how nice to see you."

The slender young woman smiled back and up at Gilbert also.

"How's your mor?" Ingeborg knew the woman had been having health problems.

"She's better."

The musicians picked up a polka, and Ingeborg smiled up at her brother. "Why don't you and Asti go dance this one." She pulled his hand out and placed it over Asti's, ignoring any look he might be giving her and smiling at Asti, who was shyer than she needed to be. She watched the two of them move toward the dance floor and congratulated herself on a job well done.

A tap came on her shoulder, and her onkel Jonas took her hand. "Surely you'll give an old man a chance to enjoy this dance."

"Since you are not old yet, I'm not sure."

She linked her arm through his, knowing they would not need to talk. Of her mother's brothers, he was her favorite.

Later on she saw Gilbert and Asti together again, and this time they were both smiling. And talking. Maybe he wouldn't be put out with her after all.

After the dance, Ivar asked Gunlaug if he could walk her home, so Ingeborg fell in with her family.

"Why did you not dance with that nice Garborg boy?" her mor asked. There was the slightest tinge of disapproval in her voice, as if she considered it Ingeborg's fault.

"He didn't ask me," Ingeborg answered, bringing her mind back from something Onkel Jens had said.

"Did you even meet him?"

"No one introduced me."

"I am sure if you had made any effort, you could have arranged it."

I was too busy helping Gilbert and Asti. But she kept that thought to herself too. If only she could remember to keep her mouth closed more often.

She wished someone would ask her mor a question, make a comment, anything.

"He seemed a very nice young man." Mor pressed forward. "He is working in his father's store in Hallingdal."

"Oh." What could she say? She would spread gossip, that's what. "Did you know that Onkel Jonas wants to go to Amerika?"

"He can't. He is the eldest son and has inherited the land."

"What if he chose to give that land to a younger brother, or even a sister?" *Ingeborg Strand, do not ask questions if you don't want to know the answer, or in this case listen to your mother talk down to you again.* As if she didn't know the primogeniture rules also.

"That just isn't done." The tone of finality should have warned her to stop.

"But what if he doesn't want the land?"

"The law is the law."

"There must be a provision for a situation like this."

"Mor, my heel hurts. I think I must have a blister." Mari,

the youngest of the children, tugged at her mor's skirt on the other side.

Grateful for the reprieve, Ingeborg dropped back and walked by herself. If only the time for the seter would come soon.

3

OSLO, NORWAY

"You know you are not working anywhere near your potential."

Fighting to keep his face neutral, Nils stared at his father. Agree? Disagree? Would it make any difference? He chose the neutral way. "I know."

"Then why are you not doing something about it?" Rignor Aarvidson stared across his steepled fingers at his son—his only son and thus the heir to the hard-earned Aarvidson wealth, a fiefdom started by his father and passed on to the eldest son, namely RA. He waited, his eyes narrowing.

Nils turned back to the window on the third floor of a cut-stone building right in the heart of Oslo. He could just see the harbor, where he knew his father's ships were moored, awaiting another load of lumber on the way to insatiable London. Why could his father not leave him be? The sun was out for a change, and the mountains were calling him. One more ski break before the snow melted.

But yes, he was not working anywhere near as hard as he needed to be. He remained in the upper third of his class, but he knew well he should be competing for top honors at his college. If only he could convince himself of the value of history and philosophy, let alone French. Though that was one class he excelled in, strictly because he could see a purpose in it. But studying the Napoleonic Wars only served to remind him that history would repeat itself if not learned.

At this point he spoke both Swedish and Norwegian fluently, had a fair knowledge of German, and could understand the opera in French. His favorite composers were Bach and Grieg, whose music echoed of mountains and living water thundering down the mountainsides. Studying music history was not a sacrifice. But his father did not deem those studies necessary to continue to build the family fortune, when the reins descended into his son's very unwilling hands.

"So what are we to do?"

We? He meant, of course, *What are you going to do about this great lack in your character*? But could we be opening a doorway or at least a window to negotiating? His father loved nothing more than a good argument well presented.

"What is it? Your face just announced it had joined the discussion."

Nils turned and focused on his father's fingers. One forefinger tapped the other, a sure sign that he was running out of patience. "I have an idea, but I'd like to have some time to think it through before we discuss it."

RA heaved a sigh, paused, and then with eyes still narrowed, gave an abrupt nod. "Will you be home for supper tonight?"

Nils knew that was not a question but a command. He'd not planned to be home for supper, but this was of sufficient importance to change his plans. After all, attending another soirée was not high on his list of enjoyments anyway. He was only going because it would make his mother happy. He could be home for supper and the discussion and still arrive fashionably late.

"Yes, sir, I will be."

"Good. Notify Cook that we will both be there." His father spun his chair and rose to his full height, a trick that Nils knew his father used when he wanted to intimidate someone. It used to work with his son.

When had that changed? Nils almost pondered that as he made his exit. Feeling like a trapped bird newly freed, he whistled his way down the three sets of stairs and out onto the street. Instead of catching a hansom cab, he chose to walk the half mile back to the university campus. Good weather like this demanded that he take advantage of it.

He nodded to the two young ladies he met and could feel their gaze on his back as he continued onward. Attracting the female population took no effort on his part. His mother had called his looks classic Norsk and pointed to his father as an example. Although Nils's wavy hair was a darker shade of blond than his father's had ever been, it was no less attractive. He nodded and tipped his hat to two older ladies, one of whom looked vaguely familiar. He had half an hour until his next class and needed to pick up his textbooks first.

⁓

Nils enjoyed philosophy, more or less. This class was less. Much less. While the professor droned on about the importance of properly weighing the statements of Marcus Jakob Monrad—Norway's foremost philosopher— when discussing governmental matters, Nils jotted down notes for his evening meeting with his father. It would look like he was studiously taking class notes. At the end of the lecture, he folded over the page in his notebook and carefully ripped out his notes, tucking the paper into his pocket.

As he was walking out the door, Hans Boonstra fell in beside him, matching him stride for stride. The cheerful Dutchman was grinning, as usual. "Saw you taking class notes very studiously. So what were you writing down really?"

"Classes like this one are better skipped." Nils was grinning too. "You know me far too well, Hans. Will you be going back to Rotterdam when school is done?"

"Probably. My father is lining up a job for me. I'd much rather stay here. Your father isn't hiring this summer, is he?"

"Not that I know of. I'll keep you posted if something comes up. Don't you want to go home?"

"To a mother who constantly tries to make me perfect so I'll marry well, and a father who constantly finds fault because I'm not exactly like him? Spare me."

"You too, eh?" So apparently Nils's life was not unique. They chatted idly for two blocks before separating. Nils cut across the park and down the alley to his family's home, where he'd been invited to join them for supper.

"I'm home, Mor," he announced as he stuck his head into the drawing room, where his mother was entertaining her sister for coffee.

"Come and greet your tante Marit." His mother beckoned him in.

He kept from rolling his eyes by sheer force of habit, gave his aunt a sort of half bow and half dip of the head, then looked to his mother. "I need to get changed before supper." Then back to his aunt. "Will you be joining us?"

"Nei, I must leave soon. Be a dear boy and ask Mrs. Skogen to call for my carriage."

"I'm sorry to hear you won't be joining us. I always enjoy your company."

"Another time. Will you be at the soirée later?"

"If at all possible. I'm planning on it."

"Good. I hear there is a young lady coming whom I would love to introduce you to."

"Now, seriously, why would you want to do that? I have another year of school and then must concentrate on learning the business, all before I can think of the ladies, including—" he paused—"Ingra Grunewald."

The tante clucked. "Cheeky boy. You know she and that Lund lad are seeing each other."

"Not seriously, of course." Another of his mother's dreams, a union between the two houses of Aarvidson LMT and Grunewald, their closest competitor. A union of the two would create a possible monopoly in the lumber shipping trade from Norway, a longtime dream of both of his parents. While he found Ingra to be lovely and a talented pianist, she lacked seriously in the love of outdoors, much preferring drawing rooms to mountain meadows and rocky trails.

"Ah yes. Unless you are publicly committed, there is always room for hope." The tante tapped her folded fan on his arm. "We must make time for a good visit one of these days."

"We must, but let's not discuss my future love life, please." He gave a vague imitation of a bow and left the room. Why did every woman over the age of thirty set about matchmaking? He and his tante used to play chess. Sometimes she even let him win. She was also quite a horsewoman, and they had spent many hours in the saddle at Laughing Creek, the summer home of her and her husband, the uncle for whom Nils was named, now deceased. That had been a sad day for all of them, as Onkel and Tante were favorites of all three of the Aarvidson children.

Nils took the curving walnut staircase two at a time and hurried down the hall to his rooms. Being late to the table was another way to irritate his far, one he was careful not to trespass upon. He shut the door behind him and sighed. A fire danced in the fireplace, and his evening attire was laid out on the bed, waiting for him. Bless Janssen for looking ahead and making sure his young man was properly dressed. Open-necked shirts with full sleeves and tightly woven wool pants that resisted wind and water were much more Nils's style, along with hiking boots and a leather vest. Riding boots too were much preferred to the fine leather shoes waiting in front of the chair. The temptation to hide out in the wing-back chair in front of the fire was hard to resist, but resist he did and donned the evening's wear, including the cravat draped on the back of the chair. He paused to clasp the walnut mantel in both hands and lean his forehead on them to stare into the dancing fire.

A campfire on the edge of a crystal blue high mountain lake slipped into his mind. If his plan worked, that would become an actuality instead of a memory. Give him trout from the lake, sizzling in a frying pan, with the hoot of an owl for music, and he was purely content.

"You better hurry, young sir," Janssen said from the doorway. "They are already gathering."

"Thank you." Nils slipped his arms into the waistcoat Janssen held out for him, then the dinner coat. "Will I do?"

"Yes, you'll do. You'll more than do." Janssen stepped back. "Will you be late tonight?"

"Most likely, unless I can beg off early. I have a good excuse though—more reading in my so delightful philosophy book, sure to put one to sleep in short order."

"Is that why you often read it standing in front of the fire?"

"Only way I can stay awake."

Janssen smiled, showing his gold tooth. "You'll do fine."

"Thank you." Nils followed him out, nearly being run into by his younger sister. "Easy does it."

"Mor reminded me to not be late, and I almost am." Katja tucked a wisp of hair back to be pinned in. Unruly hair after one had put her hair up was not to be tolerated.

"Don't worry. You look lovely, as always."

She tucked her arm around his. "Thank you. You always make me feel good. Shall we go down?"

He leaned closer and whispered, "To the dungeon?"

"I hope not. You had a meeting with Far today. How did he seem?"

"Disappointed. I am not working up to my potential."

"Well, you aren't."

"I know, but—"

"But you'd rather be up in the mountains, or at least the hills, or horseback, or . . ."

He patted her hand. "You know me well. If only sons were not the only ones expected to work in the family business. Amalia would rather be in the office than anywhere else. She was just born the wrong sex."

Katja nodded. "She thinks making money is the most exciting thing in the world. You should see the books she reads. And the newspapers. She squirrels them away as soon as Far is finished with them."

"She will do well heading up some charity and using her

skills to bring money in for their ministries." He turned to look at her as they descended the stairs. "And you, pet, what do you want to do?"

"Go climb the mountains along with you." She patted his arm, as if she were the older and wiser. "It's a shame none of us can have what we want."

"At least you can still go riding with Tante."

Katja dropped her voice. "I rode astride one day. I may never go back to the sidesaddle—a horrid contraption made by men to restrict women. You can only half control your horse, and it's easy to become unbalanced."

"You better not say that out loud."

"I know, but I can always say my mind to you." They entered the dining room just as their father seated their mother. They'd missed the drawing room conversations, which didn't bother either one of them.

"Glad you could manage to get here reasonably on time." RA waited until Nils seated his sister, then sat himself.

Nils just nodded, shook out his napkin and laid it in his lap.

"Shall we pray?"

Bowing his head, he let the old words roll over him. "I Jesu navn, går vi til bords . . ." Together they said the amen, and the footman brought in the soup tureen.

Nils kept one ear on the conversation, which was deemed proper for the dining room. Far asked each of the girls what had been the most important part of their day, and then looked to his son. "And you, Nils, what do you have to say?"

I stayed awake during philosophy was probably not a good thing to say, nor was *I was late to my first class*. His father had probably already heard that anyway. "Did you read what the king had to say this morning in his address to the Parliament?"

Since Norway was under the control of Sweden, the Swedish King Oscar II, no matter how highly respected he was worldwide, still managed to say things to offend RA, especially in regard to business measures.

"Ja."

The one-word comment stated clearly his father's opinion. While there was talk about Norway becoming independent, so far nothing was happening. When the question had been asked and answered, general conversation moved around the table. The parents had always encouraged their children to think for themselves and be able to converse intelligently, with much of the training accomplished at the dinner table. But when discussions became heated, Mor intervened with a look that took the place of many words.

Nils contributed but didn't bring up any new topics if the conversation lagged. His mind kept leaping forward to the forthcoming meeting. Would his father be willing to compromise? While he said that was an important business tactic, he often failed to use it with his family.

When Mor rose to signal the end of the meal, the girls followed her to the drawing room, where they took out their needlework and drank tea. Nils followed his father into the den.

As soon as they were settled into their leather chairs in front of the fire, Nils, ever mindful of the time, broke the silence. "Today you asked me what I planned to do about my failure to try my hardest at my studies." His father nodded, tamping the tobacco into his pipe at the same time. "I have an idea that could be very effective."

RA nodded again and leaned back to draw on the pipe, puffing a smoke ring into the air, something that had enthralled his son when he was small.

"I propose that instead of working at the office this summer, I take the summer off to spend in the mountains. I believe time there will help clear my head and get my feet on the right track so that in my senior year I will strive to be at the top of my class. I will agree to settle down, as Mor has also requested, and we will plan the next steps for me in life." He paused. Had he said enough? Too much? Would adding "I promise" make a difference? He watched his father blow another smoke ring and nod slightly.

"So you think you can do that? Be at the head of the class?"

"Yes, sir, I do." Nils kept his eyes from slitting to match his father's.

"Turn your studies around and take honors in each class?"

"Yes, sir."

"And this plan of yours to clear your head and rejuvenate your ambition is not just a ploy to avoid working in the business?"

"I have already learned the lessons of business and would simply be relearning them were I to stay here. You yourself extol the value of compromise, of tempering the absolutes of life."

RA nodded thoughtfully. Nils's hopes soared.

The gentleman leaned forward, his elbows on his knees. "In a word: no."

4

"Jonas is serious about going off to Amerika?" Hilde asked her husband at the breakfast table the following Saturday.

"I believe so. I reminded him that we never heard from our Bjorn again, but Jonas is sure nothing could happen to him." Arne shook his head. "Pass the ham, please."

Ingeborg recognized the tightening of Mor's jawline that said she was fighting the tears that had flowed so often over the last year. She'd often said it was the never knowing. And the dream that her second son was still alive. But if he were alive, why had they not heard from him? It was strange that they'd never heard a word. Surely if he had died on the passage, the shipping line would have notified them. And now Mor's youngest brother was planning on leaving too.

"So when does Onkel Jonas plan to leave?" Mari asked.

"Yet this spring, it sounds like. As soon as they've gathered enough money for his passage. He wants to farm there so he will take the railroad up on the offer to help him find land."

Ingeborg knew Far sometimes let himself dream of the

challenge of crossing to Amerika. But he owned land in Norway, even though it was not enough. Did one ever have enough land? But were it not for the seter in the summer, they would not have sufficient pasture and hayfields to feed the number of cows and sheep they ran.

She caught her mother's glance and got up to bring the coffeepot to refill the cups. Surely they would need midwives in Amerika, not that she was anywhere near trained enough. What if she were to ask Onkel Jonas if she could go along? What would Mor and Far say to that? But if she left, who would run the seter? Gunlaug could.

She paused by the fireplace. Today she needed to churn the cream into butter. Why that had become her job, she had no idea. Mari needed to be learning to do this and let Ingeborg go out and work in the garden.

She looked to Gilbert. "Will you have time to plow the garden today?"

"We are going into town," Far said in that flat voice that brooked no argument.

"Then may I use the team?"

"I will help you," Hjelmer offered, glancing at Far, who nodded.

She ignored the daggers she could feel coming her way from Mor. She was sure to hear more later, after the men left.

"Berta, you take over churning the butter. As soon as we get the garden plowed and run over with the disk, we can all go out there to rake and plant."

"You would do better to wait a day or two. It is time to wash all the bedding and hang it out in the sun to dry."

She looked to Mor, who wore the sour expression so often associated with her oldest daughter.

"Katrina and Berta can do that. We have to get the garden started while we have nice weather." Ingeborg almost flinched. That was why they were to do the bedding today.

Mor glared at her but didn't say any more.

Ingeborg knew she would pay for the victory later. Why did Mor dislike her so? What had she ever done to deserve her being angry all the time? Whom could she ask? Since Katrina was preparing for her wedding in June, she had been relieved of many other house duties to finish her linens and things for her chest—the beautiful chest Far had made for her. Katrina was doing what Mor wanted. Ingeborg blew out a sigh. She never had been able to just do what she was told. Sometimes . . . sometimes . . . She picked up a piece of firewood and stoked the fire with several vicious jabs of the poker.

A short time later, Ingeborg and Hjelmer escaped to the barn. They would harness the lighter of the two teams for the garden work. Ah, spring. The horses were shedding pounds of hair. It rose in clouds around them.

There was always a challenge between the three Strand families as to who would get their garden in first. The Arne Strand family had won last year and Ingeborg intended to make that two years in a row.

"I didn't think Far would say yes." Hjelmer stood on a stool to set the collar over the team's withers. He'd not begun to get his growth yet, something that Ingeborg knew worried him. Gilbert of course had his full height, but Hjelmer still wore the look of a boy, slender and not even as tall as Ingeborg by any means. Most of the Strand men wore their height proudly—all but Hjelmer, who was the shortest of the male cousins his age too.

"You know Far would never say this, but he wants to beat his two brothers in the garden race as bad as I want to."

"Mor thinks the race is silly," Hjelmer said.

"I know, but you have to admit that making a game of it makes the hard work more enjoyable."

"I get to plow too?" Hjelmer hopped up on the stool again to check on the horse's rump, making certain that there would be no chafing under the crupper.

"Thank you for checking for rubbing," she said. "I forgot." His grin and quick nod rewarded her. She suggested, "Let me drive the first rows and you try the next?"

Hjelmer nodded. "If I can reach the plow handles well enough."

"If not, we'll do it together." The look of gratitude he sent her made Ingeborg glad she was paying attention. They hitched the team up to the plow, and Ingeborg looped the lines over her shoulder like she'd seen Far do. This too was something most women didn't attempt. Often she wished she'd been born a male, but no longer. Now she wanted to be an even better midwife than her mother.

The shine on the blade showed it had been sharpened. Another thing she'd forgotten to ask. But then Far would have said no, the plow wasn't ready. Hjelmer swung the garden gate open, and she drove the team in, setting the angle of the blade to cut through the dirt. Good thing they'd disked the garden in the fall and then spread cow manure over it through the winter. She gripped the handles, pointed the blade down, and clucked the team forward. The blade bounced free of the ground and leaned to the side. "Whoa." She had to use more muscle. And more size would be helpful too.

Mor stood on the back stoop and shook her head before returning into the house.

The team stood patiently while Ingeborg reset herself. Hjelmer came to stand beside her.

"What if I drive so you can concentrate on the plow?"

"Good idea." She moved the wooden handles up and down to figure the best place and gripped them fiercely this time. Hjelmer clucked the team ahead, and Ingeborg gritted her teeth. Surely she could outsmart brute strength. After all, Far and Gilbert made this look so easy. "Keep 'em straight." She'd never hear the end of it if the rows turned out to be crooked.

The first steps were the hardest, but once the blade angled correctly and the horses moved forward smoothly, it was somewhat easier. After they had made a trip up and back in the garden plot, Ingeborg signaled a halt. Through narrowed eyes she studied their work. A wee bit crooked, but not erratic. Her arms and shoulders screamed in protest. "I need to get some heavy leather gloves. You wait here."

"I'm too short, aren't I?"

"Ja, I'm afraid so, but without you, I could not do this." She made herself smile at him before she headed for the shop where Far kept a stock of leather gloves. Most of them needed patching. Resolved to do that in the evenings, she found two with no holes in the palms and returned to her purgatory. They were about half done when Mari came out to say that the midday meal was ready.

She let Hjelmer unhitch the team and drive the horses back to the barn, where they could rest too. "Don't water them."

"I know. Too hot."

Ingeborg nodded and started up the rise to the house. Wet sheets and airing bedding flapped in the breeze that dried the sweat on her face and neck. Could she go back for more or cry defeat? With tears near the surface, she washed up and sat in her place at the table.

"Have you had enough?" her mother asked, her eyebrows arched and head shaking.

Ingeborg glanced over to see Hjelmer sliding into his chair. His slight headshake put the steel again in her backbone. "It is not done yet but soon will be."

Her little brother's grin was worth the effort. At least she hoped so.

The two men hadn't yet returned from their trip to town, so the others ate without them before returning to their chores.

Far and Gilbert drove into the yard as Ingeborg and Hjelmer were hitching the team to the disk. Two heavy rocks sat on the frame, the weight needed to keep the disks in the ground and not riding on top.

"You finished the plowing?" Gilbert stared at his sister, who managed to nod only through sheer force of will.

"Hjelmer will do the disking."

Far started to say something but cut it off and drove the wagon on up to the house to unload the supplies.

Looking elated, Hjelmer hupped the team and returned to the now plowed garden. Walking behind the disk, he held the lines firmly, focusing on the job ahead. In moments he stepped up onto the back frame of the disk, his slight weight added to that of the rocks. How like his far he was in that way, able to ignore things around him to work solely on the job at hand. Ingeborg felt a fierce pride in her little brother.

The sun was still high in the sky when Hjelmer drove the team out of the gate and back to the barn, where he and Ingeborg removed the harnesses and hung them on the wall.

Lifting the heavy leather up onto the waiting pegs took her last bit of energy, but they had done it. Plowed and disked the garden. Now the others could start raking.

At supper, Ingeborg could hardly haul the fork all the way up to her mouth. Her chin dropped to her chest, but sleep could not come with every muscle screaming and tightening at the same time.

"You foolish girl," Mor said. "Come. We have some liniment that will help. Women are not cut out to do the men's chores. I hope you learned your lesson."

Too exhausted to even respond, she followed Mor to the bedroom and, after removing her top, sat on the edge of the bed.

Ingeborg woke up the following Saturday, grateful to be able to move with ease. The morning after their plowing session, she'd awoken with every muscle and joint screaming. After hauling herself out of bed, slowly and carefully she'd stretched her hands over her head and turned from side to side. By the third time, she could feel the muscles relent, even to letting her exhale a big breath and drop forward, also slowly and with restraint. That was most assuredly not her normal way of preparing for the day. She'd groaned her clothes on and stumbled her way out of her room.

"Mor said to go on out to the garden," Mari said now when Ingeborg entered the kitchen. "They are raking."

Ingeborg muttered an answer and poured herself a cup of coffee, reflecting that the morning after plowing, her hand and arm had barely been able to lift the pot. Half a cup later, she dished up the mush, still warm in the pan sitting in the coals before the fire, poured cream on it, and sat down at the table.

Mari turned back to washing and rinsing the dishes. She had finally grown tall enough that she no longer had to stand on the bench Far had built for growing children to work from.

Ingeborg closed her eyes. After several days of on and off spring showers, the garden was finally dry enough to start planting. Today they'd sow all but the more sensitive crops that would not tolerate the heavy frosts that might still visit. Some years they'd even had a late snow. One could never trust the weather.

Mari finished her chores and stopped next to Ingeborg. "Mor was really upset with you last week."

"I know." Ingeborg said nothing, but she knew she'd done the best thing, whether Mor could ever bring herself to admit it or not. The men hadn't had time to do the garden then, and who knew when they would. And they couldn't afford to waste good weather when they got it. Besides, with warmer weather, perhaps the women would leave for the seter early. Just the thought made her stand up.

When she got out the door, the sun greeted her with an extra benediction of warmth, while a slight breeze invited her to go see the lambs before grabbing a rake or hoe from where they leaned against the side of the house.

Propping herself on the top rail, she automatically counted the lambs, paused, studied the pasture again, and recounted. Still short one. She opened the gate and crossed to the fold where the animals were penned at night. Had anyone counted them before shutting the gate last night? Empty. She walked behind the barn to find one ewe basking in the warmth from the wall, her lamb by her side. With a smile, she returned to the back yard, grateful that nothing had happened. Surely the dogs would have let the whole valley know if a predator attacked during the night. And the ewe would have been bleating and running around looking for her baby.

Losing lambs was always one of her big worries, since wool in the spring and fall and lambs for slaughter were two of their cash crops. With over twenty ewes they finally had more fleece than they could clean and spin into their own yarn, unless they wove more into rugs and blankets. Weaving was usually a winter occupation, as was spinning, other than what they accomplished up at the seter. While Ingeborg was adept at both, Gunlaug was the master and taught the older children during the summer. Cheese was Ingeborg's specialty.

"All is well?" Mor asked, leaning for a moment on her rake handle.

"Ja. Just a bit of a scare when I saw we were short a lamb and a ewe. They were resting behind the barn. Not their usual place, but both seemed all right."

"Do you want to start marking rows for the potatoes? Berta is nearly finished cutting what we have left. We certainly don't want a slack harvest like last year."

"Was Far able to buy more?"

Hilde shook her head. "Everyone is short."

Digging with one's fingers for the first new potatoes under the flourishing vines was Ingeborg's favorite treasure hunt. The new potatoes were crisp and sweet. Sometimes she washed one and ate it raw, like an apple.

She took the ball of twine rolled on a stick and laid out the first row between two other sticks, then hoed a hole, dropped in the potatoes, and mounded the dirt over them. The fragrance of freshly turned soil made her smile. It was one of the smells of spring that always made her rejoice. While she loved all the seasons and the changes therein, burgeoning life in spring was her favorite by far. Especially after the long dark winter.

"You mark and I'll plant," Berta said, so Ingeborg swung the bag over her head to hand to her. They'd learned as youngsters that teamwork made all the work lighter.

The iron bar rang sometime later, about the same time the sun hit the zenith. Mari had soup heated and bread sliced. She'd only recently started taking over many of the kitchen duties.

Ingeborg straightened again. While her muscles had recovered from their earlier soreness, now she was starting to ache from spending the morning bent over.

By the time the sun was starting to ease its way down to the horizon, the garden was planted as much as possible and the tools were stored back in the shed. Two days done, and it usually took at least three. Many hands did indeed make the work light, as Mor so often reminded them.

Later, at the table, Far nodded when Mari reported they'd finished—ahead of the other families. Hjelmer had run over to each of the onkels' houses to make sure.

Mari rattled on. "Tante Berthe said it was all because we have the benefit of the southerly slope. Our garden always warms up faster. I told her we really liked the bread Gunlaug brought over."

"Good." Mor nodded in satisfaction. Even though she would never admit it, Ingeborg knew she liked to win the garden contest too. Would it have been so hard for her to enjoy the game?

Ingeborg kept her mouth shut. Tante Berthe was a bit of a whiner and often provoked the others with her griping. That made winning all the more sweet. She felt a nudge under the table. Berta felt the same way. This could be worth a giggle or two when they climbed into bed. Since all the children slept upstairs, and the parents down, bedtime was often a chance for merriment. Mor had always lacked in the laughter department. Not like Far, who looked for chances to exercise his big roaring laugh. It was a shame Gilbert took more after their mother. Perhaps if he married Asti, she would make him laugh more.

After the meal, Ingeborg went back outside to pen the sheep and chickens. She didn't have to herd the sheep; she just walked ahead and called. They fell into their normal line, making their way into the sheepfold, and she counted as they came. She closed the gate behind them and went to the chickens, most of which were already roosting in the hen house. When she clucked, the others came, fully expecting the handful of grain she threw out. While they located every grain, she found several more eggs and bade them good-night as she shut the door.

Eggs in her apron, she paused to look to the west to check the sunset. Far always said, *"Red sky at night, sailor's delight."* Tomorrow would be another fine spring day. And she hoped she would not creak and groan when she woke up. And, she had to get over to Gunlaug's to tease her about the winning. Gunlaug did not particularly like to be teased. When Ingeborg entered the kitchen, Far looked up from reading the newspaper.

"If it stays like this, I think we can start moving supplies up to the seter on Monday."

"Arne, that is too soon." Mor hooked the iron frying pan on the wall by the fireplace.

Ingeborg said nothing, but her heart screamed, *It can never be too soon to escape to the seter!* She sighed. Leave it to her mor. What if Onkel Jonas would agree that she could go along to Amerika? Would she find freedom there?

5

The next several days passed slowly with spring housecleaning, along with digging out the barn, the pigpen, and the hen house, where manure and bedding were allowed to build up during the cold of winter to help provide heat for the animals.

Ingeborg checked the garden daily for sprouts, but so far the only things growing in the garden were the weeds. Hoeing weeds was always good for the soul.

"Did she really say that?" Gunlaug paused her hoeing and stared in horror. Gunlaug had volunteered to help Ingeborg hoe—an excuse to have a chat.

Ingeborg nodded. Even after all this time she was still thinking about her mother saying she'd rather go to the birthing by herself. When her daughter stuttered "Why?" Mor had just shrugged and said, "We won't discuss this further."

Ingeborg locked her jaw. Did Mor think her daughter would do a bad job? All the thinking and rethinking she'd done about the last birthing to figure out what she had done wrong or not done right. Had she somehow endangered the mother or the baby so that it took so long to be born?

She knew Mor had taken her along because she suspected problems.

"Ja." Ingeborg fought to tamp down the anger that threatened to erupt. "I thought she wanted to teach me, but she won't say any more about that birthing, and now I don't know if she wants to continue with our lessons or not." She chopped viciously at a weed.

"What are the lessons like?"

"I guess I learn by doing."

"Then how can you learn if you don't go along?" Gunlaug dug her hoe into the ground. "That makes no sense whatsoever." She tipped out a seedling weed with her hoe and paused again. "And she hasn't brought it up since?"

"No. And that was a couple weeks ago."

"Was there a problem with this last birthing?"

"I don't know. I think she is mad at me."

"She's not told you?" She looked at Ingeborg, who shook her head. "Did you ask?"

Ingeborg shook her head again. "I can't wait until we get to the seter. I just want out of here. Life up there is free and without contention." She knew what she really meant was without her mother, but loyalty or some other misplaced emotion kept her from saying it. But she knew Gunlaug knew what she meant. They were close enough friends for that assumption.

Gunlaug bent back to the task. "So what do we do next?"

"Start packing? Have you taken your loom apart to haul up there?"

Gunlaug broke out into a big grin. "Oh, I forgot to tell you. Far made me a new one that we can leave up there. He just finished it last night. He will remove the bolts so we can load it and then set it up again in our seter house."

"That is perfect. I'll be taking up the spinning wheels, and I have last year's fleece all washed and bundled up. After shearing there will be plenty of fleece there. How is our yarn supply?"

"Almost nothing left. We'll all have to spin to catch up." Gunlaug paused and looked off into the distance. "If only Ivar could come, it would be perfect."

"Oh, that would be a big help. His mor would probably come check on him once a week or send him a message that he is needed at home." Ingeborg made a face and rolled her eyes. "'I need you, Ivar, my son, my only son. I cannot get to town without you.'" Ingeborg knew she was able to mimic others, and Ivar's mor was so easy, especially the whine in her voice.

Gunlaug tried to stifle her snort, but her attempt at a stern mien crumbled into laughter.

"Ingeborg?"

Hjelmer's voice cracked on the call, sending the two cousins into rib-holding laughter.

"Ingeborg, where are you?" His call was coming closer.

"Out in the garden," she called back and hoed out another couple of weeds. Why did they sprout so much faster than the vegetable seeds? And grow three times as fast?

Hjelmer leaned against the fence. "Why didn't you answer me? Mor is asking for you."

"All right. I didn't realize school was out already."

"I just got home."

Gunlaug propped her hoe against the fence rail. "I need to get home before my mor starts calling too. See you tomorrow."

Ingeborg watched her head across the pasture. If she couldn't talk to Gunlaug, she didn't know what she would do. If she married, she would at least not have to try so hard to get along with Mor. She turned to Hjelmer. "What does she want this time?"

"You said you would make something for supper." The two fell into step, headed toward the house.

Ingeborg resisted the urge to smooth the stubborn lock of nearly white hair that stood up toward the back of his head. He used to smile at her for her attention, but now he pulled away. It was a shame that children, especially boys, couldn't remain pliable like they were when children.

"And Berta couldn't do that?"

He shrugged. "Guess she was busy."

And Katrina was plying her needle, trying to finish the linens she would take with her to marriage next month. Ingeborg was sure Katrina had coerced Berta into helping her. While Ingeborg enjoyed doing the fine needlework required, some stubborn streak resisted her sister's pleas, usually with a rather caustic comment of someone having to do the work around here. If she wasn't careful, she'd begin to sound like Mor, who of course, was helping with the wedding preparations. Katrina, as always, did exactly as Mor told her. Having the linens ready and the trunk full was a point of pride.

Ingeborg asked Hjelmer, "Are you going to finish cleaning out the barn?"

"Ja, but not today. Splitting the wood comes first."

"How is that coming?" Besides needing wood for the summer cooking and canning, they needed a supply for up at the seter.

"The pile is growing. You want to come help?" He might be boy-sized, but his work was already a man's.

"I'd rather do that than cook. Is the woodbox full?"

"Berta was supposed to do that."

Ingeborg thought for a moment. "I'll get the dough ready, and Mari can supervise the cooking. I suggest you get a head start, and we'll see who has the biggest pile by later tonight."

Hjelmer's eyes lit up. "You think you'll catch up and pass me by milking time?"

"I'm sure of it." Ingeborg watched her little brother, the lad who was so afraid he would never be tall like the other men and thus caught in the world between working with the men and helping the womenfolk. His slight build and the weakness left in his arms and legs after an attack of diphtheria two years earlier would surely change as he grew into his Strand stature. There wasn't a short man among all the Strands that she knew. She reached over and ruffled her brother's hair, which made him flinch away. It was, of course, what she expected. She'd read something about that, that if you did what you always did, why expect a different outcome? Some things were hard to resist—like letting Mor make her angry.

If Mor was with Katrina, the others were in the front of the house, so she could make the dough and slip out before she had to encounter the disapproval again.

By the time the dough was ready for the griddle and Mari all set to go, Ingeborg knew she might just as well take the milk bucket and head for the barn. Along with the milking pail, she grabbed the bucket holding the whey from the churning to feed to the hogs and chickens as she went by.

The cows were lined up outside the barn door, waiting patiently. Bess, the bell cow, tossed her head, making Ingeborg smile. Why was it she could laugh at a cow's impatience yet get so put out with her mother? That was not a comfortable thought. But it plagued her throughout the long hour of her forehead pressed against a warm flank and milk singing into the bucket. Why did not the others respond like she did? Trying so hard, or not trying but instead getting irritated. Milking was one of those chores that allowed her mind to roam freely, so she sent it up to the seter.

When she stood up between cows, she could hear the ring of the ax, the thud, a pause to set a new hunk in place on the chopping block, and then repeat. If some others didn't help Hjelmer, they'd never be ready in time. Mentioning this at supper would cause Mor to be rude again, but . . .

Why was she always the one who had to bring up contentious subjects?

Far and Gilbert split wood with Hjelmer until dusk, while Ingeborg, Mari, and Berta stacked it.

"We'll start again after morning chores." Far dug out a file and sat down to hone the two-bit ax, so Gilbert followed suit. Ingeborg straightened from the stacking and kneaded her back with her fists. Shame they'd not been able to load the wagon at the same time, but it would be needed for other jobs before the big trek.

Far glanced over at the two remaining logs that awaited the crosscut saw. "We need to drag the green logs down here."

"Is Onkel Frode going to send wood up too?" Hjelmer asked.

"He said so, but . . ."

Ingeborg knew Far hated to say anything against his two brothers. But then, he hated contention like a cat hated puddles. Not that they had any hesitation in their griping. So much so that sometimes it got in the way of their work—and living.

"I hope we can leave soon." Hjelmer eyed the piles of wood. "Can we roll that log up on the sawbucks yet tonight?"

"Is right now soon enough?" Gilbert asked, nudging his little brother. "You grab one end and I'll take the other."

Far chuckled, something he didn't do often enough, in Ingeborg's book.

"Go tell your mor we've worked up an appetite again. See if she'll set something out for a bedtime snack."

Hjelmer glanced at Ingeborg, a bit wide eyed.

Mari rolled her eyes. "I'll tell her."

Or will most likely do it herself. Ingeborg knew that was an uncharitable thought but didn't wish to erase it—like she so often wished, when her mouth or mind got away from her. If only she could do as the Bible said and bridle her tongue—always. Mor had pointed out that verse to her more than once. It rankled like a sliver under the skin.

When they gathered around the kitchen table, where Mari had set out the fresh ginger cookies and små brød, Mor acted like nothing had ever bothered her, all but looking at Ingeborg. When Hjelmer brought up the date for leaving for the seter, Far nodded.

"We will ride up tomorrow and see how the snow is melting. If we can see the bare ground, we will decide. We'll leave the wood chopping to the others."

Ingeborg felt her heart leap. *Please, Lord, let the snow be melted and let no more fall.* Wishing she could go along would do no good. But hopefully Far would take Hjelmer and leave Gilbert here to man the other end of the crosscut saw. Getting the wood ready was a big part of the preparations. Good thing they had dragged logs up the hill into the seter yard last fall. Cleaning out the buildings was always a big job too, especially the house. Who knew what had taken refuge in the snug building during the winter? One time they found a den of foxes in the cheese storage cellar cut into the hillside, and often mice, rats, or squirrels chewed their way into the house.

⁓

After milking, Ingeborg spent the next day at the woodpile and even pressed Gunlaug into the heavy work. Gunlaug soon said she had things to do at home and left before Ingeborg could try to talk her into staying any longer.

Gilbert leaned on his ax handle on the chopping block and shook his head. "She never has cared much for the heavy work."

Ingeborg refrained from reminding him that most women didn't like using a crosscut saw or an ax. If that was what he expected in a wife, he'd never have to worry about getting married. "She works hard in other ways."

"Sitting at a loom doesn't take a lot of muscle." He hefted his ax and set another chunk on the block, neatly splitting it with one mighty whack. The whack and thunk of wood chopping resumed.

No, but swinging an ax does not produce the splendid weaving that Gunlaug can do. Ingeborg didn't say it aloud. She reached for the file to touch up her ax. Chopping with a sharp ax was hard enough, but a dull one took far more muscles, and as Far often said, "Work smarter, not harder."

Mari brought two cups of steaming coffee out for them in the middle of the afternoon. "I thought you could use a break for a time." The door slammed behind her, and she returned with a water jug and a plate of leftover små brød with jam. The three of them sat on the porch step, even Gilbert breathing a sigh of relief.

"Mange takk." He lifted his cup in salute. "What's for dinner?"

"I made stew out of the leftovers from last night. Used the last of the carrots and onions."

The home garden couldn't come in too soon.

Ingeborg and Gilbert were in the yard that evening when Far and Hjelmer rode in. Thanks to the long days, a round trip could be made in a day.

"We can get ready!" Far called as he dismounted. Hjelmer took both the horses to the barn and let them go in the small field where there was no water, since the horses were both sweaty. The weather had turned unseasonably warm, for which Ingeborg rejoiced.

"The grass is coming up already. We are more than a couple of weeks ahead of time." Far headed for the house, glancing at the woodpile. "Good for you."

Gilbert grinned at her. A compliment like that showed what a good mood Far was in.

She nodded. Perhaps the parents wanted their offspring to head up the mountain as much as the younger ones looked forward to going. Now, that was a different kind of thought.

So much to do, so much to do. Packing crates, keeping the weeds out of the garden, keeping the cattle and sheep inside the fences, replenishing the spent woodpiles, managing the calves and lambs—no matter how she tried to step up the pace, more work loomed. Even the needlework was put on hold, which made Katrina less than happy.

"You won't be here for my wedding." She stared sorrowfully at Ingeborg.

"It's a shame you scheduled it for June. You could wait until next fall."

Horror rounded Katrina's eyes even more. "If you were in love like we are, you would not even jest about such a thing."

"Probably. That's the big difference between us. You want to be married. I don't."

"At the rate you are going, you needn't be concerned," Mor said with a pickle mouth.

Swallowing hot words can burn one's throat, Ingeborg discovered. Maybe they were better said, but then again, probably not. "You said you had some books for me to take up there?" Again, propriety said Ingeborg was too young to read books on birthing and other medical things.

"I'll find them for you. I asked Alfreda for anything she might have too, so you'll need to go over there in the next few days and see."

There it was again, an interest in her daughter's education. Why did she wait until now?

Before falling asleep that night, Ingeborg's mind worried at the switches in her mother's demeanor. One minute she was not speaking, then she was, and obviously thinking along the lines of education in spite of the way she acted. How was one to figure this puzzle out? Finding it hard to fall asleep in the half light of spring, where the nights never totally darkened, was not a new thing, but one would have thought all the hard labor would make it easy. The snoring from other members of the family told her she was again the only one awake. She always slept better up at the seter house too.

Someone had once told her that praying for others always made them fall asleep more quickly, as if the evil one couldn't abide praying. Ingeborg wasn't sure of the validity of that observation, but extra prayer never hurt anyone. Then she ordered her mind to go through the Bible verses she had been memorizing, one of the things Far insisted upon for his family. While he never spoke of his faith or things related to it, he made them all learn the Word. It would stand them in good stead, he claimed, an interesting comment and one not said often. But he did ask them to recite their verses, especially during the long winter nights when they gathered around the kitchen table to study or work on whatever handwork needed doing. Ingeborg often spent those hours at the spinning wheel kept in the corner, where the firelight cast a warm glow and heat to match.

She drowsed and pictured life at the seter. Something good always happened during their time up there. And sometimes crises too. Just like life everywhere. What would happen this year?

6

Oslo, Norway

Would the end of the term never arrive?

Nils stared out the window into a downpour that a few weeks ago would have blanketed the world in white. At the moment, going out into the wet sounded like something close to taking a beating. All he could think about was getting out of Oslo and leaving behind the drudgery of school, at least for a couple of months. Of course, thinking of trekking up in the mountains only served to remind him of the latest altercation with his father.

Had they been in fisticuffs, the verdict would have been a draw. But they used words instead of fists, and words left far more severe wounds, wounds that bled but did not heal. Turning from the window, he sighed and shook his head. He'd promised to attend all his classes, turn in all the assignments, and give studying his best. If he really knew what his best was. But then, perhaps he was learning that his best in the classroom was not sufficient to be at the top of the rolls. How could he do better?

That wasn't the real question, though, he had to admit. The real question was how could he make himself care about the outcome to the exclusion of all else? Or anything else? The mountains kept singing siren songs.

If he got his grades up—to the point that it was possible this late in the term—he would have a bargaining chip. In return, he could indeed spend the summer in the mountains rather than in the offices of his father's business—the company he was meant to take over after training.

But I don't want to spend the rest of my life running a business that cannot capture my dreams at all. Hiking in the mountains was not a lifelong ambition. He kept hoping he would outgrow that desire, as his father had suggested rather forcibly. But he kept hearing the mountains calling to him.

Nils stopped in front of the mirror. He looked haggard, as if he'd been out shouting *Skol!* with Hans and other drinkers, not only one night too many but for weeks. The disgusting part was that he'd been studying till the wee hours, not partying. Though he realized he would have a hard time convincing his father of that, should he happen to see his son in this degree of dishevelment.

Heaving another sigh and at the same time castigating himself for sighing, he snagged his wool coat off the peg and shrugged into it. Book in hand, he trudged down the stairs, clapped his hat on his head, and stepped out into the downpour. If any weather was conducive to staying inside, this was it.

He arrived at the classroom to find a closed door with a note on it: *Class Canceled.* He slammed his fist against the wall, wishing it were his head instead. All this for naught.

"Oh, for . . ."

The expletive behind him made Nils turn to see who else was willing to say out loud what he'd been thinking. He wagged his head and started back toward the stairs. The other student—what was his name?—walked beside him.

"You interested in the pub on the corner?"

Nils started to say no but changed his mind. "I'll buy." He knew the answer was curt but better that than stony silence. Or perhaps not. He turned to say he was sorry, but the other man held up his hand.

"No need. You want to buy, fine, but only the first one."

They both paused in the doorway. The rain had not let up. Hats back on heads, they hugged the wall as much as they could on the two-block walk and ducked into the pub, shaking huge drops off their hats and coats. Hanging them on the pegs along the wall, they crossed to the stools at the bar, ignoring the booths and tables by unspoken agreement.

Nils raised a finger and nodded to the man by his side, who also nodded. Two beers slid across the slick surface to be stopped by grateful hands.

"I should have ordered something hot." Nils set the half empty tankard back down, careful to place it in the wet ring. He stared at the cup, waiting for a sense of relief. When none arrived, he shivered and hoisted the drink again.

The barkeep pushed two more down the counter.

His father's voice beat in his ears. *"Lazy, my son is lazy . . . doesn't live up to his word . . . wastes his time. You are lazy! When will you grow into the man I thought you were becoming? So much talent and you don't use it!"*

The second beer went down, but the voice didn't stop.

"Are you all right?" The voice penetrated the fog that seemed to be rising.

Nils blinked. No, the fog was not in the room, it writhed within. "Ja, of course." He pushed the tankard across the bar. Glancing at the man beside him, he raised his eyebrows and asked if he wanted more too.

He shrugged. "Not finished with this one yet. Perhaps you should slow down."

Should. Another of those words drumming in his head in his father's voice.

"You should study. You should make an effort. You should want to run the company. You should graduate. You should graduate with honors.

"You should not run away to the mountains. You should assume responsibilities. You should make your mother proud of you.

"We are deeply disappointed in you. Lazy!"

Nils gritted his teeth. Tearing this man limb from limb would not help. His fists clenched. The third beer appeared in front of him. He turned to look at his friend.

"You said something?"

"I said you should slow down." He wore a worried look.

When Nils shook his head, the mirror behind the bar rippled. He closed his eyes and opened them again. Clear. *Should. Should. Should.*

"Mind your own business." Picking up the tankard, he drank, but more slowly. A right to the jaw should shut him up. Nils sucked in a deep breath and let it out. Violence was not his way. Where had the fist thought come from? He'd not struck anyone since his boxing class, when he knocked his opponent out and resolved never to strike anyone again. Never!

He threw some money on the counter and heaved himself

to his feet. Was his head whirling or did the room really tilt? Only slightly but . . . He grabbed hat and coat off the pegs and shrugged into them.

"Wait, let me go with you."

"No! I'm fine."

The wind-driven rain slashed at his face. Ducking his head, he stepped into the cobblestone street. Ignoring the voice behind him, he started across. A shout! A screaming horse. Falling. Crashing.

⁓

"Nils, wake up. Nils."

What was his sister doing at the tavern? He blinked but didn't try to open his eyes again when pain slashed through his head at any effort. Where was he? Maybe he was dying. Why would he be dying? Maybe that was the answer to all his suffering.

"Just move your finger if you hear me."

Move a finger. He could do that. He ordered his right forefinger to move, and it did. That was good news.

"Excellent."

The voice lilted gently on his ears. Amalia. He felt a soft hand slip under his. Warm. Was he cold? He didn't think so. He could feel blankets over him. He tapped again, twice.

"You are in your bed, in your lodgings. The doctor has been here."

Doctor? What happened? But when he tried to talk, not only his head screeched, but the air was tight. Tight? Was he having trouble breathing? Why? He tapped his finger again, flinching at the pain stabbing behind his eyes. Why? He had moved his forehead. Oh.

"The doctor was here. You have a head injury and some broken ribs. Thankfully, that is all."

"How?" The one word took a superhuman effort. Could she hear or had he imagined he spoke?

"You were knocked clear by the rearing horse, or you would have been run over by a four-in-hand. And the coach would have run over you too. That is why I say thank you, God, for saving my brother."

"Far?" Did that guttural voice really belong to him?

"I've not told him yet."

Yet. His father and mother would have to be told. Perhaps he was better off dead. She said something else, but he was fading and not able to understand.

"Mr. Aarvidson." A male voice this time. An unknown male voice.

"Mr. Aarvidson, this is Dr. Jorge. If you can hear me . . ."

Nils raised a finger. When he tried to blink, it worked. Pain but not as severe.

"You are at your home near the campus. It has been eighteen hours since your accident. You have two broken ribs and a nasty cut on the back of your head, leaving you with a concussion. Both injuries are extremely painful, but not life threatening, unless complications set in. So breathe gently and don't try to talk right now."

Nils raised the finger to earn a *Good* from the doctor.

"Miss Aarvidson has returned to your father's house but will be back later this morning. I assured her that Nurse Daggen would see you through the night, and she has. She will clean you up some and make you presentable if your father and mother learn of this and come to see you."

A nurse. Eighteen hours. Surely someone would inform his

father. After all, the accident happened on a major street in Oslo. Right in front of the tavern. Far would know his son had been drinking. Again. Not living up to his potential. Again. And here he dreamed of the mountains. He would be lucky not to be moved to his parents' home, where they could watch over him. Stand guard would be more like it.

"How bad?" Two words. Progress.

"You'll be in bed for a day or two. The pain and dizziness will keep you there. As that passes, you will want to move around. I recommend staying in for two weeks. You will find reading impossible. Concussions are like that. I stitched up the scalp wound. That will heal quickly."

If it does not get infected. Nils supplied the addendum.

"I have taped your chest to make you a bit more comfortable. Ribs take time to heal, but you can move around as much as you can tolerate the pain. Coughing is hard, but you need to cough or pneumonia could set in. That is our biggest fear, so the sooner you can sit up and stand the better."

Pneumonia. Infection. Not exactly inspiring thoughts.

"Takk."

"You are welcome." The doctor listened to his lungs and patted his hand. "The nurse says your sister is here. I will speak with her and leave you. I believe Nurse Daggen should stay with you for at least a few days and nights. If you have questions, I will return tomorrow morning."

Nils listened as the doctor crossed the room and exited at the door. Footsteps of doom or footsteps of hope? He drifted away again while waiting for Amalia to come. The land of darkness was much easier than the pain of being awake.

Sometime later, or was it only the blink of an eye . . . His eyes did that of their own accord. Blinked open. Dim light through the drapes, separated just enough to . . . to . . . He blinked again and the ceiling came into focus.

"You are awake," Amalia said.

He started to nod, thought the better of it, and blinked twice.

"Good. Nurse Daggen is bringing some chicken broth. You know that is Mother's panacea for everything."

"Mor?"

"Yes, I had to tell them. They've been here for the last two hours."

Waiting. His father did not wait well. He heard the door open and flinched, but the footsteps were not the strides of his father.

"Here you go, young man. Your sister insists on feeding you, so I will put another pillow under your head. That will hurt, but the pain shouldn't be as severe as yesterday. I'll be quick."

Either she was a liar or she'd never been in his situation. Gritting his teeth did not help. Screaming might have, but only a slight groan acknowledged her actions. He was now halfway sitting but still lying down. Like the rest of him—in a neither-nor world.

"There. That wasn't so bad, was it?"

Definitely a liar, erring on the cheerful side.

"We're going to wash your face and comb your hair. We will be careful, I promise." Her accent sounded more Swedish than Norwegian. We? Was someone else assisting her?

Round of face, round of body, with a determined smile that boded ill for her patient. He closed his eyes again, the easier to imagine her away.

"You want to look as good as possible for Far and Mor." Amalia understood. Amalia had always understood. It was a shame she was a woman and could not run the business. She loved the world of business and finance. She should be the one in college, not he. He'd thought that for the last several years, ever since his grooming for the role began.

Between his tight jaw and Amalia's cheerful persistence, they managed to get some of the soup into his mouth, improving with practice. By the time the nurse finished his grooming, he vowed to never associate with a nurse again in any capacity whatsoever, no matter what.

"Would you like me to shave you?"

Over my dead body, but when he shook his head in the barest motion, pain slammed him again. A cough burst forth, no matter how he tried to stifle it.

"You must cough!"

Had he ever contemplated murder before?

He coughed enough to relieve the pressure and collapsed against the pillows.

"I'll let you rest a bit, and then before your far and mor come in, we'll get you sitting a bit higher with more pillows."

Was that a threat or a promise? Without a decision, he promptly fell down the black well again.

$\backsim$

"Welcome back." His mother's voice cleared the fog from his brain. He opened his eyes to see her smiling at him, perfectly coiffed and dressed as modishly as always.

"Takk." He let his gaze travel the room and the closed door.

"Your father had to return to the office for a meeting. He said he'll come back tonight."

A reprieve. Now, that was something for which to be thankful. "Amalia?"

"She had an appointment. She should be back any time."
She took his hand between her own. "You gave us quite a
fright."

"Sorry." She had no idea how sorry.

"We want you to come home, where you can be cared for."

He refrained from shaking his head, but the look he gave
her must have sufficed.

"I know you don't want to do that, but . . ." She paused.
"Your father is insisting."

And if RA Aarvidson insisted the world was to stop, it
probably would. A stubbornness that he'd only recognized recently, perhaps because he was pushed to the limit, prompted
him to a soft answer. "His insisting will do no good this time.
I will stay here. I have a good nurse, and Hans will come in to
help tomorrow." A white lie perhaps, but he was certain that
would happen as soon as he sent a message. Surely Amalia
would take care of that.

Sonja Aarvidson clicked her tongue in a tsking sound.
One he knew well. She had always done what RA ordered.

"I'm sorry, Mor, but I cannot do that. I must be near the
college so that I can employ a tutor to read to me and help
me prepare for the end of the term. Far and I have struck a
bargain, and I will not go back on my word. No matter what
he orders. I know this will be difficult for you, but this accident cannot stop me." He hoped he sounded firm. Nothing
could stand in the way of his last summer in the mountains.
Nothing. "You do not have to be the bearer of the bad tidings. When he comes, I will tell him. I think you would be
wise to return home before he arrives."

"But you are wounded. Badly wounded."

"Not so badly that I cannot make decisions for myself." If

only he could be sitting in a chair before his father strode in the door. Dressed would be even better. Was that possible? If only Hans were here. Nurse Daggen would have to help him. After all, who was the boss here?

He sighed. He might want to assume the reins of power, but it would be the pushy nurse who called the shots. And his father. Even his mother. Come to think of it, Amalia had been ordering him about too. Nils Aarvidson, feckless ne'er-do-well.

VALDRES, NORWAY

Ingeborg caught herself humming. If she wasn't careful, she
might slip into whistling, but since Mor insisted that girls
weren't allowed to whistle, she'd save that for the seter. Here
it was the third week of May, and they were finally packing to
head up the mountains. The delays had been one thing after
another. Weather, a sick cow, more weather. She'd begun to
think they would never leave. And then Katrina asked why
they couldn't wait a couple more weeks so they would not
miss her wedding. That would make a big difference in the
amount of time they had to spend up there.

Two more days. Not that Ingeborg was overly eager or anything. In two days there would be a line of teams and wagons
with the chickens in crates and the hogs in a box-like wagon,
with the older boys and children herding the sheep and cows.

"I would rather ride on a wagon," Gunlaug had muttered
more than once.

Ingeborg laughed. "If we all ride in the wagons, who will
herd the livestock?" She closed her eyes. What she'd prefer

77

doing was riding one of the horses. Riding, they would arrive more quickly and could start the cleaning. But riding would not happen, not on a horse or in a wagon. Feet and legs were made for walking, or so Mor often reminded them.

Two more days until they left, if all went well. Two wagons loaded with wood had already left and should be back again by evening. They'd stack the firewood when they got there.

Up to the seter. Up to the seter. Freedom at the seter. She kept the words to herself. If Mor had ever loved the seter, the daughter had yet to hear of it. Other people told stories of their times up in the mountains. Mor never had. Ingeborg stopped for a moment to think on that. Should she ask point-blank if Mor spent summers up at a seter? Probably not today, since the others who were staying at the homeplace were stitching like their lives depended on finishing the linens for the chest and the dress for the bride. After all, June was just around the corner.

"Ingeborg!" Mor calling.

"Out here packing the wagon."

"Come here."

With a shrug and a sigh of disgust, she did as told. The dim house made her blink after the brightness outside. "Do you need something?"

"I have decided that Berta needs to remain here. With Katrina leaving, I will need help with the garden and putting food by. Hjelmer is going with you and Mari. Besides, Katrina wants Berta to be in her wedding party."

Since when? But Ingeborg swallowed the words. "Does Berta know this?"

"She will do as she is told. I have hinted at it."

"Does Far know?"

"He agrees." Mor held her stitching up to the window. "Ah, good, one more done."

I'm sure he does. If she argued now, however, it might delay their leaving. She held her peace. Poor Berta. Sacrificed on the altar of Katrina's wedding. *Please, Lord God, keep me from ever falling in love.* Look what a mess it can make for other people. Katrina and Oscar seemed oblivious to the problems, both of them working toward their new life together. And since Katrina was a good girl and never questioned, Mor granted her every wish. Sometimes Ingeborg wished she could take lessons from her sister.

Well, this bad girl has plenty to do too. "I wish Katrina every happiness."

"I know you do. Some little sacrifices are a good thing to build character."

Ignoring the barb, Ingeborg went back out to packing foodstuffs into three wooden boxes, already in place on the wagon bed. The cleaning supplies had been jammed into another box. The bedding was airing on the clothesline, the sheets and pillows folded and ready. She stopped to stare at her handiwork. Something was missing.

"Ingeborg, I'm sorry." Berta carried the box of cheese and butter molds out to the wagon. "I would rather go, but I do so hate to miss Katrina's wedding. She needs at least one of her sisters there." Her eyes grew dreamy. "And besides, I might get ideas for my own wedding."

"You better not go falling in love yet. You are too young." Ingeborg stacked the new box near the front of the wagon, since it was easier to move than the food boxes. "Besides, there are so few eligible men around here."

"Maybe at your age, but not mine." Berta's arched look made Ingeborg smile.

"Well, maybe, but those your age have a lot of growing up to do yet." She paused and studied her sister through slitted eyes. "You are thinking of someone, Berta. Confess."

"I . . . uh . . . no . . . uh . . ." Berta grimaced, again eliciting a smile from her older sister and a pat on the shoulder to go with it. "Lars Bornstadt is smart and a hard worker and trustworthy and—"

"Cute as can be. Actually too cute for a man, but his face will mature. He is big and strong, that's for sure." Ingeborg paused, a knowing look lifting her eyebrows. "Do you think he likes you? He would be stupid not to, of course, but men—er—rather, boys can be fickle." And tongue-tied and silly and . . . Ingeborg kept those thoughts to herself. Just because she wanted a man who could carry on a decent conversation, along with have a sense of curiosity and wonder, that's not to say Berta looked for the same things. Of course, when one was fourteen, one went more on attraction and good looks than truly thinking things through.

Berta nodded. "I know he does. Carly told me so."

Carly was Lars's younger sister, who was close friends with Berta.

Ingeborg strolled with Berta back to the house to bring out the stored fleeces to pack around other boxes and keep them secure. A place for everything and everything in its place. Now, that was a Mor-ism Ingeborg totally agreed with and practiced.

Not that her mother wasn't wise—they all knew she was—but, there was always that *but*, a stumbling block for sure. Understanding was important to Ingeborg, and the way her mother treated her, she absolutely did not comprehend. She forced herself back to what Berta was saying.

"Sorry, my mind went woolgathering. What did you say?"

"Oh, Ingeborg, you are so funny. I asked you how many fleeces you were taking. I saw both spinning wheels already packed, in fleece no less. There is justice or something there, don't you agree?"

"I agree that you are sounding and acting more grown up all the time. I'm afraid that by the time I return, you will be a woman and I won't know you." She tweaked her sister's single braid—she no longer wore two, a sure sign of growing maturity.

By evening Ingeborg had two of the wagons packed and covered with canvas to keep out the dew or rain, if it appeared, which was doubtful with the red sky at night. Not that true dark night ever happened these days.

The evening before they were ready to depart, the family gathered around the kitchen table like they always did. Far bowed his head and waited for them to settle. "God above, we thank you for our seter and the good cheese that will come from there. Thank you for those willing to travel up there and live away from so many good things here."

Ingeborg's mind balked at that. She'd rather be up there than here, any day. Well, not in midwinter, not that high up in the mountains, but summer days for certain. She jerked her mind back to his prayer.

"Guard our cattle and our children from wild creatures and storms and accidents. We will give you all the praise and glory. Grant us thy grace and peace. Amen." He looked around the table. "Jesus said, 'And lo, I am with you always.' We all count on that."

The nod went around the table. Ingeborg wished she could take the family Bible with her, but through the years she had copied from it, verses and whole chapters that she wanted to study. Not that there was a lot of study time up there either. She paused to snag a thought that flitted through her mind. It was true. She did feel closer to God in the higher mountains. And who knew what kinds of adventures He would guide them through this year.

"Ingeborg, is your medicinal box packed and loaded?" Mor asked.

"Ja. I wrapped it in more canvas and sheepskin to keep it safe and dry. I put in all you said." And then some.

Mor nodded and turned to Mari.

Ingeborg snapped her mouth shut. There had been reprimand with the question. Now, that was something to remember. *Ingeborg, you are being sarcastic. No I'm not. Not this time. Just relieved and thankful, is all.* Did all people have two of their own voices arguing in their minds, or was she stranger than she thought?

"Wish I were going," Gilbert said under his breath to Ingeborg the next morning. "Not to stay particularly, but I'd like to go up and back."

Ingeborg nodded. Far's comment that the man needed to stay home in case of emergencies made sense, since all three brothers were going. No matter how excited she was about heading up the hills, she hated to say good-bye too. She had already learned that one never knew what was coming, and she didn't always have to like it. Like their Bjorn, so excited about going to Amerika and their never hearing from him again. What had happened to her favorite brother?

Gilbert gripped her arm. "Take care."

She dipped her head and pressed it to his shoulder. Strand men were indeed tall. "Takk. Tusen takk." She watched him turn away to open the pasture gates. Berta came to stand beside her.

"I do wish I were going. After all, this might be my last year to do so."

"Not if I have anything to say about it." Ingeborg hugged her younger sister, who was nearly as tall as she. "You can write to me, you know."

"I will, and you write too." Even though the mail made it up to the high mountain valley only two or three times in the season, letters were always precious. News of home came up with the rider who brought extra supplies and letters and carried back the same.

Ingeborg called to the sheep as they flowed out of the pasture that would now be left for hay later in the summer. The lead ewe, her bell clanging with each step, snatched up a mouthful of grass and made her way to the woman she trusted. The lambs gamboled beside their mothers. If they strayed far, the ewes bleated their warning signal, calling them back.

Frode's herding dogs nipped at the cows' heels, driving the stock forward, nimbly leaping aside to avoid the occasional impatient kick.

They all said their good-byes, and the wagons rattled out across the valley, the animals behind snatching mouthfuls of grass if allowed to slow down even for a second. Since the sheep followed her, Ingeborg led the way, as did the sheepherders from the other two farms. The milk cows placidly nodded their way on the road, their calves settling in beside them, the herd dogs now largely ignoring them. By the second day, the young stock would realize that staying by their mothers, rather than running and jumping, was far wiser, probably what their mothers had been telling them. Ingeborg was always delighted to see the comparisons between animal and human behavior. No wonder Jesus referred to people as the sheep of His pasture.

They stopped at a favorite spot for a break when the sun nearly hit its zenith. Both animals and people drank from the brook that tumbled down rocks in some places and made serene pools in others, an ideal place for the animals to drink safely.

The cousins' fathers, Arne and Kris, along with their brother Frode, handed out the sandwiches prepared for them as well as the always necessary cheese and gorobrød.

Gunlaug sank down in the wagon's shade, while Ingeborg kept an eye on Hjelmer and the two other male cousins, who kept track of the sheep and cattle. Fast water, holes, and cliffs, not to speak of the wild hunters, were always a danger. One year a mountain lion had snatched one of the lambs, in spite of how careful the travelers had been.

"You can eat and watch." Gunlaug handed her the bread with meat and cheese. "You can do two things at once. I'll go get you some water when I finish this." She held up her sandwich. "I'm glad your mor made these, not mine. She never puts enough meat and cheese inside."

Ingeborg nodded. Her tante Berthe was known for being exceedingly careful with the food she doled out.

The animals grazed, the people ate, and an eagle screed

84

high overhead. When all had cooled down, they herded the stock over to the pool's edge and watched carefully for possible disasters. Just an arm's length beyond, the spring melt, swollen and wild, rushed down the rocky stream bed.

Back on the trail, they plodded along, no longer calling remarks back and forth, nor spending time and energy watching the scenery, spectacular though it was. The brilliant sunlight was so bright on mountain peaks marching off into the distance, it hurt one's eyes, especially against the blue of the sky bowl over their heads. A beautiful contrast to the green spring grass. Ingeborg no longer called to Gunlaug to see this or that. Everyone was getting tired of climbing and of chewing dust when on the flatlands.

The sun was low among the peaks when Far called a halt. "We will take a break and let Frode's group go on ahead. It will be several hours before we can all get to the seter. Those who go before can prepare supper for us."

Frode, the youngest of the three brothers and never married, tipped his hat. "Good idea. We'll have the fires burning and perhaps even start cleaning the kitchen."

The chimney was always the first thing to clean. No one wanted a smoke-filled room when they lighted the fireplace, let alone a chimney fire. Birds and small animals liked nesting in chimneys.

"Perhaps you should stay here and let the old man go on ahead," Kris, the middle brother, said with his typical laugh.

Arne, Ingeborg's far and the oldest, just shook his head. "Can you not come up with new jokes at least?"

Ingeborg and Gunlaug swapped grins. On some trips the conversations were a bit strained, depending on what the winter and spring had been like, along with the health of both livestock and humans. Others took on lightheartedness. This was one of those.

With a tinge of envy, Ingeborg watched the wagons go on ahead, for Gunlaug was sitting on a wagon back, grinning and waving. She was riding in style while Ingeborg walked, because her cousin had offered to do the cooking.

The drovers watered the stock, grazed them a bit, and keeping an eye out for hunters, continued up the trail. At this time of year, there was still plenty of daylight.

Every year the men said they should improve the track up to the seter, and every year other things had to be done first. Spring was like that.

The other wagons had disappeared around the curves—even the creaking wheels were beyond hearing—when Far called a halt. "One of the horses is limping. Hjelmer, bring up the extra horse, and we'll change them out." Since they always brought along extras for the teams, this was no more than an inconvenience.

"Keep a close watch," Arne ordered, "especially along that ridge up there." He pointed to a craggy section ahead of them. They were just finishing the harness change when a horse whinnied, and the two dogs raised a frenzied yapping, charging up the hill.

Onkel Kris cried, "Ranger! Blackie! Stop!"

The dogs ignored him, tearing up the hillside. Arne and Hjelmer both shouted, Hjelmer racing after the dogs. Ingeborg and the others rounded up the animals and clustered them all close around the two remaining wagons. The sheep and cows kept looking up the hill, pacing restlessly. Ingeborg sent Mari and the others circling the animals while she crooned a song she often used to settle the sheep.

Arne snatched up the rifle he kept behind the wagon seat and started after Hjelmer. The wild barking continued, moving farther away. At least it wasn't coming closer, Ingeborg thought, her attention focused on the animals and children. "Easy now," she called. "Everyone take it easy. The dogs have whatever it is on the run." *Please, Lord, take care of us all.* What would come out to attack this early? Wolves? Something desperate, for certain. But then, nothing was fiercer than a female of any species needing food for her children. The tone of the dogs' voices changed. They had treed something or driven it to the ground.

A shot split the unnatural silence. "Got 'im!" Far's voice echoed from the distance, jubilant.

The livestock settled down to graze, a sure sign that the danger was past. At least they'd kept the animals from panicking and running for their lives.

Ingeborg blew out a breath she didn't realize she had been holding. "You did well," she called to her herders. "You stayed calm. That's what we needed."

Mari sidled up to her. "What if it were wolves, or a bear? I was scared."

"Me too. We all were. You needn't feel bad."

"Hjelmer wasn't."

"No, but you can be sure Far is going to scold him for heading up by himself like that. You know the rule: Never go into the mountains by yourself, or even across the valley. We are in wild animal country—trespassing, if you like. And we or our livestock look like a good meal."

Mari shivered. "You didn't have to say that. I think I want to go back home with Far."

Ingeborg hugged her close. "Nei, little one. God will keep

us safe, He promised. Remember, He said He won't ever leave or forsake us. Far read that verse just last night. The dogs did their job too."

At a halloo, she looked up the trail to see Far and Hjelmer descending, lugging something between them. The two sisters exchanged wide-eyed looks. What could it be?

"A bobcat, Ingeborg, with almost no teeth," Hjelmer hollered. "He's an old one."

She could hear the pride in his voice. And he had been in on the kill. Sometimes size didn't matter. She'd be sure to remind him of that. "Stay with the herd," she called as the others made motions to go see the kill. Grumbles met her order, but they stayed on watch.

One of the team nickered, shifting feet and flickering ears. The others copied, with more urgency.

"Hang on to them, Ingeborg!" Far's voice rang out the order.

Ingeborg grabbed the lines right under the bits.

"They've scented the blood." The dogs leaped and yipped beside the two carrying the load, darting in to sniff and then dodging away.

She held the front team and Onkel Kris held the one behind. The closer they drew, the more restless grew the horses, but Ingeborg kept up her song of peace and calm, stroking noses and necks.

Far circled out from the party and brought the carcass in to the rear of the second wagon. The horses settled down and the dogs sat panting. "We'll take him along. Even his pelt shows he was about starving to death. How he made it through the winter is beyond me."

"Why keep it?" Hamme, Kris's youngest daughter asked, worry or fear knitting her brow.

"It'll make good dog food." Arne leaned closer to his niece. "And maybe Ingeborg will cook him up for supper tomorrow."

Ingeborg stifled a giggle at her cousin's horror-stricken face. Sometimes what people didn't know wouldn't hurt them, especially in the stew or soup kettle.

When they finally got back on the trail, the shadows darkened the way.

"We'll go on. It is not that far. I'll walk ahead and make sure all is well. Hjelmer, you drive this one."

Hjelmer climbed up on the seat, Far strode ahead, and the retinue followed, reaching the seter valley about an hour later. Those that had gone ahead had a fire going outside, both to light the way and because the fireplace probably wasn't fit for cooking. Ingeborg paused as the road descended. Candles lit the windowsill of the house, and the outbuildings lay in darker shadows so as to be hardly visible. *Home.* She felt like she had indeed come home. She blew out a sigh. Oh, the stories that would be told around the fire that night.

8

"A rat! I saw a rat!" Gunlaug complained the next morning, fists planted on her hips. "I can stand mice"—she shuddered—"but not rats."

Kris, her far, rolled his eyes, clearly thinking, *Good grief, what is the big fuss about a rat?*

"And you have always said that if you see one, there are more."

He sent his brother a *Help me* glance, but when Arne shrugged, Kris shook his head. "We will set traps. Hjelmer can shoot any he sees after we leave. Usually they are out at the barn. And come out at night, but not always. Depends on how hungry they are."

"I've shot plenty of them out there." Hjelmer did not look at Ingeborg—intentionally.

Ingeborg too was swallowing laughter. Of course they hated rats. Especially when they turned mean and attacked, or bit someone during the night. All those things happened, but usually not to them at the Strandseter. She'd never forgotten the one she once found in the oat barrel out in the barn.

It jumped up snarling. She'd had the presence of mind to clap the lid back in place before it could jump out, and set a bucket full of milk on top of it. The rat must have figured out how to lift the lid since they'd not found a chewed hole anywhere. Far had said rats were smart, sneaky, and always hungry. That was after he'd clubbed and stunned the vermin, then killed it outside so the blood would not taint the oats.

Ja, life at the seter was always an adventure.

They'd all been much too tired to unload all but the bare necessities last night, so now they finished unloading the wagons and filling the storage room with barrels of flour, ground oats, beans, and bags of other necessary things. They'd brought enough to feed the nine people, seven of them growing children. Ingeborg had all the plans in her head, things she'd been thinking about on the way up. With two new sets of hands, the work should go faster.

This was the first year for Tor, who was the same age as Anders and Hjelmer, and his older-by-a-year sister, Kari Nygaard, to join those at the seter for the summer. They lived in a distant town, not on a farm, and Onkel Frode agreed to pay part of their expenses because their family did not contribute supplies for those spending the summer in the mountains. Since the town was about twenty miles away, they didn't see their Strand cousins very often, something their tante Hilde lamented. Onkel Frode thought a summer of seter work would be good for the both of them, but especially for Tor.

Arne and Kris studied the clouds that were piling up behind the western peaks by the time those heading back down the trail were ready to leave. "Should we go ahead and start out?"

"What's a bit of rain?" Frode said. "We need it, you know."

"Far as I know, none of us have melted in the past." Arne slapped his leather gloves against his thigh as he spoke.

"Ja."

Ingeborg finished his thought in her mind. *Were those snow clouds, not rain clouds?* But while it was chilly, the temperature had not dropped a great deal. Hail was another possibility, they all knew. But the clouds could blow past too. Hail could be hard on the horses, while the men could hide under the wagons. She watched Far come to a decision. Being the oldest, that was usually the case.

"We go," he said.

Frode and Kris both nodded in agreement.

Everyone gathered to wave and shout last-minute reminders as the two teams pulled their wagons back across the valley. One wagon would remain at the seter for the summer.

"Make sure you . . ." The remainder of Far's admonition floated away on a gust of breeze.

"What do you suppose he wanted?" Gunlaug frowned after the receding wagons.

"I don't know." Ingeborg hugged Mari, who stood beside her, and waved one more time before turning toward the barn.

The first thing they needed to do was check the fences, so the sheep and cattle could be released from the corral to graze, as they were clearly telling their humans.

Tor turned to Ingeborg. "You want me to take the sheep out?"

"Yes, but no farther than that tree out there. As soon as they start to lie down, bring them back."

"Did you know that ram is a bit nasty?"

"Ja, I know. Take a stick along. He always needs to be taught a lesson right at the beginning. He will try to show you who is boss. Make sure the dogs are with you."

He gave her a disgusted look.

"I know, but those in charge have to make sure everyone is aware of the danger, especially these first few days."

"I know."

"Ja, and now we are all reminded." She turned to the girls. "Start with sweeping down the loft, so we can get the beds made properly. When the grass gets tall enough, we'll cut more to stuff the pallets. For now, take the old out and toss it in for the pigs. Put the mattress covers to soaking in lye water, and then we'll hang them on the line. We sure don't want any fleas and bedbugs attacking us. "

She looked to the sky. Were the clouds growing nearer? The sun was already warming them and the land. "I know, everything must be done at once."

She ran through a mental list, reminding herself to always count noses. With this many to be responsible for, one might get lost easily. One needed to be prepared for anything at the seter.

They stopped for a cheese and bread meal earlier than the nooning, since breakfast had been so early so the others could leave. Mari and Hamme had stopped cleaning to slice the bread and cheese.

"We need to make bread tomorrow," Mari said.

"My bread is not so good," Hamme told her cousin. "Mor says I need to knead it more, mix it up better."

"Don't worry, I like to make bread," Mari said.

Ingeborg overheard the conversation. The problem had an easy answer. Take more time for the kneading, but she knew Hamme would rather be outside than cooped up in the kitchen. She understood that feeling well, but her mor insisted her daughters learn early on to cook, especially the breads and pancakes.

"Are you ready?" she asked a bit later.

"Ja. I had to skim the milk from last night. You can already taste the difference with the cows on pasture."

Ingeborg smiled. That was another thing they needed to check over, see if clumps of Jimsonweeds were growing anywhere. They tainted the milk, and thus the cheese, if the cows grazed on them—it wasn't dangerous, but it gave the cheese a different flavor from the normal. She'd take the new ones on a plant identification lesson as soon as possible. Everything needed to be done as soon as possible.

Gunlaug came down the ladder from the house's sleeping loft. She wiped her brow with the back of her hand. "It's getting warm up there, for sure. I opened all the windows. The one at the south end was stuck, but I pried it open."

They all sat down outside on blocks of wood to eat, letting the sun soak into them as well as into the pallet covers blowing on the line. The quilts would have to serve as underbedding until they could stuff the pallets with grass again.

"You say the blessing, Anders." Looking around at all those gathered, Ingeborg again marveled at how much the cousins looked alike. Strangers would be hard put to know which family to place each one in. They were all towheads, with blue or gray-blue eyes, with rounded facial features that started lengthening out as their childhood fell behind them.

Anders nodded and clasped his hands. "I Jesu navn, går vi til bords . . ." The children had all learned the old prayer as soon as they could talk. Amen came first to baby tongues.

"And thank you for a safe trip up here and blessing our time together," Ingeborg added. When she said amen this time, they all joined in. One rarely added on to the old prayer, so they were surprised. "We need to thank Him over and over."

She swept her arm around to encompass the valley and all of them. "He will keep us safe, because we ask."

She caught Tor rolling his eyes. Did they not say the grace at his home? Or perhaps only on special days? This would bear some thinking on. After all, her far had reminded her that she was the head up here, and that included Bible and manners training. No one wanted their children returning from the seter gone half wild. She had just taken a bite and raised her face to the sunshine when they all heard the snap.

"The trap!" the big boys shouted in unison and tore into the house. Sure enough, at the back of the room, behind a crate, a rat still shuddered in the neck-snapping trap. They brought the beastie outside, waving their spoils of war. "In the daytime even."

"Don't you bring that over here!" Gunlaug shouted as she jumped to her feet.

Tor, who was carrying the prize by its tail, made a motion to do just that.

"Tor Strand, if you think you're so big you can do what you want, remember we can send you back down the mountain." Ingeborg tried to assume a mantle of authority, but the boys just laughed.

"We'll throw it out in the bushes, then," Anders said, pointing. "It is just a rat."

"Oh good, then something bigger will come to get it and get the chickens too." She swept her arm toward the free-roaming chickens.

Ingeborg shook her head, just barely, when Hjelmer looked at her. "She's right, you know. Someone can take it up the hill later. Set the trap again, then sit down and finish eating." She heard the trap go off a couple of times and a yelp from one of the three boys. The spring in a rat trap was tricky. It had to be to catch the crafty creatures. The things must have been fiercely hungry.

Ingeborg gave out the afternoon's orders, but as the children headed out, Hjelmer stopped beside her. "It was a mother rat, and she is nursing babies."

Ingeborg knew he would like to search for the nest. This brother was much like her, not wanting to hurt things but to make them better. "You know it is probably under the house and impossible to get at. Besides, what would we do with baby rats? They grow up to be big rats."

"I know." He heaved a sigh. "But no wonder she was so desperate that she came out during the day." He paused. "I could let the others finish—we are almost done repairing the downed posts—and start checking the other fence lines." He glanced back at the house.

Ingeborg knew he'd rather look for the baby rats. He didn't want them to suffer. That was what she would have wanted to do too. She looked toward the far fields. "That's a good idea. Go ahead and tell them I agreed." She smiled at him. "Tusen takk."

"For what?"

"Being so caring and responsible."

He gave her a look he'd been perfecting lately. A combination of *Oh, Mor* and *Leave it to my sister.*

It wasn't her favorite but he had to grow up too. And with Tor teasing him, this summer promised to be a real growing period, inside at least.

"Have you seen any dandelions up here yet?" Gunlaug asked after she gathered the pallet covers off the line.

"Nei. We'll put everyone on the lookout for any good

greens." Since the altitude caused the growing season to start weeks later than down in their valley, the grass wasn't nearly as luxurious, and even the weeds were behind.

Sometime later, when Ingeborg was cleaning inside, she heard the harness jingling. She left off and returned outside to where the soup was simmering over the coals at the edge of the fire. The soup had been fixed at home and brought up the mountain to be set in the springhouse to cool again. The icy mountain water did a quick job of cooling foodstuffs, as it did the milk. From the fireside, she watched as Tor opened the pasture fence so Hjelmer could drive the team through.

Ingeborg motioned to Gunlaug with a finger to her lips. Together they watched Hjelmer go over the process with Tor again, waving his arms and pointing to fallen posts and rails.

Ingeborg held to her place, wanting to go box Tor's ears. Tor raised his voice, but Hjelmer shrugged. Tor tossed the logging chain around a broken post, hooked and snugged it, and took up the horses' lines. The chain tightened some but slipped up and off the post end.

Tor now waved his arms around. He reset the chain, low on the post and tight. This time as the horses moved forward, the chain tightened and the rotten post popped out.

Hjelmer cheered so loudly they could hear him even from this distance. The two boys dug about in the posthole with shovels. Tor single-handedly picked up a new post and dropped it into the hole. He steadied it as Hjelmer filled the hole and tamped the dirt down. The two said something, exchanging what? Advice? Congratulations? Complaints?

"I wish I was a mouse in his pocket!" Ingeborg whispered.

"Or at least a bird on his shoulder." Gunlaug gave Ingeborg

an elbow in the side. "I am proud of Hjelmer. Maybe this will help them get along better."

"We can only pray so." The two returned to the house, Gunlaug to cleaning the pantry she had started as soon as they arrived, and Ingeborg putting the rooms to order and preparing the fireplace that would provide their warmth and cooking all summer.

She heard laughing from the barn where Anders and someone rather harsh-voiced were cleaning. The girls had finished the upstairs, fixed the beds, and were now in the great living room.

"At least it doesn't look like it's going to rain," Kari said on her way to fetch more water. They were keeping a big iron kettle steaming on the fire outside so the cleaners would have hot water. She clearly loved the seter almost as much as Ingeborg did. "I'll bring in a couple of buckets from the creek." The tall, sturdy girl resembled her tante Hilde with the narrow brow and pointed chin, except she had a ready smile.

Ingeborg nodded. She'd been so engrossed in what they were doing, she'd forgotten to check. As the room darkened and one of the shutters banged, she figured maybe Kari had spoken too soon. Sure enough, drops spattered on the windows.

"Get the bedding in!" All those in the house charged out the door to keep their beds from getting wet. Within minutes they had the bedding in the house and draped over chairs and tables, all the while laughing and teasing.

Ingeborg headed outside. Sure enough, the boys had the sheep back in the corral, built especially for the sheep and connected to the shed on the side of the barn. The older boys had put the horses out, and now were standing in the barn door watching the rain. The animals ignored it, and

Ingeborg shook off the drops from her shawl as she returned to the house.

Please, Lord, let the others be nearing home, away from the danger of lightning. She'd seen a jagged light flash just moments before and heard the thunder grumble. A heavy rainfall would make travel miserable. Storms of any kind could be fierce in the mountains.

"Let's get the fireplace going in case this fire is put out."

"You think it will rain that hard?" Gunlaug asked, staring out the window. "Remember when we used to go play in the rain? Dancing around the birch trees until we were ordered inside, away from the lightning? It's sad that we don't do that anymore."

"You want to go out now?"

Gunlaug shook her head. "Let's get the fire going. Perhaps we should milk early too."

Ingeborg opened the door and looked out. "You are right. The cows are up at the barn. We'll do all the evening chores now." She raised her voice. "Mari, you and Hamme make små brød as soon as the coals are hot. The rest of you come with us."

"Where?"

"Out to the barn."

Shawls over heads, they stopped in the springhouse to get the milking buckets and dashed across the puddling yard to join the laughing boys in the barn.

They had just sat down to milk when Hjelmer came running. "Ingeborg, we are missing two hens. The others are all in the pen."

"Look all through the barn first and then the sheds. Chickens don't like to be wet either."

Surely something hadn't snatched the chickens already. She could hear the boys calling as she dumped her bucket into the milk can. *Please, Lord, protect the hens and children.* The prayer went up without thought on her part. It was probably the young hens that had not been crated and hauled before. Even chickens could remember, she had always thought. The younger ones were usually the ones to get in trouble first. Something like humans. The hens wouldn't be setting already.

She dumped a bucket for Gunlaug and ambled over to the doorway, the rain-laden wind blowing air so fresh even the barn odors disappeared. She inhaled with her eyes closed. This is what freedom smelled like and felt like.

"We found them," someone called from one of the out-buildings.

Thank you for even caring about our chickens. She would remind the others of that while they ate.

"Ingeborg, do you have something for my hands?" Tor rolled his hands so she could see his palms. Weeping blisters on blisters made her shake her head.

He added, "We got the fence done. Almost."

"Did you not wear leather gloves?"

He shrugged. "I don't have any."

"What? You were told to bring gloves along." She opened the cupboard door to where she had stored her medical supplies, bringing out a tin of salve and a roll of soft cloth torn into strips for bandages. On her mor's reminder she had stocked the box even more so. "Go scrub with the soap. We can't have your hands getting infected."

"It stings," he muttered at the bucket.

"Scrub and make sure there is no dirt left in there. Why didn't you tell me earlier?" *Boys,* she thought at his flinch.

After smoothing the slippery unguent in place, she wrapped his hands and tied the strips in knots on the back of his hands. "We do not throw these bandages away," she told him. "We wash them."

He nodded, teeth clamped on his lower lip.

She hoped this didn't portend a summer full of injuries and illness, like the one they had a few years earlier. But it was sure starting out that way.

9

Ingeborg sat up in bed. What was that noise?

She closed her eyes again. Hail of course. It sounded like something determined to shred whatever it touched. Hail did that. She lay back down. Surely they had closed all the windows here. She hoped the others had made it home. Even if they hadn't, hail didn't usually cover large areas at a time. Thoughts of every other thing that could break under the onslaught made her grit her teeth.

But what can you do about it? The question stopped her. Nothing. There was nothing she could do. Other than fret and worry. The words *Fear not* tiptoed into her mind like a fawn approaching a meadow. The doe would say, *Come on,* but the tiny fawn would still tiptoe. It was that part of him that nature instilled to protect him. Was that what all these silly thoughts were doing to her?

As her mor would say, although she didn't always live it, "*Only God can control the weather, and we don't have to be afraid.*" His Word says so. *Fear thou not, for I am with thee. . . .*

Ingeborg breathed a sigh and settled back on her pallet.

The floor was hard underneath her quilt, but she'd fallen asleep readily before and must do so again. Morning would come soon enough, even though it was still lighter than dusk outside. The hail clouds made it darker than a usual late May night. She ordered herself to close her eyes and clear her mind. Do not think about hail. Do not think about all that needs to be done. Do not think, period. When all else fails, pray. Perhaps that was the problem. Maybe she should be praying before all else. That thought made her smile. Such wisdom in the middle of the night. Now to remember it during the day and all it brought.

When she woke to a rooster crowing, she realized she had fallen back to sleep. Before she went out to the privy, she put on her shoes, which was a good thing, since some of the hail was still on the ground. And still large after all these hours. She wrinkled her brow, trying to remember what it was she had promised herself she would remember. Or had she dreamed that up too? Probably not, since the hail was indeed real. So she had been awake.

Back in the kitchen, she opened the fireplace damper and, with the poker, rattled the grate and firedogs. She laid bark and bits of tinder on the now-glowing coals and blew gently. Smoke spiraled upward, and soon she saw golden flames, so she added bigger kindling and small pieces of oak. They should keep the fire up better at night. It was cold in here. She filled the coffeepot with water from the bucket sitting in the dry sink. Having to go out to the creek this early did not appeal to her, so she always made sure someone was assigned to that daily task. After adding more wood to the now snapping fire, she set the coffeepot on the hearth close to the fire. Another full bucket of water sat on the floor near the door, so she picked it up to move it to the counter.

"Oh, ugh! Ick!" By reflex she set it down hard enough to slop over the edges and stepped back.

"What is it? Ingeborg, what is wrong?" someone called down from the sleeping loft.

"A mouse drowned in one of the water buckets."

"Oh." A giggle turned into a snort, joined by another.

"Frightened by a dead mouse." Had to be Hjelmer. His voice was the only one that had started to change, a baritone that sometimes cracked with soprano. More giggles, and in a moment Gunlaug backed, laughing, down the ladder.

"All you who think that is so funny, just come on down and get at the chores," she called back up.

Ingeborg tried to ignore her but instead handed her the contaminated bucket. "You take care of this on your way out to the backhouse."

"We can still use the water. Just fish the mouse out and we can add it to the wash water outside on the fire."

"Fine. You fish the mouse out."

"You know I—"

Ingeborg rolled her eyes, grabbed a big spoon, fished the body out, and threw it out the door. The barn cats would find it. Good thing they'd brought cats along too. She forced herself to keep a stern face as the others came giggling down the ladder.

"Since you think this is funny, you do the milking and all the chores this morning without me."

"What are you going to do?" Mari asked, looking at her big sister suspiciously.

"Oh, I am going to sit at the table with my feet up, drink coffee, and eat gorobrød. With butter and sugar, of course. What else do you think I am going to do?"

At that, Mari started to giggle again, a contagious giggle that even Ingeborg with her sternest look could not ignore.

"We have gorobrød here?" Tor gave Hjelmer a confused look. "I didn't think we brought any along."

"She's teasing." Hjelmer shook his head, clearly saying his cousin must be lacking something in the brain department to not get the joke. He handed Tor a bucket.

"But I don't know how to milk a cow." Tor took a step back.

"Ah, Tor, you need not worry about learning to milk until your hands get better. You can do the other chores. Go out with Hjelmer. He'll tell you what needs doing." Although he should know these things by now. Ingeborg never failed to marvel at how much more of the vital things in life that country-raised children learned from the time they could toddle. It was a shame not everyone was raised on a farm.

As the boys and Kari left for the barn, Ingeborg went to the door and called after them. "Tor, we have to remember to tend to your hands when you get done out there. Do you have gloves on?"

He turned. "I told you I don't have any."

"I'll give you a pair of mine." Anders punched him on the shoulder. "But do not lose them, or you'll be sewing a new pair."

That is not a bad idea, Ingeborg thought as she turned back to the younger children. Did they have a tanned deer hide up here? She'd have to look. "Mari, you and I will start the bread and soup. Hamme, you and Jon go out and restart the fire so we can continue heating the water out there. You

do know how to start a fire, right?" When they both nodded, she turned to her youngest sister, who seemed so much
older and wiser than several of the others. But then she had
been coming to the seter for two years already and she had
learned to help at home, even did much of the cooking and
baking. Impulsively she reached over and drew Mari to her.
"I am so thankful for you."

Mari hugged her back then tipped her head so she could
smile up at her big sister. "Can we have eggs for breakfast?"
She gave Ingeborg another hug and giggled into her apron.

"Yes, I think we can. The hens have started laying again."

"The ride up here turned that older rooster mean. He
pecked at the others and tried to chase me, but I swung my
bucket at him. He gave me the evil eye too. I think he might
be in the stewpot soon."

"You just might be right." It was always something, or
someone not getting along. Why was peace so hard to come
by? With all the beauty up here, everyone should be happy.
But she knew that wasn't enough. Just a dream. "All right,
you get the flour and lard out, and I'll go get the milk. We'll
put an egg in the sveler this morning too."

"Sugar or jam?"

"How about a bit of sugar in the dough and jam on top
after they bake?"

Mari smiled pure bliss. "I love sveler like this almost as
good as gorobrød fresh from the iron."

"And Mor taught us how to make both really well. We
need to remember to start the dough tonight for breakfast
tomorrow."

"And lapper, and—" Mari's eyes twinkled. "Did we bring
enough sugar for all this?"

"I think so, but we have to use it carefully. Get the fire going hot." Ingeborg stopped on the stoop and raised her face to the sun. At least it didn't act like it didn't get enough sleep last night. She yawned, stretching her arms over her head. One of the dogs came wagging to see her, so she leaned down to pet her. "How come you're not out with the sheep?"

The dog turned her head then bounded toward the barn. Hjelmer must have called her.

The flat, round, sweet pancakes and eggs to go with the porridge were a hit with everyone. Good thing Mari had made plenty. Boys especially certainly could put away food! And last night it had gotten pretty cold.

"All right, do you all know what you are to do today?"

"Look for nasty weeds," two of them answered in unison. "All of us?"

"Who is going with the sheep?" she asked.

"I am and taking Jon along," Anders said. "He's herded sheep at home too."

"Good, we'll need Hjelmer and Tor to finish up the fence mending, since they didn't quite get that done yesterday. Was there any hail damage that you could see?"

The milkers all shook their heads.

"Good thing it was in the night like that," Kari offered. "The chickens weren't outside."

"Nor the sheep. Remember the year it hailed and they started to run away? I was afraid I would never find them all—alive, that is."

"A couple of them were limping afterward." Ingeborg shook her head. That had been only one of the frightening things that year. Like the lynx attack that had wounded one of the young calves so badly they had to butcher it. She'd fought the tears through that one. Being the oldest girl in a family gave her all kinds of chores, including many she didn't like.

"Can I make sveler again for dinner?" Mari asked. "We don't have any små brød."

"Enough soup left?"

She shook her head.

"Fine. We can slice the spekekjøtt to go with that rindy cheese." They didn't have much of that dried mutton left either. "We should have set the beans to soaking last night." Kicking oneself was not helpful either. "But since we didn't, they will take longer, so start them now. We can each bring in an armload of wood for the woodbox. As soon as the water is hot out there, Kari, you and Hamme wash all the windows. And then we are done with housecleaning. Gunlaug and I will sort through last year's wool and see what we have. Let's go."

"We forgot to pray."

"We did. It is not too late now." After they said the table grace, they all picked up their plates and set them in the pan of soapy water steaming near the fire.

As they scattered to do their assigned chores, Gunlaug shook her head. "Keeping all this straight in your head—how do you do it, Ingeborg?"

"Obviously I forgot something. How about you be in charge of table prayers and choosing a Bible verse to memorize each week? Maybe set up a contest, and the ones who can say them all at the end of the summer get a prize."

"Like what?"

"I don't know. We'll think of something."

"I know the boys would like a day off to go fishing. But we can't wait for the end of the summer for that. We need to check the lake to see if the trout are feeding yet."

"I heard Tor is a good fisherman."

"I'm glad he is good at something." Ingeborg flinched. "I forgot to fix his hands."

"After dinner, then." Gunlaug joined Mari at the dry sink, where the dishes were now in the rinse water, and picked up a dish towel.

The rest of the children trailed in with their armloads of wood and dumped them into the box. "More?"

Ingeborg checked and nodded.

"We need to be thinking about the shearing too."

"I know, Gunlaug." She could hear the jingle of the horse harnesses. The boys were bringing up more wood from the side lot without her having to tell them. This was a very good sign.

Ingeborg called Tor aside. An hour later he knew how to use a crosscut saw without making his blisters even worse than they were, and the pile of unsplit spools of wood had grown immensely.

Everyone sat down to dinner, glad Mari had more biscuits. While some of the girls cleaned up afterward, Ingeborg took care of Tor's hands, and then everyone except Mari trooped out to the milk house. The boys carried buckets of milk, and the girls prepared the first of the cheese pots. They put in a long hard afternoon, but so far no one was complaining. They gathered around the fireplace as supper was finishing cooking.

"Willing hands make short work. That's what Mor always says. We did it and you all deserve something special." Ingeborg winked at Mari, who had spent the afternoon in the kitchen.

"I think I smelled gorobrød," Jon said, "when I went to put more wood on the fire. With jam, right?"

"Good. Why don't you go get a jug of milk from the spring-house, and we'll sit outside." She looked at their faces. "Some of you got sunburned. That's why bonnets are no good hanging down the back."

"The boys are lucky. Their straw hats are better than bonnets." Hamme led the way out of the fire pit to the sitting logs and wood chunks that were now in the shade of the house. Mari brought out the freshly made gorobrød, butter, and jam, Gunlaug passed out the cups, and Jon poured—very carefully.

Ingeborg leaned against the log wall of the house. They had done a good day's work, and everyone got along. What more could she ask for?

"They must have smelled the gorobrød," Hjelmer said when they heard a dog bark. "I'll go put the sheep in the corral so they can eat."

Ingeborg watched him go. Hjelmer might not be the tallest, but he was the most caring of the boys in the family. He took after his grandfather Bjorn.

If only . . .

She knew better than to listen to *if only.*

But . . . not a good word either.

Please, Lord, let tomorrow be as peaceful as today. And thank you the hail didn't damage anything either.

⟶

The next morning, Ingeborg held Tor back from tending to his chores after breakfast. "Tor, your hands?"

He rolled his eyes but returned and held his hands out.

"The bandages are pretty dirty. Are you not wearing gloves?" She fetched a scissor and cut them off. "We let this go too long. Let's see how they look."

As she peeled back the bandages, she was pleased to see healthy pink skin under the dead skin of the blisters, much of which had worn away. "Very good. But we'll wrap them again to protect the new skin." As she spoke she did just that. "And you wear the gloves."

He nodded. "I know how to sew gloves if you have some tanned deer hide, or sheepskin can work too. I could make me a new pair or make Anders a new pair and keep these."

She'd not heard him speak that long at once before and to volunteer something like that. Smiling up at him, she nodded. "We do have a deerskin—two, in fact. I'll get them out for you. How did you learn?"

"My far. He makes all kinds of leather things—shoes, aprons, gloves, bags. I help him."

"I didn't know that."

"Far's gloves never raise welts or rub the skin raw either. But I'm not that good yet."

She knotted the ties on the backs of his hands. "There you go. Count yourself lucky. Those blisters could have gotten infected and messed up your summer."

He gave her a sideways glance. "Not with you taking care of 'em. They wouldn't dare."

Ingeborg tried to hide her laughter but gave it up as a bad effort and burst out laughing. "Takk, I think." Maybe there was hope for Tor after all. One thing for sure, he would learn a lot this summer.

10

OSLO, NORWAY

The clock on the wall ticked quietly, marking moments, its shiny brass pendulum flowing back and forth. Nils glanced at it again. It was five minutes after nine. The last time he had looked, it was four minutes after nine. His appointment was supposed to be at nine o'clock, and the dean was a punctual sort. What could be the problem? Ordering himself to relax, he heaved a sigh, which made him wish he'd not. He scooted a bit further back in his chair and forced himself to stop fingering the hat brim in his hands. The clock ticked.

The dean's office door swung open, and his secretary stepped out into the foyer. The gentleman was dressed like Nils's father dressed, every stitch of attire perfect from cravat to shoes. "The dean will see you now, Mr. Aarvidson."

"Thank you, sir." Nils stood up, sucked in some air as a tweak in his side stabbed him, then walked to the door.

The secretary stepped in behind him and announced lugubriously, "Mr. Nils Aarvidson, Mr. Klein." He stepped backward. Nils heard the door click.

"Please be seated, Mr. Aarvidson." The dean had been living in Oslo how many decades? And he still spoke with the clipped, authoritative German accent of his homeland.

"Thank you, sir." Nils perched on the edge of the chair, thought twice about that, and slid back to give a more relaxed impression—also not a good idea. "Thank you for allowing me this audience."

The dean nodded. "I have spent the last fifteen minutes looking at your records." He tapped a pile of papers on the corner of his desk. "I also have here a letter from your attending physician, Dr. Jorge, about the extent of the injuries you sustained in that accident. I am amazed that you are so soon ambulatory." He sat back. "So what have you been doing for the last week?"

Nils had not been expecting that question, or any question, for that matter. He had been expecting a diatribe such as his father delivered daily. "Uh, convalescing, sir. Or trying to. And studying. Actually fretting over not studying. I'm having a difficult time concentrating. My sister, Amalia, has been reading to me, coaching me. My eyes don't focus well yet."

"As your doctor's comments suggested. That blow to the head. Your father came by to see me a few days ago. He is greatly concerned."

What could he say? "Yes, he is."

"Your father has requested that we postpone your examinations until near the beginning of the fall school year. He wants you to work in his office half time over summer and study half time."

It blurted out of him before he could think. "So he can supervise my studies."

The dean smiled slightly. "Quite possibly, although he did

113

not mention that. So I queried your professors. Your philosophy professor is willing to postpone your exam until the beginning of fall semester. He senses in you a potential that is yet untapped."

As does my father. Again Nils held his tongue.

"Your logistics professor has offered to waive your exam and give you a grade based on your work to date. Would that be acceptable to you?"

Nils tried to think fast and could not. Logistics of Trade and Transport. He was making an average grade—not great, not mediocre. Could he do better with an exam? *Think, Nils!* Probably not. "Yes. Yes, sir, that would be satisfactory. I am grateful."

The dean nodded. "And your medieval history professor refuses to consider a postponement. He intends that you take the exam at the appointed time, along with his other students."

"Then I will do so. Thank you for your efforts, Dean Klein. I am grateful."

The dean stood, so Nils leapt to his feet, gasping as another stab of pain sliced through his ribs. The dean extended his hand. "Mr. Aarvidson, I am impressed. Despite your circumstance, you have not once complained or tried to pass blame. I wish you well. Thank you for coming in."

Nils stretched forward to accept the handshake and just about died. He hoped the pain didn't show. "Thank you, sir. I truly am grateful."

"And I truly am impressed with your fortitude. Good luck, Mr. Aarvidson."

Nils heard the door open behind him, so with one more thank-you, he nodded briefly and left.

As the door closed behind him, he heard the dean saying, "Take a letter. Mr. Rignor Aarvidson, care of Aarvidson Shipping. My esteemed Mr. Aarv . . ."

⁓

"This is outrageous!" RA slapped the open sheet of foolscap on his desk. "A pox on Hermann Klein! A pox on that sorry excuse for a school! A simple request and they send this!"

Nils knew what *this* was—the letter from the dean, explaining the decisions that had been made.

His father turned on him. "And you acquiesced to this nonsense!"

Apparently Nils was deserving of a pox as well. "It was the best I could get, given the choices. At least I need to study for only one exam this fall rather than three."

"Dinner is served." The footman stood in the doorway.

RA marched out, still fuming.

"Thank you." Nils nodded to the footman and followed the furious tycoon downstairs to the dining room, hanging on to the stair rail and feeling every step he took. He castigated himself with each one. He couldn't even remember the footman's name. How would he ever be ready for that test?

At the bottom of the stairs, Katja scooted past him and stood at her chair. She sat and gripped its seat with both hands, lifting as Nils scooted it in, lest his ribs decide to come apart again. Dear, sweet Katja.

Absolutely icy, Nils's father rattled through the blessing. His mother picked up her fork.

Nils announced, "I learned today that my classmate, Hans

115

Boonstra, is a descendant of Dutch bankers who helped the Germans set up the Hanseatic League. His family has always been bankers."

RA scowled at the platter of pork roast the cook placed before them before the man returned to the kitchen.

No answer? Then Nils would continue. "His family is remarkably wealthy. Apparently his father and grandfather bought up Amerikan dollars and bonds right after their civil war twenty years ago, when bonds and currency were cheap. Now the Boonstras are buying up more, because the nation is in a financial depression. They are quite certain the Amerikan economy will rebound, and when it does, they will be well enough off that they can buy most of Europe, if anyone would want most of Europe."

RA studied his son. "At least he follows in his father's footsteps." There was a bitter edge to his words.

Nils licked his lips. "Actually, no. He's going to let his brothers do that. He wants to get into trade and transport, he says. Shipping. He has taken quite a fancy to it, what with our logistics class and all, and he's quite good with geography." And Nils drove home his point: "Hans will be doing something he truly enjoys. I envy that."

For some reason he glanced at his mother. She was studying him carefully. What was going on in that well-coiffed head?

⁓

Nils had five days to master seven hundred years of European history. He returned to classes and took notes conscientiously, but learning a little something about the century immediately preceding the Enlightenment didn't help a whole lot.

In the evenings Amalia read his notes back to him, complaining frequently that his scrawl was nearly illegible. She read his text to him. He blotted up as much as he could, painfully aware that his mind was nowhere near as sharp as it had been, and it had not been too sharp to start with.

Examination day arrived, and he settled into his desk in history class and took pen in hand to write his medieval history exam. It was a shame he couldn't send Amalia to take it for him. She excelled in history and had learned more from the coaching than he had from being the one coached.

The first twenty minutes or so went pretty well. Then the headache returned. Another half hour and his eyes could not focus well. He saw his own handwriting grow larger and larger. He was losing his fine motor control. Oops, he had just mixed up Leo the tenth with Hadrian the sixth. Or wait . . . He ended up skipping the question about the popes.

At last a question that referred to the last two lectures, the dawn of the Enlightenment. He could discuss that one. When his professor counted down to zero and everyone laid their pens aside, he had completed all but the pope question and had even added some information to two of the other essays.

It took him nearly a minute simply to stand up. His legs ached, his ribs ached, his head ached. His heart ached. Surely he could have done better.

Hans was waiting for him outside the door. "I'd ask you how it went, but you look like you'd have to get better to die. I happen to have a hansom waiting for us out front. You don't have to walk."

"Boonstra, you're a prince among men. Prince nothing. King." Nils stumbled down the hallway. "I would love to join you for a beer, but I'm too knackered. I'd like to just go home and sleep."

"Understood." Hans was his usual ebullient self, and his cheer raised Nils's spirits. A little. "Oh, Nils, and I think I have a job. Not in trade exactly, but close. I will be a stevedore down on the Londres dock."

"Loading the Nordic Princess?"

Hans stared at him. "How do you know that?"

"My father owns the Nordic Princess and she's in the Londres dock right now taking on lumber. Enjoy. She used to be a ketch, but they've rigged her as a barkentine. A worthy little vessel."

"A barkentine. That's she, all right." Hans held the door for him and pointed two doors down toward a carriage at the curb. "Right over there. I'm telegraphing my father, telling him I've found gainful employment in Norway, and to save the cost of my traveling home and then traveling back to school, I'm just staying here. Save him some money."

Nils stepped up into the hansom and flopped down on the leather seat. The carriage bobbed a bit, giving his ribs another tweak. "And what will your father say to that?"

"He'll say bosh, he can afford to send me home. Or maybe not. Saving a guilder here and a guilder there has always rung his bell." Hans settled in across from Nils and swung the door closed. He rapped on the roof.

Nils chuckled as the cab lurched forward. "Can you join us for dinner?"

"Another appointment, sorry. But I'll gladly accept an invitation for another time. Just think. The shipping magnate and the lowly stevedore dining together."

Nils snorted. "A lowly stevedore who can afford to buy the

ship." How good it felt to simply chat, without the need to
learn anything, without the need to mount a pretense. How
he wished his life were like this.

By dinnertime he had retrieved enough of his faculties that
he could make decent conversation. He allowed as how Amalia had gotten him through the exam and refused to speculate
on the results. Then he let his father take off and expound,
and what the man said didn't even really register. His mother
nodded knowingly now and then, and he knew well that she
wasn't listening either. For some curious reason, he glanced
over several times to see her carefully watching him.

Nils remained at his parents' place for several days, for he
had no reason to return to his rooms, other than the obvious one, to escape his father. He made a point of letting his
philosophy book lie here and there in obvious places, as if
he were truly studying. What he did more than anything else
was sleep, frequently. He could not shake the weariness that
permeated his whole body.

One day he finally managed to stay awake for most of the
day and even read in his philosophy text for half an hour.
Perhaps he was finally getting better. Janssen laid out his
clothes for dinner, and he actually felt like putting them on,
no longer needing assistance. He ignored the shoes waiting
for him by the bed and remained in his slippers. He joined
the family in the drawing room and made light conversation.
He repaired to the dining room, seated his sisters, and when
asked about his day offered a few quotes from the philosopher
Marcus Monrad, to whom a whole chapter of his text was
dedicated. The day was going well.

The cook set out two roast chickens, a tureen of buttered carrots, and a bowl of turnips in cheese sauce. His father scowled. The magisterial RA Aarvidson disliked turnips and was not particularly fond of carrots.

They ate in silence, and again Nils noticed his mother watching him.

Father sat back, wiped his mouth, and glared at Nils. "I received a letter from Dean Klein this afternoon."

Nils's heart leapt into his mouth, starting the pain that so often sneaked in when he least expected it. Would the pain never stop?

"He says your history professor has submitted the test results. You have received only an acceptable rating. Not the top rating you promised me."

His heart dropped from his mouth to the soles of his feet. "I did the best I could."

"That is not good enough."

"Where is the compromise that you claim a good business-man must make? I did my best." *For what I can do right now. Had the professor been willing to wait, I would have done well.*

"I have a desk waiting for you in the accounting office. You begin work tomorrow." There was a chilling finality to his voice.

"Rignor." Nils's mother! She never spoke to his father in that stern tone of voice.

He looked at her, schooling his face, as he always did.

"Your son is still not well. Look at him. He cannot move smoothly, he cannot see well—have you noticed how he must squint at things that are close? Have you watched him try to climb up and down the stairs? This is not Nils in normal health, yet he did his best for you, the best he could do in his compromised state." Then her voice took on an iron-hard flatness Nils had never heard from her before. "You will honor his request. You will allow him his summer in the mountains so that he may recover. You will, Rignor." She nodded toward the table. "Katja, would you pass the turnips, please?"

Three days later, Nils Aarvidson, avid mountaineer and outdoor enthusiast, stepped down out of a coach in a village at the foot of the mountains and drew in a deep, luxuriant breath of fresh mountain air. And nearly buckled from the pain in his ribs. Were they never going to heal?

Should he spend the night at the inn in town or go directly up into the hills? Since he had no particular destination in mind, he compromised by walking up a road east of town to a small wayside inn, Raggen Inn, tucked in a crease within the foothills and there spent the night.

He ate a hearty breakfast the next morning as a swollen mountain brook crashed and gurgled beside the dining room window.

"Why don't you let me bring you more coffee to that comfortable chair outside. The view, as you can see, is spectacular, and letting the sun bake the city out of your bones will make a new man of you."

Nils smiled at his hostess. While he had planned to start out early, perhaps this might be a wiser choice. "Takk, I will do that."

Freedom tasted like the finest elixir. No one ordering him to do anything; he didn't even have to be polite if he did not feel like it. He smiled at the woman with cheeks of strawberry red and thanked her for not only the coffee but the sweet roll she had brought along.

"I just took these out of the pans, and while I know you're not really hungry right now, would you do me the honor of tasting and perhaps offering approval?"

He inhaled the fragrance. "Intoxicating." One bite and he knew he had stepped into heaven. "There are not enough words to say how good this is."

She giggled, almost like a young girl. "My son, he likes these too."

Nils returned to his room, started to pack, and instead lay down on the bed for just a few minutes.

When he awoke, the angle of the sun had shifted to late afternoon, so after bread and soup for supper he went back to bed.

Next morning after a good night's sleep and another hearty breakfast, he felt like life was returning.

The inn's mistress sent sandwiches and apples with him and insisted on grasping both his hands and asking a fervent prayer that God keep him safe. Refreshed in body and spirit, he began his trek by following a shepherd's path that the lady assured him would lead him into some of the most beautiful mountains. As if there were any mountains not beautiful.

Less than an hour later, after staggering the last hundred yards, he had to pause to rest. Being infirm those weeks had certainly taken a toll on his stamina. But he wasn't worried. He would recover it in a day or two. He continued on. And rested an hour later. And continued on.

Though it was still early, he could go no farther. Beside a rushing stream he strung a tarpaulin between two trees, built a fire, and settled for the night. His headache had returned, howling even more loudly, so to speak, than the stream beside him. This recovery might take a few days longer than he had anticipated.

⁓

Nils took his time breaking camp the next morning. He had forgotten about camping so close to a rushing stream; the air was faster and colder this close to the water. Tonight he would camp well above a stream. That way he could hear the sweet song of the water without freezing in the cold wind it dragged along with it.

As he followed the broad path dotted with sheep's hoofmarks, he had ample time to think. He realized he should have started thinking a day ago. He knew not to camp so close to rushing water. He knew how to set up a camp and build a fire for maximum warmth and comfort. Why was he acting so brainless, like a child? He had been away from the mountains far too long. That was what was wrong.

Ah, but he was here now. Now all would be better.

He rested at midday, ate the last of the innkeeper's sandwiches, and chewed a strip of beef jerky. That persistent headache lingered in the background, ready to pounce at any moment. He could feel its presence as a heaviness.

The shepherds' path leveled out now, winding off across the mountainside meadows. He would leave the path and follow this stream farther up. He had no interest in engaging simple shepherds in conversation.

The sky, which had started out blue this morning, had turned white, and now dark gray clouds hung low. He could read that well enough and tucked his collar up tighter against his neck, under his hat brim. Sure enough, the rain began and soon was falling steadily. No problem. This too was a part of the mountain experience.

His leather boot slipped on wet stones, and he almost fell. He must be more careful, but his mind seemed to be getting foggy, as if he had drunk two or three beers, but he hadn't. He stumbled while crossing the stream and waited until his heart settled its pace again before following a game trail that offered easier going.

The boulders got bigger. That was odd, because usually the larger boulders were downhill. He walked out across a rocky slope, his boots sliding now and again, and picked up another game trail. Why hadn't he stayed on the main track?

His boot slid off a wet rock and landed solidly beside it. The wild jolt sent an excruciating stab of pain up through his ribs. He gasped, doubled forward, lost his balance. He was falling.

Why was rain falling on his face? Where was his hat brim when he needed it? How could he still this howling headache, the nearly unbearable pain in his ribs and now in his leg too?

Leg? His leg hurt as badly as his ribs did. He was lying on his back in a ravine amid huge rocks, his head downhill, and one foot was pinched up between two boulders. His leg, the one that hurt so badly, was bent in a way that followed the surface of the smooth, slick, rounded rock. He realized with a chill that his leg was not bending at the knee. It had broken.

He could not move. Even if he tried to move in spite of the fierce pain, he could not. His leg was wedged between the rocks. The cold rain was soaking in despite the warmth of his wool clothing.

Tonight he would become wetter and wetter, colder and colder. The sun would nearly go down. He could not stretch his arm far enough to get his rucksack and retrieve his blankets and the tarpaulin. At some time during this long cold night, the pain would ease, he would slide into a chilled sleep, and he would not wake up, ever again.

11

At least the sun warmed him a little in the morning. How long had he been lying there? Through the night, the very long and very cold night. If only he could have retrieved his blankets and the tent he had brought along, folded so neatly in his backpack.

Nils stared around his mountain prison. What could he do to get himself out of this disaster? By himself? How often had he been warned against hiking in the mountains alone? He should have listened. Hindsight was always wise. What did he have? Besides a new lump on his head and a leg that was ten times larger than when he'd started out. His ribs were well beyond unhappy with the new situation also. The rest of him did not bear thinking about, like the swollen fingers or . . . Skip the or. If only he could get his leg into the creek. With the fresh snow melt it was plenty cold. What to deal with first?

If only his mind were clearer. Or he could stay awake. He felt around the lump that now encompassed much of the side of his head. At least the one in back had not opened again and started bleeding. That was something to be thankful for. A cough wracked him, a series of coughs that left him gasping in pain. And more dizzy. He stared at the rocks around him. If he could pull himself into a sitting position, that might help the coughing. But every time he tried to move the leg, he blacked out again. What did he have to immobilize it? His walking staff. But where had it gone in the fall? He propped himself up on his elbows. His ribs screamed. Staring around, moving his head inch by inch, he checked all the terrain within his vision. No staff. It had probably floated down the creek somewhere.

He froze, as if he weren't shaking already. Was that a dog barking? He listened with every part of his being. Yes, a dog.

"Help! Help! Help!"

Why had he not brought a gun along? Or a whistle? He ignored the pain when he sucked in as mighty a breath as possible and hollered again. *Please, God, let that dog hear me!* He listened hard, but the creek was chattering so loudly, he heard nothing. "Oh, God, please. I don't want to die out here! Help me! I know I could not make it through another night."

The effort left him gasping, so he collapsed back to a prone position. When he opened his eyes, three suns shone down on him and rocks, many rocks, danced. He listened again, not breathing until he was forced to suck air in.

A whine. Was it? Or was it the wheezing growing in his chest?

He opened his eyes. Two dog heads peered over the lip of the trail, looking down at him. One ran off while the other continued to watch him. "Go, dog. Get help." He tried to wave to the animal, but even his arm would not lift. Was

127

life draining out of him? When he looked again, the dog was gone.

Oh, please, dear God, please make him bring someone back. Please let this not be a delusion. It was a good thing God did not need to hear a loud voice. He had prayed now more than all the rest of his life put together.

Sometimes fading out was preferable to suffering. How many times had this happened during the night? What did it matter? Was he to die there, alone and with no way to tell his family good-bye?

He woke sometime later. Shadows had replaced the sunshine as it journeyed west. The shaking had grown beyond any control he attempted.

A bark. A bark nearby. He looked up to see the dog again. "Good boy, good dog." Oh, thank God, good dog.

A young boy's face joined the dog. "How bad are you hurt?"

"A broken leg, head smashed against the rocks, and I slid down that scarp." How far had his whisper carried?

"Can you move?"

"Not much. I was . . . am . . ." The coughing attacked again. Seems it did every time he tried to talk. He felt he was shouting. Until—

"What? I cannot hear you."

Nils forced every ounce of strength he possessed into an answer. "Help!"

"I will bring help. I will be back." The boy and dog disappeared.

The promise soaked him like the warmest bath. He lay back. *Thank you, God. You heard me. Takk, tusen takk.* He could no longer identify the cold seeping up from the gravel and rocks underneath him. Surely he would not have to spend another night here. But how they would lift him up from his impossible position was beyond thinking.

⌐⌐

"Ingeborg! Ingeborg!" Jon ran as fast as his legs allowed, and the trail didn't trip him. "Ingeborg!" He would have brought one of the dogs to go ahead, but Hjelmer needed the dogs to bring the sheep in. When he crested the trail to see the seter valley, he stopped and screamed again, waving his arms.

"What is that?" Ingeborg stopped on her way back from skimming off the cream from the milking of the evening before. After tonight and tomorrow morning, they would have enough cream to start a batch of cheese. She scanned the valley, catching sight of Jon waving his arms. Something was wrong for sure. She waved back to show she'd heard and looked around. Who could she send?

"Hamme, you run fast. Go see what Jon is trying to tell us. I'll saddle one of the horses."

The girl took off with a nod, lifting her skirts so she could run faster.

"Anders, catch one of the horses for me, quick."

He waved from the barn and headed out to the horses grazing in the pasture.

"Mari! Gather up some blankets." Would she need bandages? Of course, take them just in case. Apparently someone was injured. Was it Hjelmer? *Oh, God, please not.* Something attacked the sheep? She looked out. Hamme was charging back on the track. Ingeborg yelled at her. "How bad?"

"A hiker. Hjelmer found an injured hiker."

A hiker! Way up here? There were no nearby trails or major hiking routes. And just one hiker, it would seem. No one sensible would ever hike alone. Ingeborg waved to her and headed inside. "We need some of the pain medicine, bandages, the blankets. What else?" She could hear Anders with the horse. "Go see if he got the horse saddled."

Kari ran outside. "Ja!"

"Go see if the hiking staves are . . . are . . ." Where had they left them last fall?

"I saw them in the springhouse. I'll get them." Mari left.

Trying to catch her breath, Hamme puffed out, "He is down near a creek bed, not able to move. Leg is broken, I think."

"Now we know." She turned to Kari. "Tie those blankets behind the saddle. I'll carry the staves. Put the other things in a bag we can tie to the saddle."

Tor burst in the door, followed by Mari.

"Tor, you and Anders follow me as fast as you can. Jon, ride behind me to show me where the sheep are grazing and help bring the flock back. Hjelmer knows where to go. We need rope. Kari, you bring the rope and come with the boys." Her mind kept praying *Help* as she gave the orders. "Mari, make sure we have plenty of hot water and fix a padded pallet on the floor by the fireplace." She thought again. "Since we don't know how long he has been there, we'll need broth to feed him. Or soup. Fix something easy to eat."

"We're ready." Kari stepped into the room, a coiled rope over her shoulder. "Tor has another rope. The staves are beside the door."

"All of you, pray for this man, that we can save his life." Outside, she mounted the horse, took the staves in one hand,

and waited for Anders to help Jon settle in behind her. "Hang on around my waist. We'll be going fast."

"Ja."

She turned the horse and nudged it from a trot to a canter, so much easier for her passenger behind her. They quickly left the runners behind. "Are you all right?"

"Ja. I have ridden before."

Her litany of *Help us* calmed her mind as they started up the trail on the other side of the valley. It changed to *Let us get there in time.* Up ahead she could see the flock of sheep coming around a corner. "Can you take them home yourself?" she asked Jon.

"Ja, my sheep follow me."

"The dogs will help you." She slowed the horse before it could frighten the sheep. When she stopped, Jon slid to the ground.

"Can we take the horse in?" she called to Hjelmer.

"Ja. Mostly."

She pulled her foot from the stirrup so he could mount behind her. "Take care of them, Jon." They walked past the sheep and picked up a trot again, then a lope.

"Over that way." Hjelmer pointed to a smaller trail.

"How bad is he?"

"I don't really know. He's a young man. Do not know how long ago this happened. But getting him up from where he lies is going to be difficult."

"Can we ride the horse all the way?" She looked back over her shoulder. The others were just cresting the hill that bordered the valley. She turned the horse and waved to them. Certain they saw her, she let the horse pick the way. "This is a game trail."

"I know. I do not know why he was off the main trails. He

said something about his head and his ribs. For some strange reason I think he was already hurt when he fell."

Her song for help continued.

"It is not far now."

"How did you find him up here?"

"The dogs heard him call for help." He pointed to the right. "I never would have found him were it not for Ranger."

He could have died up here. "No one else around?"

"Nei." He raised his voice. "Halloo. We are coming."

There was no answer.

"Stop here. We can tie the horse to that bush." He slid off and ran a few more yards up the trail, then looked over the edge. "Down there."

Ingeborg untied her supplies and handed Hjelmer the staves and blankets. Stopping, she looked over the edge. "Can you hear me?" she called.

She was partway down the ravine when her feet slid out from under her, and she bumped down the incline on her rear until she caught hold of a bush to stop sliding. "We are coming." *Please, God, let him be alive.* She made her way to the bottom, Hjelmer not far behind her.

Kneeling beside the figure, she could see he was breathing. "Thank you, Father," she whispered. She looked back up to the trail. Hjelmer had been right. How would they ever get him up that steep incline?

The leg was grotesque. Since he was wearing lederhosen, the injury was obvious. Swollen, black and blue, with a lump where there should not be one. Below the knee and above the ankle. At least the broken bone had not punctured the skin. She turned to see a lump and swelling on the right side of his head, above the ear, although swelling encompassed half his head, even to the side of his face and other parts of his body. No wonder he was unconscious again. Blond hair, not matted with blood. That was good. If it were not for the swelling, he would be a handsome man.

Leaning over him, she asked, "Can you wake up now? What is your name? We are here to help you."

She rested back on her legs when his eyes flickered. And opened.

"Am . . . I in . . . heaven?"

She shook her head. "Nei, I don't think so. At least I know I am not."

"You must be an angel." He blinked and raised a hand to her face. "You are. I . . . am in h-heaven."

"I've never been called an angel before, but I can tell you, you are not in heaven. Somehow we have to get you out of here and back to the seter."

"Hmm." His eyelids flickered. "Takk."

"You are welcome. Can you tell me your name?"

"Nils. Nils Aarvidson."

"Well, Mr. Aarvidson, can you tell me about your injuries? I see the broken leg and the swelling on your head. Anything else?"

He paused, seemed to gather the needed strength to answer her question. Halting, he continued. "Second lump—on the head. Other back. Ribs were . . . before."

"I see. You came hiking in the mountains with broken ribs and an injured head. Are you crazy?"

"No. Thought . . . better. Find . . . camp . . . night or two . . . back . . . Raggen Inn."

"That is many miles away."

"I . . . hike."

She looked to Hjelmer, who shook his head, obviously thinking the same as Ingeborg. The man was clearly not in his right mind.

"We're going to have to splint that leg before we move him. You think all of us can carry him up"—she nodded to the climb—"with a litter of some kind?"

Hjelmer shrugged. "Maybe one of us should ride down and get help."

"We can't leave him here."

"Nei." He was looking up at the trail when he heard a horse nicker. "The others are nearly here."

Ingeborg studied their patient, who had faded out again. "If he would stay unconscious, it would be easier for him." She picked up his hand. Soft. Not a workingman's hand. Who was this man and how would they help him?

"Do you have your knife along?"

"Ja."

"See his backpack over there? See if he has a tent or a blanket so I can cover him. Start punching holes in the sides of any blanket you find, so we can bind it to the staves."

He dug in the backpack and pulled out a tent and a blanket. "What about using his tent to carry him?"

"That would be harder to punch through and lace."

"Ingeborg?" Three welcome faces appeared up at the trail.

"Good. Be careful coming down here. The scree slides easily, and we don't need rocks coming down on him. Or someone else getting hurt. Anders, Tor, do you have knives?"

"I do," Tor answered.

"Good. Bring the supplies down. We have to figure a way to get him up to the trail." *And keep him alive.* She flinched when she heard him cough. One more thing. She laid a hand on his forehead. Fever? A shiver shook him from head to booted foot. Even in his stupor, he flinched.

Ingeborg shook her head. She'd never treated anything this severe before. Not on a human. What would her mor do? What would a doctor do? *Lord, help!*

12

"Don't bother inventing the wheel if that has already been done."

"Use the brains God gave you."

Her far's truisms were all delivered in the appropriate places—often.

"Girls don't do that!"

Her mor's advice. Ingeborg dismissed it. Right now, for sure it did not apply.

After covering her patient, she sat close by the young man's head, her knees drawn up with her arms across them, and let her imagination try out different scenarios. He had mentioned his ribs and obviously suffered immense pain whenever he coughed or spoke. Onkel Frode broke three ribs once. She was young at the time, but she still remembered how they treated the injury.

When their favorite milk cow broke a leg, her far cared about the poor beast so much that he called in the doctor. The doctor had explained that when a long bone is broken, whether in cows or humans, the muscles around the break bunch up to draw it together. But if the broken ends are not exactly aligned, the muscles will push them right past each other and out through the skin. This young man's broken bone had not pierced the skin. But when they began to move him, the bone might shift, no matter how well splinted, and they would have an open bleeding wound. What would she do then?

And to get him up out of this steep ravine . . . Her mind raced, calculating . . . She stood up. "I think I have the solution. Let us pray it works."

First a fire to warm him as much as possible. Then splint the leg and build a litter that would carry him safely. There was no chance he could walk even a step on his own. Then get him up out of the ravine onto level ground. "Gather twigs and tinder as you come down. We must get a fire going."

"Hjelmer, use your knife to cut chunks out of the middle of this shortest walking staff until we can break it in half. We'll use it for the splint."

"Here?" He pointed to the middle of it.

"Ja."

Hjelmer set instantly to work.

"The two longest staves will be the handles of the litter we will make to carry him. Kari, I need your petticoat. We'll end up using mine also."

Bless the child. She didn't hesitate to get her petticoat off. Ingeborg tore the cotton petticoat into strips. She would use these to bind the blanket to the staves for the litter, rather than using up their precious bandages. "Heat some rocks to warm him. Does anyone have a cup?"

"No, but my hat might work, to carry water anyway."

"Good idea. Put a hot rock in it."

While Kari and Anders nursed their minute fire, Hjelmer propped one end of the staff on a rock and stomped on the middle. It broke in two where he'd been chipping. After feeding the chips to the growing flame, Kari fetched water from the creek.

Nils coughed and blinked. His cheek twitched.

Ingeborg shook her head. Was he trying to smile in spite of all this?

"Will this be all right? I smoothed what I could." Hjelmer and Tor held out their handiwork.

"Good. We will splint the leg now."

Kneeling in and on the rocks, Tor and Hjelmer slid their hands beneath the injured leg where Ingeborg indicated and lifted slightly. Good. She forced herself to move slowly and with great care as she bound the two sticks tightly against the young man's leg. Surely it would work. *Lord willing. Please, Lord. How do we move this rock that binds him?*

Kari nursed the fire and water as the others did the man. Slipping the warmed rock into the hat spilled part of the water. "The water is warming."

Ingeborg rocked back on her heels. "We will dribble some into his mouth. Tor, bring some of the warmed rocks over."

Nils blinked, his eyes slitting open.

"Drink this." Ingeborg held the edge of the cap against his mouth. A small victory but a step forward. A twitch of his head said enough. She handed the hat back to Kari. "See if you can heat enough to warm his hands."

"Like this?" Tor held up their handiwork, white strips of petticoat lacing the blanket to one of the remaining staves.

"Very good. Bring it here."

"But I am not done."

"I know." She reached for the unlaced side of the blanket. "We cannot lift him into a litter, so we will build it around him. Tor, Anders, you kneel by his other side there and work the blanket in under him. Hjelmer and I will draw it out this side. Kari, cradle his head in both hands. That's the way. Good girl!"

The hiker's body jiggled as they worked. He opened his eyes and mouth and said something on the order of "Eh," but then his eyes rolled up and back, and he slipped away again.

It took a surprisingly long time to get the blanket squared beneath him. Then they laced in the remaining staff and rolled up the staves tightly until they were close against the young man's body. Ingeborg knotted the leftover petticoat strips into a long rope and tied the young man snugly into his litter.

Hjelmer stood grinning at their work. "Brilliant!"

"Now to move that rock. You push and I will pull." But the rock did not move.

"We need a lever." Anders stood and looked around. "Down there. That must be his staff." He fetched it while Hjelmer and Tor dug out some smaller stone and gravel to make a hole for the end. Using another stick to dig and levering with the staff, they finally loosened the rock the few inches needed to free the prisoner. They all wiped dripping sweat from their faces and stood panting.

"We're only half done. Let us try lifting him." She pointed to the handles formed by the staff ends. "Hjelmer? Tor? Anders?" She took the fourth handle. "On the count of three. One. Two. Three."

The litter lurched and wagged as it rose. Their patient moaned.

Once they were free of the rock prison, she ordered, "Let

him down, carefully." As she feared, the smaller boys had trouble carrying the fellow when they stood there. They would never be able to get him up the steep slope. "How much rope is left?"

Kari scrambled up the scree and disappeared. She returned in a moment, sticking her head over the edge to call, "Two long ones."

"Throw the end of one of them down here. Just the end." It flopped at her feet. How to attach it to the litter? It was long enough that she could weave it among the staff ends. Would that hold? Yes. Would her idea work? *Please, God! Oh, please!*

"Now please listen carefully. We will move him up the slope feet first, so that if any rocks come loose and fall, they'll hit his feet, if at all. I will take the handles by his head. We will try to keep him as smooth as possible. Hjelmer, you and Anders will each take a side at his feet. Do you understand so far?"

Hjelmer nodded. Anders looked worried, so he understood, obviously.

Ingeborg called, "Kari, you stay up there. Get the horse. We will use the horse to draw him up the slope, but only one step at a time. Can you get the horse to take a step only when we ask?"

"Oh ja! We're friends."

Ingeborg smiled.

"Wait! I'm stronger than Anders," Tor protested. "Let me take a side."

"That is right. You are. I need your strength for the most important job. Horses mean well, but sometimes they bolt or shy. We will not tie the rope fast to the saddle. We'll loop it around the saddle. Then you, Tor, will hold on to it tightly.

If the horse starts to act up, you will release the rope immediately so that the litter is not dragged. Can you do that?"

Now Tor was grinning too. "I will do it!" He clambered up the slope.

Kari brought the horse to the lip of the ravine. Ingeborg could just barely see its rump. She could not see Tor wrapping the rope around the saddle, but she could tell the way it moved that he was doing it well.

"Wait. I need to add the other rope."

The rope finally went taut. Tor called, "We're ready."

"Hjelmer, Anders, we will raise and turn the litter so that his feet are next to the slope and his head end out here." What was the word? Perpendicular. They now had the litter perpendicular to the slope. "Now lift his feet out and away from the ground." She raised her end and called, "One step, Kari."

The rope jerked upward and stopped. Hjelmer and Anders let the litter handles rest against the slope. The young man was now an arm's length up the slope. Hjelmer and Anders braced themselves in the scree and lifted the litter free.

Another step. Another short distance. Another step. Another bit.

The litter had progressed far enough upward that now Ingeborg had to hold it while dealing with the loose scree beneath her feet. She could not raise her end far enough to keep it level. The fellow would just have to go up the slope with his head tilted downward. It was the best they could do.

And then, glory of glories, Hjelmer and Anders reached the top. Tor let loose the rope and hurried down to help Ingeborg. One more lift and the young man lay on nearly level ground.

Ingeborg was breathing so heavily she could not speak.

She flopped to sitting. Her arms and shoulders ached even worse than when she had done that plowing. But together they had done it. *Thank you, Father! Thank you!* She could not stop praising Him.

She sat up straight. "All right. Kari, will you go back to the seter and bring the others? As many as you can, all but Mari. We will take turns and rest frequently, but still, we need all the help we can get carrying him."

"May I ride the horse?" she asked eagerly.

"Of course."

The girl scrambled aboard and nudged the old horse in the sides, sending him picking his way between the rocks and sand.

Despite her speed on the main trail, it was nearly an hour before Gunlaug and the others appeared on the track ahead. Gunlaug studied their patient.

"I see he is still breathing, but do you really think there is any chance he can live through all this?"

"Please, God, let it be so." Gratefully, Ingeborg turned the whole thing over to Gunlaug and simply trailed behind for a few paces. She'd not traded off like the others.

A miserable thought struck her. They had left the young man's rucksack where he had fallen in the ravine. Perhaps tomorrow she would ask Hjelmer to go find the rest of the man's belongings and bring them in. But not today. The boys had done more than enough today. Men's work. They looked as weary as she felt.

Enough idling. She quickened her step and rejoined Gunlaug, sharing the foot end of the litter.

Gunlaug moved aside, falling into step beside Ingeborg. She flexed her arms and shoulders. "This is worse than carrying milk pails clear to town. Where shall we put him? We can't get him up into the loft."

"Near the fire, with as much padding under him as we can manage. Do you remember when our cow broke her leg?"

"Your cow? Oh, wait. Ja, I remember. Your far called the doctor, and the doctor put a strange sort of splint on it. He even had a name for it."

"We must do the same with this fellow's leg. And very soft pillows for his poor head. It has been quite beaten upon. But I don't know what to do about the ribs."

"What about the ribs?"

"Apparently some of them are smashed as well."

Gunlaug wagged her head sadly.

As they finally, gratefully, approached the house, Mari came running out. "Do I set a place at the table for the hiker?" She looked at the litter. "Nei, I suppose not." And ran back to the house.

When Ingeborg entered the house, she saw the long table set and waiting. She could smell something delicious—more than one smell. Mari had been busy indeed.

Near the fireplace they folded as many pillows and blankets as they could find and carefully laid the young man down. Ingeborg and Gunlaug unrolled the staves from the blanket and removed the laces. They folded the free sides of the blanket up over the young man.

"We have to get him warm," Ingeborg said. "Heat some rocks to put beside him."

He stirred and opened his eyes. When he saw Ingeborg, he smiled slightly. Apparently he was aware, so she introduced him to her cousin Gunlaug. He drifted off again moments later as the younger ones were seating themselves at the table.

"Ja. Time to eat." Ingeborg joined them. "Hjelmer?"

He recited grace quite rapidly. Mari brought bowls to the table—boiled pork and potatoes, molasses on winter squash, and dried peas with dandelion greens that had finally made an appearance on the hills. What a feast!

"And dessert," she announced, setting out a platter of lefse. She took the one chair left, beside Ingeborg. "I did not have enough potatoes, so I made it with extra flour and some of the buttermilk. I thought it tasted good."

"Mari, this is wonderful." Ingeborg paused to savor the squash. "A real feast, complete with lefse! And a feast is very appropriate." She looked around the table. "All of you! You all worked together in concert perfectly. I am so proud of you! We did an impossible job, and we did it as well as it could be done. You not only worked together and did what was needed of you, you did more than a person can do, sometimes even more than a grown-up would do. I can't praise you enough. Thank you. And thanks to our heavenly Father."

Hjelmer responded around a full mouth. "Ja, and you too, Ingeborg."

Mari smiled. "You all were gone so long, I didn't know if it would be a happy feast or a funeral feast. I'm so glad it's a happy feast."

"He is not on the road to recovery yet, but at least now he is safe and warm." Ingeborg spooned another helping of pork and potatoes onto her plate. Feast. Yes. *Thank you, Lord!*

She left Tor and Kari to help clean up after supper and sat down again beside the patient. That is what he was, a patient. And she was as close to a doctor as he would have for a while. What about that leg? *Traction splint.* That was the name of the splint the doctor had put on the cow's leg.

It consisted of two splints that stuck out beyond the foot—they had that on this young man now—a sort of harness out on the splints' free ends, and another harness around the foot. The two harnesses were linked together to prevent the muscles of the leg from bunching up. Did he need one of those? In her imagination she planned how to rig one up, but so far, things seemed to be all right. *"Let sleeping dogs lie."* Another Far truism.

His head. She could not do much about the head other than keep him comfortable.

The ribs. She thought about the time Onkel Frode broke his ribs. "Gunlaug?"

Gunlaug came over and sat down beside her. "Ja?"

"We need something to bind his ribs. Do you have your corset up here?"

Gunlaug gasped, "Of course not! Bringing a corset up here would be foolish! Nobody would bring her corset to the seter!" She went on a bit more in that vein, quite defensive, it would seem.

Ingeborg thought, *Of course you would, just in case Ivar should come by.* But that thought would get her nowhere. So instead, she said, "Certainly it would be foolish. I completely agree. I was thinking more like accidentally. You know, it accidentally got buried in the clothes you were bringing, and you didn't realize it was up here."

"Ah." Gunlaug studied her suspiciously. "I'll go dig around a little and see." She left, and Ingeborg smiled inside. Presently Gunlaug returned and dropped the corset beside Ingeborg's feet. "You were right. It accidentally got mixed up in everything else. That is lucky, isn't it?"

"Very lucky! Before he awakens we will lace it around him.

What's the word? Stabilize him. Not very tightly, just tight enough that when he coughs or moves, the ribs do not move."

Gunlaug nodded. "And feed him. Mari has some light soup by the fire that will be perfect." She sat down on the other side and studied the young man for a few moments. "This whole thing is miraculous, don't you think? Finding him? Getting him here safely? All of it."

"Ja." She smiled. "Our Father must really love this young man to take care of him so miraculously. He did something very foolish—tramping in the mountains alone, off the track, when he already had unhealed injuries—and God preserved him."

"We preserved him."

"Gunlaug, you know what Far says. Instruments of God. We are the hammer, but our Father is the carpenter. Do not thank the hammer for a carpentry job well done."

I wonder who he is. And I am sure, underneath all his wounds, he might be very attractive. Nils something. Wonder who he really is.

13

"Is he worse?" Mari hovered beside Ingeborg.

Ingeborg started to shake her head but thought the better of it. Mari didn't need to know all her worries. "I wish I knew. If there is no change . . ." She paused, feeling the frown that made her forehead tight. She kissed her little sister on the forehead. "We just have to wait and see. Surely God is hearing all of our prayers and someone getting better is always a good way to pray. I know God likes to hear those prayers."

Do I really believe that? Lord God, what do I believe and does it matter? You know exactly what is going on here. Lord, give me wisdom beyond my knowledge. Should I have one of the boys ride down to Valdres and bring back a doctor? Would he even come this far? Would it be too late? Oh, God, what am I to do? Could a doctor do any more than she could at this point? The picture of a leech sneaked into her mind. The doctor had told her once that he put leeches on a wound that was terribly swollen. The unappetizing creatures helped relieve the swelling. Would there be leeches moving yet in the lake? She didn't recall ever seeing them before midsummer.

Nils had a fever now. The boys were taking turns laying cold cloths on his head and on the horribly swollen leg. She had probed the leg with her fingers. It did not seem that the bones had moved, or that she had to fashion the special splint. It was just puffy swollen and quite warm. When they had changed the strips of cloth with which she'd wrapped the splints, she had asked Tor, as probably the strongest, to help, but he had turned an astonishing shade of greenish white at the request. He was no use for laying cold cloths, let alone helping with splints.

She and Gunlaug took turns spooning broth into the man's mouth, chicken broth, since they had butchered the mean rooster to make the healing food. Good thing they had a younger rooster coming up, or there would be no chicks hatching at the seter this summer. At least Nils was still able to swallow and had opened his eyes a few times.

They were on the second day since they'd brought him to the seter. The cold and hail and his fall had done their worst. She could hear noise in his lungs when she put her ear to his chest, although he was breathing more easily since they'd laced Gunlaug's corset around him. Surely the fall had aggravated the already broken ribs. At least he'd had some times of being awake and could tell them what had happened to him in the other accident.

Whatever had possessed him to go hiking so soon? And alone? Had he no sense?

She returned to the chair they had placed by the pallet, where at times Nils thrashed and at other times lay as if already dead but for the bellows-pumping of his breathing. Or fighting to.

The best way to clear his lungs was to make him cough.

148

Her mother had showed her one time how to use a cupped hand to thump all over the sick person's back. She said it loosened up the infection and made a person cough more. But in this case? Would that cause more damage to his ribs?

Finally she shook her head. With the corset in place, his ribs couldn't move. That was one reason he breathed hard. "Mari, do you know where Gunlaug is?"

"Out with the sheep."

"Oh. And Hjelmer?"

"At the barn, forking out manure. You want me to go get him?"

"Ja."

The girl hurried off. She and Hjelmer both came running back; Ingeborg could hear them coming.

Hjelmer skidded to a stop at her side. "What? Is he worse? Is—?"

"Nei, nei. I just want you to help me sit him up so I can thump on his back."

His eyes widened. "You sure?"

"I am." *Sure enough to be scared to pieces, but I don't know what else to do.*

She knelt on one side of the pallet and Hjelmer on the other. They each took hold of an arm and, at her nod, pulled the man up to sitting. He groaned and his eyelids flickered, but his chin still fell forward to his chest.

"Good. Now can you hold him?"

Keeping one hand on his shoulder to help prop him, she cupped her hand and started thumping firmly at the shoulder and worked her way down. With the corset in the way, she had to thump harder. She was all the way down one side and starting the other when he started to cough.

Shaking her head at Hjelmer's look of panic, she continued. Her arm and hand grew tired, but when he coughed again, a deep wrenching kind of cough, a glob of greenish phlegm flew out.

Standing right beside Ingeborg, Mari gagged.

"Get a bowl and a wet cloth."

She scampered to follow the order. "Here. Do we need cold water too?"

"Ja and pillows. We need to put something behind him to hold him up."

"One of the quilts?"

"Or even a horse blanket. Anything." She stopped her thumping when he coughed again, and yet again, each time it brought up more of the infection. When he quit coughing, she wiped his face and returned to thumping, up the other side of his lungs now. A drawing of human lungs she had seen in a book flashed in her mind. He coughed again, a deep ripping kind of cough. She grabbed the bowl with the wet cloth in it and held it ready in case he brought up more again.

This time he gagged, choked, and struggled to breathe.

Lord God, what is happening?

"He's not breathing." Hjelmer stared wide-eyed at his sister.

Gagging, choking, the man struggled for air.

Lord God, what do I do? Did my thumping break something? What can this be? Frantic, Ingeborg thought of Far's pounding on someone's back when they were choking. "Hold him."

"I can't. He's too strong."

Nils threw himself backward, the horrific sounds weakening.

Ingeborg grabbed his arm again. "Pull him up. Now." Together they heaved him to a semi-sitting position. "Kari, help us hold him."

The girl grabbed the arm, and Ingeborg made fists of her hands and pounded them right up both sides of his spine. When she reached the area between his shoulder blades, she pounded again. A huge, deep gagging cough and a gob of dark bloody mucus erupted from his mouth and projected all the way to his lower legs. Air whistled back into his lungs, real clean air. His chest expanded and contracted again, just as it was supposed to.

Ingeborg found herself breathing deeply with him, in perfect rhythm. When he paused, she could feel herself tighten up and then exhale in relief when he did. *Thank you, Lord God.* The litany ran through her mind, over and over. *Are we over the worst now?* She could hear retching outside the window. Sending white-faced Hjelmer a questioning glance, he half shrugged.

"Kari. She needs to get a stronger stomach. Living on a farm is better I think, than in town."

Ingeborg almost chuckled at her little brother. He was so right, but then they had never lived in a town. She looked up as Kari walked back into the house. "Are you all right now?"

Kari sniffed and nodded. "I will be. Sorry." She dipped water out of the bucket and drank. "Do you need water for him?"

"Not right now. He is breathing good again."

"He is still wheezing."

"I know, Hjelmer, but there's nothing we can do about that right now. Let's get him sitting more upright. He breathes more easily then. And without all that awful stuff in his lungs, perhaps he will get better more quickly." If she closed her eyes she could see the bloody phlegm, but he didn't seem any worse now. What if he started to bleed, bright red blood? Her mor said red blood was far worse than dark. What else did she say about it? *Think, Ingeborg, think. What if he doesn't quit bleeding?* She closed her mind against any further horror thoughts.

"Do you want me to ride down and get Mor?" Since there was no real doctor for twenty miles beyond Valdres, their mother was the only one with any real medical knowledge.

Ingeborg hesitated. What could someone else do that she had not already tried?

"You could ride him home on the horse."

"Then he might lose his leg if the break grew worse."

Hjelmer nodded. "Mor would say we should pray and trust that God will make him well again."

"I have been. That is for sure." Ingeborg heaved a sigh of frustration. What was the best thing to do? They had a wagon up here, but it was a dead axle, without springs. On the rough track it would jerk and yaw worse than horseback. What to do? *Lord God, what can we do?* She nodded once, short and sharp. "We make him as comfortable as possible, keep praying, and believe that God will do as He says."

"What is that?"

"He said to trust Him. We are going to trust Him to take care of Nils and to give us the wisdom to make the right decision."

She rolled the quilt and a blanket, and Hjelmer propped them at Nils's back. "All right, let him back easy."

"We need more for his head." Hjelmer looked around the room. "How about one of the smaller sacks from the pantry?"

Ingeborg smiled at him and nodded. "Great idea. I'll hold him while you get it."

When he returned, they removed the quilts and snugged the bag of beans up against his lower back and then finished off with the quilts and pillows. "Very good." Together they stood and nodded at each other.

When Nils started coughing again, his eyes flickered.

Ingeborg sank down to her knees and kept him from toppling over. "Keep coughing."

His head wagged from side to side, minute motions but a response.

"Good, you can hear me."

He started to say something, but the effort sent him into another paroxysm of coughing.

"Good, good. Keep coughing." *Only please not like that horrible time.* She closed her eyes, pleading.

A slight headshake and he leaned back against the bracings they had built, breathing hard and well compared to the labored way he had been breathing. Sweat beaded his forehead, so she mopped that away for him.

"We are going to keep you sitting up so you breathe better." *I hope he won't remember what happened. Lord, help me to forget it.*

A slight nod she'd have missed had she not been studying him. She glanced down to his leg and realized someone had cleaned up the mess. Who?

Kari came in the door carrying a bucket of water. "I got this from the spring. You put cold cloths on him before. I figured you would do so again."

"Thank you." Ingeborg found herself nodding and smiling at her cousin. "You are right. We will put them around his neck and on his chest."

"Do you want me to help?"

"If you like."

"I . . . I am sorry I was such a baby."

"Ah, but you came back to help. That is all that matters."
She turned toward the kitchen. "Mari, please bring us some
broth. I think he is waking up."

His lashes fluttered again, and he blinked several times
before looking at her.

"Will you try some broth?"

He nodded and managed to swallow five spoonfuls, a re-
cord, before he shook his head again. "Takk." The word came
raspy but intelligible. He laid his head back on the supports
they had constructed and slipped into what appeared to be a
gentle sleep. She and Kari soaked the cloths in the bucket of
cold water and covered him with them. They took turns sitting
with their patient through the afternoon and then the night.

In the morning, when Ingeborg was finishing her shift,
their patient woke and croaked a question. "Am I still alive?"

"It appears that way. Is there anything we can get for you?"

"Water."

She held the cup to his lips and, when he had swallowed
a few times, laid the back of her hand on his forehead. Still
hot. "Hjelmer will change the cloths again, since these are
no longer cold." But at least they weren't drying as fast as
applied. Had his fever gone down? She felt his forehead again
and then laid a wet cloth over the top of his head. "Can I get
you anything else?"

When he blinked, she stood. "I'll get Hjelmer. Hjelmer?"

"He just went outside," Mari said.

Ingeborg stepped out into the early sunlight. Another
morning. Her eyes felt raw and scratchy. While she and Mari
had taken turns sitting with him through the night, she'd

not slept well during her time off. Probably listening for her patient. After a deep cleansing breath, she saw Hjelmer coming from the barn.

"Is it milking time again?"

He nodded. "At least the cows thought so."

"Would you please change the cold cloths, and I believe he needs the help of a man. I think he is doing better. He's not quite so hot."

"Good. I'm hungry."

"You and everyone else." She let him go into the house without following him. She just needed to be outside awhile. After walking around the house three times, since she didn't want to be far from a call, she stopped and looked up at the snowy peaks, now beginning to reflect the pink and gold of morning. Beautiful colors.

Mari joined her. "I saved out the bones and some of the chicken in case we need to make more broth. Should I make pancakes for breakfast instead of porridge?"

"Whatever you want to make."

"I'll get the eggs and the buttermilk."

Ingeborg raised a hand. "Let me. I need to walk."

"It's not that far."

Out of the mouths of babes. Not that her little sister was a baby any longer. Ingeborg ducked to enter the rock-walled springhouse and stepped down to the dirt floor where they had spread river gravel. A rock trough captured the bubbling spring water while an overflow pipe on the other side drained the water out and away from the building enough to keep the floor from turning into a swamp. Like all the other buildings, grassy sod covered its steeply pitched roof.

Ingeborg inhaled the damp fragrance, slightly tinged with

the smell of the ham and spekekjøtt hanging from the heavy beams. If one of the boys could shoot a deer, they could smoke that and hang it in here too. So far they'd not had time to go hunting or even to check on fishing. The thought of fresh trout made her mouth water. She picked out four eggs and cupped her apron to hold them. Dried egg yolk on the shells told her they had a hen eating eggs. They'd need to watch for that. The culprit might be the next for the stewpot.

The boys could use a break before starting to shear the sheep. A fishing day would be good. A picnic for all of them at the lake was always a treat. *Please, Lord, let Nils get well. I need to know I did the right thing.* What little they knew of him was gleaned from the quality of his hiking gear. He had to come from a wealthy family, but until he could talk at length, they had no idea from where.

Her patient was resting comfortably by the time she set the eggs on the table by the bowl for making pancakes. Good. "Can I help you?"

Standing in front of the fireplace, stirring something, Mari nodded, so Ingeborg tweaked a braid as she passed on her way to check the woodbox.

"They already filled it."

Ingeborg paused. "When?"

Mari turned. "You don't need to worry about things like that. We all know our jobs and will do them. You just take care of yours."

Ingeborg nodded, but she couldn't disguise the lifted eyebrow or the twinkle that insisted on appearing. "Yes, ma'am."

"You need to trust us."

Ja, that's true. And I need to trust more than you kids. God, is this another lesson for me? You have given me such a responsibility. She thought a moment. "Who is doing the Bible verse for today?"

"Kari."

"Has anyone—er—everyone been working on theirs?"

Mari shrugged. "I have. 'For I the Lord thy God will hold thy right hand, saying unto thee, Fear not; I will help thee.'" She wrinkled her nose. "Now I can't remember where to find it."

Ingeborg started to answer, but a mind that turned into a blank slate had nothing to offer her. "Guess we'll look it up later. Ask Gunlaug."

"Didn't you memorize it too?" Mari's chin jutted out just a bit, and her eyes narrowed.

"Ja. Years ago. Guess I need a refresher."

She took first watch that evening after the others went to bed. By the flickering light of the fire, she thumbed through the pages of Bible verses she'd copied and brought to the seter until she finally found it. Isaiah 41, verse 13. She would remind Mari tomorrow.

"A drink, please." Nils's voice was so startling and so steady, she jumped.

"Of course!"

She brought him a cup of water and held it to his lips. He supported the cup with one hand and drank most of it. Then came another coughing fit. Had he accidentally inhaled a bit of water? That would be very dangerous.

She held a cloth to his chin. "Spit it out; don't swallow it."

She was dismayed to see streaks of blood in the sputum. *Now what, Lord? This is beyond my experience. Surely we are not going to have another incident like yesterday.*

They made it through the next day and evening with their

patient sleeping most of the time and them taking turns sitting with him, changing the cold cloths, and spooning broth into his mouth every time he woke up.

Hjelmer came down around midnight to take his shift. "Any change?"

"Not a lot, but he's not worse. That is something to be grateful for." Ingeborg retired, but she could not sleep. She relived the hours of care, the coughing, the choking. Every time she closed her eyes, she could see it happening again. What next? And what should she do if things were worse the next morning? *Lord, help me!*

Ingeborg didn't think she slept much, but when she awakened, Kari was sitting curled up beside their patient, her knees under her chin and arms wrapped around her legs, so Ingeborg must have slept the night through. Seeing Kari's lips moving reminded Ingeborg that she'd better work on her memory verses too. Why did they not stay with her better?

Nils seemed cooler, though he was still fevered. Mari was starting breakfast, so Ingeborg chose a sharp knife and walked down to the stream below the house to the willows there. A tangle of white willows huddled beside the water. Perfect. She chose chunks of bark from the larger limbs and branches, then some twigs, and carried them back to the house. She trimmed the bark carefully, then dropped it into the largest teapot in the kitchen. She poured boiling water in, laid a towel over it, and set it to steep.

At supper that night, Gunlaug said it was time for everyone to recite the verse for the day. Jon winced and ducked his head. Tor looked up to the corners of the room, and Hamme grinned.

"If you can't do it yet, you have until bedtime to get ready." Gunlaug wore her sternest teacher face. She nodded to Hamme to start. The older girls recited perfectly. By the time it got to her, Mari had the reference down too. She glanced toward her sister with a smug grin and received a *well done* nod.

Tor shook his head.

"I do not like memorizing Bible verses or anything."

Gunlaug frowned. "Then I will give you an extra one. You need the practice. Kari will coach you."

Kari glared at her brother. "You are just lazy."

When it was Jon's turn, he swallowed hard and started. Partway through, he sent Gunlaug an imploring look.

"I will help you after supper, while we are putting the loom together."

Ingeborg knew that Jon was having trouble at school too. No one was sure why. It wasn't that he didn't try hard.

"I will help you," Hjelmer said with a smile. "You can beat Tor any day."

Ingeborg watched the exchange. That's what cousins were for, brothers and sisters too. How blessed they all were to have each other.

After supper Jon and Anders hauled in wood for the box. "We are going to have to start splitting wood pretty soon."

Ingeborg nodded. Of course. "Takk. Anders, you go on out and start splitting. Tor, you help him by setting the wood in place and stacking it."

"I know how to split wood," Kari told her. "Do we have two axes?"

"We do and Far sharpened them just before we came. Tor, do you know how to use the grinding wheel to sharpen them again?"

He nodded. "I do a lot of the wood at home."

At last she'd found something the boy knew how to do. Ingeborg was beginning to wonder what all her cousin did with his time.

"Well then, as soon as your hands are healed, you can take charge of the wood splitting."

"Does that mean I won't have to milk the cows?"

"No, sorry, we all need to know how to milk. We have three more that will freshen by the end of the month." And more calves to take care of.

A thought came. She smiled at her little cousin. "Jon, do you want to be in charge of feeding the calves? You have to make sure the buckets are clean to feed them. Calves can get the runs real easy."

"Why don't you let their mammas nurse them?"

"We need their milk to make as much cheese as we can. Which reminds me, tomorrow we need to start the first batch of cheese. There's enough cream now."

"Can we make some soft cheese too?" Mari's eyes lit up. "We can eat that for dinner. Just think, fresh cheese on flat-brød for a treat." She smiled and nodded.

Ingeborg glanced over to see that Nils's eyes were open. He must have been feeling stronger because he was looking around the room. They had left the piled bean and rice bags under him to keep him upright. She raised her voice so he could hear. "I'll be there in a few minutes. Do you need any-thing immediately?" He did look better. While he still had the bright cheeks of fever, the lock of hair falling across his forehead made him look far younger than his years.

He slowly shook his head and raised a hand to cover a cough. Although his hand was unsteady, this was a big step. Something to be thankful for. Had he finally turned the corner?

After leaving their dishes in the wash pan, they all scattered to their assigned chores. Ingeborg warmed the broth, along with the willow-bark tea. They kept a ready supply, most of it in the springhouse now. After mixing them, she took cup and spoon and sat down by Nils's pallet.

"You look better. Are you feeling better?"

"Ja, a bit."

"Breathe deep."

He frowned a little. "And cough?"

"Ja. I will do the thumping on your back later." She dipped the spoon and fed him.

"I . . . I think I could drink it—slow."

"All right." She held the cup to his lips and tipped carefully. He swallowed three times before raising a shaky hand.

"Sorry. I'll slow down." She studied his face. Besides the bad bump on the side of his head, one cheek wore a scrape, from forehead to jawline. It was already purple, but the large lump was shrinking. "Let me feel the back of your head."

"Angel?" he whispered.

"Hardly." The swelling was nearly gone, and there was no bleeding. The sputum was free of blood too. Dare she hope? "Are you ready for more to eat?" At his nod, she asked, "Spoon or cup?"

At his slight shrug, she held the cup but for only one swallow at a time. When he started to cough, she pulled it back quickly. He sagged against the bracing when he could breathe again, then shook his head when she lifted the cup.

"How is the headache?"

A slight tip.

"Worse than the leg?"

"About the same." His eyes fluttered.

"Go back to sleep. That's the best thing for you."

Gunlaug already had the big canvas bag open, spilling out the parts of her loom onto the floor. "We'll put together the stand first. The legs, this part, and those two."

Later Ingeborg looked over at their patient while they worked to reassemble the loom. He was awake and watching them too. She smiled and went back to wrenching the bolts in place.

The boys came in from splitting wood and demanded more to eat. Kari was coaching Jon and Tor, who brightened at the hope of dessert.

"Something sure smells good." Hjelmer looked toward Mari. "Griddle cakes?"

"I'll whip the cream as soon as it is ready. Not long."

The boys clunked their chairs in close to the table and waited, spoons in hand. It was very difficult, Ingeborg decided, to keep boys fed.

On an impulse she went to the kitchen and got some brød. She held a flat bit of it toward Nils. "Do you want to try some?"

He smiled.

Delighted, she settled in close beside him and offered him tiny bites. He had no trouble chewing and swallowing. Good!

When he'd had all he wanted, Ingeborg and Hjelmer returned to the loom and tightened the last of the nuts. Gunlaug gave the loom a hearty shake and grinned. "Good and solid! Tomorrow we will begin weaving the rest of last year's yarn."

After the cousins enjoyed their griddle cakes with whipped cream, they all settled on the floor by Ingeborg's chair. She opened her book to the story she'd started the second night after they'd arrived. It was a silly thing, just a light bit of folklore, but everyone seemed to love it. The young hero, little Butterball, outsmarted his huge dim-witted enemy, a troll. Intelligence again triumphed over brute force, and she thought once more of the way they had rescued their patient.

The children went to bed, as did Gunlaug, and Ingeborg stayed at Nils's side. He finally drifted off into a restless sleep, or perhaps he was just dozing. A couple of hours later, Ingeborg was just getting ready to turn the watch over to Kari when Nils started to cough. The prolonged effort left him gasping. The sputum she wiped from his chin had bits of red in it again. Blood. Was it just from the coughing or something worse?

14

Several hours later Nils's coughing wrenched Ingeborg from a sound sleep, so she descended the ladder to check on him. Hjelmer was sitting with him, so it wouldn't be long until it was time to get up anyway.

Nils was panting from the effort, but in between puffs, he tried to smile. At least that's what she thought it was.

"He slept good up until a few minutes ago. I changed the wet cloths, but they stay wet now."

"Good. You go sleep for a while. The others will take care of the milking and chores. Thank you for taking your turn." She laid the back of her hand against Nils's sweaty forehead. Not bad, not bad at all. Had they finally beaten the fever? She smiled at their patient. "I know after coughing like that, it might not seem like it, but I believe you have turned the corner. For a while I was afraid you might not make it."

"Me too." The hoarse croak could be heard, at least.

"Can I get you some broth?" He shook his head. "Water?" At another shake she asked, "What would you like?"

"Coffee?"

"Sorry, the fireplace is not hot enough yet. But I will get it going. Although the water in the kettle by the fire might still be warm." He nodded, so she retrieved a cup of warm water and held it for him to drink, being careful to keep it slow. When he signaled that he'd had enough, she asked, "Did that help soothe your throat?" Even his nodding was stronger. "Coughing like that rips your throat apart but sure helps your lungs."

Her curiosity grew stronger every time she talked with him, or rather to him, like right now. Who was he and where was he from? He liked to read, she assumed. There were two books in his packsack: one looked like a college textbook and the other was by a man named Voltaire. Since she'd glanced through it, looking for information about the owner, she knew it was in French. So Nils was an educated man, or a young man getting an education. His hands did not appear to have done much physical labor.

"Takk." His whisper made her look at his face.

"You are welcome." She stood and went to throw more wood on the fire. Since Mari had banked it well, there were plenty of coals to start the new one. Last night she had almost decided to send Hjelmer down to Valdres for Mor, but now she changed her mind. As far as she could tell by probing the bone in his leg, it was not misaligned. It was hard to tell with all the swelling. *Please, God, make it so.* She had seen the doctor set a bone once but had not realized how much strength it took to get the bone in place. Good thing he had been unconscious. An even better thing that they all worked hard so they had strong muscles, and God had given them wisdom and all they needed.

What was Mor going to say about all this? Would she take

her daughter along on birthing calls now? Ingeborg felt her jaw tighten. Even the thought of that made her angry again. *I want to learn all I can. I want to learn all she can teach me. Why?* The whys beat in her head while she made the coffee.

When she woke a while ago, her first thought had been for Nils, as she had begun to refer to him. Had she sacrificed his health on the altar of her own stubbornness? Would going for Mor have made any difference? The relief that he was finally better lifted a heavy load off her mind that she'd not realized she was carrying. The feeling of lightness told the hidden tale.

Kari and Gunlaug came down from the loft, soon followed by the others. Except for Tor, and Hjelmer, who had just gone to bed.

"Is Tor up?" she asked Anders, who shook his head, disgust written clearly on his face.

"Did you tell him it was time?"

"I told him twice." Anders plopped into a chair at the table.

Mari tied her apron in place. "I think Tor needs water in the face."

"Really?" Ingeborg glanced over to see the others nodding. "And who should do it?"

All the hands went up. "Let me!"

"Let me!"

Oh, such eagerness!

Ingeborg smiled. "I see. I think it would be best if Gunlaug did it. He'll probably get angry."

"Not if we are all watching and laughing."

Ingeborg thought a moment. This would be hard on his pride. Would the threat of it be enough? "Take water up there, and tell him that if he isn't on his feet in thirty seconds, he gets the water. If he gets up first, no water."

Jon made a face.

Ingeborg knew that Anders and Hjelmer had told Tor to leave the little boy alone several times. If she heard of it again, she would have to take Tor aside and give him the talking to he so richly deserved. Unless he straightened up, he would not be invited back next year. Shame he wasn't more like his older sister, who was disgusted with him too. Mistreating those smaller than you was not to be tolerated.

"With pleasure." Gunlaug, the light of battle in her eyes, poured a cup of cold fresh water and started up the ladder, followed by the others.

Ingeborg listened, ready to burst out laughing. Gunlaug made her threat. A grumble from Tor. The yell came right when she reached thirty. The others came laughing and joking down the ladder. Tor followed a bit later. Dressed and glowering. But he had the sense not to say another word.

Ingeborg hid her smile. "She warned you."

Tor's glare flicked from Gunlaug, who was smiling so wide her cheeks were stretched, to Ingeborg, who studied him with lifted chin. Even Tor was smart enough to keep quiet, but he did jerk his chair out at the table. He apparently thought better of crossing his arms and glaring at everyone, though. Instead he sulked, head down, while they drank their coffee, some well laced with milk, and ate leftover gorobrød.

Ingeborg had a good idea he would try to get even. They needed to be on watch. She thought back to the young man who had worked so hard to bring Nils up out of the ravine. Where had that young man gone, compared to the glowering boy sitting across from her? But perhaps there was hope for him after all. Time would tell.

"Ingeborg, I think that red and white cow is going to have her calf pretty soon," Andres said later when they all came in from the morning chores. "You better go look at her."

"I will. When Hjelmer wakes up, we'll go check. Is she staying with the herd?"

They had just gathered around the table when Hjelmer came down the ladder, looking a little bleary-eyed.

"Leave it to my brother to show up when the food is ready." Mari pointed to his place, all set for him. "I'm dishing the porridge up right now. Big or little bowl? Silly question. Just sit down."

"I'll say grace," Kari said at the pause and led off with the old words they all knew so well. They passed the steaming bowls around the table, followed by the milk, cream, and molasses.

"Save some for Nils," Ingeborg reminded Mari. "This will be easy for him to swallow."

"I did. The bowl is covered and by the fire."

Ingeborg smiled. "You are getting more grown up every day. I am sure Berta wishes you were at home to help in the kitchen."

"Mor too."

After checking on her patient, who was asleep again without his coffee, Ingeborg called the dogs and headed to the cow pasture. As she thought, no red and white cow. They called her Old Boss—she used to have another name, but now she was the oldest in the herd and indeed the boss. The bell she wore announced her coming. And going. Ingeborg listened. No bell. She was either calving or grazing on the other side of the hillock.

She waved the dogs off to search and followed when one

started barking. Sure enough, in a thicket where the cows had cleared out the middle, Old Boss was licking her still wet and steaming calf. The dogs came to her signal, and Ingeborg watched the calf struggle to get his hind legs straight, fall down, and on the third try stand. His mother kept encouraging with gentle nudges and soft cow words.

Ingeborg smiled when she realized they had a female rather than a male. While they kept all the bull calves and, after castrating them, raised them for meat, a new heifer to add to the herd was always welcome. Especially so because this might be bony Old Boss's last calf. But then they had thought that last year too. And the year before. She amazed even Far. Although dear Old Boss didn't produce as much milk as when she was younger, she still outdid some of the young cows, and seven of her heifers, now grown into productive milk cows, were still in the herd.

Ingeborg waited until the calf had nursed and the afterbirth delivered before moving in to herd mother and baby to the barn, where they would have a box stall for a couple of days. Old Boss shook her head and took two steps toward the human intruder. Ingeborg stood her ground and sent the dogs around to encourage the cow to move. Boss shook her head at one dog, but when the other nipped at her heels, she ordered the calf to come with her and began moving out of the thicket and up the hill toward the barn. Ingeborg trailed behind, enjoying the sun on her face. Down by the thicket she had seen enough dandelions to either come pick them herself or send some of the others down, preferably in time to cook them for supper.

When she returned to the house, Mari told her Gunlaug had fed Nils his breakfast, and he had just fallen asleep again.

"He is feeling better—you can tell. He stayed awake for quite a while. If only that cough would quit."

Ingeborg stopped to check on him. While he was wheezing some, he seemed to be breathing with more if not most of his lungs. When he cleared his throat, he opened his eyes and smiled at her. What a great smile he had. Now that the swelling was receding on the side of his face, he looked to be quite handsome.

"I am even more convinced you are some special kind of angel." His voice sounded much better too.

"You keep right on thinking that, so when I tell you to walk, you will."

"You think I will walk again?"

"Of course. Why not? You just broke your leg, not your back. Ribs always heal, and the headaches will disappear with time too. You'll be good as new." *Now, that was a silly thing to say.* Oh great, now she had that critical voice in her head again. If Mor wasn't there to criticize her, her inner somebody managed to do a pretty thorough job without help.

"You really believe so?"

"I do."

"You do?" His voice was raspy, but when healthy, it was probably quite smooth and rich.

"Ja." She could tell by the glint in his eyes he was teasing her. He sure had to feel some better to do that. He didn't have a slow-of-speech problem, like so many of the boys she knew. "We know your first name is Nils, but you do have a last name and a place to call home? I couldn't understand when you said it before."

"I do. See, now you have me saying it." One eyebrow lifted more easily than the other. "All right, my last name is Aarvidson." He paused to cough lustily. Even his cough sounded better, foolish as that sounded. "I came from Oslo, because I would rather be in the mountains than anywhere else. I will be a senior at a college in Oslo. Do you want my pedigree?"

"No, but is there family that would be worrying about you?"

"Not yet. But the inn where I stayed is expecting me back. How long is it since I fell?"

"I think you probably fell the day before we found you, or perhaps two days."

He chewed on his lower lip while he tried to remember. "I think I lay there only one night but . . ." He rubbed his forehead. "I'm not sure."

"Well, you've been with us for several days now." She adjusted the bags he was leaning against. "Can I get you anything?"

"Did I hear someone say flatbrød last night? I wasn't sure. Maybe I made it up."

"Ja, and you had some. Not much. Just a dab, like this. But you managed solid food. Today we'll start feeding you real food. Not soup. If you can manage it."

"Good soup, though. I think. Hmm, I'm not sure of anything right now." He yawned, which made him cough. "I might have to wait awhile. All of a sudden my eyes either see two or want to close."

"I will bring it whenever you are ready." Ingeborg gave him the fever test and smiled as she turned. Very little fever, if any. Such good news. She crossed the room to where Gunlaug was stringing the larger of the two looms. "Where will we put the smaller one?"

"Over where our patient is sleeping, I imagine. Shame we

don't have an open lean-to off the house we could put the looms into, since it is only for the summer. We could store wood in it while not weaving."

"When do you plan to start?"

"I will start on this one tonight if I get it all set up."

"What about Bible verses?"

"I can coach them while I am weaving." She dropped her voice to a whisper. "I did not realize how handsome our young man is."

Ingeborg smiled at the words *our young man.*

Gunlaug got that look on her face again, dreamy with romantic thoughts. "I think he has had a far different life than we have. Do you think his family is very wealthy?"

Ingeborg shrugged. Money helped buy things, but it hadn't helped him keep from falling. Or being in a serious accident earlier. She had a feeling they would soon hear fascinating stories of his life in Oslo. He was most likely a good story-teller too. In college, no less. She wondered what classes he was taking, what books he'd read. Oh, to have a selection of books to choose from! Ever since she'd finished school, she had dreamed of shelves full of books to read, like a picture she had seen in a book one day. In that picture, floor-to-ceiling shelves were crammed with books, and there was even a sort of ladder on a track to reach the highest ones. She seemed to remember it was from somewhere in England.

Gunlaug kept her voice low. "He calls you Angel. Did you notice that?"

"Silly. He asked if he'd gone to heaven when he woke up at the creek and I was tending him."

"You know, Ingeborg, that is very romantic." Gunlaug clasped her hands at her chest. "I wish someone would call me Angel." She opened her eyes again. "Do you think Ivar would ever call me Angel?"

Not if his mor was around, that's for sure. But Ingeborg just shrugged. "Don't make something out of nothing." Ingeborg had to smile just a tiny bit inside, though. Yes, it was romantic. Perhaps *charming* was the better word.

A charming, intelligent man? Imagine that!

⁓

"Ingeborg, the cream is ready to pour into the pans." Gunlaug's voice. "Did you set them up in the springhouse?"

Ingeborg sat bolt upright in her chair. She had fallen asleep! In the middle of the day! Like some small child! Honestly!

"No, sorry. I forgot." She scooped up the mending that had collapsed into her lap.

"I washed them."

"Tusen takk. I'll do that right now." Ingeborg stood up, stretched, and plopped her mending down on the chair seat. "Ask Kari to help you carry the pots out there."

The kitchen was warm and inviting. Ingeborg had become a bit chilled during her nap. Three tall pots of cream were heating near the coals in the fireplace. Each held two and a half gallons. That would make about eight pounds of cheese.

"I can carry one." Mari's chin came out and her eyes darkened.

"I am sure you can, but Kari is bigger and stronger." She didn't say *and older*, since that should have no bearing on the fact anyway. But Mari always got a bit pugnacious if she felt someone was saying she couldn't do something because she was so young.

Mari huffed into silence. Ingeborg gave her a one-arm hug

around the shoulders. "Besides, you have done more work than anyone else today. You can sit down for a change." *You might even take a nap, like your foolish older sister just did.*

Ingeborg hastened to the springhouse and laid the setting pans out across the bench. They probably should build another bench. With several more cows, they had a lot more milk this year. Kari came out lugging a pot. Ingeborg helped her steady it as they poured the cream into a pan. Gunlaug brought the next, handed it to Ingeborg, and returned to the kitchen for the third. Kari held the pot as Ingeborg had done, steadying it for her as the silky cream flowed into the pan. Ingeborg was strong enough that she needed no one to help steady the pot, but the gesture delighted her, and she said nothing. Kari was learning well. She would be a fine cheese maker.

Kari and Gunlaug left, but Ingeborg paused, studying the pans, thinking. Daydreaming was more like it.

As soon as the rennet-laced cream curdled and firmed up, they would cut the curds and drain them as much as possible. Then the cheese presses would squeeze the remainder of the whey out. Once the rounds of cheese were solid, they would wax them and set them on the shelves in the cheese cellar to age. From now on, some step in the cheese-making process would go on every day—at least one step, and often more than one.

Ingeborg started back toward the house. With the setting of the first cream, their summer labor took on more meaning. Some of the cheese would be sold and some of it kept for use at all three houses. Since Onkel Frode was not married and had no children to share the work, he had paid for Kari and Tor to live at the seter and purchased most of the food supplies. In July they would all hay together, and in the fall, harvest the grain crops. There was a comfortable predictability to it all. Ingeborg felt secure with predictability. She liked productivity too, making something of use.

"Come on! Let's celebrate." Ingeborg waved them all toward the house.

"How?" Anders thunked his ax into the splitting spool and headed in.

"Mari made a sort of lefse substitute without the potatoes. We'll have that and pour up some of the buttermilk. We can toast this year as the year of the best cheese ever."

Hjelmer met them at the door. "You say that every year."

"Well, sometimes we have cider to drink, but not this year. Anders, did you bring your concertina?"

"You think I would leave it at home?"

"Tor, have you ever played a gut bucket?"

Tor looked at her blankly.

"Hjelmer, show him what we mean."

Cackling, Hjelmer brought out a washtub with a hole in the bottom, a piece of light cotton cord already knotted at one end, and one of the walking sticks. He threaded the thin rope through the hole in the tub so the knot held on the inside of the tub, turned it over, and tied the other end to one end of the stick. The other end of the stick was notched.

"This is how you do it, Tor." He put his foot on the bottom rim of the upside-down tub to brace it and set the notched stick in the raised rim on the other side. Holding the stick with one hand, he pulled outward to tighten the cord and plucked it with his free hand. The noise sounded more like a thud than like any kind of music. But when he pulled the stick back even farther, the tone changed. He plunked out a four-beat rhythm.

Anders came down the ladder with a leather bag and pulled out a round, aged concertina, its bellows worn and faded.

He tested it, pushing a few buttons and drawing the sides out and in. He grinned. "No leaks! I was afraid the bellows might have cracked. It was my morfar's." For sure he knew which pegs to push on the round wooden sides to make music. "My grandfather was really good on it. He taught me how to play."

"I wish I had brought my harmonica." They all looked at Tor.

Mari cried incredulously, "You play the harmonica and you didn't bring it?"

"Sorry. No one said to. I almost did."

"We should make him go back home and get it."

Ingeborg raised her hands. "We can use one of the kettles and a wooden spoon as a drum. We can sing and even dance if we want to."

With their impromptu band in place, Tor began thunking out the rhythm, happily working his gut bucket. Hamme took over the kettledrum, and the music began. Mari handed Jon another wooden spoon and a kettle lid. Every band needed a cymbal.

"You use the handle like this," she said and showed him how to add to the clamor—er, music. The rest of them sang along, with Gunlaug's lovely soprano leading the tunes. Ingeborg sang harmony and was astonished at how good they all sounded together. Why, they had their own choir right there.

She glanced over to see Nils clapping in time. When he smiled at her, she caught her breath. What had just made her heart do a funny flip? What was happening?

15

Ingeborg smiled at everyone around the breakfast table. "You are all working so hard, once shearing is over and if the trout are biting, we are going to go on a picnic and hopefully eat fresh fish."

Jon's smile gave him an angelic look. "We have had a lot of dried fish."

Mari shook her head. "You've not been eating *dried* fish. I've been soaking it and making it as good as new." She smiled at their reactions. "Well, we do our best. At least you don't have to chew on real dried cod."

"Or herring either." Ingeborg drained the remainder of her coffee.

"When do we start shearing?" Hjelmer asked as he reached for another biscuit. "Mari, your biscuits are good as Mor's."

Ingeborg thought they were even better but didn't say so. While Mor was a good cook, she was also a good teacher, so she really hadn't had much to do in the kitchen for a long time. Her well-trained daughters had taken over. But now with Katrina gone . . . Her mouth dropped open. "The wedding.

We forgot all about the wedding." She counted back the days. "It was last Saturday." She stared at Gunlaug. "How could I forget such a thing?"

"What could you have done?"

"Uh . . ." She ducked her chin and huffed a sigh. "Nothing, I guess, but we could at least have prayed for her." She glanced around the table. "Did none of the rest of you think of it either?" Heads shook all around.

"I don't even know what day it is when we are up here." Hamme shook her head again. "I like that."

"Well, this Sunday we are going to have a church service of our own, and we will start shearing on Monday."

"Maybe Sunday some of us could go for a hike, maybe up to the lake to see if the trout are biting yet?" Hjelmer suggested, leaning forward hopefully.

"I hope so. And this afternoon I need two or three volunteers to go over the pasture and pick dandelion leaves for supper. There are lots down by the thicket."

Most hands went up.

"How about Jon, Hamme, and—"

"Me. I want to be out in the sunshine for a change." Mari gave Ingeborg a pleading smile.

"Of course. So everyone knows what they are doing today?"

"Gunlaug is starting me on the loom." Kari smiled at Gunlaug.

"Ja. And, Hamme, if you want to help, you can."

"I have to card wool." Jon did not look pleased.

"Quit complaining. I am too." Mari joined in. "After we get back from picking dandelions I will card with you." Mari made them all laugh at her dramatic flair.

Ingeborg pushed back her chair. How nice it would be

178

to sit carding out in the sunshine. She glanced over at their patient, who was listening and watching. It was a shame they couldn't move him outside yet. "We need some kind of crutch for Nils pretty soon or at least a cane." He was staying awake ever longer between naps and had fed himself last night and that morning.

Still chuckling, she took a cup of coffee to Nils in the other room and held it out. "You sure look a lot better."

"I feel a lot better. In fact, if you would please hand me my pack, I think I can study for a while."

"No headache?"

"Not right now."

"Reading might bring it back."

"Probably. I'll try for a while and see. I have an exam coming up in the fall that I need to prepare for, and I am not used to doing nothing." He smiled at her over the rim of his coffee cup. "Do you have time to visit, perhaps?"

"Later. I'd take time, but right now I need to—"

"Ingeborg!" Came from outside.

She left in a swirl of skirts. Now what?

"Look!" Mari pointed across the meadow to where three deer were grazing, a doe and two fawns.

"Oooh." Her sigh was drawn out. "They are beautiful. And so young."

"She knows we're watching her." Mari had lowered her voice.

"Why?"

"She raises her head and looks our way. Watch. I wish we could see them better. I almost didn't see the fawns." Mari's smile grew wider.

Ingeborg put her arm around her sister's shoulder and

squeezed. When Mari's arm slipped around her waist, she squeezed again. The two and the others stood watching until the doe ambled away with her fawns.

"And you want to shoot a deer?" Hamme shook her head at Hjelmer.

"Only one with horns. You don't shoot the does, or there soon won't be any deer." Hjelmer was standing close on Ingeborg's other side.

She wasn't sure when he had moved there, but she wished she dared put her arm around him too, so she patted his shoulder instead. "Thanks for calling me. What a treat. Now that the wild animals are getting used to our intrusion, perhaps we will see more." She looked up and shaded her eyes with a hand. Sure enough, the eagle they had seen other years was back too. His cry sang wild and free. Why did she feel as though they had just been welcomed home?

"Come look at the sow, Ingeborg." Hjelmer motioned toward the barn. Ingeborg nodded, glancing up again to see if she could find the eagle against the bright sun.

Once in the barn, she waited for her eyes to adjust after being in the bright sun, then joined Hjelmer at the wooden pen. "That sow looks like she's about to pop too." Ingeborg leaned on the hogpen to watch the two sows make pigs of themselves in their trough. Hjelmer, who'd carted the full can of buttermilk from the churning to the barn, leaned beside her, his chin on his hands on the pen wall.

"I know. I was going to tell you. Perhaps we'd better move her over to the other box stall."

"Get the boys and we'll close the barn door so she can't get out. She'll follow you and a bucket of buttermilk anywhere, though."

The boys lined up to create a pathway to the open stall, and with Hjelmer and the bucket, she nearly raced him to the new trough and, putting both front feet in, started slurping.

"I do not think she even looked at us." Jon shook his head, smiling up at Ingeborg. "I tried to catch a little pig once and fell right in the mud." He clamped two fingers over his nose. "Pee-ew. Mor made me wash outside. Clothes too."

"Even so, he stunk for a week." Anders roughed his brother's hair. "Pee-ew was right. He should have slept in the barn too."

Ingeborg made her way back to the house. Nils was sound asleep, his book in his lap. *Sorry, but we've had a busy morning,* she thought as she went back outside to skim the cream from the milk from the days before.

"What are we having for dinner?" she asked Mari when she returned.

"Corn cakes. The beans with those hocks we brought up should be done in an hour or so." Mari pointed toward the table and a covered platter. "The corn cakes are already fried."

"Oh." Ingeborg grinned at her baby sister. "You are doing a great job, Cook Mari." How blessed she felt to know she had people around her who knew what they needed to do and went ahead and did it. And other than herself and Gunlaug, they were all children.

When she passed by the pallet, Nils opened his eyes. "I guess I fell asleep."

"Guess you needed it." She nodded to the book. "What are you studying?"

"Medieval European history. I took a class in it last semester and found it fascinating. Did you know that the Chinese were way ahead of the Europeans in language, writing, math—all kinds of things?"

"No, really?"

He held up the book, one finger between the pages to mark his spot. "It just mentions that here. You'd think they would include more if it was that important."

Ingeborg shrugged. "You would think so. Did reading give you a headache?"

"I think I fell asleep before that could happen." He gazed toward the window. "I would so like to be outside. I came to the mountains so I would not have to spend the summer days in my father's offices." He gestured to his leg, shaking his head. "And here I am. Ironic, is it not?"

"Can I get you something? Willow-bark tea for pain?"

He made a face. "That tea could use some sugar."

"Sorry. I'm so used to it I forgot to put sugar in yours. I will next time."

"Is there anything about animals and farming and all this that you do not know?"

"I have been coming up here for nine years. You learn a lot doing this. Besides, it all fascinates me. Anything having to do with growing things and animals and the mountains." *And being a midwife.* But she kept that to herself. She'd already talked too much.

"What do you want to do? Teach?" she asked, changing the subject.

"Nei. What gave you that idea?"

She smiled. "You are still in school. Not many boys from our area go to college, you know."

"Where do you live?"

"On a farm outside of Valdres. This is our family's seter, Strandseter."

"You love it here." He did not ask a question.

"How do you know that?"

"Your face lights up when you talk about the things around you."

She could feel a heat rising up her neck. "I doubt it." He saw too much, even from his sickbed. Raised voices took her to the window.

Outside, Tor and Anders were squared off, fisted and shouting.

"Oh, now what?" Hands planted on her hips, she shook her head.

"You deliberately pushed him!" Anders's teeth clenched.

"It was an accident!"

"Anders, I am not hurt!" Jon yelled at his brother.

"How can you have so many *accidents*? No one else does."

"Why do you always think I did everything that goes wrong? Just because I don't know as much as you . . . you . . . !"

Anders drew back one arm, heaved a sigh, and took a deep breath. "It better not happen again. You will be sorry if it does."

Ingeborg drew in a breath along with Anders. "Thank you, Lord."

At that point Tor made a big mistake. "Who is going to make me sorry? You?" When he turned his head slightly, he made a worse mistake. He did not see the punch coming. A solid thud to the jaw and a follow-up one to the diaphragm. He doubled over, gasping for air. When Anders started to step forward, a "No!" rang out.

Ingeborg knew Hjelmer's voice. She almost called the same but watched as Anders dropped his hands, still keeping a wary eye on Tor.

"Did they settle it?" came from behind her.

"I think so."

"Good for them."

Ingeborg had a feeling this wasn't the last they'd heard of this but wisely kept from going out there. And to think just a few minutes ago she was thinking Tor was changing. Shame. A hand on her shoulder made her turn. Mari stood behind her, nodding.

"Tor needed that."

"I know. He is a bit of a bully."

"Only a bit? Ingeborg, you always think the best of everybody, and they let you down."

"Better that than the worst and live angry all the time." She glanced over to see Nils reading his book, a wrinkle in his forehead. If they turned his pallet, he would get more light from the window on the page. At the window she called Tor, Anders, and Hjelmer to help her.

"What?" Nils asked as she nudged his pallet.

"We're going to turn you so you can read more easily." She gave the instructions, and they each grabbed a corner of the pallet and turned it so the back of his head was toward the window.

"That was much easier than trying to turn you."

"Tusen takk," he said to everyone. "Is she always this careful with her patients?"

"Unless they bite her."

"Or kick her." The boys left, laughing, and Mari headed for the kitchen.

Hjelmer paused at the door and said over his shoulder, "But that's usually the four-footed kind."

Heat coming up her neck and blossoming in her face made Ingeborg want to follow the boys. Explain them? Explain herself? If Nils thought she had a lot of people patients, she didn't want him to think differently. Dreams of his far screaming at her for not taking his son to a doctor had haunted her one night. "I've helped lots of injured animals."

"I have been thinking about getting into a chair. I could rest my leg on another. Those two strong boys could help me, I'm sure."

"Just please do not go trying to move on your own, and something else to keep in mind—"

"I know. The ribs." He patted his strapped-together chest. "When you can remove this . . . this rather interesting garment I am tied into, perhaps they can help me wash too."

"I am sure they can. And that interesting garment is a corset. We laced you pretty loosely, you know."

"And women wear these torture bands all the time?" He shook his head. "It makes no sense to me, but my sisters do the same."

Quick to change the subject, Ingeborg asked him to tell her about his family. "I'll get you some water first . . ." She paused and rolled her lips together. With eyebrows raised she added, "Or would you rather have willow-bark tea?" Laughing inside, she fetched two cups of water from the drinking bucket that always had a dish towel covering it to keep the water clean. His laugh behind her set him to coughing.

"I am sorry." She hurried back.

He raised a hand and coughed again, then reached for the water before he could talk. "Do not be sorry. Laughing to make me cough was probably a good thing, or so a certain person would tell me."

"Well, if you tell about your family, perhaps that certain person will not force willow-bark tea down your throat."

He smiled and raised his cup in salute as he drank. Setting it on the floor beside him, he leaned against his pillows. "I have two sisters. I am the oldest in the family. One year younger than I is Amalia. She tried very hard to take care of me after my first accident, but I was not a good patient. I am afraid I tried her patience, but you would never know that. She is the perfect lady, much like our mor. Katja is much younger than Amalia, and at twelve would rather be outside than anywhere in the house. She is much like me and likes the mountains and hiking and skiing in the winter. She is a fine ice skater too.

"Far expects me to take over the family shipping business, but Amalia is the one who secretly would give the world if Far would allow her to work in his business. Instead, she is forced to use her skills in organizing various benefits. She is living up to Mor's belief that helping the poor is one reason businesses make money. She does not just sip tea and gossip, as many of the wealthy ladies do. Amalia's benefits make money to provide useful things like food and shelter for orphans and widows."

"You admire your sister."

"I do. She is doing something important with her life."

What a pleasure it was to talk with a man who had both a sense of humor and an interest in many things. What would it be like to attend a school again? To ask questions and exchange ideas?

And would it ever be possible for her to do? Of course not. And yet, the hope remained.

☙

The next day Ingeborg and Gunlaug worked on the cheese together. Using the big jars made especially for this job, they poured all the saved cream to fill the jars and set them close enough to the fire to heat slowly. Then they poured the heated cream into the waiting pans and let them set until well curdled, looking more like a solid pudding than cheese.

After taking a break to check on Nils, Ingeborg said, "Guess I better get the curd cut and hung. Gunlaug, do you want to help me with the cheesecloth?" Together they cut the pans of slightly yellow curd into about two-inch squares and scooped it into cheesecloth bags to hang from hooks above the pans. When they finally got all the curds dripping, they dumped the whey into milk cans to be hauled to the barn for feeding the pigs and chickens, all of which thrived on the liquid poured over their feed.

"I think we need a cup of coffee, don't you?" Gunlaug stacked the pans for washing. They already had the cream heating by the fire again. The process would continue all through the summer.

"Out on the bench?" The bench on the other side of the house faced the mountains and had been Ingeborg's favorite spot for years.

"Of course. Then I'll wash the pans and you can either weave or spin," Gunlaug suggested.

"During the day? How slothful." Shock struck her. She sounded just like her mor. Even when she was teasing.

"I will need yarn for the loom before long, you know. Who else knows how to spin?"

"I know Mari can and Kari would like to learn weaving. Perhaps Hamme?"

"She's too young."

"One is never too young to learn to spin. You needn't have a long reach to control the shuttle." They stopped in front of the fire, and Ingeborg used her apron to protect her hands as she pulled the pot free to pour. She glanced over at their guest, who was now sleeping again, this time his book on his chest. Perhaps soon he would be able to go outside. Having to stay inside was beginning to grate on him. She could tell by the way he stared out the window. What must it feel like to be so bound by injuries?

Or social convention?

16

"Couldn't we have church after we go up to the lake?"

"Why can't we have church up there?"

Ingeborg listened to their pleas. Why not have church up at the lake? Worshiping on the banks of the lake sounded like a heavenly idea. She always felt closer to God out in His natural creation. She gave an emphatic nod. "Yes." She had to raise her voice to be heard above the cheers. "So get your chores done, and we'll pack the food."

"We might have fresh fish." Anders grinned.

"All depends on if they are biting yet. Remember, that's a higher elevation than we are here. So we'll take food."

"And coals to start a fire?"

"You don't want to just take flint and tinder?"

Mari shook her head. "Coals are much faster. Do you think the fire ring is still in place?"

"We'll rebuild it if not." The thought of fresh trout made her mouth water. Like the dandelion greens, fresh trout bespoke the change of seasons.

The others scattered out the door, and she went to the

springhouse to check on the curd they'd started the night before. Surely it could all wait until later today or even tomorrow, since working on Sunday was against God's law. But taking care of animals never stopped.

"We have baby pigs," Hjelmer hollered from the barn.

So much for checking the curd. Ingeborg headed for the barn to join Hjelmer and some of the others leaning on the gate. Hjelmer had checked on the sow in the middle of the night, but nothing had been going on. "How many?"

"Nine alive. One dead." Hjelmer pointed to the board nailed across two of the corners, just high enough off the floor for the babies to slip under, a safe place where there was less chance of the sow lying on them. However, this old girl, in pig years, was such a good mother that Ingeborg was sure she'd counted her babies before lying down.

The sow lay sound asleep, her babies mounded just in front of her back legs, close to the teats. A pig pile described them best of all. Seeing new babies like that—well, new babies of any kind—delighted Ingeborg clear to her toes and deep within her soul. No wonder she wanted to be a midwife.

"I'll go fix her some warm mash," Ingeborg said.

"It seems a shame to disturb them all, they are sleeping so peacefully," Gunlaug commented. "I wonder if they have all nursed yet."

"I don't know," Hjelmer said. "The dead one was still in the sack. I threw it and the afterbirth out on the manure pile."

Ingeborg nodded and heaved a sigh as she turned to leave. A thought struck her; someone should stay at the seter to make sure their patient was taken care of. Please, God, let someone volunteer. She did not want to pick one.

Back at the springhouse, she made sure the door was latched and returned to the house, where Mari was packing food into a basket.

"Can I talk with you a minute?" Nils asked.

When Ingeborg stopped beside him, he said, "I have a feeling you are thinking someone needs to stay here with me. Leave me water to drink and something to eat, and all of you go enjoy the lake. I just wish I were going along, but I will keep busy. I need to write a letter to my parents."

"Funny you should say that." Ingeborg thought about it. Something inside her said no. She started to answer when Hjelmer stopped beside her.

"I don't think I better go along." He smiled down at Nils. "I want to keep an eye on that sow, make sure the babies learn to go into the corners. I don't want another one to die."

Bless you, my brother. Ingeborg looked at him. "Are you sure?"

"You know we don't leave a sow alone after she farrows. It's just not good farming."

She could hear her father's words coming out of her brother's mouth. He might not be as tall as the others yet, but his sense of responsibility far outstripped his years. She nodded. "You are right. Takk for thinking like that. I just hate to have you miss the fun."

"Do you have a checkerboard up here?" Nils asked.

"Yes, somewhere, I imagine."

"I wouldn't mind a game of checkers or—"

"Chess?"

"That too."

Hjelmer nodded with a wide smile. "I will find them. I can play a game or two and keep watch on the sow too. Shame you cannot make it out to the barn yet." He thought a moment. "You ever seen newborn piglets?"

"No, can't say as I have."

Ingeborg left the two of them talking and took her wide-brimmed hat off the wall peg. "Are the rest of you ready?" At the chorus of assents she headed out the door, basket in hand. Mari followed with another, and off across the valley they went. Some walked, some ran ahead and then back, and some trailed along, studying the plants along the path, rocks, and other such things.

"Maybe we will find a branch or something we can turn into a crutch for Nils." Anders hung back with Ingeborg. "He should be able to be up and around pretty soon, shouldn't he? I'd go crazy staying inside and lying in the same place for all this time."

"Hmm." Ingeborg knitted her brow. "Our next job is to help him up to sit in a chair. Perhaps somehow we can carry him and the chair outside."

"Or we could carry the pallet outside." Anders scrunched his mouth around, thinking hard. "We carried him in."

"If his ribs are well enough, we could help him to his feet, and Tor and Anders could be his crutches."

"If he can ignore the pain, that would be the easiest way," Kari said, joining the conversation.

Ingeborg smiled. All these fresh ideas from fresh minds.

"I'm sure he would appreciate any ideas. I can tell he is getting restless and trying not to complain." Mari handed Tor the basket. "You carry this for a while. That fishing line isn't very heavy."

Tor scowled and hauled the basket two-handed.

"Don't swing it around. The tin of coals is in there."

"Yes, ma'am." He released the basket with one hand to salute, as if she'd given him an order.

Mari started to say something but instead just shook her head.

When Tor strode on ahead, Ingeborg and Gunlaug looked at each other and raised their eyebrows. One minute they kind of liked the young man and the next, felt more like smacking him.

"Did you bring some of your Bible pages?" she asked.

Ingeborg nodded.

As the track grew steeper, their pace slowed. Ingeborg was wishing she had brought one of the remaining walking staves. An idea leaped up. That was what they could use for a crutch. Cut it the right length to fit under Nils's arm and wrap a short piece across the top. Well padded, it should work.

"Look up there." Anders handed his sack off to Gunlaug and climbed up the bank. He held up a long branch. "Is this straight enough, you think?" He dragged it down the hill and measured it against his side. "It's too short. Sure is a nice piece of wood, though."

Ingeborg looked ahead to see where Tor was. Since the path turned up ahead, she couldn't see him. "Did you tell him which arm of the Y to take?"

No one answered.

"Remember, he has our food."

"I'll go catch him." Hamme took off running.

Ingeborg and Gunlaug chuckled together.

"We haven't had any time to really talk." Ingeborg turned and looked back the way they had come. The seter below them looked like children's toys left out in the sun. The sheep grazed in the fenced small pasture, since no one had taken

193

them out to find better grass. The cows were lying down, and the horses were standing in the shade of the barn. She stopped just to enjoy the scenery. For a change, no one had to hurry to do anything. Time like this was rare.

Back on the climb, they rounded a corner, and Hamme and Tor were sitting on a rock waiting.

Relief felt good. They all took the right arm of the Y that seemed to go straight up. But just over the ridge they could see the lake below, sparkling a welcome in the sunlight.

Ingeborg and Gunlaug paused, their faces creased in joy. So beautiful.

Hamme stopped with them. "Do you think the fish are biting?"

"Are you hungry?"

"Don't be silly. She is always hungry." Gunlaug snorted.

"Well, not all of the time." Hamme looked up at her sister. "Sometimes I'm sleeping."

Giggling, they followed the boys, who were already halfway down the switchback trail.

"The fire pit is good. We'll go find tinder," Anders shouted back to them.

Ingeborg, Gunlaug, and Kari settled onto the smooth stones that served as benches and let the others start a fire and set a pot of water to boiling for the coffee. Soon Mari joined them.

"I'm going to see if the fish are biting," Anders called, and the girls waved in response.

Ingeborg lifted her face to the sun, eyes closed, listening to the sounds of the lake—wavelets lapping the shore, birds singing and two jays scolding above them, the wind sharing secrets with the crags, and children laughing and shouting.

The mountain music filled Ingeborg with such joy, it leaked out her eyes and down her cheeks. She sniffed but never opened her eyes.

Her mind roamed the lake and the ring of mountains, and as she took deep breaths, she could feel the tightness drain out of her shoulders and her entire body. *Tusen, tusen takk for bringing us to this place. Your beauty makes me cry and reminds me you are indeed my God. You have to love us a lot to have created such . . . such . . . I don't have the words. I lift up my eyes to your mountains and my spirit dances and sings, and all I want to do is to worship you, to be the woman you have planned for me to be. Lord God, I am so far from that woman, I can never be her, unless you do it. How and who and when?* She kept her eyes closed, listening to the music around her. Listening inside. *I love you,* came a whisper. *I love you.* The whisper circled around her, filling her eyes and her soul. *I love you. You are mine. I love you.*

Ingeborg fought the tears, but that was like trying to stop the lake from sparkling. So she let them flow, watering her gratitude that could not find words to express. Only the tears. A soft hand touched her shoulder. When she opened her eyes and sniffed, she almost expected to see the hand of God there, but it was Gunlaug.

"Are you all right?"

"Oh, Gunlaug, I am so much finer than all right. Takk." She laid her hand over Gunlaug's. Perhaps for now, this was the hand of God. She took a soft cloth out of her pocket and blew her nose. Sighing with contentment, she allowed her eyes to drift closed again until she heard Gunlaug whispering.

"Look at the heron over there."

Kari leaned forward, and Ingeborg opened her eyes. A gray blob at the top of a stately stick stood motionless until, with a flash, he scooped up a small fish, gulping it down in two swallows.

A pair of ducks dabbled in the shallow weeds just offshore. Ingeborg locked her hands around one knee and rocked backward.

"Don't fall," Mari cautioned.

"I wasn't planning on it." She smiled a dreamy smile at her sister. "You think God had a good time creating this scene? I think He must have. Who else could come up with such blues and greens and shapes and variety?"

Gunlaug mimicked her friend and cousin's actions. "I chose the Psalm 46 verses to memorize this week."

"What a good idea. Did you know then that we were coming up here?"

"Nei. It just seemed appropriate." Gunlaug inhaled and a grin split her face. "Smell the coffee."

Kari nodded. "I pulled it back; it should be ready soon. I'm going to walk that way for a while. Mari, do you want to come with me?"

"Of course, but not for long. My stomach is complaining." As was Mari, obviously.

Ingeborg replied, "It wants food, not just coffee. You two go ahead and run along. We'll eat when you come back."

As the two ran off, Ingeborg returned her attention to the lake. "I am so grateful Hjelmer volunteered to stay at the seter. Otherwise I was going to have to."

"You could have asked one of us, you know."

"I know, but everyone was so looking forward to getting away." She spotted more ducks swimming out in the lake and counted to ten. There would soon be ducklings swimming behind their mors.

"He likes you, you know."

"Who?" Ingeborg's eye brows arched high.

"Nils, silly. He follows you with his eyes whenever you are in the house."

"He is just grateful we saved him."

"No, I know the difference. He is really . . . I think he is falling in love with you."

"Oh, Gunlaug, don't be a silly romantic. You see love everywhere."

"Maybe that is why I recognize it, and you turn a blind eye."

Ingeborg planted her feet firmly back on the ground. "He is a son of wealth and city and business and society, and I am a farmer's daughter from a small village. He would no more fall in love with me than . . . than that heron would become a duck." Words were not enough. "Gunlaug, do not ever mention this to anyone. Do you hear me?"

"I hear you, but you wait. You'll see. He is everything you have always said you wanted in a man. He is educated, loves to discuss stuff we never even think about—well, you do but not the rest of us. He makes you laugh, and you make him laugh. You have to admit, he is one very good-looking man. Just wait until he gets to shave and bathe, and if he were to wear good clothes, you would be surprised."

"Well, all that is not going to happen, other than getting him on his feet so he can leave and go back to a life I cannot even imagine." Ingeborg stood. "Let's start setting out the food. This area is flat. We can spread the picnic cloth here."

"Or by the fire. I wonder what happened to the dry bushes we had by the fire ring last year."

"Someone probably burned them. Shepherds. Hunters. We aren't the only people who come here."

"Can we go ahead and eat without the two fishermen?" Kari asked when they returned, panting.

"We'll holler, and if they show up, good. If not, too bad." She cupped her hands around her mouth. "Dinner is ready!"

"Coming." Hamme answered from wherever she and Jon were playing. A halloo came from around the lake.

"They all heard."

Jon and Hamme ran in, panting when they stopped. They were about to say grace when Anders called that they were coming.

"No fish?" Ingeborg asked when she saw them.

"No, just swimming around the lake, not biting on anything." They set down their fishing gear. "I kept Tor from jumping in to snag one. He didn't realize the water was probably twenty feet deep—and ice cold."

Tor complained, "You could see them clear as your face. Huge trout just swimming around. It's not fair."

"No flies or other bugs yet either. Do you think they know the difference?"

Ingeborg shrugged. "It's a good thing we brought food, eh? Let's say grace." She started and they all joined in.

"Help yourself." Mari pointed to the laden picnic cloth. "There should be plenty."

There wasn't any left when they finished. Mari poured another round of coffee and set the pot away from the fire.

Ingeborg looked about. "Shall we sit around here for worship?"

When they were all seated, Gunlaug started one of the hymns that everyone knew. Ingeborg marveled again at how lovely their voices blended. They sang for a while, then Ingeborg read from her Bible pages.

Gunlaug announced that it was Bible verse time and began with her own. "Psalm forty-six, verses one through three. 'God is our refuge and strength, a very present help in trouble. Therefore will not we fear, though the earth be removed, and though the mountains be carried into the midst of the sea; though the waters thereof roar and be troubled, though the mountains shake with the swelling thereof. Selah.'"

The others recited the verse with her, some of them stumbling more than once.

Anders wagged his head. "Imagine these huge mountains shaking and getting tossed into the sea!"

Kari reminded him, "God can do it. He can do anything."

"I wonder how many mountain references there are in the Bible." Kari leaned forward to pick up a little rock to throw in the water. They all watched the circles widen and spread.

"There must be hundreds, especially if you include hills." Gunlaug recited, "Psalm one-twenty-one, verses one and two. 'I will lift up mine eyes unto the hills, from whence cometh my help. My help cometh from the Lord, which made heaven and earth.'"

They recited the verse until everyone had it. They now had two memorized for the day.

Ingeborg clapped her hands. "We all need applause. Well done."

Mari giggled. "I knew that one already."

"Then we should find you a new one."

"Not fair."

Ingeborg laughed and started another hymn. When the music trailed off, she bowed her head. "God in heaven, you who made these mountains and all the beauty that is here, we thank you for sharing it with us. Thank you for this most perfect day. Healthy baby pigs in the morning, climbing the trails, making Nils well again when he so easily could have died, providing all that we need and then some. Thank you for being right here with us, for you said that where two or three are gathered in your name, you would be there. Help us get done all the work still ahead. Protect both us and the sheep as we start shearing. Remind us to always be thankful and live our lives to make you happy. In Jesus' name we pray, amen."

Ingeborg raised her head and inhaled a deep breath of mountain air, including the peace she could feel seeping through her.

"Let us close with our Lord's Prayer, saying it all together, Fader vår, du som er i himmelen . . ."

Silence blessed them all. She blew out a breath.

"I like our kind of church best," Hamme whispered.

Ingeborg didn't say a thing. She did too. Such freedom they had up here. Going back down into the valley was not something she ever looked forward to. "All right. Let's pack up. I see you found a few more sticks, Anders."

"I hope one of them can fit. If I were Nils, I'd be so grumpy by now that no one would want me around."

Tor reached for a couple of the sticks and the basket, earning him a surprised look but a thank-you from Ingeborg and Mari. By the time they arrived back at the seter, the cows were lined up for milking, and a couple of them complained at the wait.

"No fish?" was the first thing Hjelmer asked. When they all shook their heads, he shrugged. "Maybe next week. I sure am ready for fresh fish."

They gathered their buckets and headed for the barn.

Ingeborg saw that Nils was asleep so she meandered out to her bench where, as always, the mountains beckoned her, even more so now that she'd had a taste of the serenity she so desired. She felt it settle back inside her.

"Who won?" she asked back inside when Nils woke up, nodding toward the checkerboard.

"Tie. He is a good player."

"I know. Hjelmer does not like to lose."

"I don't think anyone in your family likes to lose."

"Does anyone at all?"

"Some take it more gracefully than others." He stretched his arms and flinched when it pulled too much on his ribs. "Tomorrow I have to get up."

"We'll help you. Anders will be measuring you for a crutch. He hopes one of the sticks he brought back will be a good fit, or maybe we can cut one of the staves down."

"That Anders—he is a good boy. He and Hjelmer more than make up for Tor. But I think by the end of the summer you will have been able to work some changes in him."

"I hope so." *Lord, please let that be so.* "Is that thunder?" Sure enough, dark clouds were gathering in the west. Could they shear under the sheep fold if it was raining in the morning? They had to start the shearing.

17

Jesus is the Good Shepherd.

We are the sheep of His pasture.

Why, oh why, could Jesus not have been the Good Cattle Herder? Cows were smart. Cows could handle emergencies, generally. Sheep had no idea how to escape danger. Cows could find good forage. Sheep simply stood there and ate whatever was there, even if the plants were poisonous. Cows were fun to care for. Sheep? Nei. As Far had often reminded her, this was her opinion and not everyone else's.

On the other hand, Ingeborg could pretty much tell what a sheep was going to do before it knew itself. Sheep were highly predictable. To an extent, so were people.

She watched in dismay Monday morning as Tor made another attempt in vain to grab a sheep. He managed to snatch a fistful of wool from the ewe's rump, but she twisted away, pulling his glove off. Furious, he threw his other glove to the ground. "I hate sheep!"

Ingeborg stepped into the stone-walled fold while all her cousins looked on. "You must learn to pay attention to a sheep and predict what she will do. Watch." She walked toward the ewe Tor had been trying to catch. "She is confused. See how she moves, keeping an eye on both of us? Now she will move off to my right because that's where she's looking most often. And I will not chase her. I'll move to the right also, try to get there ahead of her."

The sheep bolted right; Ingeborg darted to intercept her. The ewe ducked away too late. Ingeborg grabbed two fistfuls, one on each side, and tipped the ewe up and back. The sheep landed on her tail, all four legs sticking straight out, and the chase was over.

"You see, Tor, once the sheep is sitting on its rear end like this, it will not fight me anymore. It paralyzes her in a way. Now she can be shorn; she'll not resist." Ingeborg clamped the ewe between her knees. The poor sheep let its legs droop and stared blankly at nothing.

Kari handed her the shears, and she made the first pass. "You start here. Keep your shears filled. By that I mean to make sure you cut a large glob of wool with each snip. Trim off the chest and belly like this; this fine wool is especially valuable." She continued on with her narrative as she finished shearing the ewe. Tor did not seem to be paying close attention, but Anders certainly was. But then, he had helped with shearing in the past, and this year he had grown enough to shear sheep on his own.

She released the ewe and tipped it forward toward its legs. It fell on its side, squirmed, gained its feet, and ran off. "This was not the best shearing. You can see a couple places on the ewe where I nicked her skin, a little blood here and there. A fine shearing job does not nick the skin." She carried her fleece over to the big table by the wall.

Gunlaug pointed with her big pair of scissors. "I'll cut off the scraggly bits like these here and here. Then I will smooth it out and check for burrs and weeds. This fine wool I will cut off and put aside. The coarser wool from the back and sides will go on this pile." She trimmed the fleece and draped the main piece over the stone wall of the fold.

Ingeborg smiled at Anders. "Why don't you try next."

Anders picked a ewe from the flock. "I learned this part good last year. I don't chase it; I try to be where it's going to be."

"That's right! See how she's watching you? She knows you have her singled out."

"How do I get her to move?"

"Take a step toward her."

Anders did so. The ewe stood there. Impatiently, Anders ordered, "Come on, sheep. Move!" He took another step. She lunged forward and galloped right past him before he had a chance to reach for her.

"Take note of where she's looking. She'll hesitate and then bolt. Watch what she's telling you with her eyes and ears."

Anders missed her on his second attempt. "Stupid sheep!"

Ingeborg agreed, but she didn't say so out loud. Another reason she much preferred cows.

Anders accidentally chased her into the midst of the flock. "Now I don't know which one!"

"She'll tell you. Move in closer."

Anders took two steps toward the group of sheep, and his ewe ran out the back and around the rock wall. She raced past Gunlaug, who made no move to catch her.

Anders huffed, "Why didn't you grab her?"

"It's your sheep. I just sort the fleeces."

It took him several minutes more to catch her as she feinted and he feinted, she bolted and he snatched. Finally he grabbed her on the fly, dragged her to a walk, and heaved mightily. He almost lost her, but he managed to get her up on her tail. "She quit struggling!" he cried triumphantly. "I did it!"

"Huzzah for Anders!" Kari cried.

Ingeborg handed him her shears. He was doing quite well for a first time, but then he lost his grip. The ewe fell to its side, gained its feet, and ran off, a great glob of loose fleece hanging from her belly.

Ingeborg caught the sheep, set it on end, and clamped it between her knees. "I'll hold it. You shear it."

With all the cautious and patient care one would use diapering a baby, he snipped away at the fleece as Ingeborg kept urging him, "Fill your shears. It will go faster."

Fifteen minutes later, he stepped back, triumphant. Not once had he nicked the ewe's skin. True, his work was rather uneven, and he left inch-long sections of unshorn wool here and there on her, but for a first attempt, the job was not too bad. Should Ingeborg criticize or not? She decided not. Let him have his moment of victory.

He carried the fleece over to Gunlaug, and she threw it out open across the table. "Where do I cut away?" she asked him.

Anders pointed. "Here and here—the fine wool. Right?"

"Right. There." She laid the snips aside. "Now what?"

"Make sure there's no weeds in it," Anders said. "Look, there's a burr right there."

Gunlaug cupped her fingertips around it and pulled it out, then turned the fleece over. "Is it good?"

He peered at it. "It's good." He stood erect, grinning broadly. "That is my first fleece all by myself."

"But certainly not the last." She flopped it over the stone wall on top of the other one. "Now it's my turn." Gunlaug tucked Anders's shears into her apron pocket and strode out into the fold. She was showing off, Ingeborg knew, and it was delightful to see. Their fledgling shearers should see how it was really done.

Gunlaug, as well as Ingeborg, knew which ewes were the most wily and resistant. She caught up one of them so that the apprentices would not have to deal with it, flipped it and sheared it, all in less than three minutes.

Ingeborg applauded appreciatively. "There is more than one pair of shears, you know, and they're freshly sharpened. Now let's all get to work here." Ingeborg stepped back to let the others take over, but she quickly realized that the small ones were never going to hold a sheep that weighed as much as or more than they.

"Mari, you and Kari work together—one hold the sheep while the other shears. Hamme and Anders, can you two work together?" Then deliberately she pointed to Tor and Hjelmer. "And you two."

Tor was obviously going to object; scowling, he opened his mouth. And closed it again. With a deft hand, Hjelmer seized a sheep and turned it on end. He stood watching Tor, a smug expression on his face, poorly concealed. Tor snatched up a pair of shears and started hacking. Several times he drew blood. Each time, Hjelmer warned, "Be careful!"

What should she do? Ingeborg felt torn. Keep the two feuders together and hope they'd learn to tolerate each other? Put them on separate sides of those mountains behind them?

As if reading her mind, Gunlaug stepped in beside her and

murmured, "Maybe Tor would like mucking out the stalls better than shearing."

"Good idea." Ingeborg raised her voice. "Tor, come with me, please. Anders, finish Tor's shearing job there."

She walked off toward the barn. Morosely, Tor followed, carefully studying the dirt ahead of him.

Ingeborg wheeled suddenly. "What is the matter? Why are you angry?"

He gave a huge shrug and stared at the ground. She waited. And waited. And waited.

He suddenly blurted, "I'm just angry. That's all. You let the little kids do all kinds of stuff, the boys and the girls both. I'm bigger. I can do it better. You should be asking me to do it."

"When we were getting Mr. Aarvidson out of the ravine, I asked you to do something only you could do, and you did it splendidly. You were strong enough to take all the weight on the rope, and when it was all right to let go, you did so and came down to help me without being asked. It was a perfect job. When I need your strength, I don't hesitate to ask. But the smaller children have to learn how to do all these things too. They won't learn if they can't do things."

He muttered something and started to move away.

"Tor!"

He stopped.

"Bullying and teasing the smaller boys, and that includes Hjelmer, only shows how childish you are. You will not do it anymore. Do you understand?"

He muttered something.

"Clean out the stalls, please. We have another cow due to calve soon, and we'll need a clean box stall for her."

"But I'm supposed to be helping with the shearing!"

"I distinctly heard you say you hate sheep. You needn't work with them if you dislike them so."

"I like them better than cleaning out stalls."

"There is plenty of shearing yet to be done. You won't lose out. And we need the stall." She paused. "I care about you, Tor. I don't want you to be angry." She returned to the fold.

Anders was stalking a ewe. She bolted; he grabbed her and hauled her to sitting.

Kari clapped enthusiastically. "You're getting better at it, Anders!"

Clearly pleased, Hamme set to work with her shears.

Ingeborg was watching children do adult work, and it delighted her. These children would do a perfect job next year.

A few minutes later, with her ewe punctured only a few times, Hamme dragged the fleece up to her shoulder and carried it to the stone wall. Grinning, Gunlaug spread it out.

"Here and here—the fine wool." Hamme pointed as Gunlaug snipped. "This is fun!" Her grin dimmed the sun.

"You did a good job too," Gunlaug told her. "When the underside of the fleece is flat and even like that, it's easier to card and spin."

Ingeborg called, "Mari, let's you and I go make supper."

Mari pouted. "Do I have to? This is much more fun."

Ingeborg was going to say, "Yes, you have to," but she stopped herself. Work that is fun goes far more quickly. So often, work that has to be done is not fun. Mari would get enough no-fun work in her life. Let her enjoy this. Besides, Mari was learning a valuable skill. The girl was not real good at shearing yet and needed practice. But for sure she already knew how to make supper. "All right. You convinced me. You help with the shearing, and I will go make supper."

Mari squealed, "Takk!" and turned her attention to the unshorn ewe between Kari's knees.

Ingeborg gathered half a dozen eggs in the hen coop and continued up to the house. She walked in the door, stopped, and gasped.

Her patient was sitting in the chair beside the fireplace!

"Nils Aarvidson, what do you think you're doing?"

He gave her an impish little smile. "Well, I think I am sitting in a chair. When I awoke from my nap, I had to, uh, do something that a proper young man would never ever mention to a proper young woman, so I shall never mention it. But there was no one around to help me. I am quite proud that I managed on my own."

She should have left one of the boys there! Too late now. "Well, uh, you have earned the right to be proud, for sure. Do you want to remain there awhile?"

"I do."

"Very well, then." She took the eggs out of her apron and put them in a bowl on the table. She ladled water into the big iron pot, hung it on the fireplace hook, and swung it in over the fire. The fire was down to weak embers among a few charred sticks. She stuffed another three thick sticks of stove wood into the dying coals, for they were too low to boil water in a decent time.

She gathered up a big bowl of potatoes and brought them to the fireplace. Nils was sitting in the chair she usually used, so she brought one over from the corner, settled into it, and began peeling potatoes.

Nils watched her for a few minutes. "Is there nothing you don't know how to do well?"

She glanced at him. "I'm a farmer's daughter, and I have

been coming up here to the Strandseter for years. If I were to make a guess, I would say that the only reason you are impressed with my skills, shall we say, is because you are not a farmer's child, and they seem unusual to you. Believe me, they are very ordinary to me. All of us are good at what we do, even the smaller children."

"Nei." He studied her a moment. "Nei, it is more than that. Much, much more than that. You make cheese and show the youngsters how. Weave and—"

"Gunlaug does most of the weaving. I spin the wool." She stopped. She had interrupted him. How rude.

Nils continued. "You husband the cows and sheep. Farm tasks. But . . ." He pursed his lips in thought. "I was a very, very foolish man who did foolish things. I would have died from my foolishness—indeed I was very close to death—but you saved me. I am getting well because of your wits and good nursing. That is not ordinary. That is most extraordinary. You are a most extraordinary woman, Ingeborg Strand. And I salute you."

Ingeborg bit her lip. What could she say? Gunlaug's words at the lake galloped back to her, about Nils being attracted to her. No, this was just gratitude talking. That was all. Surely that was all?

18

Three days and they were still shearing. *If only I could be out there,* Nils thought. His curiosity needed more than a view through the window to be satisfied. Would he have been able to do all the things Ingeborg took so for granted? And always made look easy? He watched, wishing he could see through that rock wall.

Jon and Kari had taken the shorn sheep out to pasture at the far end of the valley. They'd not gone up into the hills like usual. He'd learned the patterns of life at a seter through all his hours of forced watching. Finally he could read for longer times, but the life going on around him was far more fascinating than Plato and Voltaire.

The kettle hanging over the dwindling fire emitted fragrant smells that set his stomach to growling. One of the others would be in soon to stir the pot and feed the fire. He knew better than to try to walk by himself. He would not take a chance on undoing all the progress that had been gained. He'd thought about many things on his pallet, the lessons he was learning—patience being one and fortitude another. Hopefully both of those would help lead to wisdom.

How would he ever forgive himself for taking such a foolish chance? Hiking by himself. One of the first laws the lovers of mountain hiking learned was never to hike alone. The folks at the inn had tried to stop him. More than one friend had tried to talk him into remaining in Oslo. As had his family. He shook his head. No wonder his father was always disappointed in him.

Ingeborg had said someone would be coming up from town soon with mail and messages. He would take down the letters Nils had written to be mailed. His mor and far must be frantic by now.

Perhaps he had needed an extended time of introspection, since he so rarely indulged in that aspect of life. He'd always believed the mountains had the ability to change a man. Now he knew that for certain. Ingeborg would say it was God who changed men. Watching those at the seter made him wonder. What was the difference between his family and this one, other than the obvious house and life and all the accoutrements of wealth? Those here had something he'd not seen before his sojourn at the seter. He started to think of his father and quickly stuck that back in a box down in the depths of his mind.

He'd done enough pondering for the day. Time to study for his test in August. He picked up his textbook. Even that was preferable to thinking about his father and his demands. Voltaire. Unlike many other philosophers, Voltaire possessed a wit worth studying—dry, acerbic, often profound.

Animals have these advantages over man: they never hear the clock strike, they die without any idea of death, they have no theologians to instruct them, their last moments are not disturbed by unwelcome and unpleasant ceremonies, their funerals cost them nothing, and no one starts lawsuits over their wills.

Nils liked that one. It didn't strictly apply to his family, though. They were, his far especially, so hidebound, no one would dream of suing, because primogeniture was so thoroughly ingrained. What would he do with his life if he did not enter the business? He would probably have to leave his native land, for starters. Leave the mountains? Leave the sparkling waters of the Vik, the supreme majesty of the deep fjords and the soaring eagles? Just when he thought pondering might bear some fruit, it discouraged him further.

Mari returned, scrubbed her hands, and started getting out flour and other ingredients.

He laid Voltaire and company aside. "What are you making now?"

"Biscuits to go with the rabbit stew. Hare stew, actually."

"Rabbit? Hare?"

"Hjelmer's trapping paid off. He moved his trapline to another place and we have enough to feed everyone. He usually does that a lot up here."

"Is there anything he cannot do?"

"Umm, make biscuits." Her grin made him chuckle.

It would be hard to put anything over on that girl. Besides being a fine cook, she was really observant. She and Gunlaug. All of them, really. Well, most of them.

Sometimes when Gunlaug was sitting at her loom, she talked with him. He surely hoped that her man, Ivar, was all she thought him to be. Of course, then he could probably walk on water too. Strange that Ingeborg didn't much care for the young man.

An itch started again down on his leg. Scratching it through all the wrappings was not an easy feat. When Ingeborg re-wrapped it the other day, he was appalled at how his injured leg had become smaller, not that either leg was very strong now. How quickly the body lost muscles when not used. He wasn't sure he'd even be able to hike back to the inn where he'd started.

He had to walk again and soon.

Mari brought the Dutch oven over to the fire and set it off to the side, wiggling it down into the coals as she always did.

"You are letting the pot heat, right?" He shook his head. "Our cook at home sure has it easy compared to you."

"Ja, that's probably true. You've been getting cooking lessons whether you wanted them or not, haven't you."

"I have been getting lots of lessons I did not know I needed." He inhaled as she lifted the lid on the other pot, which was hanging over the fire, and stirred. "If that tastes as good as it smells, there will not be any left over. That is for sure."

She dipped some stew out on the wooden spoon and held it out. "Here, taste and see what you think. It is hot."

He blew on the spoon and waited, inhaling the fragrance. When he tasted it, he could feel the grin that stretched his cheeks. "How do you make everything taste so good?"

"I just add salt and pepper and other things until it tastes right. Easy. Anyone could do it."

He shook his head slowly, from side to side. "You are wrong. I know people who have cooked for years and nothing they make ever tastes really good." He was thinking of his mor. She could cook, her own mor had made sure of that, but *delicious* was not a word one used to describe a meal his mor prepared. It was one of the reasons they had a cook.

214

He heard shouts outside. "What is wrong now?"

"Nothing. This is a big rite. They just sheared the last sheep. Now we concentrate on other things: we wash and clean the fleece, and we spend a lot of time carding the wool to keep the two spinning wheels in motion. And we keep making cheese."

"Does all the work never end?"

Mari stared at him. "Is it supposed to?"

"Well, in the city, people go to their jobs, where they work, and at the end of the day or the shift, they stop working and go home."

"Here we live with our work."

"I see that."

Mari put coals in the bottom of the Dutch oven and placed the biscuit dough in the upper level on the rack. After making sure there were plenty of coals surrounding the oven, she stoked the rest of the fire, and wiped her forehead with the corner of her apron.

"I agree. Gets right hot in here."

"Go wash," Mari ordered as the others hit the doorway. "Down in the creek and bring back two buckets of water. Takk."

One would think Mari was much older than her ten years, as the others did her bidding. She would make a fine general some day.

When Ingeborg and Gunlaug came in laughing, the wet edges of their skirts said they had not only been *to* the creek but *in* it. Water dotted their shirts too. Someone had been splashing.

"The others are having too much fun to come right now."

"The biscuits are not ready yet. Would one of you please bring in the buttermilk and butter?"

"Come on, Gunlaug, we will cut and hang the curd at the same time." The two left again along with the sun they had brought in.

"So what are they doing out there?"

"Cheese is made from cream that has been heated and mixed with rennet to make it solid."

He nodded. She had told him this before, but he was listening harder now.

"We cut the curd, what the cream forms, and drain the whey away. We have been drinking that, and I use it in cooking. The animals love it too. It is good food. The curd is hung in cheesecloth bags to drain. When it is dry enough, we put it in a cheese mold, or maybe just a large flat pan, and press it down tightly to force the rest of the whey out, what little is left. We can eat some at that point—"

"The soft cheese that we have been eating?" Tasty soft cheese. Fresh, yet not fresh.

"Ja! Most of it is molded in big rounds—wheels—and we wax them so they don't spoil or dry out. Then we store them to age in the cheese house. Some farms use a cellar, but we have a cavern cut away back into the hill. It always stays the same temperature."

"And goat cheese is made the same way?"

"Ja, and I have heard that in different parts of the world they use different kinds of milk. Camel, sheep, whatever kind of animal they can milk. But cows produce the most and goats after that."

"What about gjetost?"

"We do not usually make that, although Ingeborg knows

how. Sometimes people add other things to the cheese too, to give it different flavors. And different countries make different kinds. The Swiss make a kind with holes in it—Emmental. I, for sure, don't know how they manage to put holes down inside."

"I never really gave much thought to cheeses, well, not really to most food. Cook buys things at the market, and then he cooks them and serves them in the dining room at home."

Mari studied him curiously. "After dinner would you tell me about your home? What it looks like?"

"I will." *Maybe Ingeborg will join us.* His personal angel of mercy. He had a new thought. "How is Tor coming with the leather gloves? I would have him make me a pair if he has the materials."

Mari shrugged. "You'll have to ask him. I do not really know."

"And do not really care?"

"Is it that obvious?"

"Probably only to someone who has nothing to do but observe. You hide it well."

"Takk." She lifted the lid on the Dutch oven, nodded, and with a smooth motion pulled it out of the fire. She immediately swept the trailing coals back into the fire, even though the floor in front of the fireplace was made of slate to prevent fires from happening in just such a situation.

She stepped outside to ring the bar, returned to lift the biscuits out onto a plate on the table, and then came over for the stewpot she had removed from the fire.

Nils would have given anything to offer to help. They all worked so hard, and there he sat. *I will not live the way I have in the past,* he promised himself. *I am no longer taking wealth for granted. There is too much to be done in this world.* All his life he had had servants to wait on him. What were their lives like? Did they work as hard as these people did?

In noisy high spirits, the shearing crew came tumbling in and seated themselves at the table. Hamme said grace, and Gunlaug began filling plates and passing them down the table. Mari prepared a plate of stew and biscuits for Nils and brought it to him.

He thanked her and discovered the stew was even better than that foretaste he'd had. Here he sat in his chair by the fire; there they sat at their table. All together and yet apart. He was not with them, not of them. Very near them, yet not in their world. It was an unsettling thought.

"I think we should lift Nils's chair and haul him outside." Hjelmer made his announcement when they were nearly done eating. "Tor has a good idea."

Tor took the cue. "We stick two poles under the seat of that chair and four of us can carry him out, kind of like we did with carrying him home."

"What a good idea." Ingeborg smiled at Tor. "Why did we not think of that sooner?"

"He hasn't been in the chair that long." Tor tried to look like it was nothing, but his almost smile gave him away.

Nils applauded. "Thank you, young man. I am looking forward to real sunshine on my face. It's a good thing you are all strong. I could not have carried weight like that when I was your age. And to think you all carried me clear from that creek. Up to the trail." He shook his head as he spoke, and when his voice broke, he stopped to clear his throat. After rolling his lips together, he continued. "You saved my life. All of you." He caught Ingeborg blinking and Gunlaug sniffing.

After heaving a heavy breath, he added, "I heard a story once about two men; one saved the other man's life. The one saved said, 'I owe you my life, so how can I help you now? It is yours.' I feel that way about all of you."

The room was silent as most of those around the table studied their hands or the plates or the spoons in front of them. Jon finally broke the silence.

"Are there any more biscuits?" The laughter made him look around. "What?"

"Yes, there is one more, and you may have it." Mari passed the plate. "Go ahead and have more of that cheese on it too. I wish we had more jam."

"Maybe whoever comes up will bring some." Jon moved the biscuit to his plate and carefully split it open.

Ingeborg and Gunlaug exchanged smiles and slight nods.

Nils watched them. The two took their responsibilities to not only teach skills and get the work done, but to teach morals and the Bible and how to live the kind of life they lived. Did they even begin to understand all they were doing? Or was it a natural thing? They quoted Bible verses like he quoted Plato or poets, mostly dead men. This family made the Bible seem alive and useful and a pleasure.

He realized his education was lacking something that might make his life richer too. Ingeborg prayed as if she were talking to a friend and yet much more than that. This was not the God he heard about in church every Sunday, where they went all dressed up and saw other well-dressed people and smiled and went home and figured they had done their duty for the week. Even confirmation had been an experience to get through to please the grandparents or Mor and Far. He had passed, and that was the end of that.

Until now.

Ingeborg stood up. "All right. I'll get the staves, and we will haul you outside. If that is all right with you, Nils. I mean, do you want to go outside?"

"Do sheep smell bad and get bugs in their fleece?"

Hamme snickered, Jon giggled, and the others fell into laughter that spread like the circles at the lake after the rock.

"How do you know that?"

"I heard you all complain. That's how." He leaned forward. "Let us go forth and prosper." Now, where had that come from?

Ingeborg, Gunlaug, Tor, and Anders took the ends of the poles and lifted. And grunted, but headed for the door, where they turned sideways to get through. *Good thing my knee bends,* Nils thought as he was eased out the door. One chair leg caught on the sill and almost dumped him, but they compensated and planted him in the sunshine.

"Oh, tusen takk, tusen takk." He closed his eyes and raised his face to the sun.

The others were just going about their next things to do when they all turned at the "Halloo, the seter!" that echoed across the valley. A man on horseback leading a packhorse waved his arm and continued up the track toward them.

Gunlaug's eyes widened with a smile that brought brightness to her face, rivaling the sun. "Ivar! That's Ivar!"

"Not *the* Ivar that I have heard so much about?" Nils grinned up at Gunlaug, but she ignored him and ran partway out the track, then apparently thought the better of that and walked sedately.

"Hush!" Ingeborg said, glancing at Nils with her eyes dancing.

He sniggered. "What all is he packing?"

"It might be fresh vegetables from the gardens down below. We never know. But the important thing is that he will bring letters from home. We will get to hear how the wedding went and all the other news." She clasped her hands to her chest. "Oh, Ivar, kick that horse into a canter."

Nils watched Ingeborg, her cheeks pinking, her smile as broad as one of those cheese presses. *I thought she didn't like him.* He thought for a moment. No, for Ingeborg it was getting news of home. Would there be a letter from a man who was waiting for her to return? The thought dimmed the sun. Was there someone she cared about? If so, she had not mentioned anyone. Gunlaug or the others did not tease her about a beau, not like they did Gunlaug. Of course, she might have a beau by correspondence only, or perhaps even a favorite that no one else knew about.

Teasing Gunlaug was such fun because she got all flustered and red-faced and dropped things. Perhaps now, if he met this Ivar, he would understand why Ingeborg did not approve of this match. Not that she'd ever said those words, but he was learning to read her well. And he didn't care for the idea that there might be a man down below waiting for Ingeborg. Not one bit.

19

The next morning Ingeborg watched as Ivar walked with Gunlaug up the track toward home, leading his horse, followed by the packhorse, now loaded with rolled and bundled fleeces. She'd just turned away when something caught her attention. They had stopped to say good-bye, but instead of kissing her, which is what she knew Gunlaug was hoping, Ivar shook his head and mounted his horse.

Was Gunlaug crying? Was she that sad to see him go? Ingeborg had a hard time believing that. Had he said something to her? Yes, Gunlaug was weeping, not just crying the way you express sadness at a loved one's departure, but sobbing lustily.

Ingeborg charged out to meet her. "What's the matter?" What had that weaselly mamma's boy said to her best friend, the one who loved him, or at least thought she did?

Gunlaug collapsed in her arms. Her great gulping sobs made it impossible to understand her.

Ingeborg patted her back and made loving shushing sounds to help calm her.

"He . . . he said . . ." The onslaught ripped onward again.

"All right. I know something is terribly wrong, but I don't know what it is. Gunlaug, tell me before I have to go in and get the gun and shoot him."

That put a pause in the storm. "He . . . he said his mor . . ."

I knew it had to be something to do with his mor, that grasping old tyrant. "His mor what?"

"Has found a woman with two children for him to marry—" sobs and a hiccup—"and they will all live with his mor." More sobs and hiccups.

"Oh." Ingeborg hugged her cousin close, although she felt more like stamping her feet and screaming. How could a grown man . . . ? Of course. That was part of the problem. *That woman* wanted her son to remain a boy all his life and take care of his mor. *Gunlaug, Gunlaug, if only I could convince you that Ivar is not worth your tears.* "What else?"

"They are to be married before the end of August."

Ingeborg nodded, tonguing her lower lip and then catching it between her teeth. Swallowing words was never easy for her, and right now she was about to choke on them. She could not say what she was thinking, that was for sure.

Gunlaug shuddered in her arms. "I know you always said he is not good enough for me, that he's a mamma's boy, but Ingeborg, I love him."

"I know. Hush now. All is going to be all right. We will talk about this, and then we will go bushwhack him, knock him off his horse, and roll him down the hill to land on an anthill and get bitten so bad he dies."

"We do not have anthills like that." Sob. "Those are in Africa."

"Oh, *humph*, that's right. I know, a bee tree instead. He

will bump against a bee tree, and the bees will chase him all the way down the mountain."

"We do not have wild bees and bee trees here either." Shudder. Despite Gunlaug's sorrow, a smile tried to break through the clouds. She sniffed and used the corner of her apron to wipe her eyes.

"Then you and I will stand at the road and throw pinecones at him and laugh when he tries to dodge them."

Gunlaug mopped her face. "Is that before or after the bee tree that we do not have? But it sounds like a good idea."

"Both." Ingeborg hugged her friend. "Please listen to me."

Her voice was low, sad, defeated. "I am."

"You are better off without him. Just think. Would you like to live with his mor for the rest of your life? And you would, serving her."

Gunlaug shuddered. "No, not at all. Eee-ew."

"We should pray for that poor young woman and think of her children."

"Ivar's mor likes children. That's what he said."

"Do you know what her name is?"

"Whose? His mor or the woman?"

"His mor."

Gunlaug wrinkled her forehead, trying to think. "Mor must know but I . . . I guess I do not. I just know she never liked me."

"Ja, well, may she someday rest in peace." *Without you around, my dear friend, to wait on her.* Ingeborg locked her arm through Gunlaug's, the way they used to when they were little girls and went skipping down the path to school. "Come. He might be worthless, but he brought us some licorice. I think right now is a good time to open that." And it's a good thing he did, since he forgot the letters, leaving them all feeling bereft.

They ignored the questioning looks from all the others and went into the house to the cupboard, where Ingeborg had hidden the tin of candy, keeping it for a special occasion. She unwrapped the tin and finally pried the cover off. Together they inhaled the intoxicating fragrance of licorice.

"Since you need consoling, you get the first piece, and then you can share the rest with the others."

"You take one too, and we will pop a piece into our mouths." She did. "Oh, I do love licorice." Her eyes grew dreamy, like when she talked of Ivar. "Someday there will be just the right man for me, and he will be a real man, not a permanent boy."

Thank you, Lord. Ingeborg figured this was not the end of Gunlaug's sadness, but it was sure a good start.

"Come and have licorice!" Gunlaug hollered from the doorstep. "If you do not come quick, I will eat your piece."

When she brought the tin to Nils, he nodded and thanked her gravely. "If licorice is so important to all of you, I will have to send you some from my favorite place in Oslo. When I get home, that is."

Gunlaug nodded. "We would all like that. So that means we have to work extra hard to get you well enough to walk again and soon."

He surely saw her puffy red eyes, but he said nothing about it. "We do. Anders said he is working on a crutch for me. I would make one, but I have no idea how to do such a thing, and we don't need lopped off fingers or portions thereof in the bargain." He put his piece into his mouth and smiled wide. "Have you ever had horehound drops?"

"That is a cough medicine."

"But a candy too. Along with lemon drops."

"And peppermint." Gunlaug smiled in spite of herself.

That evening, when the rest of the family was still at the supper table, Anders brought the two pieces of wood he had been smoothing and forming and showed them to Nils. "I need to carve a hole here to put them together, but I wanted to make sure this is all right before I go any further."

"Do you have an awl?" Ingeborg asked.

"Not that I know of. It is not in the tool chest. Saws and hammers mostly."

She thought a moment. "Any glue?"

"Nei."

"Well, you dig out a hole or a notch, whatever will work, and we'll wrap it tight with thongs. I saw something that said wrap the things together with strips of rawhide and soak it in water. When it dries, the rawhide shrinks down and the bond will be solid hard."

Anders looked at her. "Where did you learn that?"

Hjelmer grinned at his sister. "From a book she read. Ingeborg learns all kinds of good stuff from the books and newspapers she reads. She is always looking for more stuff to read."

Ingeborg felt a smile wrap around her heart. What a compliment from a boy who observed far more than he spoke! She ruffled his hair. "Takk."

Tor reached for the wood. "I have strips from the gloves I am making. I know how to weave the shorter strips together to make a long one without knots, so it can be smooth. If we use some of that sheepskin that has the wool on, that should make good padding for the underarm part."

Ingeborg felt her mouth drop open and snapped it shut. She exchanged looks of delight with Gunlaug, who was now grinning from ear to ear. It wasn't even the end of July yet, and look at the way these children were learning to work together. *God be praised.*

"This will save my life—again. I'll be able to walk." Nils reached out to shake each of the boys' hands.

Ingeborg watched the boys run merrily outside, then offered, "You've been amazingly patient."

"You have no idea, since you didn't know me in my other life."

My other life. Ingeborg thought on that. He was right. And not just about his life. Their lives here at the Strandseter were set apart from all their other lives. The time here did far more than just produce a lot of cheese and spin wool and feed the livestock so that the lowland pastures could be hayed for winter fodder. Both children and adults learned to work together and grow up in so many ways. Surely there was someplace in the Bible where it said, *God is in this place.* Never before had she seen this so clearly. When she got home she would have to look that up. Someplace in Genesis perhaps. If only she had a Bible along. She knew it wasn't in her copied sheets, because so much of those were the Psalms and parts of the New Testament.

Hjelmer waved a hand in front of her face. "Ingeborg, come back."

"Uh, sorry." Back to work.

All of them. Anders set to carving out an indentation to take the top of Nils's crutch. Mari went to mixing something in the kitchen, Ingeborg to spinning along with Kari on the other spinning wheel, while Gunlaug and Hamme took to the looms. Tor worked on his gloves, leaving Jon and Hjelmer to card wool.

"If you showed me how, I could probably learn to help with that," Nils said to Hjelmer. "Then we could perhaps play a game of chess."

"This doesn't go fast."

"I'm aware of that."

So Hjelmer showed him how to stroke the wool straight through the fine wire teeth of the tools that looked like large, flat, shallow wire hairbrushes. Then he handed Nils two cards. "Now you slide one against the other, like this. It combs the hairs—the fibers—out straight so they'll spin into a smooth yarn."

Nils made a couple of passes. "This isn't as easy as it looks."

"Most things are not."

Ingeborg forced herself to pay strict attention to her spinning. Otherwise she might burst into laughter. Hjelmer was doing a fair job of teaching, rather coaching. *Leave them be.* When she caught herself wishing it were her hands on the backs of the carding combs guiding Nils's hands, she nearly broke the spinning thread. *Ingeborg Strand, what are you thinking?!* She knew she didn't say that out loud but . . . She heaved a sigh and reached into the basket beside her for another handful of the fine belly wool. This stuff took more skill to spin than did the coarser wool. She spun a fine thread to knit into stockings. Once she had several skeins, they would need to find materials for the dyes. Some they'd already brought up from the farms: onion skins that made yellow, walnut husks a nice brown, and of course, the indigo plant. Everyone used indigo.

The only bad thing about spinning was it allowed her mind free rein. And she felt uncomfortable about where it kept wandering. "Gunlaug, what is that psalm you wanted us to memorize?" That would help keep her mind in check.

Gunlaug recited it. "I have it written down."

"I know, but—"

Gunlaug's chuckle set the evening air that floated in the windows to dancing. She stopped the gentle thuds of the heddle and batten working in rhythm and rose, stretching as she did. "I need to move around. We can all work on it together."

Mari brought in some dough flattened into a round on the griddle to set into the coals of the fire. "We will have a treat tonight."

"What is it?"

"You will see."

Ingeborg heard a grunt or a groan of disgust from Nils when Hjelmer stopped his carding and showed him how to pull in long sweeps so that the wool strands lay straight and even. Nils took them back with a sigh.

"Why is it that I can discuss ancient Roman and Greek philosophers and speak four languages but I cannot master wool carding?"

"You will get it. Hjelmer is not telling you the hours it took for him to learn." Ingeborg did not say that Hjelmer picked up the skill years earlier from watching Ingeborg. He took right to it. All she was doing was stretching the truth a bit. After all, how many hours had he spent watching her?

Hjelmer gave her a sideways grin and a raised eyebrow. He knew exactly what she was doing. She wondered sometimes at the perceptions of this younger brother of hers. Someone had said one time he was an old soul when he was born. She believed it. His was the first birth she was ever in the room to observe. She had stolen in and hidden in a corner because she wanted to know more so desperately. Even then, all things to do with birthing and healing and the way life worked fascinated her.

Perhaps that was why she felt such a connection with him. Her mother had lost two more babies that Ingeborg knew of, both of them early on. Had she not been instructed to run for the midwife, she would probably not have known then. Her mother, like all women, kept womanly things intensely private.

"That certainly smells good. Are you sure it is not done?" Hjelmer asked, staring at the baking griddle in the coals. "You wouldn't want to burn it, you know."

"I will not let it burn, but no matter how good it smells, it would still be doughy in the middle. You need to learn patience."

Gunlaug laughed. "Your little sister has you there."

"My little sister thinks she is the boss in the kitchen. Just because she is almost eleven."

"That is just because she is. Who does much of the cooking around here? I do not see anyone else volunteering."

"I think I got it!" Anders waved the shorter piece in the air. "Tor, what do you think?" The two worked the two pieces together. "Tight fit, I know, but that is important."

"I have some thong done here. You hold it and I will wrap it."

"How about if I try it out first?" Nils suggested.

"Good idea. If we need to we can shave some off the end."

Nils started to push himself up when Tor stepped closer and provided a leaning post. "Takk. Even that good leg has gone weak on me." Anders settled the crutch under Nils's arm and stepped back, but not far. Both boys were making sure the man did not fall.

Ingeborg let out the breath she did not realize she had been holding. Nils stood upright, on his own, the crutch beside him. He moved the crutch forward, thought the better of it, and planted the crutch beside the splinted leg. He moved the other leg and, balancing on that, moved crutch and mending leg together as one. "It works!"

Everyone clapped and Tor cheered.

Ingeborg felt like leaping to her feet and twirling around the room. *Thank you, Lord*, she repeated over and over. What a monumental accomplishment! Maybe they could soon remove the splint too.

She could hear Mor's sage advice. *"Do not rush in a birthing or in getting well. Running ahead of the good Lord is never wise. He will tell when the time is right."*

Mari disappeared out the door and returned with a jug of buttermilk to set on the table. With everyone staring at her, she lifted the griddle out of the coals and set it on the table with wooden trivets underneath. "We have something to celebrate and something good to celebrate it with. Come on, so we eat it while it is hot."

Cautiously, deliberately, Nils used a step-and-thump action to get across the room to sit down at the table with the others. His grin told Ingeborg how pleased he was.

And hot the food was, but the oohs and ahhs around the table said more than words.

"Mari, what is this?"

"Not biscuits and not bread or cake but something in between."

"It is my secret," Mari told them. "But I am glad you like it."

Nils sat with eyes closed, a contented look on his face as he worked his mouth. "It may be a secret, but you need to tell the cook at our house how to make it."

Ingeborg could see the color rise over the cheeks of her baby sister. What a fine man to think to say something so perfect to a young girl who so seldom heard words of praise. Something fluttered in her chest. Whatever it was, it made her feel deeply pleased.

20

"I told you he likes you." Gunlaug failed at looking innocent.

Ingeborg shook her head. "He just likes to talk with some-one who has read at least a few of the authors he has read." She tipped her head back and gazed across the valley. She never tired of looking at the cattle and sheep grazing under the watchful eyes of the herders. Most of the books Nils mentioned she had never heard of, but he loved to tell her about them. And she loved to listen. And to argue. What a splendid time they had arguing.

He seemed to enjoy asking her about life on the family farms and the intricacies of all the relatives that played such an important role in each other's lives. This was all quite ordinary to her, but it seemed amazing and exceptional to him. It made her wonder even more about his family.

"Did you not know your grandparents?" Ingeborg asked him one evening in front of the fire.

"They died when I was young and did not live near us."

"And your aunts and uncles and cousins?"

"You have to understand, my far left home and moved

233

to the city to build a business of his own. I do not know how often he returned to see his family. He never talks about them."

"And your mor?"

"Her far thought she was marrying beneath her station, and since she went against his wishes, he ordered his family to have nothing to do with them."

Ingeborg shook her head and prodded the coals of the fire with the poker, just to see the sparks dance. "That is so very sad."

"Perhaps, but not unusual. Far and Mor have created their own place in society, and they are happy with that. They want their children to receive a good education and to make good marriages." He rubbed his leg, which no longer wore the splint but only a wrapping. "It is not something to get upset about. That is just the way life goes."

"I cannot think of life without my cousins and tantes and onkels. We do everything together just like one big family. Onkel Frode never married, but he is included in everything. He says Onkel Kris and my far, Arne, had enough children for all of them. He is the funny one in the family. Far is the deep thinker and a very careful farmer, and Onkel Kris sometimes likes the bottle a little too much, especially in the winter when the days are dark. But Tante Berthe does not allow drinking in the house. I think he keeps a bottle in the grain bin, but I've never gone to look. Life is different in the summer."

"But you are never home in the summer."

"I know. I'd rather be up here than anywhere." She locked her hands around her knee and stared into the fire. As warm as it was outside, still the fire was a pleasure. It kept the coffee-pot hot. "Would you like a cup of coffee?"

"No, thank you. There is no need to get up. Just stop and rest for a change. You never slow down."

"There is so much to do, and even in the long days I resent stopping to sleep. Sleeping seems a tragic waste of precious time. I can sleep in the winter when it is dark again."

She leaned her cheek on her knee, knowing that this was not acceptable ladylike behavior. "What do you do in the winter?"

"Most of my life I have gone to school in the fall, winter, and spring. It seems like most of the year."

"Probably because it is." She prodded the fire again. Soon she would need to bank the coals and go to bed, but the pleasure of his company was too strong. "Do you go to fancy society events?"

"Ja."

"And you enjoy them?"

"Ja, sometimes. But one always has to be polite and proper and—" He stopped and shook his head, a lock of blond hair falling across his wide forehead. "Those things can be so boring. Here at the seter, you are all doing something that is important and will make a difference in your families' lives. And you're polite and proper, certainly, but that is not the sum of your whole existence."

"Providing for one's family through a business is equally important." She thought about the folks who lived in the village. "What would we do without someone to run the store or the blacksmith shop or the other businesses?" But little as she knew of the lives of wealthy people, the businesses in Valdres did not make their owners a great deal of money. She knew that what she would call wealth had no comparison to the kind of life Nils talked about. They were in different worlds. And that made her sad.

Ingeborg paused as she measured out some rennet. "Do not be silly, Gunlaug. I am tired of your insisting. Men of wealth are not interested in farm girls. This is just a pleasant turn of fate for him. Soon he will go home and never think of me—er—all of us." For some reason the thought made her heart heavy. There was no hope, so rather than think of that, she chose to enjoy each moment.

Nils had made remarkable progress over the past few weeks and had healed so well that he had started helping with the chores. Today Nils was out with Hjelmer herding the cows. For some silly reason she always knew exactly where he was. As if she had a little bird that kept her informed.

Gunlaug slammed the batten against the body of the rug she was weaving. "You are wrong, but I will not argue. You always have to learn by experience."

"Look who is talking."

Gunlaug shrugged.

"Come on, that is not fair."

But Gunlaug also refused to argue or discuss, not a new reaction but irritating nonetheless.

On Sunday afternoon the older boys went fishing. The last couple of times they had brought home enough trout to last several meals. Or it should have, but everyone ate enough fried fish to practically swell up. And never want any again—until the next time Tor and Hjelmer went fishing. Anders did not enjoy it so much and chose to stay at the seter.

"Do you think the lake will be warm enough for swimming soon?" Mari asked.

"It never gets as warm as the lakes down below—you know that—but if you want to go in next Sunday, that is up to you."

"We can go wading."

"You go wading in the creek."

"I know, but we have not gone to the lake enough this year."

"That is true, we have had so much cheese to make we cannot even take Sundays off." But Ingeborg knew that was not the real reason. It was too hard for Nils to make the climb up to the lake yet. Since she did not want him to feel left out, she had been making excuses to stay near the seter.

Nils had changed to a short stick for awhile and for the last two days had been walking without any assistance. But he could not go far yet.

August rolled in and with it a sense of urgency that the time to go back down to the home farms was approaching. They all spent hours spinning, weaving, tending sheep and cattle, and making cheese. Always making cheese.

When a horse and rider appeared on the track from home, Ingeborg thought at first it might be Ivar again, but then he would nearly be married by now, and for certain his mother would not allow him to come back up here. Besides, the rider was leading two horses. That was strange. She watched Gunlaug notice the rider and stalk off, shaking her head. She too had had hopes for a minute, but common sense probably told her the same thing it told Ingeborg. She'd not mentioned Ivar since the day he'd left.

"A rider is coming," Jon came running into the house to announce. "Maybe he will bring candy again."

"Perhaps. But he will bring letters." She glanced at Nils, who looked like a thundercloud had smothered him. She almost asked him what was wrong, but when the light dawned, she thought the better of it. He might hear from his far, and she knew he didn't want to.

When she recognized the rider, she ran out with the others. "Gilbert, how wonderful to see you. They usually send the old men, you know, not the young ones."

"The older ones are too busy or just did not want to ride all the way up here." He dismounted and drew letters from one of the bags. "I imagine this is what you want the most."

"Is there anything about the wedding?" Mari asked.

"Of course." He handed her a letter from Katrina, three to Ingeborg, several to Gunlaug, and one to Kari. He had one thick letter still in his hand.

Ingeborg led him over to where Nils stood stock-still. "Gilbert, I'd like to introduce you to Nils Aarvidson. Nils, meet my brother Gilbert."

The two shook hands and Gilbert said, handing him the last letter, "I believe this one is for you."

Nils looked at the handwriting. "Ja, it is for me."

Trying not to be obvious, Ingeborg watched his face go from that of the man she had come to know to one that was not familiar at all. He did not frown, but his face turned to stone. While the children helped unload the packhorse, Nils turned away and walked on around the house. He had named her favorite spot the Mountain Bench, and Ingeborg had often found him there.

He obviously loved watching the ever-changing mountains as much as she did. If that were possible. She forced herself not to go searching for him. From the look on his face, she thought he would rather be left alone. Dread. Not anger or fear. Dread. What an awful word and thought, to dread hearing from one's far.

When they gathered for supper, Mari had made flatbrød on the griddle again to go with the leftover hare stew. She added some of the potatoes and turnips Gilbert had brought up to make it go farther.

He settled on the bench beside Ingeborg. "You are eating well up here this year. It used to be porridge and more porridge."

"We have that for breakfast, but when we have meat, we are glad. Hjelmer runs a trapline, like the one you did, very successfully. He trapped many hares, and Tor is going to tan the skins. He said he made mittens once out of rabbit skins. I want a pair. You should see his gloves. Deerskin, and they are so soft."

Gilbert nodded at Tor. "Good for you."

"We used the leftovers from the deerskin to make strips of thong to join the two pieces of the crutch Anders made for Nils."

"You will have to show me how to do that."

Gunlaug giggled. "I guess you need to come up to the seter to learn all kinds of new things. We have an inventive group here. Now that Hamme and Mari both know how to spin, we take turns on the spinning wheels. We should have plenty of wool for knitting this winter."

"Mor reminded me to tell you she misses all of you." They talked about life at the seter and life at the farm until late, when they gave Gilbert a pallet to sleep on by the fire.

"You wouldn't like to stay and help us with the haying?" Ingeborg asked the next morning as Gilbert was loading the packhorse. "By the way, what is the other horse for?"

"To bring Nils back down. His father sent it up here. I'm sure he told Nils that." He looked around. "Where is he?"

Her heart leapt, not a happy leap. "I do not know. He was not here for breakfast either. Did you hear him during the night?"

"No, but the roof could have caved in without waking me."

Ingeborg ordered her jumping heart back into place. "Let me go look for him."

She found him out in the barn, cleaning out the farrowing pen. The sow and her piglets were now out in the bigger pen with the others. Between both the sows they now had sixteen healthy and growing piglets.

"Do you know your far sent the horse for you?"

"I do. He informed me of that in the letter."

"I see." But she didn't, not at all. Not that she wanted him to leave, but she understood that when a parent called, the son or daughter was to answer. "And what are you going to do?"

"Remain right here until you all go down. You have taken care of me all this time, after saving my life. Now it is my turn to repay you."

"You need not repay us."

"But I am going to." He threw another forkful of dirty bedding in the barrow. "Is Gilbert ready to leave?"

"Ja."

"Then I will give him the letter I wrote to mail to my far."

"What will he do then?"

"He could come up and get me, but I doubt he will go that far." Nils propped the fork in the corner. "I hope he will just

240

be content to let me stay up here. After all, I was supposed to have the summer in the mountains, and while this is not the way I had planned it, I am very content here and have no desire to do more hiking. Not that I can at the moment, but with hard work, the strength will come back. When I return to Oslo and school in September, I will attack my studies with the same zeal I am going to attack the hayfield, as soon as someone teaches me how to use a scythe. There is plenty of work here to keep me busy. Now, is that all right with you?" His blue eyes gazed firmly into hers.

How to reply decorously when she would rather sing and dance? He was not leaving! She'd awakened this morning sure that the other horse was for him, and it was. Instead, they would load it with more rolled-up fleece. Gilbert was already taking some of the soft cheese home with him. With an extra horse, he could carry more. She sucked in a deep breath and smiled. "Yes, that would be fine with me and all the others."

Together they walked back to the house, where Nils went inside and brought back a packet. "Please mail this to my far," he said to Gilbert. "The address is on it. Whatever the postage is, I will pay you when I get back to where my other belongings are."

"Where is that?"

"They call their place Raggen Inn, not far from where I left the coach."

"Not near Valdres, that is for sure. You came clear across the mountains from there?"

"Ja, I did, but I sure am hoping I do not have to return that way, since I would be lost within a couple of hours." Nils smiled. "It was my pleasure to meet you."

"And mine." Gilbert nodded as he mounted his horse. "Do you think a month before you come down?"

Ingeborg shrugged. "It all depends on the weather, as you know. If you hear of a snowstorm, you come get us."

Mari smiled up at her brother. "Tell Katrina I hope she is happy. Oh, and thank you for the letter."

"You know, I think both you and Hjelmer have grown taller up here."

"The good mountain air makes all things grow faster." Ingeborg stepped back and bumped into Nils. She hadn't realized he was so close. She turned to apologize and stopped at the look in his eyes. What was it? "What?"

"Nothing. I'm going back to finish my job. I dumped the first load on the manure pile off the barn. Is that right?"

"Ja." For some reason, her mouth had gone dry, and her heart skipped like a little girl out to play. How easy it would be to drown in his gaze. She didn't hear the horses ride out or the others laughing and waving and yelling, "Takk." Gilbert had brought peppermint drops, a highly popular gift.

"Ingeborg. Ingeborg!"

She heard the sharpened tone and turned. "Ja?"

Gunlaug stood in the doorway, hands on her hips. "You said you would help me take this rug off the loom so I can get started on something else." While she tried to look stern, laughter peeked out around her eyes.

"I am coming right now." Ingeborg turned to see that Nils was just entering the barn.

"I called you three times."

"Oh. Well, I am here now. Let us get to it."

Would Nils's far really come up here to get him? The thought made her shudder. While he was surely a good man, it seemed that he required a lot of his children, his oldest son especially. All the fancy things they were required to do. What would it be like to wear a lovely silk gown and dance in a ballroom rather than outside or in a barn loft? The thought of strapping into a corset until she couldn't breathe turned that vision on its head. And almost made her laugh.

"Now what?" Gunlaug asked in a suspicious tone.

"I was just thinking about women in the city who have to wear those horrid corsets under their lovely clothes, and I cannot believe anyone could be so willing to do that. You did get yours back?"

"I found it on my bed one day. Did Nils ever comment on being lashed into a woman's corset to help his ribs?"

"No, not a word." The two looked at each other and giggles just erupted. They hadn't laughed like that for a long time. "We have been too serious."

Now it was Gunlaug who turned thoughtful. "I agree. A little teasing would lighten things up around here. Especially the gloom from Nils when he is usually so cheerful. Even all through that pain, he never was grumpy."

Ingeborg shook her head. "I know. The letter from his far was not a good thing. You know, I have been thinking. Being wealthy does not necessarily make people happy."

"Being terribly poor doesn't either. I think we are fortunate to be right in the middle. We have enough, we work hard, and we have learned to laugh and trust God for all things."

Ingeborg stared at her. "Gunlaug, sometimes you amaze me. Let us remain best friends all our life."

"Ja. Of course. Unless you go to Amerika some day."

Ingeborg shook her head. "That will never happen."

21

Nils stood in the doorway of the house, looking out over the field they were to start to hay today. Hjelmer had told him several weeks ago that they would not be grazing that section any longer but would take the cattle and sheep into the higher meadows each day to graze. How he could know so much for being only twelve years old was beyond Nils's comprehension.

"We have to wait for the dew to dry off before we start cutting with the scythes." Hjelmer stood beside him. "You did real well sharpening them yesterday, you know. Takes a natural rhythm."

"Thanks to you." Nils tossed the dregs of his coffee out to the dirt. They'd had porridge for breakfast again. He understood that that was pretty much a staple around here, but he was looking forward to having eggs. Or breakfasts like the cook at home made for them every day, one of the few things he looked forward to back in Oslo.

The boys, who were more men than boys, gathered by the barn, where they had sharpened the scythes on the grindstone the day before and finished the edges with files. Daily Nils was learning new skills, skills he had never even dreamed of, let alone planned on learning. Getting the knack of pedaling the spinning wheel and then holding the scythe blade at the right angle to the stone looked easy. It was not. As far as he was concerned, nothing the others took for granted was easy. The blister on one hand had already taught him the value of leather gloves.

"We will walk close together, each a few paces behind the other, in order to not leave clumps of grass uncut." Hjelmer looked at Nils. "We do not chop the grass; we stroke it and draw the cutting blade across it." He nodded to Anders. "We will show them." The two reached the edge of the field and Hjelmer swung his scythe in a half circle that laid the grass out flat and smooth. Swing, step forward, swing, step forward. Andres started behind him with the same rhythm.

Hjelmer stopped and looked to his two new men. "Anders, you take up my line, Tor, you go next, and Nils, you will be the third." He handed his scythe to Nils. "I will walk along and help the two of you until you do it well, and then we will trade off."

Tor was quiet today, making Nils wonder if something was wrong. But rather than think on that, he paid close attention to what he was doing. He held the tool just the way he had practiced and cut his first swath of the day. It did not lie down smooth and straight like Hjelmer's had. He stepped and swung again.

"You need to keep the swing smooth."

Nils glanced ahead. Tor's looked better than his did. "Has he cut hay before?"

Hjelmer shook his head. "Not that I know of, but he has

probably used a scythe at home sometimes. Keep on. It will get better."

"Ja, it will." He said it more like a vow than an agreement. By about the tenth stride, he could see some improvement. But before long his arms started to ache, then increase to pain, and his right shoulder cramped. With gritted teeth he continued. *You will not get behind.* This was indeed a vow.

By the time Hjelmer called for a switch, Nils rolled his shoulders and tipped his head from side to side, stretching muscles that screamed in protest. He glanced up at the sun. Had it even moved?

"Go walk around and lean against something in the shade. If you sit down, you will never want to get up." Hjelmer spoke softly so the others wouldn't hear.

Nils nodded and relinquished his death grip on the scythe.

"You have blood on your glove. Do you have a blister?"

Nils nodded. "Do I need to see Ingeborg?"

"Ja." He waved at Hamme, who was bringing out a bucket of water. "You are just in time."

"I was watching." She dipped out some water for each of them, noticed the bloody glove, and rolled her eyes. "Ingeborg is going to yell at you."

Nils just nodded. *She couldn't yell any louder than he already was.* He would continue with the scythe. He would.

"Tomorrow you will go out herding with Jon" was all Ingeborg said after she had smeared something vile smelling on his palm and wrapped his hand.

"I will continue in the hayfield, so wrap it well."

Ingeborg started to say something, then obviously recognized the steel in his eyes and didn't say any more. "Dinner will be soon."

"Takk." He turned and headed back for the hayfield, fighting hard not to limp more than usual. Now that he thought about it, his leg ached something fierce too. But he could tell the difference between the bone ache and the muscle pain. He'd had those many times when hiking up steep grades.

He stepped into Tor's place. When he saw Tor trying to cover the aches, Nils felt better. It wasn't just he.

When the sun was straight up, they broke for dinner.

They all filled their plates and brought them outside to sit in the shade, since the sun had indeed grown hot. The tiny breeze blowing on his sweat-soaked shirt made him and the others close their eyes in delight. Nils tipped his head back against the log wall, grateful for the block of wood he was sitting on.

"Hot out there." Anders wiped his face on his sleeve. "But that means the hay will dry like it should."

"So we can turn it tomorrow." Gunlaug sat down, the last one out of the house.

"Hope so. I doubt we will finish cutting today, but with three of us, we are moving pretty fast." Hjelmer looked to Ingeborg, who nodded.

"Let's say grace." He started it and the others joined in. "And thank you, God, for good weather. Amen."

Nils smiled at Ingeborg and nodded, then whispered. "Those three are fine young men."

"That they are."

"Far older than their years."

"Not really, but they do know how to work hard. They will make good farmers one day."

"Ja, like right now."

"They have a lot to learn."

Nils just nodded but thought so clearly he was afraid he had said it out loud. *Just like all the rest of us.* And no matter what he learned at school, was any of it of value compared to what they were all doing? Yes, learning to run a business was important, but how did Latin and Greek help that? And philosophy and ancient history and speaking several languages? He drank another cup of water. Philosophy? Not so much. But speaking French and German could well be a help. He had heard and believed it to be true that if one did not learn from the mistakes in history, one was bound to repeat them. He knew the one who wrote it was referring to nations, but he could see it applied to individual people too.

His mind returned to a discussion he and Ingeborg had had late one evening in front of the fire. He had commented on the Israelites not learning from their mistakes and making God angry. She had asked in return if we were any different today. Her words had stayed in his mind for him to mull over.

"Like Paul said, I want to do right, but something makes me not do that, but instead what I know is wrong. Well, not exactly, but that is the meaning of it. I should have that one memorized by now."

"You have a lot of verses memorized," he told her.

"I know, but it is never enough. Like now, when I do not have a Bible up here. The Bible is not always handy, but what is in my mind is. Mor and Far always taught us that, as did Reverend Berger, who knew whole books of Scripture by heart. He made a deep impression on me, on all of us, actually."

And that had set Nils to thinking about the large formal church his family attended.

Family. Far. Again thoughts of his far swept in and took over. Would Far actually come up and get him? Grasp an ear and drag him home like a six-year-old? He might. He sometimes treated Nils like a six-year-old. But then, compared to these boys right here, Nils *was* a six-year-old. These boys took on men's labor and absorbed grown farmers' knowledge.

And another thought came. Nils's far would consider a farmer beneath his station. Farmers were dolts, oafs, lazy people. How wrong Far was! These people were smart and creative and highly specialized. It simply was not the same specialization that Far knew. No, up here Nils had learned a healthy appreciation and respect for farmers, something very new to him.

Ingeborg's voice brought him back. "Let me see your hand."

Nils held out his hand, feeling like a little boy again, who had come crying because he fell down and hurt himself.

She unwrapped the bandage and shook her head, tsking at the same time. "You are not as bad as Tor was, but the more you continue to cut hay, the worse it will get."

"Even with it wrapped?" Although how he was to put a glove over the thick wrapping he couldn't imagine.

"There is plenty you could do without injuring it further."

"Like what?"

"Like holding your hands out for measuring yarn." Gunlaug held her open hands about fifteen inches apart.

"Or reading to us while we spin and weave," Kari added.

"Or make butter." Hamme made a face. She was the one assigned to plunge the dasher in the churn up and down to turn cream into butter. Not her favorite job.

"Or you could straighten the hay." Was there a suppressed sort of giggle in Gunlaug's voice?

He looked at Gunlaug. "What do you mean?"

Ingeborg gestured over the cut hay out there. "Make sure it is all lying the same direction and flat. Although you boys did a very good job. Straightening it will not take a lot of work."

"Who usually does the straightening?"

Kari giggled. "The girls. The boys mow and the girls go behind and straighten."

Nils raised an eyebrow. They were teasing him. The thought made him feel like he was a real member of the family, no longer a guest to be taken care of. "Perhaps Gunlaug will teach me to weave on the loom."

"Men weave too, so ja, I will teach you."

"And they spin?"

"Not usually as much. Unless they are wounded and cannot work at men's work."

"You think I am so wounded I cannot do a man's work?"

"No, no . . . uh . . . um . . ." Gunlaug stared at Ingeborg, as if imploring her assistance. Was that red creeping up into her face?

Nils tried to keep a stern look on his face, but when Hamme snickered into her hands, no matter how tight he held his jaw, he could not keep from choking on the laughter bursting out. As soon as he laughed, they all snickered, then true laughter broke out and rocked them all.

Ingeborg dipped her fingers in the vile-smelling salve and slapped some on his palm. "Uff da, such carrying on," which only made them all laugh more.

Nils watched her and recognized the laughter dancing in her eyes until she gave in and laughed out loud too.

"I am sorry Mari and Jon missed out on this," Ingeborg said when they quieted. "She needs a good laugh."

"We can tell her what happened, and she can laugh then," Hamme said with a grin at Nils. "But we will not let you tell her, because you will not tell her the whole truth."

Nils tucked his chin and looked at her from under his eyelashes. He pointed a finger to his chest and shrugged.

Ingeborg tied the knot on the back of his hand. "We all need to get back to work. Any other blisters that I need to look at? Tor, how are your hands?"

"Tougher than shoe leather." He held them out. "I put an extra layer of leather in the palm of my gloves. See?" He turned them partway out. Nils knew this was the first pair that he had finished.

"When will mine be done?" Nils asked.

"I didn't put an extra layer in yours, but soon. I keep falling asleep in the evening when I would be stitching them."

Nils nodded. He was well aware of that, since he had sent the boy up to bed more than once. "I will be pleased whenever you get them done."

Kari followed the boys out to the hayfield, pitchfork in hand to smooth out the rough spots. Hamme washed the dishes, and Ingeborg carried the spinning wheel outside.

"That is not fair," Gunlaug complained. "I cannot take the loom outside."

"I will trade you jobs." When she returned with her basket of wool for spinning, she also brought out part of a fleece and the carding paddles and handed them to Nils. "Here, you should be able to do this—if you want, that is. Hamme will be out to help card in a bit."

He nodded, keeping a sober face, since that was what she was wearing. But if his eyes danced as much as hers, he knew they were in for more laughter.

"Do not laugh now," he ordered, as he laid some of the wool on the metal teeth.

She tried not to laugh, but when he gave her a stern look, she giggled like a little girl, then laughed along with him.

"You need to laugh more."

"We all need to laugh more."

"Very true." He smiled at her and held up the paddles. "Am I doing this right?"

"You will get better with practice." She looked out across the field to where the others were hard at work. With a bit of a nod, she picked up her straight-lying strands of wool, pulled out a small piece, and drew it through her fingers, feeding it through the flyer hooks onto the bobbin. She made it look so easy, and the yarn winding onto the bobbin was absolutely even—no lumps, no thin spots. Nils would not attempt spinning this year. He would never, in the time remaining, master that skill.

With the wheel humming, she looked back at Nils. "You are doing better."

"Takk."

"Eventually the slap and pull of the cards will be easy, and you can forget what you are doing and take part in the conversations or even enjoy a joke or two. You almost look angry at what you are doing."

"I am not surprised. This should be easy and it is not."

"That is like life, is it not? What looks to be easy can sometimes be most difficult."

"When we were little my tutor often said, 'Life is what you make it. You choose hard or easy.' I have a hard time believing that. I did not choose to step in front of the carriage or fall down to the creek. Some things just happen."

"The Bible says all things come from God's hand."

"I have a hard time believing that too. It must be something men say as an excuse or confusion as to the actual meaning."

"Have you read the book of Job?"

"Part of it." He did not mention how few parts of the Bible he had read at all. He had heard more of it than read it himself.

"When you get home, you might read that. Your family has a Bible, right?"

"Ja, that is where all the family history is usually kept. But in our Bible, the family records are remarkably short."

All the while they talked, she kept the spinning wheel humming, and the spindle of yarn grew in size. How she did that, he would never understand. Thoughts of his mother spinning did not fit. She stitched fine pieces, but as far as he knew, neither knitted nor even mended. They had a woman come in to do the mending, and all the women's clothes were made by a seamstress and the men's by a tailor. Had Far's mor done these things? He had no family stories to laugh over and repeat to enjoy like these cousins did. He'd listened to their stories in the evenings, and they all shared one another's lives in a way not only unknown to him but almost of a different world.

He slapped the carding paddles, but only once. The pull and stroke were coming more easily now. Unless he started watching Ingeborg. Then all carding went out of his mind. The smooth actions of her hands, the rhythm of her foot on the pedal that kept the wheel spinning, the dreamy look on her face. What was she thinking?

Did he dare to ask? Nei, but to hope?

22

Two weeks later, Ingeborg gazed out over the hayfield to the stacks of hay dotting the brown of the mown grass stalks. What a job that had been, added on to all the other chores that continued every day. Thanks to Hjelmer's trapline and Tor's fishing skill, they often had meat to go with the porridge, for they had run out of vegetables other than what they could harvest from the wild.

Tor also had hare hides nailed to the walls to dry. He planned to finish tanning them and make mittens in the winter. The pair he had finished as a pattern would go home with Nils, along with the gloves that Nils swore were the finest he had ever had.

With him would also go her heart. Not that he knew that, but one day while she and Gunlaug were talking, she realized that yes, what she felt was indeed love. Love that needed to be kept secret, for she understood that the son of a successful city man and a girl raised on a farm near a small village were not meant to be together. Nils would become a wealthy businessman, even if that went against all he desired. And she? She would become the best midwife possible and go on with her life, because no other man would ever compare to this one.

Soon they would start preparing to head back down the mountains to home. The thought of leaving made her stomach clench. As the days grew shorter, so did her spirits. Back to the strictures of society and to Mor, who would criticize everything she did.

So what is it you want to do? she asked herself.

I want to become the best midwife possible and help babies come into this world and help mothers get strong again afterward. I want to help make people well; I want to learn all about herbs and natural remedies for both animals and people. I want to do what God wants me to do. Lord, I feel so much closer to you up here. Do you live only in the mountains and not in the valleys?

"Are you all right?" Gunlaug stopped beside her.

"I'm thinking about going home. I need to go count the cheeses. It may take two wagons to haul it all. We have done well."

"We also have fourteen new pigs, four new calves, and enough wool to keep your spinning wheel running twenty-four hours a day, if you want."

"With fleeces left over to sell. I believe Onkel Frode will be glad his investment paid off so well."

"Are you never curious as to what has gone on at home?"

"At times, but I so dread returning. Every year it gets harder."

"This one will be even worse."

"Why is that?"

"You will be saying good-bye to Nils."

"I know. I cannot allow myself to think about that."

"Will we wait until they arrive or should we send someone down?" Gunlaug asked.

"Wait. We will get everything ready so that when they come we can load, close up the house, and be gone the next morning."

"All the fleeces are already rolled. We have been using up the kitchen supplies, so the baby pigs will have a wagon to ride in. We have more chickens too, so I don't know if they will all fit in the crate."

"Many things to think about. I am going to go spin until it is time to fix supper."

That night after the others had all gone to bed, Ingeborg and Nils sat in front of the fire, she at her wheel and he on the floor with arms crossed over his bent knees and his chin resting on them. The yellows and reds of the flames danced merrily across the side of his head.

Ingeborg stood up to add more wood to the fire. Sitting close to him was growing more difficult as the days left at the seter grew shorter. "Would you like some coffee?" Anything to get to move around.

"Takk." When he smiled up at her, her heart paused and then started dancing even more wildly than the flames. If only they could remain here and not return to that other life.

She brought a cup and poured the dark brew into it. When she handed it to him, his fingers brushed hers, and she nearly dropped the cup. If this was what love felt like, she was not sure she ever wanted to feel like this again. Or could feel like this again.

She had met the love of her life, and her love for him was
not to be. She returned to the spinning wheel and picked up
the wool where she had left off. At least she understood all
there was to understand about spinning. The bad thing about
spinning was that she could do it with her eyes closed, and
that left her mind free to wander. Perhaps this year, when the
snow was deep and the skiing was easy, she would come up
here with the men when they came to load the hay onto the
sleighs and take it down to feed the cattle. And she would
remember the summer that she met Nils and she would smile,
but the pain of leaving would have dimmed by then, so she
would not weep but be grateful for the time she loved a fine
young man.

She stood suddenly and stretched, unable to settle.

"Can you not sit for a while longer?" Nils asked.

"If you want. I . . . I guess I am just restless this night."

"Did you hear the owl call?"

"Nei, I just heard the spinning song."

"When I came here, I would not have recognized an owl
call."

"I'm sure you don't hear owls calling in the city."

"I might have heard them when I was hiking and camping
but did not know what I heard. Now I know about cows and
sheep and what they eat and how the babies are born and how
to herd them and keep them safe and how to cut and stack
hay. And I have found a woman who has a mind and is not
afraid to speak it and who can laugh and repair broken legs
and blisters and teach children how to do the things she
knows so well. And with a heart big enough to welcome a
very spoiled young man and take care of him and help him
walk again. A woman who knows how to read and can discuss

what she reads and learns new things and weeps when talking with her God and teaches others what love is by the way she acts."

Ingeborg closed her eyes and tipped her head back. The silence was broken only by the crackling of the fire and a sleepy *woof* from one of the sheep dogs sleeping in a covered spot next to the doorway.

Surely he couldn't mean all that. No one had ever said such things to her. No one had ever touched her heart like this.

He patted the floor beside him. "Can you return to sit here?"

She wanted to say *No, I need to leave now.* But instead she did as he asked and sank down beside him yet not close. The urge to reach out and touch his hand raged inside her like an angry wolverine, the fiercest of the predators.

"Do you understand what I am saying?"

She stared into the fire, picked up the poker, and stabbed it into the coals. She nodded, her heart closing her throat.

"Ingeborg, look at me, please."

She breathed a sigh and turned her bent legs the other way so she could see him better. His eyes were dark, his face changing shape with the flickering firelight. Gold glinted in the lock of hair that always fell over his forehead, the lock she so often wanted to smooth back, now grown long and tied back with a sheepskin thong.

Run! Her inner voice screamed a warning. *Do not listen to him!*

But if that was good advice, when did she ever listen to good advice? She opened her eyes again and met his gaze. The shock of it sent tremors clear to the soles of her feet.

"I love you, Ingeborg Strand, and I can only hope you love me in return."

She shook her head. "It doesn't matter how much I love you. This love cannot be."

"You do love me!" He reached for her hand and laced her fingers through his. The warmth of it, the joy of it, choked her up even more. *He loves me. Nils loves me. How can I stand the joy of it?*

"Come, let us go outside and look at the stars." He rose in one graceful movement that showed how strong he had become and pulled her up with both hands. Together, hands locked between them, they opened the door softly so as to not wake anyone and walked a few paces away from the house. One of the dogs stirred, but she told him to go back to sleep, and he settled in again. They stopped and stared up at the arched bowl of the cobalt sky, pinned into the heavens by the pricks of light.

"I will look up and see those same stars when I return to Oslo and school. I will know that you are looking too, and if the stars can shine on both of us, there is hope. We will find a way, in spite of what our families are going to say. I know mine will say plenty, but you, my Ingeborg, are worth braving any storm that I might be with you. Society is no longer important to me. We will find a way."

To be together. She wanted to shake her head. She wanted to dance with joy. She wanted . . . she wanted his words to be true. With her whole heart, she wanted his words to be true. But where or how? Her practical side fought to take over, but this time she refused to allow it even a voice. Let his words be true. That she was not loving in vain.

"You do love me?"

"Ja, I do."

"And you will wait for me? I must finish my commitment to my far to do a good job and no longer act the dilettante.

And then I will come for you." Hands locked between them, he turned to face her. "May I kiss you?"

She meant to say *ja* but the word wouldn't form. Instead, she nodded. When he lowered his head, she raised her chin, letting his lips settle over hers. Warm. Tantalizing. No one had ever told her kissing could be like this, that a simple kiss could send shock waves clear to her fingers and toes and make her heart skip and dance.

When he raised his head, her lips begged for more. But she needed to catch her breath. Could kissing make one feel dizzy? Even the stars were dancing in their assigned places in the heavens. She grabbed on to his shirt front with both hands and felt his heart hammering against his chest. Ah, so it did that to him too? She leaned her forehead against the solid wall of his chest. Had her sister kissed her beloved and felt the same way? Why did she not warn Ingeborg what could happen? Or was she the only one to ever feel just this way?

He placed both hands against the sides of her face and tipped her head back so she had to look at him. "That is what love feels like. Stars bursting and the earth blooming. Fires raging, and your voice calms them all. You are my world, Ingeborg, and I want no other."

This time when he kissed her, her lips took on a life of their own, and she kissed him back. Perhaps wanton behavior, but it seemed the natural thing to do. When she needed to breathe again, she drew back.

"I need to go to bed now. Morning will come too early."

"I know." He heaved a sigh. "I feel our time is running out faster and faster. Ingeborg, I don't want to go home."

"Neither do I, but there is no choice. Once winter comes here, the only way in or out is on skis. And the seter house is not built to withstand winter. Besides, you made an agreement with your far. And you have to live up to it."

"I know." He kept hold of her hands. "But too soon everyone will be telling us that we cannot love each other, that our lives have to go a different way. I will write to you."

She nodded. "And I will answer."

The next morning the weather had turned cold, and they shivered on their way out to do the chores. Back in the house, Mari had the fireplace hot and was cooking the ubiquitous porridge, but she also made biscuits with cinnamon and sugar on top.

Ingeborg paused a moment to watch the porridge bubbling so sluggishly. "Tomorrow we can have eggs, and maybe Hjelmer will bring us some meat when he checks his trapline. We need to go look for dandelion leaves again. It takes a lot to feed all of us."

Mari smiled. "That is one way to know when our life at the seter is nearly over. We run out of vegetables. It is a good thing we always have cheese, and thanks to our chickens, eggs—and thanks to the cows, plenty of milk."

"Ja, being grateful for what we have is the most important thing we do." Ingeborg cupped her hands around her coffee cup. She felt sure the men would be coming to get them either today or tomorrow. How the weather could change so quickly she didn't really understand, but when fall arrived, that was the way of it.

Snowflakes had just started to whirl down that afternoon when they heard the halloo that announced someone was coming. Jon and Hamme ran outside and started to jump up and down and wave as three wagons and a string of horses started down into the valley.

"We almost waited too long," Gilbert said as he dismounted. "When did the snow start?"

"Just a bit ago."

"Can you be ready to leave in the morning?"

"Ja, we are ready to load. We believed you would be coming any day."

"Nils, I have more letters from your far. It looks to me like you have recovered well."

"I have, and takk. I almost thought he would come up here to get me, but I am grateful he listened to reason. He is not a real lover of high mountains these later years." He took the three letters and stuck them into his shirt. "What will we load first?"

"Frode and I will take the cheese. Kris's wagon over there is set up for the hogs. We will drive the rest of the animals down. All the household things will go in the wagon from here."

"We will pray the snow is just a warning." Ingeborg did not look forward to this leaving, all the packing in such a hurry. She and Gunlaug would take charge of the house, and the men would take care of the cheese and the animals. They would have to leave very early in order to get home in one day. The days were growing shorter quickly.

Did the men have the hardest work or did the women? The men had to build a chute to run the pigs up into the wagon. The chickens would be easy to crate once the sun went down. They were easier to catch in the dimness before dawn. And the wheels of heavy cheese. And so many crates.

But someone had to pack those crates with all the bedding and household goods. The grass stuffed in the pallets had to be emptied; it would be pig food. And they must pack the things they would use for breakfast in the morning. Their last breakfast on the mountain.

Early the next morning Mari made the porridge for breakfast again, then broke eggs into the skillet. Eggs did not travel well so she would boil what was not eaten. They poured the morning's milk into the milk cans and fed the rest to the hogs. Everyone folded up their own bedding and stuffed their clothes into canvas bags.

Mari doused the fire for the last time. Ingeborg didn't allow herself time to even think—she just kept on working. They made sure all the windows were closed and the door was shut tightly. Although it was snowing and some had remained on the grass overnight, the sun was trying to come out, making the snowflakes shimmer.

"Good thing we are getting you out of here," Gilbert said as he climbed up on the wagon seat. Ingeborg and Nils climbed onto the wagon next to his. With four wagons, including the one they had kept at the seter, the line snaked across the valley as the cows and sheep fell in behind the wagons and the packhorses.

When they reached the opposite ridge, Ingeborg stopped and looked back. Saying good-bye every year like this did not make it easier. Especially since she knew that looking ahead was not good either. Just dealing with today was enough, and today meant getting everyone and everything down the hill safely.

As they dropped lower, the snow stopped, but rain made the track slippery, causing the horses to work extra hard to keep the wagons from going too fast.

"When does the coach to Oslo come through Valdres?" Nils asked Ingeborg about halfway down.

"Early in the morning. There is an inn in town where people often stay to be ready for the coach."

"Then I shall stay there."

She could feel her heart growing heavy. Every step down the grades brought their good-byes that much closer. While he said he would write, something inside her said this was the last time she would see him. She smiled, not willing to let him see how hard this was for her.

When at last they reached the farm, she introduced him to Far and Mor. Nils thanked them for the time he'd spent at the seter and said he would be leaving for Oslo in the morning. His father's letters had included money for his travel.

Mor looked at Ingeborg with a tiny shake of the head, making sure her polite face stayed in place.

Ingeborg walked him to the road and stepped back when he wanted to kiss her.

He understood. "I will come back."

She nodded and fought to keep her smile in place.

"And I will write. You'll see, Ingeborg. Please trust me."

I trust you, she thought, *but I know how strong the influence from your parents and mine will be.* "I hope school goes well for you, and you show your far what kind of man you are." *You are the man I love. The only man I will ever love. That is the kind of woman I am.* She smiled again and, staring into his eyes for the last time, made herself keep her smile. *I can cry after you leave.* "Takk for all the work you did at the seter." *And for all of our time together. I shall never sit in front of a fireplace the same again.* "Study hard."

He walked backward as if devouring her face. "Until we

meet again, my love." He blew her a kiss, turned, and strode off, his rucksack on his back and not a trace of a limp.

"Good-bye," she whispered. "God bless you." She ignored the tears pouring down her face as she turned to walk back to the house she had grown up in.

Good-bye.

23

Silently, grimly, Nils's mor seated herself at the table. His far pushed her chair in and walked around behind Katja to seat himself. Silently, grimly, Amalia seated herself at the table, and Nils pushed her chair into place. He sat down in his usual place and tucked his napkin into his lap.

Cook set out the roast pork, the potatoes, and applesauce. A young woman Nils had not seen before served bowls of soup to each of them. His parents did not introduce her or even, apparently, notice her.

Dinner had commenced.

Far studied Nils, scowling. "Since this is your first evening home, I assume you have much to tell us about your adventurous summer." His voice was hard enough to shatter ice.

"Other than that the summer did not go at all as I had originally planned, not much. Katja, how has your summer gone?"

She shrugged. "I spent most of it preparing for the academy exams. I passed them."

Amalia picked up her spoon. "And I managed the shipping and receiving ledgers this summer."

Her far stared at her. This apparently was the first he'd heard of it. "I trust you are joking."

"No, I'm not." She was keeping her voice quite steady. "The young man you hired in Nils's stead had no idea how to proceed, and—"

"When I interviewed him, he said he was familiar with our system."

"Familiar with it, ja. But actually making entries, nei. So I showed him how and supervised his work. He's a bit dull, but he eventually caught on and did a serviceable job."

Far opened his mouth to speak, but she raised her voice, pressing on. "I also showed him how to prepare invoices. You may have noticed, Far, that receipts to date this year are considerably in excess of last year's. That is because your clerk was quite in arrears with his work, and not all your invoices had been tendered. We caught you up. Your accounts receivable are now current."

Mor was staring at Amalia. "I do not permit business discussion at the table," she said, keeping her voice steady, and it too was ice, "as you surely know. We will discuss this later."

Amalia nodded and dipped into her soup.

Far studied Nils. "You rather skipped past my question. Have you a fuller account of how you spent your summer?"

"I have been trying to decide how to articulate it." That was not true. Instead, Nils had been thinking about the meals at the seter. No icy glares, no frowns—well, perhaps from Tor once in a while, but never like this— and happy, enthusiastic conversation. People eating heartily, be it soup or porridge or fresh-caught hares. Enthusiasm. Accomplishment. He was thinking about the value Katja would have received up at the seter instead of studying for lifeless examinations. His family was missing so very much! And that was it, right there. His family knew so little about being a family. And he would still have been ignorant, except that he learned about family during those wonderful few months at the seter.

The soup was all right. No hare in it, of course. Mari, not yet eleven, made soup as good as Cook's. "My difficulty is this: I learned so much about myself and about us this summer that I don't know where to begin. I wrote to you about the accident and my injuries. I could not be more pleased to report that my ribs and leg are healed, and I've not had a headache for over two months."

"Excellent news." Mor dipped her head in a perfunctory nod.

"Also, I have very nearly all my strength back after the long convalescence." He paused to finish his soup.

"So you got to go tramping after all." Amalia had finished hers.

"Not really, except toward the end, going to the upper pasture to herd the cattle. My strength mostly was restored by doing chores and cutting hay. Which gave me blisters."

Mor and Far did not approve of cutting hay; he could tell that in an instant.

"Can I see them?" Katja, at least, seemed interested.

"Ja." Nils held his palm toward her. "Can you see them from there?"

"Oh, ja! That's terrible!"

Amalia turned his hand over to see his pink blister scars. "I wouldn't wish blisters on myself, but your summer actually sounds like fun."

"It was!" Nils served himself some pork and potatoes. "And satisfying. You look out across the field at the end of the day, all the hay you scythed piled into a great stack, and you feel a sense of accomplishment. You know, you don't just pile hay up in a big mound. You have to arrange the top two feet just so, just exactly, or rain will get down into it and rot it. Cows can still eat it if that happens, but moldy hay can kill a horse."

"Really! And here they say *healthy as a horse*. They're that delicate, ja?" Amalia was smiling.

Mor and Far were not.

Nils paused for a mouthful of pork. Then he speared a bit and waved it. "There's a great deal of skill involved in raising good pork. And you should see how fast piglets can grow. Double their size in less than—"

"I believe we've heard enough farm stories for now." Mor glared at him, the storm cloud black.

"Baby pigs!" Katja exclaimed. "They must be so sweet. I want to hear more."

"Some other time. Filthy pigs are not a satisfactory mealtime topic." Mor's tone of voice closed the conversation with a slam. *And yet,* Nils thought, *there's part of a filthy pig on your plate.*

"This Saturday," she continued, "there will be an interesting soiree. You, Nils, will accompany me. There will be a young woman there I want you to meet."

Nils tackled the applesauce with gusto. He did like applesauce. "By that I assume you mean she is a marriage possibility."

"We could go so far as to say 'marriage probability.' Her family is nicely situated, and she is well educated. She speaks French, Spanish, and Dutch. Her father owns an extensive parcel of timbered land, good for at least ten years of intensive logging. Your far and I met the family at a formal dinner and were quite impressed with the girl. They are equally impressed with your credentials, particularly your love of schooling."

Love of schooling? More matchmaking games. Nils asked, "A timber baron? Join the two houses, and Far, you would have a fine arrangement indeed. You ship his timber; he provides a ready shipping market. Particularly in Spain, where they're starting to run low on harvestable forests. He can have his daughter translate correspondence. So what about Ingra Grunewald? Is she out of the picture?"

"Her family recently announced her engagement." Mor sounded disappointed.

"Then there will be no union of the two biggest shipping firms in Oslo." Nils finished off his dinner.

"Your snide comments are unwelcome."

They finished their meal in a rigid, cautious silence and rose to leave.

Mor glowered at Amalia. "We will repair to the parlor for tea." It was a command, not an invitation. Nils almost cringed at the tongue-lashing he knew his sister was about to receive. Meddling in men's business affairs? Unthinkable.

Far glowered just as darkly at Nils. He did not have to say *Come.* Nils followed him to the study, telling himself as they walked down the hall, *Stay calm, Nils, no matter what.* But he doubted he would be following those instructions.

Far marched toward his desk, wheeled suddenly, and roared, "You deliberately disobeyed me! I provided for your return, and you deliberately disobeyed!"

"That is true." *Stay calm.*

"Your promises that you would try harder and become the person you ought to be—hollow!"

"Not true." *Serenity. Remember gently sloping pastures with sheep grazing peacefully.*

"And exactly what would you call it if not disobedience?" His voice roared no less ferociously.

Nils managed a peaceful—he hoped—smile. "I could take refuge in a lie and say I was not yet well enough to ride down the mountain on a horse, but I will not. I was well enough. I was ready to travel but not ready to leave. I have learned important lessons this summer."

"Of course you have! How to stack hay. How to count pigs! You are a disgrace to this family!"

Calm flew out the window and over the porch rail. "Stop!" Nils realized he was screaming. Screaming at his far! "Stop listening to your own delicious rage and listen to your son once! Just listen. Hear me out, I beg you. Can you not do that?"

The lion's roar shook the earth. "You dare shout at me? Your far? Leave the room! This instant!"

"No! We're not done here yet. I changed, Far! I'm *not* the Nils who left. I can—"

The door opened and Janssen walked in, balancing his silver tray with the brandy and snifters. He paused, considered, and started to back out.

Nils threw up his hand. "Stop, Janssen! Come back. Serve the brandy, please."

The gentleman's gentleman glanced at Far, hurried over to the desk, and set his tray down. He poured, handed a glass to Far, then one to Nils. With a swift, stiff bow, he hurried out.

The brandy in Nils's glass was jiggling; he was shaking that hard. He forced his voice down to normal. Almost. "Have I ever before shouted at you, Far? Or opposed you? Even once?"

The man scowled.

"Will you take that as proof enough I've changed? That I must reach you. Tell you." He took a deep breath. Several of them. "Your opinion that I was a spoiled child was absolutely correct. Your opinion that I was not adequately applying myself to my studies was also absolutely correct. You believed I had no heart for the company, and you were right. Then my accidents. Both of them. I nearly died, Far. Twice. I spent weeks lying on a pallet or sitting in a chair, unable to walk or climb a hill. I had a great deal of time to think about my life and the direction I want to go."

Why would his far not sit down? The man stood rigid, but at least he seemed to be listening.

"I was rescued by women and children who work like men seven days a week—even the small children. Working for their family. Family is that important to them. And I realized you have done exactly the same. You did not receive your company on a silver platter. You began with nothing and worked tirelessly to build your company. And you built it up in order to provide well for Mor and us children. There is no sacrifice nobler than that."

The man relaxed slightly. Only slightly.

"Now you offer that precious company to me, your son, as my inheritance. You want me to be ready to receive it. And I was behaving shamefully. I am not just saying this to mollify you. I mean it."

The corners of Far's mouth lifted slightly.

"I think I more clearly see how much our company means to you. It is your life. And how much you want your children to prosper as you have prospered. And I am beginning to see that becoming a shipper—a businessman—is not so bad a lot." He took a deep shuddering breath. "So yes, Far, I will apply myself better this year. I will graduate honorably. For the first time in my life, I want to succeed. And I will make certain I am ready to take over, that you can entrust your life's work to me."

The man was studying him. Not glowering. Studying. He too took a deep breath. He turned and walked over to the globe in the corner. He came back and stood near Nils but not in front of him.

"Your promises in the past were all broken. I can't trust you. But we shall see."

What had he expected? Full acceptance? Nei. In fact, this was more than he had hoped for.

"Takk, Far. Takk."

～

"Oh, Nils, she was mad! Beyond furious," Amalia said the next day as she shifted the heavy basket on her arm and continued down the street.

Nils would have carried it for her—after all, it was filled with his belongings—but his own arms were full. They were on their way to his new rooms near the university.

She continued, "My behavior was unacceptable. She said it over and over. And finally, like you, I lost my temper. My patience. I told her, 'I saved Far all that money just by doing the books more efficiently than his fancy clerk, and I trained his new hire so that the man can do what Far needs doing, and you say my behavior is unacceptable?' And then she *really* got mad."

"This sounds pretty weak, but they mean well. They want the best for us."

"The best for you, maybe. For me, they want someone who looks good at a soiree." She shifted her basket again and stopped. "Why are we suffering like this? Hail a hansom. Are you going to go with Mor to that social?"

He chuckled. "Ja, I'll go. The bomb will drop soon enough."

"What bomb?"

"I am in love with a farmer's daughter. She is everything I want in a woman, and she's sweet, tender, gentle, good-natured. . . . She knows as much about treating injuries as any doctor, knows as much about farming as any man, she's an expert spinster—an expert everything. And she is beautiful."

She stared at him agape. "Oh, Nils! Can you imagine Mor and Far when you mention that bit of news! They'll disown you. Cast you out!" But she was smiling. Grinning, actually. "What's her name?"

"Ingeborg Strand. Actually, as farmers go, her family is pretty well off. They have quite a— There! Yo!" he shouted, waving his laden arm, and a hansom drew to a halt beside them.

"Moving?" the driver asked dryly.

"Matter of fact, I am. To rooms near the university to commence my senior year of study. I can't wait!" He helped Amalia dump her burden on the cab floor and climb in over it. Then he called up, "Einar Alley just off the King's Strand. Big square building of three stories."

"Ah, I know the place."

Nils climbed in, settled to the seat, and rapped on the roof. The cab lurched forward.

"Nils, are you sure about this? I mean—a summer romance I can understand. But a farm girl? Nei. You will be courting trouble, huge trouble, from both families. You don't want to do that to her."

"She is worth it, Amalia. Oh, and incidentally, don't fret about Mor's diatribes. When I take over the business, I intend to bring you in as a full partner. Then you can run it while I pose and preen as a handsome figurehead."

She laughed. "And go tramping in your beloved mountains. Ja! I can hardly wait!"

Hardly wait? Nils could certainly wait to go to yet another soiree. Why did Amalia have to mention it? Now he could glumly anticipate posing and preening for a whole parcel of snooty society women. And dream of the mountains and his Ingeborg.

He asked the hansom driver to wait while they carried his belongings, which grew heavier with every step they climbed to the third floor to his new rooms. Then they took the hansom back home. Amalia was right. Why suffer? Besides, it was starting to rain.

⁓

Saturday came all too quickly, and it was still raining. Janssen laid out his attire and helped Nils dress. He joined his mor in the parlor, and they walked out to their waiting carriage as Janssen held the umbrella over Mor. Nils handed Mor up into the vehicle, climbed in to settle in the opposite seat, and Janssen closed the door. The leather seats crackled.

Mor sat quietly with a look of vague disapproval on her face. Nils seemed to be seeing that more and more.

"Mor, who is the new serving girl in our kitchen?"

"The cook's daughter. He wants her to learn service so she can find a good position in some household. I gave him permission to bring her in and train her."

"And I assume you are not paying her."

"Absolutely not. She is inexperienced, and Cook asked me to take her. I did not hire her."

Cook's daughter. Nils had not known that Cook was a family man. He came early in the morning and left late at night. That is all Nils had ever known about him. Nils knew nothing about Janssen either. Or the cleaning maid. These were people with lives beyond the Aarvidson household that Nils had, frankly, never even pondered. Why had he been so obtuse for so long?

"The young woman I want you to meet is Kristina Lindstrom," Mor said. "Lovely girl."

The carriage stopped under a marquee, and Nils hopped down. His leg tweaked a little. It often did if he sat for too long before using it. He gave Mor a hand down and escorted her to the door.

A stolid butler opened the door and stepped aside.

Nils handed him the calling cards.

Sonorously, the fellow announced to no one in particular, "Mrs. Rignor Aarvidson and her son, Nils." Did this man have a family, sons and daughters, who greeted him at the door?

"Ooh, Sonja! I am so pleased to see you!" A rather overweight woman came shuffling up. She was wearing one of those skirts they called a hobble skirt. She could not take steps of more than several inches. Nils found himself contrasting that to Ingeborg's peasant skirt, and her free-spirited stride.

"Monika, I present my son, Nils. Nils, this is Monika Lindstrom, our hostess."

Nils took her fingers in his hand and murmured, "Enchanted, Mrs. Lindstrom."

Mrs. Lindstrom smiled broadly, turned, and waved vigorously. "Kristina! Kristina, come here, dear. I want you to meet our guests."

A most beautiful young woman threaded her way through the other guests to join them. Her hair and eyes were darker than most, and unlike her portly mother, she was quite lithe and graceful, with a full stride. The fashion of a hobble skirt, thankfully, had not reached her yet. So this was the young woman who spoke three languages.

Monika waved expansively. "Mr. Aarvidson, Nils, this is my daughter Kristina."

She smiled fetchingly. "Es verdad, señor. Estoy a sus ordenes." Large brown eyes, like Viennese chocolate. She suddenly got a slightly impish look on her face. She glanced at the two mothers, who were both beaming broadly. "Usted es muy guapo, señor. Me gusta." *You are very handsome, sir. That pleases me.*

Nils caught the joke immediately. Speaking a language neither of the mothers knew, she could make a shockingly forward comment, be very bold, even quite wanton, and they would keep right on beaming. He smiled and purred, "Y tú, señorita, con tu ojo de vidrio y pierna de madera, pareces a una noche llena de estrellas." *And you, miss, with your glass eye and wooden leg, are like a night full of stars.* Was that laying it on too thickly?

She laughed, a delightful tinkling laugh. So she had a rich sense of humor. Again, he found himself comparing Ingeborg. And as he thought about it, although Ingeborg liked a joke as well as the next person, she did not have this sophisticated, ready wit.

The evening was going to be far more interesting than he had anticipated.

24

"I told you he would not write."

"Ingeborg, it has been only two weeks. When was he supposed to start school?" Gunlaug adopted her scolding voice that told Ingeborg right away that Gunlaug was beginning to believe her. "He does love you. I know he does. I saw it in everything he did. He never took his eyes off you when you were in the same room. And all the evenings the two of you spent in front of the fire? He said he loves you. You have to have faith."

Ingeborg nodded, to calm Gunlaug, if for nothing else. "So what have you heard about Ivar?"

"Ivar who?"

Ingeborg nodded, her eyes losing their sadness for just a moment. It settled back in almost immediately. "I'm glad to hear that. I thought you were over him, but now I am sure."

"He is a married man, and I wish him and his family all the best."

Ingeborg weighed her cousin's voice. She could tell when Gunlaug was saying something she thought Ingeborg wanted to hear. It didn't happen often; it was not happening now. "Of course you do."

"Mor said I should go check on Onkel Frode, but Far said he would go. He was supposed to come to our house for supper last night, but he didn't."

"That is not like him."

"No, it isn't." Gunlaug wore a shawl around her shoulders. The cold air had arrived in Valdres too. "I wonder if we are having an early winter this year."

"It will be cold and rainy for a few days, and then fall will come, and we will have a glorious time watching the trees turn as we bring the last of the garden into the cellars. I pulled the cabbages yesterday and hung them from the rafters. Mor had herbs hanging too, both in the house and in the cellar. I found a book on compounding herbs for better results. I cannot wait to try some of those things after the fall work is done."

"Is your mor glad to have you home?"

"I guess. At least she has someone to criticize again. It seems strange to me that she never seems to get after the others. There must be something about me that she does not like. She and Far have both been reminding me that there is no hope for Nils to ever come back. That I need to find a nice man of my own station, marry him, and settle down to raise a family."

"What? Men like that are hiding behind the bushes waiting for us to drag them out and force them to the altar?"

"Isn't that Onkel Kris coming now?" Ingeborg nodded up the lane.

"Ja, and something is bothering him. I better get home."

"Takk for coming. I miss all of our time together. I guess I'll go dig turnips, then the rutabagas. The bins are clean and ready for them."

But Onkel Kris did not continue on home. He turned into their lane and, without smiling, asked, "Where is Arne?"

"At the barn, I believe," Ingeborg told him. "Can I help you?"

"No. I need to talk with him."

Ingeborg watched him stride off. Something was wrong; this wasn't like her Onkel Kris at all. He did not smile, and he always had an extra warm smile, just for her. It was nice to be someone's favorite.

The two men strode out of the barn moments later, wagging their heads, looking shocked and terribly sad. Ingeborg stopped in front of them. "What has happened?"

"Frode died either sometime yesterday or during the night. I found him on the floor. His dog was lying next to him." Kris blinked a few times and continued. "We need to tell our families."

"You want me to run to old Reverend Berger's house? He was Onkel Frode's favorite pastor."

"No. Hjelmer is a faster runner. I will send him." Far sniffed and turned to wipe his nose and probably his eyes.

She could tell he was not thinking clearly. "But Hjelmer is in school." Ingeborg felt like she'd been punched in the stomach, and from the looks of the men's faces they felt the same. Had Onkel been sick? Had something happened during the summer that they at the seter had not heard about?

"Ja, you go. We will go do Frode's chores."

"I know he has not been himself, but . . . he is the youngest of us." Far shook his head slowly, no doubt fighting to understand. He stared at his brother. "When did you see him last?"

Kris closed his eyes. His wrinkled brow said he was trying to remember. "He was out in his garden early in the afternoon.

He was supposed to come to supper last night." He stared at his older brother. "I should have gone to see why he did not come. Maybe if I—"

"Why would you have done that? Did you ever before?"

"No, but . . ." He made fluttering motions with his hands. "You go on, Ingeborg."

Ingeborg took off running, although she wondered why she was hurrying so. There was nothing they could do for Onkel Frode. *Lord God, he is with you now.* She refused to think what this would mean for the families. She arrived at the pastor's house out of breath so stopped to walk the last bit. When she knocked on the door, he answered it, clad in a sweater and his house slippers.

"Why, Ingeborg, welcome." He narrowed his eyes. "What is wrong?"

"Onkel Frode died sometime since yesterday afternoon, which was the last time anyone saw him. Onkel Kris said he is on the floor."

"I see. Come in, come in." As he stepped back, he held the door wide open.

"Nei, takk. I must get back to see what I can do. We will miss him greatly."

"I will be there as soon as I can. What a tragedy. Tell your far we are praying for all of you."

"Tusen takk." Ingeborg turned away, feeling as though she were carrying the whole of Norway on her shoulders. One by one the tears slid out from under her resolve and trickled down her cheeks as she walked as fast as she could home. But the closer she got, the slower she moved.

She entered by the back door. Both families were gathered at her house, other than the men who were still doing chores.

"Mor, I am going to go bring Onkel's milk cows here so we can milk them easier. I'll put them in the side paddock for now?"

Mor nodded, staring at the table. Did she even hear Ingeborg? "We need to make plans."

"Ja." Ingeborg tossed a shawl over her shoulders, gathered up several halters and ropes, and headed toward Onkel Frode's. If her far was still there, he could help.

Onkel Frode. Oh, Onkel Frode! She collapsed to her knees in the middle of the road, buried her face in her hands, and wept bitterly.

Onkel Frode had never been the best at cleaning his house. Ingeborg and either Mor or Gunlaug had always come by to clean at least a couple of times each year. Especially in the spring. Every house had to be spotless before Easter, even if the resident was a bachelor. No good housewife in the whole of Norway or perhaps in the entire world would leave a house unclean for that most holy of days.

Ingeborg was helping clean out Frode's house several days after he was buried. Everyone else, children and grown-ups alike, was pitching in to help finish the harvest and take care of the animals. She mopped the bedroom. Who would live here now? Perhaps Gilbert, even before he married, which didn't seem to be happening soon. That seemed the likely idea. He was the oldest of all the cousins. Unless Katrina and her new husband were invited to live here. So many decisions to make. But at least the house would be clean for whoever moved in.

She found Onkel Frode's Bible lying on a shelf in the bedroom. It was leather bound, big and heavy, with a strap and lock. The lock was not only open but rusted. She lifted the top cover. Despite the fact that he had no wife or children, he had carefully recorded all the huge Strand family's births and deaths on the flyleaf. Perhaps Ingeborg should enter his own death as the last one on the page.

What was this? A folded paper marking the first page of the Psalms. Far's and Onkel Kris's names had been written on the outside in Onkel Frode's unmistakable hand. The urge to unfold it and see what it said had her doing just that before she gave it any thought.

At the top of the page she read, *My last will and testament.* Her gaze traveled swiftly down the page. She closed her eyes and leaned her forehead against the window glass. She felt like ripping the paper into shreds. *Oh, dear God, this will not be good.*

Tradition dictated that the two surviving brothers should divide everything right down the middle, including the precious land. Land that was at a premium because there was so little of it. But Frode decreed that Arne have the land and Kris all the cattle and other things. This was going to bring down ill on everyone. Her far and her onkel were both stubborn men who would do what was right. But was this right? Why had Frode done this? It went against all custom and tradition.

She tucked the letter back into the Bible. *Let someone else find it and break the news. I do not want to be the one.* But how she would love to have Onkel Frode's Bible. *What do I do, Lord? Why will you not answer me? I need an answer now. Or I'll leave the letter in the Bible.* Perhaps that was the answer. As she turned away, another thought exploded in her head. When someone found it, how could she lie and say she'd never seen it? But why would anyone ask her? They most certainly would if she kept the Bible. *I will leave it here and do something else if I am so led. Or Lord, please, you lead someone else to break this news.*

She stripped the bed and hung the quilt outside on the fence to air. The other things she bundled with his dirty clothes to take home and wash. After dusting and washing the inside of the windows, she went on to the next room. She could hear Mor in the kitchen talking with Tante Berthe. Gunlaug was at home, Tante Berthe said, and most likely weaving. Or still gathering the garden produce. That was what Ingeborg had planned to do today, but Mor had insisted she help here.

By noon, when the house was clean and Onkel's personal things were gathered together in a trunk, they shut the door and headed for home and the coffeepot. Ingeborg's soul was in turmoil.

Gilbert was cleaning out Onkel Frode's barn, so she dropped her bundle of wash in the doorway and stopped to talk with him.

"Have they spoken with you yet about living here?"

He shrugged. "In an offhanded way. Far said Frode told him once that he had written a will regarding how he wanted his things cared for. You did not find anything like that in the house, did you?"

Ingeborg ignored his question and blew out a breath. "I'm sure dinner will be ready soon." She picked up her bundle and, carrying it over her shoulder, cut across the field to her far's house. Surely by now the coffee would be hot. Berta was making applesauce from the bruised and wormy apples today. They would pack all the good apples into barrels to store in the cellar.

When they sat down for dinner, Far said grace, then asked,

"Ingeborg, you did not see something like a will in Frode's papers, did you?"

"I did not go through his papers. I gathered them up and put them in the trunk, along with his Bible. You want me to bring them over?" She spoke the truth and yet successfully skirted the real question.

"No, Kris and I will sort through them this afternoon." He shook his head. "I am sure he mentioned a will one time. Although why he would want to make a will, I don't know. Everything is always divided between the remaining brothers when there is no immediate family involved."

Takk, Lord. Let them find it. But the feeling in the pit of her stomach did not lighten. She was sure there were going to be hard feelings. Or would they choose to ignore the will and follow tradition?

As soon as they finished eating, she headed out to the garden. Putting food away for the winter did not cause controversy.

She heard it coming before she saw the two brothers coming across the field from Onkel Frode's. She was back in the garden gathering up the last of the root vegetables, but she could hear their voices clearly. Intent upon each other, they did not notice her as they approached, so she stepped behind the chicken coop and listened. From the looks on their faces and the tone of their voices, they were both very angry. And yelling at each other, something unheard of from her far, who was usually silent when he was angry.

Onkel Kris said, "I say we ignore the will and follow tradition!"

"A will is a binding document," Far said. "The law would say we have to follow the wishes of the deceased."

"But this is our brother!" Onkel Kris shouted. "He must have been out of his mind."

"This was written some time ago. When did you ever see him out of his mind?"

They emerged on the path beyond the coop and continued toward the house.

"One time long ago he was mad at me for something, I cannot even remember what. He probably wrote this then." Onkel waved his arms and shook his fist at the heavens. "If you can hear me, brother, know your paper is causing a terrible division."

"I do not think he meant for that to happen. You know how he loved his land. Only because our father wanted all his sons to have land, did it not all go to me in the beginning."

"That is such a stupid, selfish law. What about the rest of us?"

"You have your land," Far said, his voice gentle, "so give thanks to our father for that."

"But I should have half of Frode's land too. And what about the seter?"

"What about it?"

"Will we divide that too?" Onkel Kris was raging.

Far shook his head. "Come, let us go inside, where the whole of Norway will not hear our disagreement."

"This is not just a disagreement. And I do not want to go into your house. I am going home to my house, on my land."

Ingeborg watched him storm off. The way he stomped his feet could have caused earth tremors. Sighing, Ingeborg hauled her wheelbarrow of rutabagas toward the cellar that was dug into the side of a small rise behind the house. Inside, the fragrances of earth and herbs and stored fruit and vegetables greeted her. Comforting, familiar fragrances.

She would soon take the herbs to the house. Then they would bank the front of the cellar with used straw from the barn, like they did the house, to help insulate it from the winter cold.

They went about the evening chores with sad faces, all of them. Never had there been a rift like this between the families. They always did everything together.

Surely they will come to some kind of agreement, Ingeborg told herself over and over. *Please, Lord, let them not harden their hearts like you speak of the Israelites.* She knew Mor and Far were talking, trying to figure out something else to do. Was there any chance Far would give in and divide the land? Why had Onkel Frode done such a horrible thing? Just because he did not have a son to pass the land down to? By giving Onkel Kris all the animals and machinery and household things, Onkel Frode had given him a lot. Besides, his money went to Kris too. Oh, why had she not torn up that paper when she first saw it? All this could have been prevented.

She was milking when Far picked up a stool and sat down to milk the cow behind her. He looked so heavy, she asked, "Are you all right?"

"Nei. A break between brothers is a horrible thing."

"Ja. Far, do you have any idea why Onkel Frode did this?"

"Ja. I do, but there is nothing I can do about it. We are bound by the law."

"Can you tell me what it was?" She hesitated to ask, but for some reason it was important to her to understand the whole thing.

"You know he did not like Kris's drinking."

"Ja." None of them did, really. A few drinks when at a celebration was one thing, but last winter, it seemed Onkel

Kris was at least half drunk, if not sleeping off a binge, all winter. Maybe it was not that bad, but it bothered his family a lot. She and Gunlaug had talked about it many times, as had Mor and Tante Berthe. Even Reverend Berger had gone to talk to him about it.

"But when spring comes he does not drink so much."

"I know, but he neglects his land at times. You know how Frode felt about the land. A man's job is to take care of his land, so his land will take care of his family."

She had heard that said so many times, it must be true. And neglecting the land would have been the worst thing a man could do. Frode was protecting his land, even from the grave.

That evening Gunlaug brought a letter to the house. When Ingeborg asked her to come in, she wailed, "I cannot. Far said I cannot go in your house. We cannot go in your house, or you in ours, until this is settled." Tears rolled down her cheeks and dripped off her chin. "Oh, Ingeborg, this is so crazy. I am afraid. Far has been drinking, and he is angrier than I have ever seen him. I do not even want to go home." She ended on a wail and turned and trudged down the path.

Ingeborg took the letter to Far and watched as he opened it. His forehead furrowed and his brows collided. He threw the paper on the table. "My brother is losing his mind. Better proof that Frode did the best thing. I will let him be until he cools off. We will not be bound by such an edict."

Better proof that Ingeborg had also done the right thing in not destroying the will. Still, she fought the tears that were like the ones pouring down Berta's and Mari's faces. Surely this could not be happening.

25

If everyone on the other side of the fence was as unhappy as her family, Ingeborg would cry for them both. She knew they were. She and Gunlaug had tried to get in touch, but somehow their fathers learned of it, and she never heard from Gunlaug again. Her far forbid her to read her books for a week. By the end of the seven days, Ingeborg was ready to kill both patriarchs—her term of disgust for them.

No one should be so stubborn. No one. Families were supposed to come first. Not feuding. Of course there was no feuding because there was no contact, for weeks now. There might as well be an ocean between them.

Half of her family was banished, and she hadn't heard from Nils. Where was God in all this? She cried out to Him repeatedly, and as far as she could tell, He was turning a deaf ear. David in the Psalms always went back to say God heard him. And listened. If this was God hearing and listening, she really didn't want to try any longer. No letters, no Gunlaug, no God. And the days were getting shorter and shorter, the darkness growing longer and longer. The Bible said God could see in the dark, that the darkness was like light to Him.

Then why did He do nothing about this heartrending situation?

"Your book says you heal the brokenhearted. Is my heart not broken enough for healing? Can this get any worse?" she muttered, although she would rather be shouting and, if truth be told, shaking her fist.

The cow switched her tail, her way of saying, *Pay attention.*

Ingeborg understood the message, but a manure tail across the face did not make her any happier. She wiped off what she feared was there and sucked in a deep breath. At the same time she reached up to stroke the cow and reassure her that she need not put her foot in the bucket or kick it over.

"Sorry, old girl." She kept her voice soothing and gentled her hands. She was grateful the bucket of milk was not on its side, the milk draining down the gutter. She finished with that cow and made sure she was calm before moving on to one of the cows that had had her first calf up at the seter. The younger ones were not as patient as the older cows, but then perhaps that was a life lesson too. But if age was supposed to make people more patient, what about her far and Onkel Kris?

She swallowed. She could not think of that, or she would get mad again and possibly get kicked this time.

At least it was peaceful in the barn, although too cold to stay out there for long. While there wasn't much snow on the ground—it seemed to come and go—fall had succumbed to winter and was letting them know.

And she still had not received a letter from Nils. *I know I am not going to get a letter, so why keep thinking about it? We*

*had a lovely time, I fell in love, and that is that. Now I must
go forward and stop feeling sorry for myself. It is not doing
me or anyone else any good. We should be getting ready for
Christmas with great happiness. After all, it is December now.*

It was hard to believe that November was really gone.

⁓

"There is a letter here for you," Hjelmer said when he
brought home the mail on his way from school the next day.
He handed it to her, and when she looked up in shock, he
grinned.

"I am glad for you. I know this has been terribly hard."

Leave it to her little brother to observe such things. She
had hoped she was hiding her feelings fairly well. She found
a quiet corner and slit the envelope open. It was not a long
letter, but when she read that he was planning to come to
see her before he had to return to school after Christmas,
she let her hands clutching the letter fall into her lap. Until
she needed them to wipe away the tears. He was coming. He
had not forgotten her.

She read it again. He made no mention or excuse for not
writing earlier; the message was fairly terse. But all that mat-
tered was that he was coming.

And she could not tell Gunlaug, whom she knew would
just say that it was about time.

Dearest Ingeborg,

*If only I could write to you every time I think of you,
but then I would get nothing else done. So instead I am
doing all within my power to live up to my word with my
far. He does not believe I can be trustworthy, and I must*

prove to him that I can and I am. That my life was indeed changed this summer, thanks to the time I spent with all of you at the seter. There was nowhere else where I could have learned all I did in such a short period of time. All the thanks goes to you and your family for taking this dilettante in, doctoring him in both body and soul, and showing him what true faith and love are.

My family is adamantly against the love we have for each other, but once I prove to them that you are the reason for my change of heart, I believe they will have a change of heart also. Both of my sisters are firmly in our camp and want to come up to the seter too. Perhaps we can do that next summer, even if only for a few days. They so want to meet you.

I will be coming to Valdres on the coach to see you right after Christmas and before I have to return to school. I have to see you and hear your voice, no matter how short the visit. I wish it could be longer, but that is the way things are at the moment. I promise to write more often, and we will begin to dream of our future together.

I love you, Ingeborg Strand, with all my heart can hold. I want you to be proud of me too, but I have a feeling that convincing Far is more difficult than convincing you. When I get too sad, I dream again of life at the seter and ways I can use what I learned there to make our family business even more successful and make a difference in more people's lives.

> *Until I see you,*
> *All my love,*
> *Nils*

He signed it *All my love, Nils*. That she would treasure.

That night she took out paper and quill pen and wrote an answer. She kept it short, like he had, but said she would meet him at the coach in Valdres when he told her the day he would be arriving.

All of a sudden, getting ready for Christmas took on new meaning. Or perhaps an old meaning restored. The sorrow of not having Christmas with the other half of their family had surely put a damper on the Jul days. But she would no longer allow herself to mope around.

By the time Christmas arrived, she had finished her gifts for everyone, putting away the scarf and mittens she had knit for Gunlaug in her trunk, where they would wait. Surely, some day, they would be able to be friends again.

"Squeeze together! Make room! The coach is crowded today; make room!" From his seat in the box, the driver waved an arm, but no one was looking at him. Crowded indeed. The seats were full and one young man was sitting on the floor with his knees tucked up under his chin.

Nils smiled. Bright sun. Blue sky. A beautiful day! And he was so bundled up in wool, from his underwear to his coat, that the winter cold could not come near him. And these wonderful rabbit-skin mittens! "I'll ride on top. Look at this fine weather!" He stepped onto a back wheel spoke, then up to the rim, and grabbed onto the luggage rail.

"Eh, it's bitter cold!" the driver warned him.

"Not too cold. You ride up here, ja?" Nils grunted, pulled, kicked, and got himself up on the roof.

"Ja, that's how I know." The driver grinned too and twisted back to face the front.

"You'll not have all the fun!" A young man with a slight German accent, no doubt also a university student, clambered up the wheel. Nils reached out and helped him to the top.

"Me too! Me too, please!" It was the young fellow who had been curled up on the coach floor. The hostler gave him a boost, and Nils and his companion dragged the lad up to the roof with them. "Tusen takk!" The lad settled in between the trunks and carpetbags. "I would rather freeze my nose than be kicked by all those feet on the floor."

Nils extended his hand to the man beside him. "Nils Aarvidson of Oslo."

"Hermann Schneider of Bremen. Studying at the university."

"As am I. And you?" He looked at the lad amongst the luggage.

The boy smiled. "Alvald Thorvaldson, from Bergen. I am an apprentice to my onkel, a blacksmith in Oslo."

The coach lurched forward. He was on his way to Valdres and to Ingeborg!

Apparently the lad had a tendency to motion sickness, and apparently he was just now learning that coaches yaw and sway the most on the top. But he was game and stayed curled up in the nest he had created.

The coach rattled to a halt as men shouted somewhere up ahead. Nils and Hermann got up on their knees to see over the driver's box.

The fellow standing in front of the horses pointed up the road ahead. "A snowslide blocked the road beyond the crossing. It'll be dark before we can get it shoveled out. Best turn back."

"What's the river road like?"

"Passable, but not very good. Some drifts."

"Eh, *passable* is the word I was waiting to hear." The driver nodded. "I'll turn at the farm road just ahead and take it down to the river."

"Should be all right." The fellow nodded as he stepped back.

The coach rattled and waddled forward.

Ja! Oh, ja! Nils's heart thrummed. They would not be turning back! They would stay almost on schedule. A little slower, no doubt, but who would care? They would get there soon.

The driver drew his horses to a halt. He urged them to the left, off the main road. They knew perfectly well where they were supposed to take the coach, and this puny farm track, barely visible under the blanket of snow, definitely was not it. They shook their heads, backed and sidled. Finally, he convinced them to do as he wanted, and the coach lurched its way along a track that was even worse than that track from the seter to Ingeborg's farm. And that was rough.

They came out onto a road that followed close beside a river. The fast-moving river rushed among boulders beside them. Although the larger boulders were snow-capped, the river had not frozen over yet.

The driver suddenly urged his horses faster with a crack of the whip. The coach hit a drift and blasted through. Half a mile farther, they tried to blast through another drift. The coach stopped at an odd angle, bogged down. Nils, Hermann, Alvald, and the other men got out and pushed; sheer muscle shoved the coach through the drift to the other side. All clambered aboard again.

Should Nils take off his boots one at a time to dig the snow out of them, or would his feet freeze? Possibly, but the snow packed down around his ankles was painfully cold.

The coach sped up again. Another drift ahead. The coach bucked. The right side rose up onto the packed drift. The left sank in. Alvald shrieked as two trunks slid together, pinning him between them. The coach was tipping. Nils could feel it go. It was going to land on its side. First that collision with a hansom, then the fall down the ravine, and now a coach accident. With his luck, no one was going to want to travel with him.

People screamed. Horses squealed. The driver cried, "No! No!" The coach roof tilted completely vertical and just kept tilting, flinging Nils away. Icy water rushed over him, filling his face, covering his head. He gasped, sucking in frigid water.

⌒

After Christmas Ingeborg received another note from Nils. He would leave Oslo on the twenty-ninth and be in Valdres on the thirtieth. He was looking forward to seeing her even for a short time.

"You are getting your hopes up in a hopeless situation," Far said, shaking his head. "You need to find someone in our station and start your own family. You are getting to be an old maid, you know."

"There are always widowers looking for someone to help raise their children," Mor added. "That will be a most likely choice for you, since you disdain the young men of our area." Mor had to get a snide remark into her advice. She shook her head while she spoke, her face long and sad. "But look at Katrina, how happy she is. And expecting their first child. Isn't she just beautiful?"

"She is," Ingeborg agreed. Her sister had found a man she could love. Ingeborg knew she had done the same, but the man who stole her heart was said to be beyond possibility. One side of her understood that. Another side insisted on dreaming of a life with Nils. Perhaps if they went to Amerika . . . The thought made her catch her breath. In Amerika, no one cared about stations and traditions like they did in the old country. Someone had read a letter from one of those who had gone to Amerika and moved to the middle of the country—they said the land was free for something called homesteading. Or one could purchase land. In Norway there was no land to purchase.

It was too late to write Nils a letter with this news, for his letter arrived the day before he planned to arrive. But he was coming to see her. A thought made her pause. Mr. Aarvidson expected his son to take over the family business. That did not include a move to Amerika and a farm on the free land.

"I am going to meet Nils at the coach in the morning." She didn't ask permission. She just named her intentions gently. "Do you want me to bring anything from the store?"

Her mor just sniffed and shook her head. Her far looked up from the farming magazine he had borrowed from a friend and shook his head too.

⁓

Berta and Mari whispered with Ingeborg that night in the dark. At least someone was excited for her. "You are going to ski into Valdres?"

"Ja. How else would I get there?"

"How will you ever sleep tonight? I am so excited, and I

am not the one going to meet the man I love." Mari giggled. "I heard him tell you he loved you."

"You did not."

"I did so. I was awake and I heard him—and you too. I could hardly breathe, I was so excited."

"Mari, you are too young to think about love yet."

"But I am almost old enough." Berta's voice sounded dreamy through the darkness.

"Do not be in a hurry."

"I think Jens likes me." The same tone.

"Gilbert is the one we need to be concerned for."

"Oh, you were not here. He took Asti on a picnic last summer."

"On a picnic? Just the two of them?"

"Ja, and he was gone all the rest of the day. Got home again just in time to do chores."

"There were not any cows here to milk."

"I think he felt guilty and used that as an excuse."

"That does not make sense." Ingeborg heard a giggle and realized she had joined in. It was she who had introduced Gilbert and Asti. She took Asti to be a very nice young woman. Ingeborg knew her but not very well. She laughed a lot.

"What did Mor say?"

"'Well, it is about time.'" Berta sounded just like their mor.

Ingeborg tried not to laugh out loud, she really did, but choking was not good either. She muffled her laughter in the pillow. "Good night." This was one of the things she missed at the seter. Darkness that could harbor secrets and time with her sisters. Berta had told her all about the wedding, and Katrina looked so happy. Ingeborg had heard people say that women were even more beautiful when they were pregnant, and Katrina would prove the point.

c⁓

When she woke, she was surprised that she had fallen asleep at all, let alone right away. She could hear Gilbert and Hjelmer stirring, so she knew it was time to milk the cows. She caught herself humming as she dressed. Today she would see Nils again. She could not get through the chores fast enough. It seemed to take forever to milk and feed the cows, spread grain for the chickens, and fork hay in for the sheep. They would be going up to the seter to bring back more hay pretty soon. With all the animals they had to feed, hay disappeared like a magic trick. It was a good thing they cut so much up on the mountain.

After breakfast and Far's reading the Bible lesson for the day, she buckled on her skis and poled off to the village. And to Nils.

The sun glinted on the snow so bright she kept her eyes only half open, and still they watered. She waited outside the inn for a time but finally accepted Mrs. Fiel's offer to wait inside. And waited.

"Would you like a cup of coffee?" Mrs. Fiel asked. "There is no charge."

"Takk, but not now." Maybe later, after the coach arrived, she and Nils could come inside and enjoy a cup of coffee before she needed to leave for home. Dark came too quickly, already hovering.

"I cannot believe the coach is so late. They must have had a breakdown or something." Mrs. Fiel moved her curtain aside to peer out.

By now Ingeborg had removed her outer garments and sat on the bench. Two people were waiting to board the coach and decided to listen to Mrs. Fiel's suggestion to have something to eat. Ingeborg hoped they liked the cheese, since the inn was one of their regular customers to purchase cheese.

Dark slithered in and took over. Still no coach.

"Your mor and far will begin to worry that you have fallen."

"The moon will be up soon. I will wait for that." But she knew she could ski home. The snow reflected the slightest light, and tonight the northern lights would assist to show her the way.

She heard a man talking outside and recognized Gilbert's deep voice. He had come to make sure she was all right.

When he walked in through the door, he looked all around. "He is not here?"

Ingeborg shook her head. "The coach has not come."

"They must have had a breakdown. They would not travel now anyway." Gilbert warmed his hands at the fireplace. "Come, we will ski home together."

Ingeborg stood, feeling stiff from sitting so long. Usually when a coach broke down, they had it repaired and ready to leave again before long, but of course it depended on where it broke down and how much repair was needed. She knew that, but the sorrow at not seeing Nils today wore heavy around her shoulders.

"I will return in the morning. If he arrives before I do, please tell him what happened."

"Oh, I will, Ingeborg, I will." Mrs. Fiel patted Ingeborg's shoulder. "I don't know what could have happened."

Immediately after chores the next day, she skied back to the village. And waited. A coach arrived at about the usual time, although a day late. The driver climbed down, shaking his head. "There was a terrible accident, so bad that some people even died, partly because it was so cold. I do not know any more than that, but none of those passengers was able to continue their journey. I'm sorry to be the bearer of such bad tidings."

Ingeborg thanked him and turned away. How could she find out more? If Nils were able, he would have sent her a message. That horrible foreboding feeling she had felt when he left returned with a vengeance. She was never going to see him again.

She skied home and put her skis away. Without a word, she went up to her bed and crawled beneath the covers, there to lie dry-eyed until she eventually quit shivering and fell asleep. Only to have a terrible nightmare that woke her, screaming.

"Ingeborg, what is it?" Berta knelt beside her and took her shaking hands.

"I . . . I do not know. But a dream . . ." She licked her lips and shook her head.

Berta's voice came gently through the darkness. "Shall I light a candle?"

"Nei. I will be fine." But she knew, deep inside, she would never be fine, not like she used to be, ever again.

26

"I have to know more." Ingeborg mopped at the incessant tears that she fought to hide. She did not need another sermon on the foolishness of her love and her dreams. Mor and Far were both experts at dispensing those lectures, usually at her inability to control the sorrow that threatened to drown her at any time.

Something whispered that perhaps he was alive and terribly wounded and could not write to her. But in that case, surely Amalia would write a letter for him. Did she dare write Amalia a letter and ask? Nei. Perhaps he had not told his family about her; perhaps he had not even been on that destroyed coach, and was going to college and doing what his parents decreed that he do. *Perhaps* was an ineffective word at best. And right now, nothing was best. If Nils was indeed dead, his family would be suffering terribly. They would not want to hear from her.

One side of her mind tried to pray for strength, but it was time to get over the silliness of childhood and trusting that God would indeed live up to His Word, that He cared about

His children. There was probably not even a God, but then she would have no one to be so angry at.

Furious was a better word. If God was who He said He was, then He could have kept an accident from happening that would leave families grieving and heartbroken. But He didn't! What had she or Nils done that was evil or even bad enough to warrant a punishment like this?

Skiing seemed to be the only outlet where she could scream at the heavens if she so desired. But skiing in the middle of a snowstorm was not a good idea. So she wrote out her pain, leaving ink blots and tear washes on all the pages. She longed to talk with Gunlaug, but that too had been taken from her.

What are you trying to do, God? If destroying my life is in your plan, you are well on your way. How could one feel so alone in a family like hers? But she did. She must have been crying in her sleep one night, because she woke with Mari whispering her name, patting her hand, and singing the soothing words that their mor used to use to comfort them. At Ingeborg's invitation, Mari crawled under the covers and stroked her sister's hand and face until they both drifted off to sleep.

January 1879 had not an auspicious beginning. And the darkness of winter did nothing to contribute to feelings of strength and fortitude. More and more, Ingeborg found herself wanting to hide under the covers. Instead, she spent hours at the spinning wheel. At least something good was coming of this. The skeins of yarn multiplied. The song of the spinning wheel reminded her of those days when she would spin and Nils would lie there, or sit there, and watch.

The thing that surprised and saddened her even more as the winter continued was her anger at Nils. Why was she angry at him? Because he'd left her. As if he had any say in the matter. If only he had not been coming to see her. He might still be alive; that is, if he was truly dead. The not knowing was driving her ever deeper into a black pit that she could only label despair.

What if something terrible was happening with Gunlaug, with the cousins, at their house? When Ingeborg allowed herself to think about that, she added Far and Onkel Kris to her angry list. Because they were acting like spoiled children—well, at least Onkel Kris was. All of the rest of them were miserable.

But in spite of her wish to hide or die and be away from her thoughts and her tears, life continued around her. Mari and Hjelmer went to school. The animals were fed and watered. Good smells came from the kitchen, and the woodbox was kept full of both wood and peat, since wood was at a premium. Hay brought down from the seter was feeding the animals; food brought in from the cellar was feeding the family. The romance between Gilbert and Asti was one bright spot in a dark world.

When Gilbert admitted he was going to ask Asti to marry him, Berta and Mari wanted to help plan the wedding. What date?

"I have not asked her yet," Gilbert said, his face growing red. "I will tell you what she says."

"She is waiting for you to ask," Mari advised.

"How do you know that?"

"We girls have ways of gaining knowledge that you men know nothing about."

Ingeborg felt a giggle arising, an astonishing thing. "Good for you, Mari." *You tell him.* Her face nearly cracked in a smile from lack of practice.

Mari ran over and threw her arms around her big sister. "You are coming back," she whispered in Ingeborg's ear.

"Perhaps I am." Ingeborg threw more wood on the fire and returned to her spinning. Even the song of the wheel sounded different. She looked out the frosted window to see sun glinting on the crystals and water dripping from the icicles. Was this February's promise of spring? Spring was so needed, not only in the world around her but in her soul. *Takk, oh Lord,* she whispered in her heart.

That afternoon when he came home from school, Hjelmer had a letter for her. When she gave him a questioning look, he shrugged. Nils's handwriting was not on the envelope.

She took it in to sit by the fire and in front of a window so she could read it. As she opened the packet, a newspaper clipping fell into her lap. She read the letter first—straight, elegant handwriting in a fine hand.

My dearest Ingeborg,

By now you will have heard the news concerning my brother, your Nils. I fear you may not have received details, so I am enclosing the Oslo newspaper's account of the accident that took his life.

Please allow me to address you as Ingeborg rather than as Miss Strand. Although we have never met, I feel I know you intimately, for Nils spoke so often and so highly about you. Oh, he was smitten! He was absolutely determined to court and marry you, even though my sister and I tried our best to dissuade him. And, we see in retrospect, his course was the right one. A love like his would have overcome any adversity, and your strength and character would have won over any objectors.

He told us about his time at the seter, his forays into farming and livestock husbandry, his often humorous attempts to become a man of the soil, if only for a short while. Those weeks on the mountain changed him, Ingeborg. You changed him. He climbed your mountain a spoiled dilettante and came down the mountain a greatly matured man, determined to do well and make a difference.

When the constable came to the door with the awful news, our parents could not immediately accept it. My father had despaired of Nils ever becoming worthy to take over Aarvidson Shipping. But he saw the profound change in Nils. Far is a cautious man, a demanding man, and he did not immediately acknowledge that change or his new trust in Nils. Yet, as the holidays approached, he grew more relaxed, became much happier, if you will. He was seeing his most fervent dream come true at last.

Nils saw another world and it made his life, short though it was, richer for the experience. I wish that one day I could meet the woman who made such a difference. I think I want to be more like you. I do so love working in my father's business, but my mother is adamantly saying that is not proper for a young woman like me. But thanks to my brother's courage, I will step outside the bounds of society and into the world of business. I am good at it, like you are good with so many things.

If there is any good thing that has come of this trag-edy, it is this: My brother learned to love not just a woman but a whole family, and he showed us how to love each other. Our family has become more caring and has drawn closer together in these last few weeks. See! This letter has rambled on and on. But I wanted you to know how very much you have given us, yes, we who have never met you. You gave our son and brother happiness. And through him you gave us love and one another.

> *With warmest love and*
> *my deepest condolences,*
> *Amalia Aarvidson*

With her eyes wet and burning so that she could barely see, Ingeborg laid the letter aside and unfolded the newspaper clipping. Amalia had penciled the date in the margin.

Tragedy struck when the weekly circuit stage serving the villages of Nes and Valdres, continuing to Voss and Bergen, overturned, plunging into an adjacent stream, which incident resulted in four deaths. According to statements by survivors, the coach lay partially submerged among large rocks, and the passengers inside, four men and two women, were able to assist one another in escaping to shore. Two men continued up the road into Valdres to summon assistance while the remaining four managed to build a fire, maintaining it by breaking up wood from the coach and wheels. Rescuers arrived at dark and escorted the survivors to safety. In addition to the six persons inside, the coach carried on the roof three passengers and the driver. All four perished.

The deceased:

Hanni Holstrum, 43, driver

Hermann Schneider, 19, student

Alvald Thorvaldson, 12, blacksmith's apprentice

Nils Aarvidson, 22, student

"At least now I know." She laid the letter in her lap and stared into the fire. And suddenly, as ardently as she had wanted to know, now she did not. Before, there had been the tiniest flicker of hope that he had survived the accident, that he was not on that coach at all, that he had forgotten Ingeborg and found another. Anything. Just that he was still alive.

Nils was gone. He would not be coming back. She felt like a door was closing on that part of her life. She now knew what love—deep love—felt like, and she would always treasure the memory of that young man who said he loved her. And was sure she had changed his life. Amalia confirmed that.

Takk, Lord God. I asked to know for sure and this arrived. That door is indeed closed. Amen. She folded the letter and tucked it into her pocket. She thought of throwing it into the fire but left it in her pocket. It might serve some good one day.

⁓

A week or so later, her mother came in to sit and knit in front of the fire. "I have a situation where I can use your help."

Ingeborg looked up. "Ja, what is it?"

"I have two mothers due at the same time. If by chance they go into labor at the same time—this is a slim chance, as you know, but I want to be prepared—I want you to come with me, and I will leave you with Mrs. Hanson. This is her third, so she is an old hand at having babies, and I will go on to Mrs. Larson. This is her first, and there might be a chance of difficulties. You will come with me?"

Ingeborg nodded, her heart smiling. "Ja, I will. Takk." She thought a moment. "Mor, have you been able to talk with Tante Berthe at all?"

"Nei, and it breaks my heart. I heard from someone else that Kris is drinking even more than usual, and a mean streak is emerging. I am so afraid they are all suffering under this edict. He even removed his children from the village school. So no one sees anything of them. As if they moved far away."

"Are they going to a different church too? They never came to ours."

"I doubt they are going to church at all."

Ingeborg's heart ached for Gunlaug—all the others too, but losing her was almost as bad as losing Nils. "How easy it would be to hate Onkel Kris."

"No, do not say that. We cannot hate those of our own family."

"I know Onkel Frode did not want something like this."

"I know that too. But he made a choice, and we are all paying for his choice. That is just the way life can be."

⁓

A few nights later, a knock came at the door, and they learned that Mrs. Hanson had gone into labor. Hilde bade them to wait and went for her things. She hadn't been gone for an hour when another knock announced that Mrs. Larson was asking for her.

So Ingeborg bundled up, took her basket, and told Mr. Larson to take her to the Hanson farm and wait. She took over for her mor, as they had planned, and stepped in beside Mrs. Hanson.

The lady, voluminously pregnant, was walking up and down in her kitchen between the fireplace and the table. Back and forth, back and forth.

"It's good to see you, Ingeborg. You came with your mother for the last one born. Let me see . . ." She paused and waited until the spasm was past and continued walking. "That was about fifteen months ago. He is sleeping soundly in the children's room, and now we will see this one into the world." They paused again.

From the floor came a splashing noise. She sighed, "Oh, my water broke. I am sorry to make a puddle. Now this should speed things up."

"Do you want to lie down yet?"

"Nei. The pains are not close enough together yet. Besides, I enjoy walking and talking with you." She panted again. "But perhaps we should go to the bedroom. I do believe they are getting worse, but let us walk some more. I am so sorry to hear about the horrible feud going on between those brothers. All these years we have pointed to the three and marveled at how well everyone got along and worked together. Not seeing Kris's family in church every Sunday has made many sad."

Ingeborg nodded. The quiet of the birthing room made sharing easier. "We are all suffering from the rupture. I am sure his family is in terrible shape, since at least the rest of us do not have to live with someone drinking to excess."

"I thank our God for that. I told Mr. Hanson if he ever came home drunk, he would sleep in the barn, and he knows that I mean business."

"Good for you."

"And if it happens a second time, he need not come home, because both the house and the barn will be locked."

Ingeborg wiped the smile from her face. What a shame that her tante was not that strong. Or had been back in the early days when she might have been able to stop it. *Might* was another word like *if*. One could always look back and say things might have been different, if . . .

What was it that made one man fall into the temptation to drink too much and another be able to resist? Another of those questions to which she would probably never receive an answer.

Mrs. Hanson gasped. "I think we are ready for the next step." She lay down and positioned her legs just in time. The head appeared. Good, a normal birth. The baby, a healthy pink, beautiful little girl slid into Ingeborg's waiting hands and immediately screwed up her face. She did not whimper but gave a lusty yell.

Ingeborg laughed. "She is not happy with this release from warmth and comfort."

"I do not blame her. I think we shall name her Ingeborg after you. I want my daughter to be a fine, upstanding woman with love and compassion, just like you."

Ingeborg let the tears roll. The miracle of holding new life in her hands made everything else dim in comparison. She laid the baby on her mother's chest and draped a small blanket over her. "You two get to visit a bit while I clean things up, and then I will wash her." *And dress her and give this new bundle of life back to her mother to nurse.*

Lord, I believe you are calling me to be a midwife and help other women, but somehow, I do wish that I could be that mother and feel the joy of nursing a new baby that grew in-

side of me. God willing? I do not know, but things look rather dismal for this dream right now. I do not even have a man in my life.

Near the end of February, Ingeborg's mor received a letter from a cousin who lived in the next village to the north, asking her to come and visit. Their daughter was pregnant, and she was concerned. "'I hope you can look at Anna and tell us if there is anything special we need to do.'" Mor read from the letter.

She looked up at Ingeborg. "I think we will go."

"We?"

"Ja, for some reason I think it is important that you go with me. Your training needs to include more house calls. And this will give us a break. We used to go visiting between families, but for some reason we do not do that as much anymore. We will take a horse and sleigh."

"Without asking Far?"

"We will ask, but he will say yes."

Two days later, Ingeborg was driving the horse and sleigh to visit Mor's cousin. She stared down the lane to Onkel Kris's house as they passed by. Although no one was out, smoke was rising from the chimney.

Mor said wistfully, "I think of her, of them, every day."

"So do I."

When they arrived at Mor's cousin's house, one of the boys took the horse and sleigh, and Alfreda Knutson met them at the door. After the greetings and the catch-up with family news, Cousin Alfreda leaned forward. "There is nothing definite to point to that I can see, but I want you to talk

312

with Anna and see if you can discover what it might be that is making me suspicious."

"Of course we will." Hilde smiled from her cousin to Ingeborg. "Ingeborg has a good sense when something might be wrong. I want her opinion too."

Ingeborg swallowed the shock of hearing such news. What was happening to her mor? Never had she praised her, not even given a veiled suggestion of praise.

Anna smiled from across the table. "Mor has a tendency to worry about me, but I keep telling her that I feel wonderful. I am so looking forward to giving Roald either another son or the daughter I carry. She will be old enough to travel with us to Amerika without being an infant."

"When are you planning on leaving?" Hilde asked.

"Next fall."

"Mor." A little boy with eyes the blue of Norwegian fjords and hair so blond it was near to white ran in to ask his mother something. Anna bent over to listen to his whisper, answered him softly, and he ran back to play with the other small children.

"That is our son Thorliff. He is the light of his far's eyes." Anna's eyes shone with pride, and she smiled at Ingeborg. "I had no trouble when he was born. The midwife said I was made for bearing children easily."

"Well, we came all this way, so let us go in another room and see if we can find anything of concern."

Ingeborg watched Anna walk before them into the downstairs bedroom. She seemed to favor one side. "Does your back bother you?"

Anna smiled over her shoulder. "It did not until the baby has gotten larger and is pulling on something. I felt about the same with Thorliff."

"I see."

"Please lie down on the bed," Hilde instructed. With Ingeborg on one side and her mor on the other, they felt all around the growing belly. Ingeborg focused with her hands, seeking anything unusual.

"Anna, what is it your mor has noticed?"

"I am not sure. She just senses things at times. Always has."

"I am not finding anything different or unusual. You seem to be a healthy young woman in the later months, nearing confinement. Ingeborg?"

"Nothing. But . . ." She moved her hands over the mound again. Still nothing, but why was something bothering her? She decided to talk with Anna's mor. She felt down Anna's legs and feet. No swelling. When she listened with her ear to Anna's belly, she could hear two heartbeats. Just as she should. She extended a hand to help Anna sit up.

"We will all pray that you have another healthy baby like you did before."

"Ja, I know I pray that and Mor does too. Takk for coming and taking time like this, all because of one of Mor's feelings."

"Rather safe than sorry. If your feet and legs start to swell up, you make sure you put your feet up several times during the day."

"I will. Takk, tusen takk."

Later, when Anna's mor described her sense of unease, Ingeborg almost said she felt the same. But she had not evaluated pregnant women often enough to make a solid judgment. They were spending the night with Alfreda, so Roald came for supper and to pick up his wife and son.

Thorliff looked so much like his father that Ingeborg smiled when she met him. "You have a fine son."

"Ja, we do, and we are grateful." They talked about the plans for the trip to Amerika during the meal, and afterwards Roald took his family back to their own home.

The next day on the trip back, Mor asked Ingeborg what was bothering her.

"I think I feel the same as Alfreda. But I have no idea why, and there were no symptoms to support my feeling." She heaved a sigh. "I pray all will be well."

"Ja, me too."

27

Ingeborg stopped on her way in from milking one morning and sniffed. Ja, the air definitely smelled like spring. Of course there would be more winter, but the breath of it right now made the promise that spring was indeed on the way. The days were growing longer again, and with the sun out, the icicles would be dripping. A definite harbinger of spring.

She thought back to the day before. She couldn't remember thinking of Nils even once. Perhaps like spring coming, she was on the mend too. Going back up to the seter would revive all those memories, though she could deal with that now. But not having Gunlaug and the other cousins up there was a different matter. How would they manage? Tor and Kari had already said they wanted to return, but Anders was such a hard worker, and little Jon would not have time to grow into the boys' work when they worked like men. But the biggest loss, in her mind, was Gunlaug. How had she endured this winter without her best friend? She shook her head. How were they? Did they never go to town or church or school?

She carried the buckets to the springhouse and poured

the milk into the cream pans. Several of the cows were dry now, so they were not getting as much milk. It looked like it was time to make butter again too. That could be sold to the store and the inn. They were running low on cheese too, but that was the cycle of it all. They had sold all they could, and now the rest waited for them to eat before the summer's cheese-making progressed again.

She returned to the house, where breakfast was ready to put on the table. "Did you bring in milk?" Berta asked.

"Nei. No one asked me to. But I'll go get some. Are you planning on churning butter today?"

"Is there plenty of cream out there?"

"Ja and no more butter."

When they all sat down at the table, Far said grace, and then Mor passed the food. Bowls of porridge to start, then ham mixed with eggs.

After they finished eating, Far looked at Gilbert and point-blank asked, "Are you serious about that Edberg girl?"

Ingeborg closed her eyes and shook her head slightly before watching the red rise on Gilbert's throat. He embarrassed so easily. Had he even kissed her yet?

"Asti? I . . . uh . . . ja."

"Is she serious about you?"

Gilbert shrugged.

"Ja, she is." Berta filled in the painful silence.

Gilbert stared at her. "How do you know?"

"Unlike you men, girls talk together."

"So?"

"So, Rhea said that Asti told her that she was so hoping you were going to ask her to marry you. Every time she saw you, she hoped that would be the time." Berta rolled her lips together to keep from laughing at her brother's face. How many shades of red could he turn?

Ingeborg glanced at Far and had to look back down quickly. Merriment was dancing in his eyes, and he too was trying not to laugh.

Mari piped up, "I think you should ask her soon and make sure the wedding is before seter. I missed the last one and do not want to miss this one."

"I . . . I was waiting until I could afford to get married."

Mor's head bobbed. "That is good, but Mari is right. We should all be here for the wedding. Where are you thinking to live?"

"Well, I was hoping we could live in Onkel Frode's house. I know there is not furniture or anything there, but it is a good house, and it needs someone to live in it."

"Have you and Asti talked about anything like that?" Mor asked.

"No. Why would we if I have not asked her to marry me yet?"

"I hope you talk with her more than you do with us around here." Berta crossed her arms. "Just the two of you will be mighty lonely if you do not."

"What do you know of people being married?" Mor asked, sipping her coffee.

"I have eyes to see with, and as I said, girls talk."

"So if girls talk, what have you heard about the family next door?"

Berta shook her head, sadness taking the shine out of her eyes. "Nothing. It is as if they moved away, and no one knows where they went."

"We know they are there, because there is smoke from the chimney every day," Far added.

Ingeborg glanced at her father out of the corner of her eye. So he did care, even though he was still angry at Onkel Kris. Two brothers should be able to settle things like this. The Bible said so. She had read the day before that they were not to let the sun go down on their anger. There had been many sunsets since the big fight happened. Maybe it would have been better if they had truly fought it out with fists and not let this terrible silence ever start. But then, it was easy to look back and wish you had made a different decision.

Hjelmer looked up from stirring his coffee that was half milk, as was Mari's. "No one has lived in Onkel Frode's house. The mice probably moved in like they do up at the seter."

"Most likely. It will need a good cleaning. We will have to either make or look for some furniture."

Gilbert pushed back his chair. "I have not asked her, and she has not said yes. Do not act like we are married already." He stood and, snatching his hat and coat off the pegs by the door, slammed out.

Mari and Berta looked at each other and giggled. Mor and Far looked at each other, both with an eyebrow raised. Ingeborg pushed her chair back. "I will be spinning, and then I may go out and check that cow again. She has a sore on one teat, and I will put some salve on it." Such a distance there was between today and her solitary skiing during the winter. Today felt like spring, and she wanted out of the house.

"You could churn the butter," Mari called.

"Ja, but so could you. I will help you memorize that poem if you want."

"I'll bring the churn in there, and we can do both at the same time."

Mor joined them a bit later with her mending basket in

319

hand. She sat by the fire and darned wool stockings while her daughters did their jobs. Mari worked on her poem, and Ingeborg, who still remembered the poem from when she had to memorize it, prompted Mari. The spinning wheel hummed.

⌒

Three days later, when Hjelmer returned from school, he had a letter for Mor.

"Oh, from my cousin. The baby should be born by now, right, Ingeborg?"

"We will see if our idea of it being a girl was correct."

Mor opened the letter, read a few lines, and gasped, her hand to her chest.

Ingeborg's heart went thump. "What is wrong?"

"Anna died in childbirth. Both Anna and the baby. Two weeks ago. She started to bleed and the midwife could not stop it."

"Oh, nei." Ingeborg shook her head and kept on shaking it. "Nei, that cannot be. Oh, that poor man and little Thorliff. His mor is gone."

"Alfreda says Roald was beside himself but since has gone even more quiet than usual. Thorliff is staying with them for right now."

Ingeborg closed her eyes. She could still see the little tow-headed boy with eyes of such a vivid hue that one would never forget them. How could his far take him along to the new land by himself? But to leave him behind? That was even more unthinkable.

Her heart ached for that little child. His mor had loved him so. It was evident when he came to ask her something. They were all so looking forward to the trip to Amerika. Probably

Roald would not go now. Not that she knew anything about him, but she could not get the thought of the little boy out of her mind. He was too young to understand. He would just not be able to find his mor.

Ingeborg wagged her head. "I feel so sorry for him and for Thorliff. What do you think they will do now?"

"My cousin goes on to say that the Bjorklunds plan to go ahead after all. His brother Carl and his wife will be going too. They already have the tickets and they would lose money if they gave them up."

Ingeborg returned to her spinning. Far was talking about shearing the sheep early this year if the weather did not turn real bad again. He too was aware how few they would have to work at the seter. One more example of how their lives had changed. For one who always looked so forward to the summer at the mountain farm, Ingeborg had a hard time reminding herself that she needed to start preparing.

"So did you ask her?" Mari pointedly asked Gilbert several days later when the family was sitting around the table after they had finished their dinner.

Gilbert gave her a dirty look and heaved a sigh. "Ja, I did. Last night."

"And?"

"And what?" He glared at his little sister.

"And what did she say?" Mari's eyes were twinkling. Was she doing this just to embarrass him? Would a little sister do such a craven thing? Ingeborg almost smiled too.

His face reddened again. "She said ja, she would be honored to become Mrs. Gilbert Strand. Are you happy now?"

"So when is the wedding?"

"Probably in the fall sometime. She suggested that, and I said takk."

"That is all you said?"

He glared at her. "Mari, this is a private matter. We will get married, and that is all you need to know." He pushed his chair back and, grabbing his hat and coat off the peg, stomped outside.

"I think he is mad."

"I think you may be right. That was a bit rude, you know?"

"Well, if I do not ask questions," Mari said, "how will I ever learn the answers?"

Ingeborg looked down the table at Far, who was moving his silverware around at the side of his plate. It was good to see him smiling for a change. There had not been a lot of smiling in their house this winter. She asked Mor, "Will you send Roald a letter of condolence?"

"I could," she said, "but perhaps, Ingeborg, you would do that? You are better with words than I am."

Something was happening. Another compliment from her mor. "I would be glad to."

She helped Mari clean up the remains of dinner and tidy the kitchen, but her mind was flying off to far places. Last winter had been like all other winters. Last spring had been like all other springs. But last summer at the seter the world suddenly turned over on its head, and nothing was like what had been. Nils, Onkel Frode, the family rift, Anna's death, each one ruining Ingeborg's life in a new way. Ruining? Ja. God promised He was overseeing all this, but to Ingeborg, it absolutely seemed like ruin. Why, she might even put Mor's sudden compliments on the list, for they were an abrupt change from the usual, the expected. There was nothing old and familiar and comfortable to hold on to. Nothing. She was cast afloat.

Spinning was old and familiar, and there was quite a bit of that fine wool yet to spin. With the kitchen cleaned up and Mari off to do her schoolwork, Ingeborg settled herself into the warm little inglenook with her spinning wheel and a bundle of fine wool. She did not even need good light for this, for spinning was done more by feel than by sight. She anchored a new tuft in the bobbin and patiently drew it out, stroke by stroke, winding it through the flyer hooks. Another tuft, draw it out, another . . . and then she sat back and let her fingers do the work while her mind wandered, sometimes to places she savored, other times to places she didn't want to think about. But then, that was old and familiar too. Her brain certainly had a mind of its own.

Nils. Ah, Nils. According to Amalia's kind letter, Nils learned to love at the seter. A new thought popped into her head. The coach from Oslo was crowded, so he rode on the roof to allow more room for others inside. A selfless gesture; he had been making sure someone else had more comfort. Too young to die. Nils had been too young, but God had a reason and let this happen. She would always remember the young man she had argued with and introduced to new ways of thinking and laughed with—and fallen in love with.

Her life had been ripped apart. And the Aarvidsons' too. How horrible for Nils's family to lose their son like that. Then she thought of her mor and far losing their son to Amerika. She knew what became of Nils, but they lived day to day never knowing for sure what had happened to Bjorn. Knowing made a world of difference, for good and for bad.

And while she was thinking about beaux, why was Gilbert

so angry and defensive about asking for Asti's hand? Was it purely embarrassment, or was something else afoot?

And Gunlaug. Poor Gunlaug. Poor all of them.

And Anna and her newborn, and Roald and Thorliff.

And Onkel Frode. For some strange reason, he was beginning to fade in her memory. No, not in her memory but in her pain. It was a curious difference. His empty house would become home to a new family, probably Gilbert's family, a change totally unanticipated half a year ago.

No wonder the whole world was topsy-turvy!

But now it was spring. New life, new beginnings, new hope. *Takk, Lord God. Please forgive me for doubting you these months, for my anger, for blaming you. I now know that you did not leave me, but I left you and wandered in my own dark land. But you are bringing spring back into my heart too. Such a lonely and sad winter. Now if you could please heal the anger between two brothers, who should be holding each other up with love and grace instead of closing the door and locking it. Amen.*

⁓

Three weeks later winter was back and howling around the house, as if fighting the last battle of the season before spring could come and bring new life. But that was old and familiar too. Winter always did that—brought one last pounce when you least expected it. Ingeborg was on to it. She built up the fire and escaped the storm by spinning.

That last storm also brought a birthing. For some reason, babies seemed to prefer arriving during storms, so Mor wrapped up well and went out. When she returned, there was a letter waiting for her on the table.

Ingeborg met her mor in the kitchen. "How did it go?"

"All is well. Mor and baby son are sleeping soundly, and the far is very grateful." She picked up the letter. "From my cousin." Slitting open the envelope, Mor pulled out the page and leaned close to the kerosene lamp to read it. "Why, Alfreda writes that Roald is looking for a wife to go with him to Amerika and help with his son." She looked up at Ingeborg. "She says she thinks you would make a very good wife for Roald and a good mor for Thorliff."

Why, of all the ridiculous . . . Ingeborg shook her head. "What nonsense! I cannot become his wife Anna all over again. He needs time before he remarries. Time to heal."

"But they are leaving in the fall or winter, I am not sure which. And that little boy needs a mor. Roald Bjorklund is a fine man, a hard worker and, according to Alfreda, has always been a good provider for his family. He is a good Christian man and his brother Carl and wife Kaaren will be going too." She looked up from the letter. "Ingeborg, this is a good idea. You thought you loved a young man, but he is gone. Many marriages start with a situation like this, and the two people learn to love each other over the years. Besides, you will make such a good mor for that little boy who needs you so desperately."

"He will find someone, but it will not be me. Good night." Ingeborg nodded and headed up to the loft to her bed. How could Mor say such a thing? *"You thought you loved a young man."* There was no *thought* about it. She had experienced true love. Lasting love. Amalia claimed Ingeborg taught Nils to love, but Nils taught her what true love is. And besides, what could Alfreda be thinking of to write a letter like that?

Only three days later, spring won the war. The snowbanks

melted back, and the grass greened up as soon as its snow cover left and it could reach for the sun. For the first time since Nils walked out of her life, her spirit did not just lift—it soared. *Thank you, Lord God!*

A week later Ingeborg was gathering up the kitchen waste to take out to the pigs when she happened to glance out the window. A man rode into the yard and dismounted, flipping the reins over the rail out front.

He looked familiar. *Why, that is Roald Bjorklund. Whatever does he want?* She hastened out to answer his knock at the door. "God dag, welcome to our farm."

He removed his hat. "Takk. I see that you remember me."

"Ja, I do. How is your little Thorliff?"

"He is still staying with Anna's mor so that I can continue working to raise the money for our trip to Amerika."

"Oh, excuse me. Come in please. I am not sure what has happened to my manners. Would you care for a cup of coffee?"

"Nei, takk." He stepped inside, and she realized that tall as she was, he made her feel small. That was unusual.

"Are your mor and far here? I would like to talk with the three of you."

"Far is up at the barn, and Mor is out hanging bedding on the line. We are in the middle of spring cleaning, so everything is in disarray. I will go get them."

She hurried up to the barn and asked Far to come down, then out to the clothesline to ask Mor.

Mor frowned. She didn't like spring cleaning to be interrupted. "Who is it?"

"Roald Bjorklund, your cousin's son-in-law." She wasn't

sure if that title still fit, but she couldn't think of what else the relationship would be. "He says he wants to talk with the three of us."

"He came all this way? To talk to us?" Disbelief colored her voice. "Of course, I will come. Did you offer him coffee?"

"I did."

"Berta!" She waved an arm toward the line. "You finish hanging these up. I will be back soon." She walked beside Ingeborg to the house. "Did he say for what?"

"Nei. Just that he wants to talk to the three of us. He is sitting at the table."

When they entered the house, Far was shaking hands with Mr. Bjorklund.

Ingeborg hung back and let Mor join them. Whatever could he be there for? It had to be important to have come this long way.

28

"The nerve of that man!" She could not believe what Mr. Bjorklund had asked of her yesterday. How could he think any woman would agree to it.

The cow she was milking shifted her back feet, a warning.

Not wanting a tail across the face, Ingeborg sucked in a deep breath and unglued her shoulders from her earlobes, which took concentrated effort. She could feel her hands relax. The cow settled back down.

"Sorry, girl, I get carried away. I'll go bang on the barn wall later."

Consciously choosing to think of something else, she thought about the lesson she had heard in church that morning. *Forgive as Christ forgave you.* She wished Onkel Kris had been there. She had sneaked a look at her far's stony face. He was always sober in church but not granitelike as today. *Lord, let there be forgiveness from and for these two proud men.* She had been praying this all winter, but so far they were as far apart as ever. At least that she knew about.

When she finished milking, she poured the milk in the can

328

and waited for Gilbert to finish too. Tonight was Hjelmer's turn to milk, but she told him she would, just to get out of the house.

"I am going to take a walk."

Gilbert nodded. "I will finish the chores, then."

"Takk."

"Do not be long. Supper will be ready soon."

Ingeborg set out, trying to stomp Mr. Bjorklund right into the sloppy mud, thanks to the thawing going on. She thought of the discussion around the table yesterday after he arrived. . . .

"I know this is no longer the way we do things in Norway, but I have a great need, and I am running out of time. So may I be forthright?"

Far nodded for him to go ahead.

"You know that my wife, Anna, died a few weeks ago in childbirth. The baby did not live either." His voice cracked and he cleared his throat.

"We were so sorry to hear that. Our condolences to you and your family."

"Ja." He cleared his throat again. "Takk."

Ingeborg felt like reaching out and patting the broad hand digging fingers into the tabletop. So much sorrow.

He began again. "You know I have a small son, Thorliff."

Ingeborg's mind went immediately to the little boy with the striking blue eyes, eyes that matched those of the man sitting across the table from her.

"He is a good boy, and I do not want to leave him here in Norway with Anna's parents. I want him with me, and to do that I am in desperate need of a wife."

"Good thinking." Far nodded as he spoke.

Mr. Bjorklund looked across the table at Ingeborg. "Anna spoke very highly of you, and her mor told me you are not married."

She felt herself nodding and wanting to run at the same time.

He turned back to look at Arne. "I am here to ask for your daughter's hand in marriage. I vow that I will be a good husband to her. I will provide for her to the best of my ability. I have a good reputation as a worker, and I am willing to do whatever it takes to take care of my family. Mr. Strand, I live up to my word. My brother Carl and I are emigrating to Amerika. We have our tickets already, so your daughter would have passage too."

He stumbled. "I know I am saying this badly, and it sounds more like a business venture, but I also know that arranged marriages can be solid and beneficial to both parties." He heaved a sigh and looked down at the table then back up at Ingeborg's parents.

Arne Strand looked at his wife and then down at his hands.

Ingeborg felt as if she were standing up in the corner looking down on someone else. Was he really talking about her? About a marriage to her and she to him? Surely this was all a dream and not really happening. He was a stranger. A very cheeky stranger. She stared at Far, willing him to look at her. When he continued to study his hands, she jerked around to Mor, who was not saying a word.

She pushed her chair back, but Far said so softly she almost did not hear him, "Stay here."

Surely you cannot be serious! This is insanity! Far, look at me.

Finally he raised his head, but still without looking at

Ingeborg. "You have given us a great deal to think about. I cannot give you the answer you want right now. We must talk about this."

Mr. Bjorklund nodded. "I understand, sir. I know this is a very heavy decision. When can I expect an answer?"

Never! Ingeborg's mind screamed, but she did not move. At that point, she did not think she *could* move. She was frozen to the chair. If she tried to stand, she might shatter into a thousand pieces.

The effrontery of the man!

Mr. Bjorklund licked his lips. "May I return in two days?"

Far's eyes narrowed, like they always did when he was thinking hard. He nodded. Pushing back his chair, he stood. "Ja. We will see you again in two days." He held out his hand, shook hands with Mr. Bjorklund, and saw him to the door.

"You . . . you did not . . ." Ingeborg choked on the words. "You did not tell him no. That you would not put your daughter on the auction block!"

"Ingeborg, Ingeborg. He did not offer to buy you. This is not an auction." Mor finally looked at her daughter, but Ingeborg wondered if she really saw her or was looking at something else. "We will have to pray about this and talk and think."

"There is no reason to think."

"Ja, there is. He came here in good faith, and we will honor that. He is not a monster."

"He is still in love with his wife. He has to be!"

"But she is gone, and over time, he will come to terms with that. Something to keep in mind: That little boy needs a mor—now."

No. This was so wrong! Her thoughts were so scrambled she could not make sense of them.

She could not sleep that night. The confusion became fear, and now it had turned into anger. Anger and sorrow fighting each other to be first in her heart. . . .

So here she was out walking as Gilbert was finishing up the chores, trying to distance herself, trying to calm the fury. And not succeeding.

Ingeborg reached a cove of birch trees that she dearly loved. Mr. Bjorklund would be here tomorrow. It was obvious to her that Far and Mor both thought this was a good idea, her marrying Mr. Bjorklund.

"Lord God, what can I do? I mean, they will not force me into the marriage." She paused to think, studying the yellow-green catkins hanging from the birch branches. The leaves were tiny bumps that promised to grow.

Yes, they could force her into marriage. She was growing past marriageable age. She had loved Nils, and they forbade her to even consider a union. But here was a man with an outrageous proposition, and her parents seemed to be open to it. If banging her head on a tree trunk would help, she would do so. Maybe that hurt would outdo the ache she felt in her heart right now. She breathed deep, hoping that would soothe the sorrow.

But you said you wanted to start over, and you thought about Amerika, her inner voice reminded her.

"But that was with Nils. I thought perhaps the new country would be different than here."

But Nils is gone, and you have a life to live.

She couldn't argue with that. She had realized that over the last couple of months.

Her heart, though, still insisted, *Nils, I cannot let you go.*
And the cold, relentless answer, *You must.*

But marriage to a man she did not love, did not really
even know? Her thoughts wandered to a story she had heard
about mail-order brides. Norwegian men who had gone to
Amerika were writing back and asking for a woman to agree
to marry them in exchange for a ticket and a home in the new
country. Any woman. Any unknown man. She and Gunlaug
had laughed about it. Was this any different?

There were no easy answers. She gave up and trudged back
home. *Let not the sun set on your anger.* Was that the quote,
or was it something similar to that? Well, she was certainly
violating the Bible's rules, because she could not think of
anything else.

"Is Mr. Bjorklund indeed coming back tomorrow?" Berta
asked from her bed in the stillness of the night.

The dark night was not just from the lack of light. "Ja, I
believe so."

"What will you do?"

*I will not laugh in his face. And I will not say yes when all
of me is screaming no.* "I will wait and see what Far says. I
am sure he will say no."

"I am not so sure about that. I do not want you to go to
Amerika. Bjorn left and we never heard from him again."
Mari's voice ached of tears.

"Those kinds of things do not happen often."

"Maybe not, but it happened." Mari padded across the
darkness and crawled into Ingeborg's bed. "Mor said the little
boy needs a mor. You would make him a good mor. Maybe
you could offer to take care of him but not get married.

Then when he grows bigger, you can come home. What do they call it?"

Ingeborg said, "A nurse," just as Berta said, "A governess."

Ingeborg hugged her little sister close. If she left with Mr. Bjorklund, would she ever see her family again?

When Mr. Bjorklund rode into the yard the next day, he had the little boy seated in front of him. The child had such beautiful eyes.

Ingeborg watched through the window as the man dismounted and then lifted his son down. Thorliff patted his father's cheeks with both his hands, and Mr. Bjorklund hugged him before setting him on the ground and leading him to the door. Against all her instincts, she invited them in.

"Thorliff, you remember meeting Miss Strand at your grandma's house?"

Thorliff shook his head and tried to hide behind his far's leg.

Arne Strand crossed the room and shook the man's hand, taking over the manners that his daughter neglected. "Welcome to our house. Mrs. Strand has the coffee started."

"Takk, sir." He turned to look at Ingeborg and nodded. "It is good to see you."

Not really. But she knew if she were impolite, Mor would be displeased, very displeased. "Velkommen."

"Please be seated." Far gestured toward a chair at the table.

Ingeborg motioned for her mother to take her seat, and she would pour the coffee when it was ready. If she had her way, it wouldn't be ready for a long time.

"So how are your preparations going for the trip?" Her far talked as if they were journeying to Oslo or Bergen, not clear across the ocean to Amerika.

Thorliff clung to his father like a lifeline.

Ingeborg did not blame him a bit. His far had better not betray him like hers had betrayed her. When she saw the child before, he had been so happy and had even smiled at her before he ran off to play again.

How could this sad little waif be the same boy? But she knew he was. The eyes were a giveaway.

Ingeborg cut the coffee cake, dished it up on plates, and set them around with a cream pitcher in the middle of the table. She poured the coffee and again set the cups around, listening as the men talked about the weather and farming, getting around to the seter when Arne mentioned that Ingeborg ran the seter every summer and was an exemplary cheese maker.

"People around here vie for her cheese. I know we could sell a lot more if we had it, but we cannot take care of more cows over the winter than we have now."

"Because my oldest brother owns the family farm, my brother Carl and I have worked many different jobs besides farming. But we are looking forward to having our own land in Amerika. We will be going to the middle of the country, to a place called Dakota Territory. I have heard nothing but good things about the land there."

"And it is free?"

"One has to prove up a claim. There are, of course, requirements. I have all of that information."

When Ingeborg sat down, Far cut into his cake, so the others did too. The talk continued, but Ingeborg watched Thorliff's eyes following every bite his father took. He almost smiled when he was given a bite.

"May I fix Thorliff some coffee cake?" Ingeborg asked when there was a slight lull.

"Ja, and perhaps a cup of milk."

She brought it to the table. "Would you like to sit on my lap to have your cake?"

Thorliff looked up to see what his far said, then took the long way around the table, keeping one eye on his far. He stopped by Ingeborg's side.

"I will lift you up."

He nodded.

She did so and held him on her knee so he could reach the table easily. He turned to look up into her face. "Takk."

She smiled down at him.

He finished off the cake and drank the milk without a word, then slid to the floor and returned to his far. It was all Ingeborg could do not to brush his hair back off his forehead and hug him close. She turned back to what Far was saying.

"You have a fine son."

"Ja, he is a good boy."

"How old is he?"

"Four."

"I . . . we have given your request much thought and prayer. Ingeborg has a fine mind and a strong faith in our Lord. Our second son left for Amerika, and we never heard from him again, so letting Ingeborg start a journey like that is not easy for us."

Good. Far was letting Mr. Bjorklund down easy.

"While we feel this would be a good thing for our daughter—"

Ingeborg stopped breathing.

"—we believe that she should be allowed to have a say in this. So we have decided that if you can convince her that she should marry you, then you have our full permission to court her. I know you feel you need a final answer right now but, but we just cannot do that."

"I see." Mr. Bjorklund studied the crumbs on the tablecloth and then looked up at Ingeborg. "Will you write letters back to me when I write? And I will come see you again."

If you are no better at corresponding than Nils, I will have no trouble with this. She nodded. "Ja, I will do that. But remember, I leave for the seter in a few weeks, and we do not have regular mail service there."

"Then I shall come and see you at the seter."

She nodded, as he had not asked a question but made a statement. What kind of summer was this going to be?

29

It was just over a week later when the first letter arrived.

Dear Miss Strand,

You did not give me permission to call you Ingeborg so that is why the formality. I too know how strange this is, and if there were any way I could undo the last two months, I most assuredly would. But since I cannot and you cannot, we will go forward with what is.

I would like to tell you a little about my family. There are four boys and two girls in our family. I am the second son. Johann is the oldest and has inherited the farm, or will when our far decides not to farm any longer. There is not enough work for us here all year around, so the rest of us find work elsewhere. Sometimes we have gone out on the fishing boat with an onkel.

Carl, who is emigrating with me, is married to Kaaren. They are looking forward to owning land, as am I.

Sincerely,
Roald Bjorklund

338

Ingeborg wanted to pretend the letter never arrived, but since Hjelmer announced to the entire world that she had a letter, she would answer.

Dear Mr. Bjorklund,

Thank you for your letter. We are preparing to leave for the seter. Does your family have one too? I love it up in the mountains, more than any other place on earth. I also like making cheese. We planted our garden early this year.

Sincerely,
Ingeborg Strand

There, she finished that. He would probably not write again, but at least she did her duty to politeness.

A black cloud hung over the preparations. Since they would not have as many cows this year, there would be far less cheese to make. They sheared most of the sheep the week before they were ready to leave, so that would be easier too. But still, without the usual full complement of helpers, the work would be hard. Gunlaug. She sighed.

Tor and Kari were excited to be going with them again, and since their younger brother was now old enough, he would come along too.

A week later, another letter arrived.

Dear Miss Strand,

Thank you for writing so promptly. I hope you receive this before you leave for your home away from home in the mountain valleys. Your mor said you are also an expert on the spinning wheel. I wish we could take ours

*to Amerika, but I will build another when I get there.
They say there is plenty of wood to be had for the cutting. Wood of all kinds.*

*Have you ever driven a yoke of oxen? Farmers in
Dakota Territory use oxen instead of horses. Mules
are very popular too. A family from our valley sent a
son over there, and his letters are very educational. Will
there be a place for Thorliff and me to sleep when we
ride up to the seter?*

*Sincerely,
Roald Bjorklund*

Ingeborg had to admit the man wrote a good letter. And
he spoke well, so he had had an education. She wondered if
he liked to read. A couple of nights before they were to leave
she wrote back.

Dear Mr. Bjorklund,

*Yes, there will be a pallet for you to sleep on. Unless
you would rather sleep outside. We leave the day after
tomorrow, so we are loading the wagons in prepara-
tion. My sister Berta wants to come up this year, but
Mor insists she stay home to help with the garden and
food preservation for the winter. Katrina, our married
sister, will be having a baby sometime soon, so that
makes Mor happy.*

Does Thorliff play with the lambs at your family farm?

*Sincerely,
Ingeborg Strand*

If only she could at least say good-bye to Gunlaug. But she could not. The day came and the wagons waddled out across the track. Why did she not feel the anticipation this year that she had felt last year? When they started up the mountain, Ingeborg missed Gunlaug even more. All the things they had done together . . .

Kari walked with her behind all the cows and sheep. "I miss Gunlaug already."

"Me too. And Anders and Hamme. This has left such an empty place in my heart." Ingeborg was surprised at herself. She had not said much to anyone other than her immediate family all winter. And since Tor and Kari lived in a town another valley over, there was not much contact there either.

They arrived at the seter without incident and unpacked the wagons. They spread out to clean the house and settle the animals, all the things that always had to be done. Hjelmer found a bird's nest in the top of the chimney, on the cover they had put over it to keep this from happening. But at least the babies had already flown.

"You know, Hjelmer, you have really gotten taller this year," Kari said that evening with a grin. "They cannot call you shrimp any longer."

He grinned back, ignoring the red creeping up his neck.

Ingeborg tapped him on the head when she went by. "He is almost as tall as I am now. You watch, by next year he'll be hitting his head coming in the door."

Gilbert and Far stayed an extra day to help get more wood cut, since they had not brought a load up the day before, mainly because that was something Onkel Frode always supplied. So there were a lot of adjustments this year.

Ingeborg stepped outside as the sun was nestling itself in behind the mountains. She stood looking over the valley and the snow-clad peaks beyond and prayed for the calm the scene always brought her. She turned to go back inside and almost bumped into Kari.

"I could not wait to get here, just to make sure this was all still here."

"Oh, Kari, that is just the way I feel. I can almost hear God saying, 'Look up to the mountains.' Only the power of God can build mountains and make the creeks sing and bring spring back around again."

"How will we do it all without the others?"

"We'll just have to work harder. We only have five sheep to shear, so that will be easier. I guess Tor is going to have to learn to milk cows."

Kari snorted. "That will be a sight to see."

"Your brother learned so much last year. You wait. At the end of this summer, you will not recognize him."

"If that is a promise, I will indeed be watching." She looked out over the valley once again. "We all will have to learn to herd sheep, that's for certain. And we will all have to help with the cooking so Mari can help with other things. We will manage. I know we will."

Ingeborg loved the way Kari used the word *we*.

Kari grinned at Ingeborg. "And this year we will not have broken legs and blisters and . . ." She breathed deeply, as though she had not had air like this to breathe for a long time. "I am so glad to be here. This year I want to learn more about making cheese, if you do not mind."

"Oh, not at all." Ingeborg draped an arm over the girl's shoulders. "Someone needs to get that loom talking too."

"You string it, and I can go from there."

"We will string it together so that you learn how."

The two walked back around the house and saw the cows lining up at the barn. Some things never changed.

With two trees sawed into fireplace lengths, Far and Gilbert split wood for a while the next morning before heading down the mountain. All those staying at the seter waved good-bye and returned to their cleaning and other chores.

"Something sure stinks in here," Mari said after checking over all the supplies in the storeroom. "Do you smell it?"

"I know. Are all the cupboards washed out?"

"I think so. Where else can we look?"

They started going through each of the cupboards and soon found a dead rat in the very back of one of the lower shelves. "Eee-ew."

Ingeborg gagged as she hauled the carcass outside and heaved it as far from the house as possible. Let one of the wild animals find it if they could stand the stench. They scrubbed the cabinet until the stench was gone and left everything empty to dry.

"How do you suppose that happened?"

"I think it died of old age and did not have the grace to do so outside."

Mari laughed. "Another experience we learned at the seter. How about a cup of coffee with fresh cream?"

Two weeks later they had the sheep shorn, two calves had been born, one of the hens was already broody, and the first batch of cheese was in the presses, with more in various stages, just as it was supposed to be. The seter did not feel quite the same as usual, and the work was heavy, but all was going smoothly.

Ingeborg was back in the cheese room rearranging wheels when a "Halloo, the seter!" echoed across the fields. Hjelmer came running into the cheese house. "Someone is coming, and I have no idea who it is."

Ingeborg hastened out and followed him to the front of the house. "I do not know." But when she realized that a small boy was riding in front of a man, her mouth dropped open. "It's Mr. Bjorklund and Thorliff."

"All the way up here?" Hjelmer looked from Ingeborg back out to the rider. "Did you know he was coming?"

"He said he was, but I did not realize he'd be here so soon." She looked at her brother and shrugged. "Maybe he will want to split wood. At least we can hope so." The two of them walked out to greet their guests.

Mr. Bjorklund didn't just split wood. He milked cows, fed the pigs, and did anything else that he saw needed doing. When Mari told him the rat story, he laughed. All of the children made sure Thorliff was kept safe and close at hand, which wasn't a problem, because he followed Hjelmer around like a shadow.

On the third morning at breakfast, Hjelmer announced, "The grass is not up yet in the high country, but we can move the sheep to that lea above the bluffs. Can Thorliff come with me herding today?"

"If he wants," Roald said, "and if I can go too."

Ingeborg watched as they led the sheep out and off to a higher pasture.

That evening after the sheep were back in their fold, she found Roald sitting on the bench, Thorliff sound asleep in his lap. He smiled when Ingeborg came around the house. "I will never forget this." He nodded to include all of it. "Can you sit down for a while?"

Ingeborg did, but somehow she could not lose herself in the beauty like she so often did.

"Call me Roald, I beg you. May I please call you Ingeborg?"

"Ja, Roald, I believe you can."

"I am sorry I have to leave in the morning."

"You have been a big help. Tusen takk."

"You made us feel welcome. Takk."

She waited for him to say more, but he did not. His attention seemed to be taken by the snow-capped peaks across the valley, as they turned first to a soft yellow, then to orange, then to a flaming pink. So beautiful. Was he rapt in their beauty too? She hoped so.

After milking and feeding the next morning, the guests departed. Ingeborg stood in front of the house watching Roald and Thorliff ride down the track. Did she feel any of the emotions, any at all, that she had felt as she watched Nils depart? Nei. Not a bit. Did she love Nils? Oh ja! Did she feel the same for this man?

Nei.

She went inside and settled herself at the loom, the one that last year Gunlaug wove upon. She sighed as she picked up the rhythm. Soon her feet were working the treadles just right, the fine wool slipping through her fingers, the flyers spinning, and she let her mind wander.

Roald Bjorklund was a good man. She was pretty sure he was smarter, more profound than he'd first seemed. His letters indicated that. Too, he did not talk a lot. That was not to his detriment. She knew many boys who loved to hear themselves talk. And prattled. Bah!

He was a good man. Never did she see any sign of anger. Sadness, ja. It was to be expected. And she thought she could see in him great concern for those around him. Or perhaps that was just her imagination.

He was a good man. And industrious. He worked hard and efficiently. He got things done. She knew from watching Far that an industrious man was much more than just a nice thing to have around a farmstead. He was an absolute necessity.

And then another thought, a new thought, struck so suddenly her fingers stopped, and she lost the thread. Never, not even once in her whole life, had she felt about a boy the way she felt about Nils. Never. If true love comes once in a lifetime, hers had come and gone.

She had loved and lost, and it was gone forever. Gone. The thought brought hot tears to her eyes.

Roald did not come up to the seter again. As the weeks passed, she found herself thinking not about him but about the little boy with the fjord-blue eyes. How would Roald manage if he did not find a wife? Or what if the woman he married did not love his son? Some women were like that, especially when they had children of their own. What about Thorliff?

There were two letters from him when Gilbert brought up supplies and the mail in August. Ingeborg answered with one letter and said they would be back to the valley by the end of the month. Unless it snowed and they returned sooner.

But the snow held off, the days stayed warm, and they could graze the sheep in the high pastures right up to the last moment. Still, the summer ended all too quickly, in fact, before she could sufficiently think about all these things. The summer had been warmer than usual, the grass greener and more lush. The cows produced so much milk that they had nearly as much cheese as they had made last year.

The wagons came, they loaded and departed, and it was over. The trip back down was as uneventful as the one up. Almost. She walked down the track behind the cows and sheep, as usual. As they passed Onkel Kris's place, he was working outside. He stopped and looked at them. And nodded! Was he ready to bury the hatchet? She could only hope and dream.

And then she saw Gunlaug looking out the window. She waved at Ingeborg, her arm swinging in an arc over her head, a huge smile on her face. Ingeborg waved back and then ducked her head, afraid to look at her father. But her heart rejoiced.

She walked into the farmyard and stepped over the threshold into the house. Seter was over for another year. She was home.

A letter from Roald waited for her. As soon as she could send a message, he would come. She did so.

࿊

True to his word, he rode into their farmyard with his son in the saddle in front of him. Far greeted him at the door. Mor and the girls laid out a supper that was more a feast. They ate in a strained politeness. They all gathered afterward before the fireplace as Mor served coffee.

In the nervous, palpable silence, Mr. Bjorklund asked a question. Far answered, but Ingeborg was not really listening. Her mind was leaping off elsewhere. She had made her decision.

This would not be so much a wedding as a business arrangement. She would promise to honor and obey her husband, and he would promise to provide and care for her. But her true vow would be to the small boy with the big blue eyes who had stolen her heart. Him she would love and care for, and if God blessed them with other children, then she would rejoice. But no matter where they went, she knew deep down inside that God was calling her to help bring babies into this world and help them and their mothers live. To that she could give her wholehearted vow. God had not taken His eyes off her, even when she thought He had. He loved her. Perhaps there would be love too between the man with the fjord-blue eyes and the woman who would marry him.

And now Roald was kneeling in front of her. He took her hands into his. "Ingeborg Strand, will you marry me?"

"Ja, Roald Bjorklund, I will marry you."

Her heart was filled with more tears than smiles. "Ja."

I loved you, Nils. But you are gone, and my life must go on. Good-bye.

Acknowledgments

Gunlaug Noklund and Sandy Dengler deserve thanks and praise for their unfailing wisdom and perseverance with this, Ingeborg's early story.

I have the most wonderful friends, including all the staff at Bethany House publishers, who always work so diligently and wisely in helping my ideas and dreams become reality. Sharon Asmus, you have been one of my heroes for years. Dave Horton, I am so grateful I get to work with you. My BHP family—wow! I am blessed by you all.

Thanks too for all my readers who have pleaded through the years, wanting to know where Ingeborg came from. I wanted to know too, and in *An Untamed Heart* we find out.

Thank you, Heavenly Father.

Lauraine Snelling is the award-winning author of over 70 books, fiction and nonfiction, for adults and young adults. Her books have sold over 2 million copies. Besides writing books and articles, she teaches at writers' conferences across the country. She and her husband make their home in Tehachapi, California.

Don't Miss the Continuing Story of the Bjorklund Family!

To learn more about Lauraine and her books, visit laurainesnelling.com.

Facing the untamed but beautiful Red River Valley, the Bjorklunds must rely on their strength and faith to build a homestead. Through the challenges of this difficult land, they suffer tragedy and loss, but are also blessed with joy, hope, and an enduring love.

RED RIVER OF THE NORTH: *An Untamed Land, A New Day Rising, A Land to Call Home, The Reapers' Song, Tender Mercies, Blessing in Disguise*

Astrid Bjorklund loves Blessing, the prairie town settled by her family, and enjoys studying medicine under Dr. Elizabeth Bjorklund's direction. But when she feels God might be calling her to the mission field, will she have to leave her beloved town—and her chance for love—behind?

HOME TO BLESSING: *A Measure of Mercy, No Distance Too Far, A Heart for Home*

More Books in the Bestselling BLESSING Saga

The now adult children of the Bjorklund family look to their own futures and find themselves caught between two worlds. When they are forced to choose between the farm in Red River Valley and pursuing their own dreams, can the family legacy live on?

RETURN TO RED RIVER: *A Dream to Follow, Believing the Dream, More Than a Dream*

As the prairie yields bountiful harvests, the Norwegian pioneers enjoy a measure of prosperity. Now their young daughters seek to fulfill their own dreams and aspirations—but each will need faith, courage, and perseverance to find God's plan for her future.

DAUGHTERS OF BLESSING: *A Promise for Ellie, Sophie's Dilemma, A Touch of Grace, Rebecca's Reward*

⬥ BETHANYHOUSE